The Year She Disappeared

James A. Michener Fiction Series,
JAMES MAGNUSON, EDITOR

ANN HARLEMAN

THE YEAR SHE

Disappeared

A NOVEL

University of Texas Press ⤙⤚ *Austin*

Requests for permission to reproduce material from this work
should be sent to:
    Permissions
    University of Texas Press
    P.O. Box 7819
    Austin, TX 78713-7819
    www.utexas.edu/utpress/about/bpermission.html

♾ The paper used in this book meets the minimum requirements
of ANSI/NISO Z39.48-1992 (R1997) (Permanence of Paper).

LIBRARY OF CONGRESS
CATALOGING-IN-PUBLICATION DATA
Harleman, Ann, 1945–
The year she disappeared : a novel / Ann Harleman. — 1st ed.
    p. cm. — (James A. Michener fiction series)
ISBN 978-0-292-71747-3 (alk. paper)
1. Kidnapping—Fiction. 2. Grandparent and child—Fiction.
3. Life change events—Fiction. I. Title.
PS3558.A624246Y43 2008
813'.54—dc22   2007034386

For Janet Hagan Yanos

The Year She Disappeared

One

It was her sixtieth year to heaven—the eighth of December, 1998—and Nan Mulholland had never expected to spend it on the lam.

"How long will it take?" She tapped the ticket agent's map with a smooth oval nail. "Say if we—if I—fly to New York, then go from there to New Haven?" She saw herself, somewhat melodramatically, as laying a false trail. The first of many?

"How long?" she persisted.

"Lady! I was born right here in Seattle. Never been east of Minneapolis."

The fragrant young man in line behind Nan stepped up to the counter. She breathed in: Obsession; Gabriel, her son-in-law, wore it. "What time a day you gonna get in?" He had trustworthy brown eyes and a New York accent. "It's wicked slow, this close to Christmas."

A second witness, besides the ticket agent. Nan was most definitely in luck today. Quickly, like knocking on wood, she glanced back to where her granddaughter, four-year-old Jane, sat hunched on their one small suitcase, her long brown hair falling over her face, both arms tight around a large stuffed animal.

"I'd take Metro North, I was you. Get the airport shuttle to Penn Station."

"Thank you," Nan said. Then, inspired: "I've burned my driver's license, so I'll probably do that." That should embed her firmly in his mind for later, when he was questioned.

She paid cash—nearly eleven hundred dollars—for the last two seats on Flight 1066 to La Guardia, departing at noon ("That's less than thirty minutes, ma'am") from Gate 11-A. Clutching the tickets tightly—was she really, truly going to do this thing?—Nan turned away. The helpful young man took her place at the counter and pulled out his wallet. For good measure she lurched against him. He jumped back, credit cards spilling onto the floor. She excused herself in pretty, dotty-old-lady confusion. He wouldn't forget her, or her supposed destination.

Heartened by this evidence of her newfound criminal mind-set—maybe she really *could* pull this off—Nan clicked across the shining expanse of the Sea-Tac terminal toward Jane. The smell of the place was heartening, too (an exquisitely tuned sense of smell was Nan Mulholland's own peculiar joy and sorrow)—pine-forest disinfectant, minty vinyl. The smell of newness. Of fresh starts. Why, she wondered, do they call them terminals, as in disease, when their whole ambience suggests beginnings? Remember the Plan, she said to herself. Her new mantra: Remember the Plan. Underneath her amethyst wool dress (she'd told Gabriel that she was taking his daughter to a matinee performance of the *Nutcracker*) she wore a silk half-slip bought years ago in West Berlin; its wide lace border concealed three zippered pockets. "*Versteckte Vermögen*," it was called. "Hidden Assets." Two thick rolls of hundred-dollar bills, her passport, and an extra vial of nitroglycerin thumped comfortingly against her knees as she walked.

|

They made the plane with minutes to spare. Jane, tired now and sulky, cold-shouldered the welcoming flight attendants, and they were in: safe. None of the other passengers (Nan checked faces as Jane stalked ahead of her down the aisle) took the least interest in them.

Jane demanded the window seat, though there was nothing to see in the lozenge of smeared glass but evergreens and tarmac. Good, thought Nan, no one can try to talk to her. The middle-aged man in the aisle seat offered to put Nan's coat in the overhead bin; he folded it carefully, buff silk lining out, then clicked the bin shut. Seated again, he shook out a copy of the *Seattle Post-Intelligencer* (the *Pee-Eye*) and occupied both armrests. His rolled-up shirtsleeves revealed forearms densely carpeted with sandy-blond hair. Squinting (she never wore her glasses in public), Nan read the largest headlines. CIA SEEKS LOOSER RULES FOR KILLINGS DURING COUPS. TACOMA COUNCILMAN TOOK OVER 100 BRIDES. She blinked. *BRIBES*.

Jane was watching the flight attendant step through the emergency-landing ballet. Her intent face had a pinched look, and she rubbed her forehead with two fingers, the way she did when she was tired—her mother, Alex's, gesture. What had Alex told her about the reason for this very sudden trip? Nan had had no time alone with Alex this morning, no chance to ask last-minute questions. Gabriel had come home from the hospital early.

The flight attendant held up a bright yellow oxygen mask and strapped it over her face. Nan felt Jane stiffen, and put her arm around her. Jane shrugged away. "First put on your own mask," the recorded voice intoned. "Then assist your child."

When Alex was little, all that traveling because of Tod being in the Foreign Service, Nan used to worry: Could she? Would she really be able to deny instinct, to watch Alex gasping, clawing at her throat, while she calmly fastened the strap around her own head?

The attendant tucked away the mask and waved a languid arm at each of the Exit doors.

"Nana! See that button?" Jane pointed to the round knob on her side of their shared armrest. "That's the Inject Button. You press it, and it injects the person next to you out of their seat."

You won't get me that easily, my chickadee, thought Nan. She smiled down at her granddaughter, determined to be cheerful. For an instant, her heart-shaped face hardening, her chin as determined as her mother's, Jane stared back. Her eyes, the bronzy-green of spoiled grapes, rested on Nan accusingly.

"Whose special girl are you?" Nan said. "Huh, Grape Eyes?"

But Jane turned back to her own reflection in the airplane window.

Nan sighed. This was new—this cold dislike. Up until now—until this very afternoon, this very trip, which Jane clearly didn't want to take and which Alex apparently hadn't explained to her—Jane had adored her grandmother. Nan, as Jane's only living grandparent, had the field all to herself. The one, the only . . . Nana! And she basked in it. More: she needed it. In her occasional moments of stark honesty, Nan recognized this. Grandmothering filled the gaps that came with widowhood. Grandmothering gave her something to be good at. Grandmothering was what Nan, motherless since the age of four and raised by her own grandmother, knew how to do.

The flight attendant finished her demonstration, shook back her long blond hair, and went to take her seat. But the plane didn't move.

What have I agreed to? Nan thought in dismay.

Alex had asked for help, and Nan had agreed to give it. But (Be honest!) the deal was that Nan would give up, for a while—a *short* while—her comfortable widowed West Coast life. It didn't include giving up her cherished grandmotherhood. They had their private jokes, she and Jane. They had their shared pursuits: finger painting; collecting wildflowers, which they pressed, as Nan's own grandmother had done with her, between the pages of Webster's Unabridged; riding all the roller coasters at Six Flags. They had their small conspiracies: roller coasters were strictly forbidden by Alex. Where had it (so suddenly!) gone—that mutually adoring comradeship? Without it, Nan realized, she had no idea how to connect with her granddaughter.

"Nana!" Jane whispered. "You're all red."

Nan laid her hand over Jane's, but she pulled away and wrapped both arms around her balding stuffed squirrel. Back inside her bubble of sullenness. So that was how it was going to be.

The captain's voice announced in a honeyed Southern accent that there would be a delay in taking off. Jane drooped; her eyes closed. She sank sideways against the wall of the airplane, her light brown hair—long and coarse and thick as a horse's tail, like her mother's—falling across her face. Nan took her own pillow and tucked it between Jane's cheek and the wall, then leaned back in her seat. The numbing flurry of preparations for departure that had filled the past two and a half days was over, leaving her face-to-face with the *reason* for departure.

What am I doing? she thought. What in the world am I doing?

|

Why me? Nan had asked on Monday morning.

She and Alex were alone in Alex's old and calm and beautiful house, Gabriel already at the hospital, Jane at preschool.

Why don't *you* take her? Both of you just get clear away from Gabe, if—

If what you say is true. Nan bit back the words: what kind of mother would side with her son-in-law against her own daughter?

She's better off without me.

Alex! Surely not. She'd miss you terribly. She'd be losing both her parents at once.

Alex's face hardened. She looked down at her trembling hands and folded one tightly over the other. Her knuckles turned white. He'll try to find Jane, she said. He'll come after you. You know what he's like—

Alex, honey, that's just what I mean. If I take her, it's—it's kidnapping. Abduction.

I'd be too easy to trace, Alex went on, as if Nan hadn't spoken. But you. You could do it. Nobody looks at an old woman.

My daughter can be cruel, Nan had thought—oh, she can.

|

"Folks, this is your pilot speaking. Mighty sorry for the holdup. Shouldn't be too much longer before we're up and away."

Nan looked at her watch. They'd been sitting on the runway for half an hour. *Holdup. Holdup.* Inside her head the word pounded. She looked around anxiously, up the aisle, then down, half expecting to see uniformed policemen converging on her and Jane. But there was no one. The flight attendants were strapped into their jump seats, and the other passengers sat wrapped in the same heavy, thrumming cocoon of airplane noise as Nan. In the cloudy afternoon twilight Jane slept, wedged at an uncomfortable-looking angle against the cabin wall, a translucent bubble of spit coming and going between her lips. Nan reached out a hand to smooth her hair back from her face, then stopped, afraid of waking her. In front of Nan a shaved male head rustled a papery airline pillow; beside him an unseen mother told her unseen child, "Justin! If you don't behave, we won't go. We'll get off this plane right now." The man next to Nan, isolated in his yellow cone of light, opened his newspaper to the Wednesday Word Wizard, a list of nonsense words to unscramble and then use to fill in the blanks in the Grand Prize Sentence. The plane shuddered promisingly several times, then was still.

What if, after Nan and Jane had left this morning, Alex had had a change of heart? What if she'd told Gabriel about their conspiracy? What if the police were now holding all outgoing planes to search for Nan and Jane?

No, she thought. Alex wouldn't do that. Alex had never been given to changes of heart. Remember the Plan. A sound, well-ordered plan, like all of Alex's plans. Right down to Nan's awareness of being backed into a corner, backed into being generous. But there'd been Alex's face, white and despairing; Alex's voice, shaky, ashamed.

To distract herself, Nan peered at the newspaper over her neighbor's sandy-haired arm, which reminded her of a bath mat she and Tod had had once (was it in Bucharest?). She read:

BULTAR

LESCUM

INGADE

HESTOO

BETHIL

STYMIC

It looked like a shopping list in Serbo-Croatian. (Not one of Nan's languages, though she'd dutifully attempted the language of whatever country Tod was posted to, through all the downward moves—Bonn, Genoa, Warsaw, Bucharest.) After LESCUM Sandy Man wrote in MUS-CLE; then his gleaming gold pencil tapped inquiringly beside INGADE. Nan tightened her lips against the whisper, *Gained! Gained!*

Her thoughts homed back to her own predicament. Yes—Alex could be cruel. An old woman, she'd said. And didn't Sandy Man, still in oblivious communion with his newspaper, bear Alex out? Even now, when her deepest desire was for this damned plane to move, for herself and Jane to depart unnoticed, Nan spared a moment to feel miffed. Leaning back in her seat, in her chic but feminine dress—brushing invisible grit from the skirt and smoothing the fine, soft wool over her knees—she looked (she knew) neither old nor sick. Her hair was, though by artifice, still blond; her skin, suffused with a heart patient's rosiness, still vibrant; her eyes, still a deep bachelor-button blue. Who was Sandy Man, to be so immune?

Sixty. I'm only sixty.

"I mean it, Justin!" The voice of the unseen woman in front of Nan was louder now. "We can get off this plane right now and go home."

Jane stirred. "Nana, I'm thirsty."

Nan offered her own plastic cup of ginger ale, the ice cubes nearly melted. Jane pushed it away. "I want Coke!" she said loudly.

"Shhh!" Nan grabbed her granddaughter's shoulder, about to shake it, then stopped herself

Jane squinted up at her. Nan could see her considering whether or not to burst into tears; luckily, she was too sleepy. She punched her pillow against the window and turned away, hugging Squirrel.

Damn Alex! Nan thought, and immediately felt better, anger being a more bracing emotion than fear.

After all, I don't *have* to do this. We can get off this plane right now and go home.

The captain's voice, honeyed testiness now after almost an hour on the ground, announced that they were third in line for takeoff. "Thank God!" Nan said, not realizing she'd spoken the words out loud. Sandy Man glanced up from his newspaper. A pretty black flight attendant paced the aisle with last offerings. Nan accepted a blanket, unfolded it, and eased the soft wool over Jane's curled-up legs and stocking feet. Her eyes flickered open, then closed again.

"Don't lie to me, Justin!" the invisible woman in front of them said in a low voice. "I don't like you to lie to me." An imperious arm came up to flag the flight attendant. "My son is sick," the woman's voice accused.

Nan caught the nutlike smell of vomit. Beside her, Sandy Man rose abruptly, flinging his newspaper into her lap, shoved past the flight attendant, and ran down the aisle. Nan looked down at the paper. In the blank next to BULTAR Sandy Man had printed, carefully, BUTLAR. Good, she thought, that's sunk him. He'll never win the Grand Prize now. The word he should have written echoed in her mind. *Brutal.* Was he that—Gabriel? The son-in-law whom (Be honest!) she adored?

Could Gabriel have done it? How *could* he have done it? And if he hadn't, what was Nan—a woman who always at first glance read the word in newspaper headlines as MOLE-STER (some kind of burrowing, earth-dwelling gangster)—doing here?

The roar beneath Nan's feet deepened. The plane shuddered. They began to move.

All the traveling she'd done in her life—the trains and planes and (in the early days of her marriage) ships with Tod—and still she wasn't used to it. The brashness of embarking. The suspension (like dying, surely?) between earth and water, earth and air. Nan's heart slipped into three-quarter time—The nitro, she thought. No, wait, count to five, remember?—then righted itself. *Remember the Plan.* But that was, at this moment, no comfort at all. She longed to unfasten Jane's seat belt and pull her onto her lap, longed to be anchored and comforted by the warm weight of Jane. Instead, she began to count silently in German, the language of order and calm.

Ein . . . zwei . . . drei . . .

Beside her, Jane sat up, brushing her hair out of her eyes with a brusque, grown-up gesture. Her legs caught in the blanket and she kicked to free herself. Her elbow jabbed into Nan's ribs. Nan looked—really looked—at her granddaughter. Her small bright teeth caught her bottom lip. She was trembling all over.

Vier . . . fünf . . .

Nan reached for Jane's hand and felt first Jane's fear, then her own. Their two palms were slick with sweat. The cloudy afternoon rushed in great gulps past the little oblong window.

Sechs . . . sieben . . .

She pulled Jane close, feeling her stiffen and resist, kept pulling until she yielded and buried her face in her grandmother's armpit. Nan laid her cheek against the small, warm head and breathed in the smell of Jane, sleep and sweat and the mild, sweet fragrance of baby shampoo.

Acht . . . neun . . .

Calmed, not stopping to think who was comforting whom, Nan watched the window. Abruptly the earth, with its tight flocks of blue and yellow lights, tilted downward. Liftoff: the moment between *yes* and *no*. Then the ground below them dipped and circled away.

Two

On Monday morning, two days before, a lifetime before, Nan had awakened in darkness to the ringing of the bedside phone. Tod! was her first thought as she reached for it. In her dream he'd been alive, his naked body in the hospital bed completely shrink-wrapped, only his mouth left bare.

Alex's voice in her ear said, very softly, "Mama?" How long since she'd used that name instead of the chilly "Mother"?

"Sweetie—what is it?"

"I can't talk now." Alex's voice shrank to a whisper. "Can you come over?"

"Now?" It's 5:06 in the morning, Nan carefully did not say. Alex sounded tremulous—a rare departure from her usual clipped, self-reliant calm. Or was it just the effect of whispering?

"This morning. After they're gone. Around nine?"

"I've got Spanish class. Then Mariela." After Tod died, Nan had volunteered for the West Seattle Literacy Project, on the advice—the nagging, really—of her grief counselor. It was supposed to be a short-term thing, quick-fix therapy; instead, almost against her will, she had become so attached to her first tutees that now, five years later, not only was she still tutoring, but she'd started learning Spanish to try and meet her pupils on their home ground. "I could get there by eleven."

"Mama, *please*. I need you."

"Okay. I'll be there a little after nine. I'll cancel—" A click; then silence. "Alex?" Nan said into the dead phone. "Sweetie?"

The beautiful old house—Gabriel and Alex's house—clung to the south slope of Queen Anne Hill, three stories of precisely cut reddish stone with a wide slate terrace overlooking the city. A territorial view, Seattleites called it: perfect, Nan thought when she first heard about the house, for Gabriel, who was nothing if not territorial. She parked on the crescent-shaped gravel drive under the sheltering branches of an ancient blue cedar, wondering how Alex—practical, sensible, methodical Alex (like so many women, Nan seemed to have given birth to her opposite)—could possibly need her. Rolling down the window, she breathed chill morning air, the smells of pine and cedar. A damp breeze touched her cheek. Be calm, she told herself. Be interested, but don't *engulf*. But her heart quickened, and her breath came short. Was this, finally, the moment? All these years—three decades since that afternoon in Genoa, when Alex was four—all these years of yearning after her daughter and never being able to reach her—

Nan got out and went slowly up the front steps. To her left the terrace beckoned. Beyond distant city buildings, held off by a fence of tall iron palings like beasts at the zoo, she could just make out a wedge of Elliott Bay, dark blue in the blue-gray morning mist. From somewhere high up came the terse cries of a crow. Before she could lift the knocker, the door opened.

Alex's abundant coarse brown hair (Tod's hair) was lank and dirty-looking and pulled carelessly back into a ponytail that strayed around her ears—the same stubborn curls that had resisted Nan's hairbrush when Alex was little. Her eyes (Tod's eyes) had dark smudges of sleeplessness under them. She stood aside for Nan to enter, and as she passed, the unwashed smell of her daughter's body assailed her.

Something is very wrong.

Nan heard herself sigh. Her grandmother, Dorothea, had raised her on the principle that a child is a sort of bank account, kept by the adult only until the child is old enough (eighteen, in Dorothea's view) to manage it herself. Then you hand it over. Despite—or because of?—Alex's deep self-reliance, Nan had not found this principle easy to follow. Children *open* you: that had been Nan's experience. Once you have a child, anyone has the high road in to you. All they have to do is wonder aloud what's best for your child.

Alex led the way to the living room, and they sat down on opposite ends of the long, voluptuous white leather sofa that always made Nan think of marshmallows. On the coffee table were a bottle of Calvados and two brandy glasses, like fragile balloons on stems. Alex waved a hand at them. "Something to drink?"

"At nine thirty in the morning?"

"Suit yourself." She leaned forward and poured a generous amount of the golden liquid into her glass, lifted it, and drank. Her throat above the grimy sweatshirt looked white and vulnerable. Calvados was Gabriel's drink; Alex drank only the occasional glass of wine.

On one side of them a wall of glass looked out onto the terrace. The dense green of rhododendron and laurel gleamed at its edges, and there were cypress and juniper and (even now, in December) some sort of flowering shrub in pots and tubs. On the other side, the living room gave onto a small conservatory, where more plants of every size could be glimpsed through the mullioned glass doors, pressing against them like a crowd of curious onlookers. So much green; so much gleam. Nan quelled an impulse to shade her eyes.

"I could make coffee if you want," Alex said. "Or tea?"

Nan shook her head, then, on second thought, said, "Tea would be good. Herbal tea, if you've got it?"

Alex rose, still holding her brandy. Nan saw that her hand trembled, and the goblet rang on the coffee table, glass against glass, when she set it down. She went out through the dining room into the kitchen. Her step—tentative, wavering—bore no resemblance to her usual purposeful stride.

Gazing after her in dismay, Nan thought of all the dinner parties at the long, shining rosewood table, where she'd found herself seated among mildly illustrious fellow guests. The grateful parents of Gabe's patients (the King County prosecutor, a state senator, a local software millionaire); the board members of his various charities; his medical colleagues. Nan (if she'd been asked) would have preferred a family dinner in the kitchen to such worshipful gatherings among drifts of snowy table linen and candlelight and flowering vines in pots climbing the pale green walls. French cuisine and Cuban cigars and Calvados. The orchestration of sensation, in their home, in their garden, at these dinner parties—such elegance had to be Gabriel. It was uncharacteristic of Alex, though she was the one who prepared the *blanquette de veau*, who tended the small conservatory full of the difficult and rare: orchids, Siberian irises, pomegranates. And Alex herself? Marriage transformed her. Her heavy nut-brown hair, released from its pre-Gabriel rubber band, flowed gleaming to her shoulders, and her mouth was shiny red, and she wore, instead of her pre-Gabriel beige or navy suits, an emerald-green or sapphire silk shift. It was as if Gabriel had *sprung* her.

What had they talked about at those dinners? Nothing trivial—not with Gabe. Nan ate pumpkin mousse or persimmon sorbet or *crepes Directoire* and listened to Gabriel talk about his patients. The five-year-old boy blinded in a street bombing who that day had had his bandages removed. There was this poster on the wall, Gabe said, a girl eating an ice cream cone. Julio asked for *helado*. Couldn't understand why that would make his mother cry.

From the first time she'd met Gabe, one thing had been clear to Nan: he loved the uncertain. With new patients, he was utterly intent—*learning* them, not only their physical deformities but their hopes and dreams. Then, once he'd done what he could for them—often, according to Nan's fellow dinner guests, performing miracles—they passed completely from his thoughts. Nan would sometimes ask about a patient whose story, passionately detailed a few weeks before by Gabriel, had stirred her. The response was a look of utter blankness. Julio? What Julio? By the time Jane was born, not quite a year after their wedding, Gabriel had stopped *learning* Alex. She could not be either pitiful or imperious enough to hold him. She was his—her calm and her self-possession and her beauty—a possession permanently secured, like the orchids and the shining dinner table and the lovely old house. And Gabriel became, despite what might have been predicted of a man who'd delayed marriage till his forties, a good father. Very good; visibly good. (Babies, Nan thought at the time, require endless wooing; they're never quite *yours*.) Alex, at Gabriel's request, had quit work shortly before Jane was born. (She'd been an internal auditor for a large HMO—a job Nan couldn't even begin to imagine.) At the center of her life now were only the baby and Gabe. Fatally, she tried harder to please him. Nan had watched it all in candlelight over a long series of dinners, guiltily enjoying the attention she received from Gabriel's guests and saying nothing. Alex had always been aware of her mother's attraction to her husband. Anything Nan might have said, any advice she might have given, would have been suspect.

Alex handed Nan her tea, in a delicate porcelain cup that rattled softly in its saucer. Then she sat down on the other end of the marshmallow sofa (Gabriel's taste in furniture inclined toward the baronial) and picked up her brandy snifter and held it in both hands. She was pale, Nan saw, even paler than usual, and somehow hunched. Not her shoulders, or her body—it was more as if her spirit were hunched. "Mama," she said. The word had the intonation she used to use as a child, the one that heralded a question that the adults in her life would most likely be disinclined to answer—generally one involving the two great themes of death and sex. A melody Nan would long since have forgotten, except that she heard it, these days, from Jane.

She raised her eyebrows invitingly, but Alex was gazing down into her brandy, so she said, "What, Sweetpea?"—the old endearment popping out.

Still not meeting Nan's eyes, Alex took a shuddering breath. Then she said, in a rush, "I want you to take Jane away from here."

"What?"

"Just go away, as far as you can, as soon as you can. Just the two of you."

"Alex! Why? What's the matter?"

"Jane needs— She needs—" Alex took a long drink of brandy, then set her glass on the coffee table. She rubbed her forehead with two fingers.

"It's a new thing for her, preschool," Nan offered. "You go through stages in a new place. First you're looking in, from the outside. Then you're sort of a minor character. And then, one day, all of a sudden, you're on the inside." She hesitated, then plunged. "Remember when you started school? In Genoa—"

"Mother, please. Italy was light-years ago. I was—what?—five years old."

"Four."

"*Jane* is the child now. I'm talking about Jane. About— Jane's in danger, Mother. Your granddaughter is in danger, and you're not even listening. As usual."

Demoted from Mama to Mother, Nan said meekly, "Tell me."

"Jane is being abused." Alex's eyes found Nan's and held them, her level gaze heart-stoppingly like Tod's. "Sexually," she said.

A bomb dropped inside Nan. She took a deep breath. Licorice-scented steam from her untouched tea met her nostrils and steadied her.

"Alex—are you sure?" She shouldn't have said that—a good mother would have believed her daughter instantly, unquestioningly. Still, Nan thought, now that I *have* said it . . . "How do you know?"

"She's . . . different."

"How?"

Beyond the long windows a neighbor's leaf blower started up, fracturing the stillness, startling in its ordinariness.

"She has bad dreams. She never used to. Scream dreams, she calls them. And at preschool, she's different. Her teacher says she stays in the doll corner all morning, or out by the rabbit hutch. She doesn't play with the other kids."

"Maybe—"

"No!" Alex said. The amber liquid jumped in her glass. "She does things with them. The dolls. She—she strips them naked and ties them up, ties them to the backs of the rabbits."

Nan would have given anything for a cigarette. But there was no smoking in this house—a doctor's house, a house with a young child in it. Outside the room's long windows the sound of the leaf blower approached, receded, approached again.

"I don't understand," she said, momentarily forgetting everything that Tod, a diplomat to the core, had taught her. ("No one wants advice," he used to say. "No one wants *solutions*.") "Why don't you just take her out of there, if you think the staff might be abusing her? But, Alex, those stories in the news—Sometimes it turns out that the children are making it up, not making it up exactly, but, you know, saying what they think the grown-ups want them to say—"

"It's not the preschool."

"Then who—"

"Why are you always so willing to believe people are good?" Alex burst out. "Why do you always just shut your eyes?" She rolled the globe of her brandy glass back and forth between her palms, looking down into it as if it held some message. "It's Gabe," she said, so softly that Nan wasn't sure she'd heard. The jackboot noise of the leaf blower grew louder, closing in. Alex looked up to meet Nan's horrified gaze. "It's Gabe," she repeated, shouting now. Her cheeks were rosy, her eyes unnaturally bright. "Gabe! Gabe!"

The leaf blower stuttered, then stopped. In the silence, Alex reached out a shaking hand for the bottle of Calvados, uncapped it, poured. Nan's field of vision darkened and drew in, blackness smoldering around its edges, until all she could see was the stream of golden liquid falling into the frail bubble of glass. She seemed to see this from a great height, as if she were standing on a ledge looking down. Her heart thudded against her stapled breastbone. Automatically, one hand went to her skirt pocket. Her fingers closed around the plastic vial of nitroglycerin.

Breathe! she told herself. One . . . two. Breathe. Three, four . . . five.

She unscrewed the cap and fumbled out a pill and put it in her mouth. She took a too big swallow of tea, scalding hot, burned her tongue.

Alex didn't notice. She was leaning forward, gripping her brandy glass, and her hands shook so hard that bright drops leapt out onto her white shirt. "The way he touches her, Mama. The way he looks at her." She looked away, out through the French doors to the terrace. Her face tightened with pain. "Last night when I came home, he was—he'd been putting her to bed, and he was coming out of her room, and he—his bathrobe was untied—"

Nan's hands came up in an involuntary motion of dismissal. The cup and saucer on her knees slid forward and fell onto the Persian carpet, splashing the coffee table's carved wooden base and Nan's pant legs with tea. "It can't be," she said. "He wouldn't."

But a memory came to her from the summer before, of walking past the bathroom door in the morning sunshine. Of Jane sitting cross-legged on the linoleum floor next to the clothes hamper, holding a pair of Gabriel's white cotton boxer shorts across her lap. Leaning back against the pedestal of the sink and wiggling her thumb through the fly. It'll grow, she was crooning. It'll grow.

Alex slumped back against the white leather cushions. She looked unspeakably tired. Nan put out a hand and touched her arm. Seconds ticked by.

"Can it wait a little?" Nan said. "Can't you just . . . watch her? Make sure she's— Make sure it's what you think it is?"

"I *have* waited. I've been watching her for weeks now. Don't you see? Somehow I—" Her voice shook. "Somehow I let this happen. I can't let it go on."

"What about taking her to see somebody—a counselor? Have her . . . evaluated." Even as she said it, the ugliness of the word *evaluated,* the coldness of applying it to Jane, made Nan ashamed. She looked away. Outside the long windows the sky had lowered, and clouds plump with rain were moving in from the west.

"A therapist would have to file a report with child welfare. That would mean letting Gabe know." Alex didn't have to say more. Nan knew perfectly well that Gabe would fight such an accusation—true or false, it didn't matter—with all the means he could muster. And with his reputation, his connections, those means were considerable.

"And Jane. They'd question her, Mama. Right now maybe she doesn't know, really *know*, that what's happening to her is bad. But when the therapists—and the courts, Mama, because that's what it'd come to—when they got done with her, she'd know. She'd never be able to forget." Alex paused and looked straight at Nan, her face stripped of everything but need. "Her innocence would be taken away forever."

The way mine was, that day in Genoa. Was that what Alex meant? If so, she did not have to say it. Her white face, her eyes puffy from a night's worth of tears but still keeping their steady Tod-like gaze, said it for her. It's not the same thing at all, Nan wanted to say (but you couldn't refute an accusation that hadn't been made). You can't guilt-trip me into giving you what you want (but the guilt was, arguably, all in Nan's own mind).

Anyway, Alex was right. Nan's doubts didn't matter. It didn't even matter whether Gabe really was abusing Jane. True or false, she'd be questioned. Interrogated. *Hounded.*

Children open you.

"What do you want me to do?" Nan said.

Of course Alex, being Alex, had a plan. She left the room, her step quicker and lighter, and Nan could hear her moving around overhead. She returned with a manila envelope. Inside was a smaller envelope stuffed with fifty-dollar bills ("You've got money, right, Mama? This is all I have, I had to save up so Gabe wouldn't notice"), Jane's passport, and a stiff, folded sheet of children's drawing paper.

So she knew I'd say yes.

Alex sat down close to Nan and unfolded the piece of paper. On it was a heavy dark vertical line studded with notches in red or green, each linked to little balloons filled with matching red or green writing. "I made a Time Line. Here's where we are now. On Wednesday, that's two days from now, you say you're taking Jane to see the *Nutcracker*—there's a matinee that day. You leave town instead. Right away." Alex's finger moved back and forth between the line with its notches and the little balloons. Her fingernails, Nan noticed, were bitten to the quick. Nan couldn't read the writing inside the balloons without her glasses, so Alex read it for her. "Here—four days from now, that should give you time to get away, to hide her—I move out. And here—the day after that—I file for temporary custody of Jane. That way Gabe can't go to the police."

"The police?" Nan said in alarm.

"With a custody order, I'll have possessory rights. That means I can leave Jane in the care of whoever I want. So they can't charge you with kidnapping."

"*Kidnapping?*"

"He'll have to hire a private detective instead. So I talked to one. He told me what he'd do in a case like this, how he'd go about looking for you. I made a list of what not to do. Here—"

"Wait!" Nan said. "I didn't realize—"

"Mother. This is serious. We're not playing around here." That look again. The expression she'd adopted at the age of four, the expression that said, *You've lost the right to question me.* The one that said, *You owe me.*

She's right. I have. I do.

Alex went on. "The detective said no cell phones, that's the first thing he'd check. Get rid of yours, don't even take it with you, so you won't be tempted. Don't call me, not even from a pay phone. Incoming calls can be traced. Don't tell me where you're going—that way I can't tell anybody else. Don't use your real name, or Jane's. Don't use your bank card, charge cards, checkbook, anything like that. Pay for everything in cash. Okay?"

Nan was silent, feeling her life as she'd known it up till now tug at its moorings. Feeling herself come adrift.

"Okay? Mama—are you with me so far?"

"I don't understand," she said. "Why wouldn't Gabe go to the police?"

"He won't."

"But . . . she's his daughter."

"He just won't. There're things he wouldn't want them looking into, things that might affect his license."

She's got something on both of us, then.

"He'll do it through the courts, where his reputation'll protect him from any awkward questions. We can't let that happen. Because he really might win. Who's going to believe that such a fine, distinguished citizen is a child molester?"

Who, indeed? Nan thought.

"Where were we? Okay. Pay for everything in cash, that way you can't be traced. Can you get hold of enough cash, between now and Wednesday?"

"I—I think so. How much? I mean, how long would I need it for?"

"I'm getting to that." Alex's finger tapped the Time Line. "Here's where you and Jane lie low till I get temporary custody. Then—somewhere in here—I get a place ready for us, Jane and me. Then you bring her to me, or I come and get her. Four to six weeks should do it."

Nan struggled to clear her mind, to match her daughter logic for logic. "But how will I know when you're ready? I can't phone you, and you won't know where to phone me."

"From what the detective said, our motto should be 'Back to the fifties.' We'll use the Personals, in the paper. Nobody reads newspapers anymore. What we'll do is, twice a month I'll put a message in the *P.I.* A progress report."

"How . . ." Nan began faintly.

"On the seventh and the twenty-first of each month. All you have to do is get hold of the *P.I.* and read through the Personals. We can't use real names, though. The message will say "To Pookie," and it'll be signed "From Hippie.""

Nan felt her lips curve in a smile, despite the grave substance of this conversation. "Hippie" and "Pookie" were the names three-year-old Alex had bestowed on herself and Nan, her own versions of names from a German children's book they'd had in Bonn. Nan would have thought Alex had long ago forgotten those names. The sound of them made her feel oddly shy. She looked out over the terrace, half expecting to see the sun break through the mountainous mass of clouds.

"You'll do it, then? Mama?"

When Nan turned back to her daughter, Alex's face was calm. Like Tod, she'd always been comforted by organizing and planning. And now, as so many times in the past with Tod, that comfort deepened and widened and extended itself to Nan. The beauty and calm (now that the neighbor's leaf blower was silenced) and settledness of the old house seemed to enfold her, to surround and soften the terrible thing her daughter had revealed.

She leaned forward to say *No*, to say, *Maybe we should wait*—the tip of her tongue already curling to meet the roof of her mouth—when suddenly Alex stiffened. Her head turned toward the foyer. Nan heard the sound of a car door closing, then the large heavy front door of the house opening, then Jane's voice shouting, "Nana, Nana, Nana!"

Gabriel stood in the archway with Jane perched on his shoulders, her chin at a queenly angle, her small hands clutching his curly silver hair. Together they were so tall that Gabriel had to stoop so that Jane's head would clear the carved molding above them. He winced as Jane, already struggling to get down, caught him in the ribs with one bright-red rubber boot.

She ran to Nan, clambered onto her lap, nuzzled her in an almost animal way, lamb to her ewe. Whispered into her ear, "A runcible cat!" to which Nan whispered back, "With crimson whiskers!"—their special greeting, a secret guarded with giggles and sidelong glances. Nan relaxed beneath the warmth and weight of Jane. She laid her cheek against Jane's thick horsetail hair, damp with rain.

"An unexpected pleasure," Gabriel said to Nan. Then, to Alex, "Don't you have yoga class till noon on Mondays?"

"It was canceled," Alex said. (Lied, Nan thought, checking her watch: only ten thirty, yet she seemed to have been here a lifetime.)

The openness was gone from Alex's face. She looked—smoothing her hair, running a finger inside her sweatshirt collar—no more surprised than an early homecoming would merit. Maybe Nan shouldn't have wondered at this—Alex had always had the ability to hide her feelings. But still. How could the unspeakable thing they'd just been speaking of disappear so completely? The Time Line had vanished; Nan heard a faint crackle as Alex crossed her legs.

"*You're* home early," Alex said.

"That maxillofacial was canceled. Remember, the little girl whose mother—" He broke off, with a glance at Jane. "Skin graft didn't take." Bending down, he picked up Nan's spilled cup and saucer and teabag and set them on the table. Then he leaned close to brush Nan's cheek with his. She smelled, beneath the familiar fragrance of Obsession, post-surgery disinfectant soap mingled with the faint tang of blood. Gabriel looked at the bottle of Calvados and the brandy snifter, both of which had mysteriously migrated to Nan's side of the coffee table. "Tough morning?" he said to Nan.

Quick as thought, she reached around Jane and lifted the glass and drank. "Irregular verbs," she said. Gabriel, in that way he had of knowing all about you, knew about her literacy tutoring and her Spanish class. The brandy burned in her throat, down her esophagus, into her stomach, laying a trail of light as it went. Gabriel watched her with an amused expression. His eyes—greenish silver, the clouded color of Coke bottles just out of the refrigerator, oddly lighter than his olive skin—reminded Nan, as always, of one-way mirrors. She was seen, but she could not see in.

Jane slid off Nan's lap and went to Alex. "Look, Mama! I'm a turtle." She turned around to show off her new backpack, a turtle's shell. Then she shrugged free of its straps and unzipped it and began to show Alex the drawings she'd done at preschool.

"We decided to play hooky, didn't we, Janey?" Gabriel said. "It's a shame to be indoors on such a nice day."

Nice day? Nan looked out at the gray, misty morning. Did Gabriel suspect something? Was that why he'd come home early? Or was this— Nan went cold all over—a way he'd found to be alone with Jane?

Children open you.

Gabriel went into the dining room and stood by the long rosewood table opening his mail. Like Alex, he now seemed completely normal. This made Nan feel the distance between husband and wife: two people who barely looked at each other, the smoothness of whose interaction came from never quite engaging. She recognized it from her years in the Foreign Service—the gingerly demeanor of couples who found themselves repeatedly stranded together in alien territory.

"Nana!" Jane knelt down in front of Nan and flung her arms around Nan's knees. "Come upstairs and see my guinea pigs. We got them on Saturday. They don't even know you yet!"

|

The sky had darkened to gunmetal, the mist turned into fine, almost imperceptible rain. Nan, crunching across the gravel to her car, inhaling the blessedly fresh, damp air, ducking under the low-hanging cedar and feeling its wet-feather branches brush her cheek and neck, thought, I don't know what to do.

|

The summer Jane turned three, Gabriel and Alex had bought a cottage on the Olympic Peninsula near Port Angeles, where Nan (it goes without saying, Gabriel nevertheless said) was welcome anytime. After lunch on a July day singing with heat, she was nearly asleep under the limbs of a huge old madrona on the bluff overlooking the Dungeness River. The *Peninsula Gazette* (29 NATIONS AGREE TO BRIBERY PLAN) was spread across her face to keep off flies.

Soft summer voices. Nan removed the newspaper, looked down to the river. Gabriel and Alex came into view, Gabriel carrying Jane slung over one shoulder and whistling a song Nan didn't quite remember the words to. (Singing, he couldn't carry a tune, but he could whistle anything.) Alex shook out a blanket the color of marigolds and they settled on the riverbank.

Nan was no more than fifteen yards away, but above them, where they didn't think to look, and hidden by the shadow of the madrona. Honorably she put on her glasses and returned to the newspaper. BRIBERY BAN, she saw with disappointment. She gave up and watched the three of them. It was a perfect midsummer day. Puffy white clouds, doubled in the shining river; the liquid calls of cardinals; the fragrance of sun-warmed strawberries in the field behind Nan. The sun printed two shadows on the yellow blanket: one for Alex, one for Gabriel/Jane. They sat like that for a while. Then Alex got up and walked down to the river's edge and stood with her back turned, looking out over the water.

In Gabriel's lap Jane stirred, stretched. The radiance of sleep gilded her bare arms and legs, and her hair clung damply to her perfect skull. Gabriel's hands moved over her, his palm smoothing her forehead, his fingers tucking the light brown hair behind her ear. Even at this distance, Nan could feel his tenderness. Jane arched her back. One round coppery-rose arm was flung out; a hand clenched a fistful of yellow blanket. Her eyes opened, and she seemed to look straight up at Nan. Gabriel stroked Jane's leg. Cicadas sang in the long grass where Nan lay. Gabriel's hand cupped Jane's knee. The sound of the cicadas soared and fell. At last Jane's eyes closed, and she fell asleep again, and finally Nan did too.

When she woke, the light had changed, the sun was veiled in thin clouds, and the riverbank below was empty. There was only a square of bruised grass where the blanket had rested. A loon skimmed the surface of the water. Nan's back hurt from rocks hidden in the grass under the madrona, and her neck was stiff, and she was sweaty. She remembered a small waterfall, a quarter mile or so downriver. She climbed down and walked along the riverbank, taking her time, concentrating on her footing.

The waterfall was steeper than she'd remembered. A stream fell straight down over rocks into the river with a homing sound, water into water. Ten yards or so away from it, Nan stopped. It was like listening to the organ in a great cathedral. She sat down on a fallen log and rubbed her palms over the thick, woolly moss and waited for the sound to fill her brain. To wash away the lingering, uncomfortable strangeness of the afternoon. Instead, the words of the song Gabriel had been whistling surfaced in her mind.

Be careful—it's my heart
It's not my watch you're holding,
It's my heart

Between the log where Nan sat and the waterfall, the riverbank rose steeply, then leveled out into a wide granite shelf that disappeared behind the curtain of falling water. Climbing slowly over rocks and crumbling shale, grasping fistful after fistful of sumac and cedar, she edged onto the shelf. Inches away now, the roar of falling water filled her head; the pounding of it entered her body. She hesitated. Cold spray needled her face, her bare arms: a small, inviting pain. She took a deep breath, then ducked behind the curtain of water.

Peace. Not silence, then, but sound? For a long time she stood there in the gloom, pressed against the rocks in her thin, wet summer dress, and let the sound wrap around her, fill her, wear away whatever it was she'd seen back there on the bluff. A touch; a look. The heat, she told herself. The light off the river. Dreams of a drowsy summer afternoon.

|

I don't know what to do, Nan continued to think, all that long Monday afternoon. And all that evening, smoking forbidden cigarettes and drinking forbidden brandy and pacing through the three rooms of her apartment in West Seattle. It *could* all be Alex's own unhappiness coloring perfectly innocent events; it could even be Alex's jealousy of Gabriel's love for Jane.

I don't know what to do.

But of course she did know. And this time, unlike that July day on the river bluff, what she did would not be nothing.

On Monday night Nan barely slept. On Tuesday morning she sat sleep-deprived over a breakfast of black coffee and cigarettes in the chair that had been Tod's—something she'd trained herself to do, a gesture of acceptance, preferable to sitting across the table from his ghost. The window of the kitchenette was open to the little garden. Birds were beginning their sunrise call-and-response, and the white trunks of birches emerged against the green wall of spruce and hemlock. Inside these three gracious, spacious rooms—the apartment found for a distraught Nan, a Nan nearly undone by her husband's long, slow death, by Gabriel—was the life she had, finally, made for herself. Her calm and beautiful refuge.

How can I give this up? How can Alex ask me to?

But in fact (Be honest!), it was already gone. Destroyed—blasted to ruins—by what Alex had told her, in the same way that, long ago, Nan's innocent seven-year-old's world had been shattered by the newspaper photographs of the concentration camps that she'd found in a hatbox on a high closet shelf, the year after the war ended. Her grandmother, Dorothea, never knew what made little Nan turn suddenly grave. A delayed reaction to her mother's death three years before? The onset of what the Church chose to call the Age of Reason? All Dorothea ever knew was that some essential innocence had departed.

Innocence: a strange word to use for the state of not knowing, Nan reflected as she watched the smoke from her cigarette spiral upward. A word (the nuns had pointed out long ago) that originally meant "doing no harm." The chain was all too clear: Nan to Alex to Jane, the loss of innocence handed down like some evil legacy. Though Nan would have liked to escape this thought, she found she could not. How much, she wondered unwillingly, did Alex remember of their year in Genoa? Of that one terrible revelatory day?

Naptime. Muted sounds from across the hall. Waking in the heavy afternoon light, the taste of sleep sour in her mouth, to see four-year-old Alex standing silently on the threshold. Her thumb was in her mouth, and a shabby square of blue blanket trailed from her fist. Where's the *bambinaia*? was Nan's first thought. Why isn't she looking after her? Then she felt Jack standing by the side of the bed, frozen in the act of lifting up the covers. He was naked. The blood banged so loud in her ears that she had to turn away. When she looked again, Alex was gone, her footsteps clattering away down the loggia to the sun-filled balcony, where she fell two stories onto the rose-colored paving stones below.

Afterward, nursed devotedly, guiltily, by Nan, Alex never spoke of the afternoon that led up to her broken leg, only of the fall itself. But from that day, she changed. She formed attachments, but only mild ones, easily relinquished. There was always a part of herself that she kept back, for the time when the other person would fail her and she would be once again on her own. The tilt of her head said that it was wise to keep an *own* to be on. Nan's guilt was great—she'd been the cause, however indirectly, of physical harm to her daughter, and probably of psychological harm as well. She never knew how Alex interpreted what she'd seen in her mother's bedroom, or even whether she remembered it, because she was afraid to ask. Yet, despite her guilt, Nan did not stop having affairs. She just made sure to hide them better. Wasn't this what made Alex see her childhood as (Nan knew) she saw it now? The Family as constructed by Nan, arranged like an old-fashioned photograph with everyone in place, frozen in a crazy attempt to look natural, smile, pause, explosion of powder and flash.

Nan got up and poured herself another cup of coffee, then sat down again at the little table. She turned the pack of Marlboros over and over between her fingers. Forbidden coffee; forbidden cigarettes; forbidden anxiety and stress. She felt the way she used to during the years in the Foreign Service, before each of their many downward moves. That Verge Feeling, she used to call it. Now, as then, it was all to do over again, the acclimating to a new reality—but requiring an adjustment far greater. Requiring the acceptance of a secret, ugly reality *inside* the one you've always known. Useless admonitions from the once-memorized State Department publication *Handbook on Orientation for Wives and Dependents* (unaffectionately known to its readership as *HOWDY*) floated to the front of her mind. *Do not deal with the black market. Do not take pictures from planes or trains or bridges. Do not wear shorts or bathing suits on the street.*

Alex's Time Line, which Nan had found tucked into her coat pocket when she got home the day before, lay on the table in front of her. She should get up now, right now, and begin. So much to do if she and Jane were to leave the next morning. Money; pack; stop the newspaper and ask her upstairs neighbor to collect the mail; let Mariela know she'd need to request another tutor. (*Abusador!*—Mariela's word for her ex-husband—echoed suddenly in Nan's head.) There was no one else in Seattle to inform. No friends close enough to miss her. (Tod's long dying, begun almost as soon as they'd retired to Seattle, had left little time for forming new friendships, and then after that there'd been Jane.) No lover. (The man she thought of as the Last Lover had decamped two years earlier.) She should get up right now and go to the phone and call Deenie, let her know that she and Jane were coming to Providence.

Instead, she lit a cigarette from the stub of the old one, the way she and Deenie used to do, two high school girls coughing and giggling in the tall grass behind the gymnasium, nearly fifty years ago. She sat with her elbows on the scrubbed wooden table and smoked and looked out the window. In the center of the little garden was a twisted apple tree silvered over with lichen. Green moss and tiny, tight-curled ferns filled the cracks in the paving stones around it. That was the beauty of the Northwest, as Tod had so often pointed out: green all year round. The smell of wet leaves and bark and alderwood smoke from her upstairs neighbor's chimney rode the chill, damp breeze into the kitchenette. In Providence, where she and Jane were going, there would be snow. White roads and black, bare trees and the city smells of cinders and car exhaust. It would be weeks before she sat like this again in this verdant, peace-filled place that Gabriel had found for her.

Gabriel.

What didn't I know, and when didn't I know it?

Not that Nixon, in Nan Mulholland's far from humble opinion, had ever known much of anything. More than Reagan, though, even before the revelation of Alzheimer's. She'd met Reagan once, their palms sparking briefly, at a reception in Warsaw during the pre-revelation years of nodding affability. Wasn't it shortly after that that she'd misread, with delight, the headline SURGEONS REMOVE FLUFF FROM REAGAN'S BRAIN?

Stick to the subject.

Tod had often found it necessary to excuse his wife's proclivity for glossing things over. "Remembering," he used to say, "means selecting the things that we can bear and letting them crowd out the things we can't. Memory isn't about remembering. It's about forgetting." Here in her own place, alone, listening to the birds celebrate the mild morning, it was easy to dismiss what she had seen, what Alex had seen. Yet easy, too, to give it too much meaning? Alex's desperation had been real; she truly believed what she'd told Nan; but was her belief well founded? Nan simply didn't know. Her last glimpse of Gabriel had shown her only a middle-aged man tired from the morning's surgery, his daughter's lunch box in one hand, turning away to scan the day's mail.

One thing, though, was clear. Nan stubbed out her cigarette, rose, went to the phone. Gabriel—a man who stopped at nothing to repossess what he might have lost—would be a formidable antagonist. He had power, connections, a sterling reputation; above all, he had passion.

Jane was his passion.

Three

When their plane landed at La Guardia, Nan and Jane took a shuttle to the Port Authority in Manhattan, where they just managed to catch the last bus to Providence. (First Nan bought two tickets to Baltimore at the Greyhound window, asking a lot of loud questions and pretending to throw up.) The bus line that went to Providence was called Bonanza, which Nan, settling the two of them near the back, out of range of the driver's rearview mirror, took as a good omen. Jane snuggled into her seat, one arm clutching Squirrel, the other tucked into Nan's. The huge, loud, neon-scribbled expanse of the Port Authority seemed to have made her realize how far from home they really were. Her spirits rising—maybe this trip could after all be seen as an adventure?—Nan gave Jane one of the Kit Kat bars she'd managed to buy before they boarded, and took the other herself. They ate them, as always, the same way, breaking off a stick at a time, making three bites of each stick.

By Bridgeport Jane was asleep. The cheek she turned toward Nan was still printed faintly with the fleur-de-lis of the airplane upholstery. Nan smoothed the thick horsetail hair. Everything (her spirits rose further) had gone smoothly. She checked her watch, set now to East Coast time—nearly eleven fifteen—then snapped off her overhead light and leaned back in the high seat. Behind her came the intermittent sound of a child's cough, voices rising and falling in Spanish. About three hours to their destination, now. She'd chosen Providence because her oldest friend in the world had just moved there, and—truly providential!—she hadn't mentioned this fact to Alex and Gabe. Deenie. Geraldine Tice, her name had been, until marriage had unfortunately changed it to Geraldine Horsfal. Her last letter, three weeks ago, had had her maiden name written above the new return address—a senior moment, Nan supposed. *Tice,* she whispered to the darkened, orange-and-urine-scented bus—and that one syllable brought Deenie back. They'd found each other in assembly the first day of freshman year, two scholarship girls from the heart (not the "inner city" then) of Philly, both tall for their age, both lost. Nan was thirteen; Deenie, fourteen. They'd been what Nan's father used to call "close as close" ever since. (Hey, Two Peas! he'd yell up the stairs. Dinner's ready!) In nearly half a century, and often separated by half a world, they'd never lost touch.

There'd been no time to call Deenie from the Port Authority. But she would have heard the messages Nan had left on her recorder yesterday and again this morning. By now she'd have made up the bed where Nan had slept five years ago, when she'd visited her in Chicago after Tod died. A vase of fresh flowers on the nightstand, and a bottle of spring water. A lavender sachet under each pillow. Sleepy now, her head falling back against the little paper bus pillow, Nan thought, Deenie will take care of me. Of us. Quick, warm Deenie. Two seats ahead of her a man began to snore: that once-maddening, now nostalgic sound. Nan thought of Tod, then of Deenie again; then, lulled by the bus's ponderous, rolling rhythm, of nothing at all.

|

"You got lucky, lady," the taxi driver said, engaging Nan's reluctant eyes in his rearview mirror. "You and your daughter. You got the last white cabbie in Providence. I'm on the endangered species list. Ha-ha!"

Jane leaned forward. "I'm not her daughter," she said, in a pleased voice. She loved having useful information to impart to grown-ups. "I'm her *grand*daughter."

"Shhh!" Nan pulled her back, held her firmly across the shoulders.

Jane squirmed. "Nana! Don't!"

"Be quiet!" Nan whispered, so fiercely that Jane subsided. Nan could feel her surprise: her beloved Nana never got mad at her. Her beloved Nana *liked* her to be full of facts.

Evading the taxi driver's mirrored eyes, Nan worried. Once again they'd made themselves conspicuous, but this time she hadn't wanted to. Would he remember them? Remember their (genuine, this time) destination?

Nan sighed. If so, there was nothing she could do about it. Asking to be taken back to the bus terminal would make them even more memorable. And anyway, this had been the last cab in the deserted plaza when the bus pulled up in Providence. She and Jane had beat out a pale, baleful-looking priest for it—Nan feeling a flash of the same surprised fierceness she'd so often felt when Alex was little: how ruthless you could be when a child's safety was at stake. The unheated cab smelled of Juicy Fruit and old cigars. Nan buttoned the top button of her coat and turned up the collar: she'd forgotten Northeast Decembers. Then she zipped up Jane's too-thin Seattle-weight parka and put one arm around her and pulled her close. Jane, resigned and silent, huddled into Nan's armpit. Why hadn't she asked where they were going? Jane, usually so curious, so watchful. Had Alex told her not to ask? Or was docility in strange circumstances a characteristic of sexually abused children? Which you know nothing about, Nan reminded herself. To still her rising panic, she snatched at her mantra. *Remember the Plan.*

It was two in the morning. A poor time for houseguests to arrive, but Deenie would be expecting them. They swept along empty city streets, through darkness that could have been anywhere, until they passed a large white theatrically lighted dome. "State House," the driver tossed over his shoulder. It wore a ring of white Christmas lights, like blurred pearls in the foggy cold.

Jane began to kick the back of the driver's seat.

"We're almost there," Nan said. "Not long now."

"Where ya's from?" the driver asked.

"Virginia." The lie came easily, almost automatically.

"Yeah? Ya don't sound it."

Jane said, "Actually, we're not from there. We're from— Nana! Ow!"

Nan loosened her hold on Jane and put her lips close to Jane's ear. "Be! Quiet!" she said, in a soft but (she hoped) sufficiently menacing voice. Jane pulled away, stiff with fury. Dismayed and fearful, but unable to think what else to do, Nan let her be.

"Now me," continued the driver, as if he'd noticed nothing unusual, "I'm from New York originally. The Bronx. I hadda get out, know what I'm sayin'? Helluva town, Manhattan. But the Bronx, that *is* hell. Pardon my English."

Jane kicked harder. They were on a cobblestone street now, the cab bouncing rhythmically. Suddenly it swerved. Of its own accord, Nan's arm shot out to hold Jane in her seat. The cab slammed to a stop.

We've been followed.

Nan twisted around, still holding on to Jane. A bulky figure pushing a shopping cart trundled past her window and crossed in front of the cab.

"It's shame on them if they get nailed," the cabbie said. "Hey, that's what ya got insurance for, am I right?"

"Nana!" Jane said. "Ow!"

Trembling with relief, Nan released her. She gripped the back of the seat and pulled herself upright. "Now sit still!" she whispered.

"This here's the river they're putting back," the driver said, waving an unlit cigar. "Used to be all paved over. See how they're building those little curved bridges, for walking? Now the mayor's callin' Providence the Venice of the Northeast."

Nan's hands were so cold her knuckles ached. She couldn't find her gloves—must have left them on the bus—so she tucked her hands into the opposite sleeves of her coat the way the nuns at the Academy used to do. Her earlier sense of adventure had completely evaporated. All she wanted now was to be enfolded by Deenie, relieved of her suitcase, tucked between warm flannel sheets.

The driver found Benefit Street and had their one suitcase out on the brick pavement in front of number 215 before Nan had finished calculating the tip. A narrow frame house, attached on either side to other narrow frame houses, it rose abruptly from the pavement, unsoftened by grass or shrubs. No lights in any of the windows. The driver insisted on waiting until they got inside. Nan went up the steps, holding tight to Jane's hand, and lifted the brass knocker and let it fall. Waiting, she saw a match flare inside the cab; its engine was the only sound on the deserted street. A cold, fog-laden breeze licked her face. She let the knocker fall again, heavily, twice.

Nothing.

Maybe Deenie's left the door unlocked for us and gone to bed?

But when she tried the knob, it didn't turn. She banged on the door with her fist. Beside her, Jane seized the skirt of her coat. Nan put one arm around her and continued to assault the door. No answering lights came on; no sound of eager approaching footsteps. Twisting the cloth of Nan's coat, Jane began to cry, not loudly but a soft, dry, hopeless sound.

Oh, no, Nan thought. *No!* The single syllable filled her head, no room now for hopes, for plans, just the sound of her fist, over and over, against the cold unyielding wood.

|

The next day, Thursday, after phoning three times and getting Deenie's recorder, she knew she had to go back.

She hesitated, worried about taking Jane there. Already, not even twenty-four hours into this trip, she'd come up against the stark realization of the single parent: she would not ever be alone. A child of four could not be left, would be with her everywhere, every hour of the day, waking and sleeping—a new experience for Nan Mulholland. Life in the Foreign Service had always included built-in child care: a long line of women, au pairs and *bambinaias* and *panis*—the name changed with the country—whom she'd come to think of, collectively, as The Nannies.

She sat down in a shaft of morning sunlight in the Frederick's little down-at-heel lobby—the kindly taxi driver had taken them, at two thirty in the morning, to a shabby residential hotel owned by his cousin—and tried to come up with a plan. In the corner by the counter Jane was building what looked like a castle out of Legos provided by the hotelkeeper's wife, a wide, smiling woman who seemed to speak only Spanish. Nan had dressed Jane that morning in clean clothes, a yellow turtleneck and jeans, and wrestled her horsetail hair into the French braids Jane had demanded. Now Jane examined each Lego thoughtfully, keeping some and discarding others, her small face rapt. For the first time since their journey began, she looked the way a child should look. More than anything, Nan wanted to hang on to that. Besides, there was the question of what she might find at Deenie's. Clearly something had gone wrong. Tired from the long night of traveling, Nan fought the urge to bury her face in her hands and weep. What should she do? What *could* she do?

Jane herself solved the problem. When at last Nan rose and went over and held out her hand, saying with false cheerfulness, "Time to go, Grape Eyes," Jane threw herself onto the floor, forehead to the dirty olive tile, small bottom up in the air. Her old baby posture of outrage. She *would not* leave her Princess House. She *would not* go back to the Spook House. The hotelkeeper's wife, moved by such passion, offered to keep Jane with her; and Jane, her face smoothing out instantly, begged Nan to say yes.

She looks kind, this Consuelo. And we need her.

For a bleak moment Nan's mind filled with images of all the refugees in all the countries she and Tod had lived in.

We are the refugees now.

She put one hand on the counter to steady herself. From now on, the kindness of strangers would, more and more, have to be relied on. Trusted.

"All right"—Nan grasped for her baby Spanish—"*Sí, gracias. Muchas gracias.*"

"Coca-Cola, *querida*?" Consuelo said, smiling down at Jane, who was already scrambling to her feet. "*Lo quieres?*"

Nan bent down and hugged her. "A runcible cat!" she whispered into her ear. But Jane didn't answer. She put her hand into Consuelo's, shooting a sidelong glance at Nan. See? said that look, so like her mother's. I'd rather be with *her*.

Nan watched her granddaughter follow Consuelo's bulky, slow-moving figure down the hall to the kitchen ("*Está aquí!*" "Here?" "*Sí, aquí!*"). Would Jane remember to say nothing about where they'd come from? Would she remember their alias? Nan had chosen "Tice" when they'd registered the night before; she and Jane had practiced at breakfast at a nearby Burger King. Consuelo's lack of English protected them somewhat; but Jane, too, would have to be trusted. There was no alternative.

Outside, in the cold blue morning, Nan felt free and light. She walked to the corner and caught the number 32 bus to the East Side, as instructed by Consuelo. When it stopped at the corner of College and Benefit, she got off and walked the two short blocks to Deenie's place. Again there was no answer to the knocker's clank, or to Nan's knuckles on the green-painted door. But this time when she tried the doorknob, it turned. Her stomach lurched. She pushed, and the door swung inward.

"Deenie?" she called through the narrow opening. Then, louder, "Deen? You there?"

There was no answer.

Nan hesitated on the step. Why was the door unlocked now, and not last night? Or had she been mistaken—it had been so late, and she'd been so tired, so worried that the cabdriver might get suspicious. The sun warmed the top of her head; deep breaths of frost-filled air made her heart bob. Yes; no; yes. What made her think she even had a choice?

A quick look up and down the street revealed no one except a lone dog walker whose back was turned. Nan slipped through the opening and found herself in a small foyer. Closing the door behind her, she stood still, unable to see, the bright day printed in spangled afterimages on the blackness. The space in which she stood felt stuffy and sealed off. She could smell the cindery odor of soot, the ghosts of old spices, a touch of mildew. She moved forward slowly, hands out, until she touched cool wood, a glass doorknob. It turned.

Here, in whatever room it was, the darkness was less absolute. There was an odd sound, a sort of clucking, not rhythmic enough for a clock. Ahead of her, at the other end of the room, fingernail lines of daylight suggested windows. As she moved cautiously toward the light, chairs, a low table, a sofa made themselves known to her knees. At last she felt along the sills for the window shades, snapped one up. Bright sunshine fell over her. Behind her the clucking sound multiplied and grew louder. Turning, she saw a figure in a dark coat, uttered a little choked scream, then understood: it was herself, her own reflection in the mirror over the mantel. The fireplace was flanked on either side by a row of tall humped shapes, like giant eggs, in red corduroy shrouds. Legs wavering in relief, Nan sat down abruptly in a wing chair. How could she have forgotten Deenie's birds?

When she felt steady again, Nan took off her coat and put up the rest of the shades, sent them clattering to the top of the tall windows, flooding the room with light. Then she pulled the covers off all six birdcages. There was a great eruption, chirping and scolding, pinwheels of blue and yellow and green. Cheered by the commotion, Nan walked around the room, inspecting. Goldfish puttering in a bowl; a pot of mauve chrysanthemums on the hearth in front of the fireplace; propped on the mantel a framed, familiar newspaper clipping: CHICAGO WOMAN NAMED MS. SENIOR ILLINOIS; WAY TO GO, GERALDINE! above a dim Deenie in ball gown and tiara. The parakeets' water dishes were nearly full, the goldfish bowl unclouded, the chrysanthemums' soil, when Nan dug a finger into it, damp. Deenie couldn't have been gone long. Maybe, Nan thought, she just went somewhere overnight. But where? There was a cousin she'd been close to, growing up; but he'd lived abroad for years.

The mail (Nan was frankly snooping now) did seem like a lot. A stack of unaddressed Christmas cards—"Peace on Earth, Good Will to Men"—lay next to an uncapped pen on the pretty Empire writing desk.

Deenie seemed to be in the middle of inserting "wo" before "men" on all of them. The pen no longer wrote. Nan put the cap back on anyway. If Deenie had gone away, where was she?

A few feathers, like languid snowflakes, floated on the stale air and drifted slowly to the floor. The parakeets had settled into loud, steady chirping, a clear, virtuous sound. One of them ventured, "What's up, Doc? Pretty boy!" Biting back a nervous giggle, Nan went back into the little foyer and opened the remaining doors. A closet: more mustiness, threaded with the heady smell of mothballs. Kitchen. Bathroom. The last door led to Deenie's bedroom. The big pearwood canopy bed where Nan had slept on her visit to Chicago stood in the center of the room, sunlight falling across it through half-closed shutters. Nan could smell Deenie's perfume, L'Air du Temps, unchanged since she was sixteen. (Attila the Nun bursting into the upper school lavatory—"What's that I smell?"—and afterward, in detention, Deenie's whispered joke: What's black and white and can't get into an elevator? A nun with a spear through her head.)

Deenie, thought Nan, with longing.

Instead of a closet there was an old-fashioned wardrobe in looming mahogany. Feeling unhappily like Miss Marple, Nan peered inside. But how would she know what garments were missing? On a table by the bed, an answering machine blinked. Nan pushed the PLAY button and Deenie's greeting came on:

Enough of all this fiddle-dee-dee—
I'd like to know why you called me

followed by Nan's own voice announcing her imminent visit. Frail and wavering, an old lady's voice. Her two messages were the only ones on the tape.

On top of the wardrobe something caught her eye, a glint of metal. Was it her imagination, or did the square shape seem to beckon? Nan rose and dragged a small oval-backed chair from the corner and positioned it in front of the wardrobe. The seat was covered in the same slippery satin as the bedspread. Nan pulled off her shoes. She grabbed a corner of the wardrobe and knelt on the little chair, then, with her other hand on the wardrobe's carved top, pulled herself to her feet. Slowly she straightened up. It was a metal box, like a small suitcase, with a metal handle and a lock—too big to manage with one hand. Grasping either side, Nan tried to lift it. Too heavy. Her heart made a tiny fish-dive in her chest. Impossible to climb down from the chair and hold on to the box at the same time. Let the box fall? No—throw it onto the bed. She began slowly, carefully, dragging the box toward her.

"Who you are?"

A man's voice, deep, foreign. Nan's heart dived again; a flash of heat ran through her. The heavy box leapt out of her grasp. She had just time to think, *The nitro!* before the chair beneath her vanished.

Then, with the abruptness of dreams, she found herself sitting on the closed lid of a toilet in cold fluorescent light.

"This, it shall pain. I am sorry."

On his knees before her, a dark-haired young man upended a green bottle onto a folded square of cloth, then softly, delicately, stroked her knee. "I am sorry, I am sorry," he repeated as she winced. The tiny white-tiled bathroom filled with a smell like Clorox. Nan made the mistake of looking down at the dark-red glistening mouth of her wound. Blood, bright blood, crawled down her shin. She swayed and would have fallen sideways if the young man hadn't stopped her with a quick hand between her shoulder blades.

"*Nyet!*" he said. (So he was Russian, then.) "Do not look." She did not have to tell him that the sight of blood made her faint. He passed a large hand lightly across her eyes to make them close.

She felt again the sting of the disinfectant, then something cool and jellied, then a soft pad and the winding of tape around and behind her knee. The young man's hands moved slowly and with care. He whistled under his breath.

"*Konyets!* Now can look."

Nan opened her eyes. Her knee was covered by a neat square bandage, which the young man, sitting back on his haunches, regarded with satisfaction. Bright black eyes met hers. They both, at the same instant, became aware of the pink-mottled expanse of Nan's legs, bare from underpants to ankle socks. The young man looked away and began rolling up the cotton gauze in its tissue paper, capping the bottle of disinfectant, laying a green stalk of aloe (so that was the soothing coolness she'd felt) on the edge of the sink. His large hands were stained blue and yellow and red. He kept his body apart from hers, not easy in the tiny space, his head with its black springy curls tactfully turned away. He washed his hands with a scuffed chunk of soap, then dried them on the back of his jeans.

"You are okay? I bring to put on," he said, and left, closing the door behind him.

Nan looked down at her bare legs. The scar along one thigh, where they'd taken the vein for her bypass, looked starker under the fluorescent light. No old-lady scribbling of blue veins, at least. If only I'd worn a skirt, she thought. No—then the cut would've been worse.

Her charcoal pants lay in a heap in the bathtub. When she held them up, she saw that one leg was torn and bloody. Maybe she'd somehow landed on the metal box? The pockets were empty—the nitro pills must still be in the pocket of her Hidden Assets slip. But she didn't seem to need them now.

A knock on the door; then a large paint-stained hand, offering a black garment.

"Thank you," Nan said.

"Please!"

The door closed.

Nan unfolded the garment, which turned out to be a pair of black jeans. Not something Deenie would ever wear, not unless she'd turned punk and lost thirty pounds. For God's sake, said Nan to Nan, instead of worrying about who the owner of these pants is, you should be worrying about who the man outside the door is. And why you can't remember being brought in here. Probably a concussion, in which case—she remembered from the Personal Safety section of *HOWDY*, the State Department's handbook for wives—she shouldn't have been moved. Well, too late now.

Squeezing into the jeans, Nan recalled *HOWDY*'s warnings about just such situations as the one she now found herself in. *Watch out for agents provocateurs. They most often appear to be ordinary people, unmemorable in appearance and speech* (Well, she thought, that doesn't apply to my rescuer) *and proffering aid or consolation.* (Uh-oh.) *They tend to appear precisely when needed.*

The jeans, left unzipped, would do. They were wide-legged enough not to disturb the bandaged knee, which was something. Nan pulled her sweater down over the gap at her stomach and smoothed her hair. Then she rolled up her own torn pants and tucked them under her arm.

"How you are feeling?" the young man asked when she opened the door. He'd been hovering in the hallway. He reached out and took her rolled-up pants, then put a hand under her elbow. This was the first chance she'd had to really look at him. Tall and lanky, with a round rosy face and that head of black curls like a Renaissance putto. A cherub's head on a man's body. Another kind stranger? What choice had she but to think so?

"Better," she said, surprised to find it was true.

Visibly relieved, the young man led her through the hall into the living room, moving slowly to accommodate her limp. Glancing into Deenie's bedroom as they passed, Nan saw that the metal box had disappeared.

"My friend, Efrem, also drives taxi, he is like you. Sick with blood. But he never learns. Tries to be—how is it?—*boyets*?"

Nan guessed, "Brave?"

"*Nyet, nyet*—he fights other men on stage. For money. Naturally, his mantle health is never no good. At last he has nervous breakthrough."

They stopped in front of the sofa. The birds acknowledged their presence with a storm of scolding.

"Look," Nan said as the young man released her arm, "I don't even, I mean, who are you?"—then was ashamed of her brusqueness. They seemed to have leapfrogged over preliminaries into some strange intimacy that made it too late to ask this kind of question.

He said gently, "Please, you will sit? My name is Valeri Peshkov. I and my wife, we are friends to Mrs. Horsfal. We are caring for her house."

Nan found herself shaking all over with relief. She hadn't realized till this moment how afraid she'd actually been that this man was (somehow; so soon) from Gabriel. She sat down on the sofa. Valeri Peshkov sat down beside her, occupying only the edge of the seat, as if that was all he felt entitled to.

"I'm Nan, Nan Tice." Two false names had, in last night's weariness, been more than she'd felt up to. "She's gone away, then? Deenie—I mean, Mrs. Horsfal?"

"*Da*. She has gone." His round boy-face turned unaccountably sad.

"She's ill," Nan suggested. "She's in the hospital?"

He shook his head. He put one hand over hers. It was cool and dry and heavy. Her knee began to throb, a slow steady drumbeat of pain. The birds seemed to multiply, caroling hysterically, the talker among them asking, "What's up? What's up? What's up, pretty boy?"

Valeri Peshkov turned to them and shouted, "*Konyets!*"

The silence was instant. He turned back to Nan and slowly picked up her hand and folded it inside both of his own.

He said, "I am most sorry."

|

For the next two days Nan went about the business of what HOWDY had termed "acclimatizing" and she and Tod had privately called "ass-climb-atizing." At odd moments she found her mind running through the litany—Bonn, Genoa, Washington, Warsaw, Bucharest, Washington. She'd done it so many times; she could do it again. Only now she was on the other side of that experience: a refugee. Alone (*friendless*, she thought, in the long cold nights that invited self-pity) in a strange city, a continent away from everyone close to her, except for Jane. And no one in the world knew where she was. Not even Alex, as Alex herself had insisted.

Both mornings, Jane went happily off with Consuelo, whose plucked brows and high white forehead gave her the imperial look of a Velásquez, but whose dark eyes were kind. Nan paid her twice the Seattle rate for babysitters. Paid kindness felt safer.

On Friday morning Nan borrowed a city map from Consuelo and made her way to the new downtown mall, where she bought a warmer winter coat—a shiny red hooded parka—for Jane. Then she walked across the river to the Old Stone Bank, a small chapel with a reassuring gold dome, to open an account in the name of Nancy Tice and deposit her rolls of hundred-dollar bills, thirty-five of them. But the assistant manager asked for ID—which Nan, of course, didn't have. He was handsome, patronizing, and black, with skewed features like O. J. Simpson's. "Separation?" he asked, eyeing Nan's rumpled cash. "Bad breakup?" Nan looked past him discouragingly, but her chest widened with fear. She couldn't afford to attract anyone's interest. Remembering what Tod used to do when they traveled, she went back to the Frederick and begged an envelope and Scotch tape from Consuelo. She smoothed out the bills and put them in the envelope, then took out the top drawer of the dresser, taped the envelope to the underside of the dresser's top, and replaced the drawer.

Deenie's death had revealed a fault line in the Plan. Without a place to stay, would Nan have enough cash to last the six weeks that Alex's Time Line required? She had no way to get more money without revealing her identity; no way to reach Alex without revealing where she and Jane were. All she could do was wait till the appointed day—the twenty-first, almost two weeks away—and scan the *Pee-Eye*'s Personals. The Frederick, dim and dirty and cockroach-ridden as it was ("*Sí! Sí! Las cucarachas!*" Consuelo had cried when Nan complained, making them sound like some festive surprise), was too expensive. On Saturday morning Nan met with two Realtors who seemed to have only overpriced, over-carpeted condominiums for rent. In the afternoon, on Consuelo's advice, she scanned the bulletin board at the entrance to the little grocery store across the street from the Frederick; but when she and Jane went to see the one affordable place, she panicked. The owner—an old-young woman with long, graying Pre-Raphaelite hair—had troubles of her own, which she seemed eager to impart. Nan knew how quickly the desire to share confidences could become a demand to trade them. Too dangerous.

Standing in line at Burger King, where they went for a very late lunch, Jane demanded to know when her parents were coming. Nan should have prepared for this moment, but she'd been too busy the last two days to worry about it. She hesitated. (What had Alex told her? There hadn't been a chance on Wednesday morning to ask, because Gabe had come home for lunch unexpectedly.) Jane began to stomp—When? When? When?—bringing her feet down hard on each *when*. People in line stared. She was tired and hungry, but so was Nan, and Nan lost it. They're not, she told Jane, self-pity flooding through her. Mommy and Daddy aren't coming. It's just you and me, kid. Then call them to come and get me, Jane demanded, and when Nan refused, she stuck out her behind and squatted over the fake-brick floor. "If you don't, I'll just pee right here!"

This scene was followed that evening by another in the lobby of the Frederick. The second one was more dangerous. Nan said *No*—a word almost unheard in Nanaspeak—to a second Kit Kat from the vending machine. Hands on nonexistent hips, Jane shouted, "I'm going home right now! My daddy's coming to get me! He hates it here!" They were both exhausted: it was the very end of a long and fruitless day. Nan, who'd never spanked her own child, found herself smacking Jane's blue-jeaned bottom. Dragging her off to the elevator under Consuelo's reproachful gaze, she thought, This can't go on. I've got to do something, got to get us out of here.

The night was tropically hot in their small room, whose radiators clanked incessantly. Nan sat at the rickety table in the kitchen alcove while Jane huddled on the sofa bed with Ballet Dreams Barbie, today's Bribe of the Day. On the table lay the unfolded Time Line and Nan's cell phone. Disobeying Alex's instructions, she'd put it in her suitcase at the last minute. Though she almost never used it, she'd become attached to it as a talisman—what Gabe, when he'd given it to her the year before, called a "worry-bypass." Nan sat and smoked—three years now since she'd quit for good, right after her real bypass—and looked out at the swatch of cold, starless sky above the brick building across the street. She'd struck her granddaughter. How could she have done such a thing?

Horror at her once-unthinkable action mingled with dismay at her loss. Jane was her tenderness object. Had been so from the day Alex and Gabriel had brought her home, two days old, and Nan had cut her fingernails, thin and frail as insects' wings, because she kept scratching her cheeks with them and Gabe had already left for the hospital and Alex was afraid to bring scissors near her squalling, battling baby. From that day when, looking down at the small, red, ferocious face, Nan had felt, for the first time since Tod's death, light.

There was a singed smell coming from the radiator. Nan got up and went to turn over Jane's white blouse and red corduroy jumper, which she'd draped over it to dry. Every night now she washed one of Jane's two outfits in the bathroom sink, thinking wistfully of The Nannies. Leaving Seattle with one small suitcase—all Nan could comfortably carry— meant taking few clothes for either of them. She'd planned on borrowing from Deenie and having enough money to buy new ones for Jane. She sat down again at the kitchen table. She had to think of something to tell Jane, something that would persuade her of the necessity for this trip. Something that would comfort her for the loss of her parents, her home, her preschool, her friends. But what? What on earth could do that?

Alex should have explained to her, Nan thought—made up some plausible story. It's a *mother's* job.

She put out a hand and touched the cell phone. She turned it on. The MESSAGE icon in its little window began blinking. Instantly her anger was swamped by a wave of fear, her whole body going hot, then cold. Only Alex and Gabe had this number. Without stopping to think, she punched DELETE, then switched the phone off. She crumpled the Time

Line—What use was all of Alex's planning now?—and tossed it on the bed, then threw the cell phone after it. She lit another Marlboro, letting the match burn down until it seared her fingers, the way Deenie, laughing, used to do.

Deenie.

The tears Nan would, when younger, have shed were now a pressure, hard and unyielding, between her throat and her diaphragm. It had been years since she'd cried; tears, she'd realized during Tod's long dying, were nearly always for the one who cried them. That discovery seemed to dry them up. In any case, Deenie was linked, for Nan, not with tears but with laughter. That pope with chronic hiccups, Pius XII, whom they'd prayed for every morning in homeroom—while Deenie, beside her, hiccuped softly into her folded hands. Whispered exchanges after school in the empty, beeswax-smelling chapel. Deenie: Why did God make man first? Nan: Why? Deenie: Because every masterpiece needs a mock-up.

The smoke from Nan's cigarette dreamed its way toward the ceiling and out the window, which she'd opened at the top in deference to Jane's young lungs. Her wounded knee throbbed, but distantly. She supposed it was healing. She hadn't seen a doctor; some confused recollection of old noir detective movies—never take your gunshot wound to a hospital—had prevented her. On the building across the street a billboard offered what looked like DENIAL INSURANCE; lifting up her glasses to look through them, she saw it was DENTAL INSURANCE. The building housed a small grocery store called the Food Basket, patronized chiefly by old people. Their backs in dark winter coats were S-shaped, like vultures: dowager's hump, Deenie called it. *Would have called it.*

She didn't even know what Deenie had died of. Her Russian housesitter had said, incomprehensibly, "a delicate fever"; the hospital, when Nan phoned, had refused to say. Whatever it was, did that explain Deenie's sudden move from Chicago to Providence?

The Food Basket's windows threw golden parallelograms of light across the sidewalk. Nan watched two women try to enter by the same door at the same time, their walkers tangling. A young man in a green shirt came running out to help.

Driving her back from Deenie's house in his taxi, whose bumpers seemed to be held together by duct tape, Valeri Peshkov had explained. The cremation—of course Deenie would have wanted to be cremated—had been the week before. He, Val ("Please, you must to call me, it is typical American"), was keeping the ashes for Mrs. Horsfal's cousin. Nan thought of other funerals. Her mother's (which she could barely remember); her father's; her grandmother's; Tod's. No wisdom had accrued to her from their deaths. Lines from a poem memorized long ago echoed in the night silence.

Are flower and seed the same?
What do the great dead say?

At eight thirty the Food Basket's lights went out. Wishing heartily that she'd observed The Nannies more closely when she'd had the chance, Nan rose, stubbed out her cigarette, and went to coax Jane into bed. (Bed was a narrow mattress on the floor of the big walk-in closet, covered with a clean, fraying sky-blue quilt: yet another reason for leaving the Frederick.) Nan helped Jane pull on the soft white T-shirt—one of Nan's—that served as a makeshift nightgown, read to her (*Goodnight Moon*—yesterday's bribe), sang to her ("Zombie Jamboree"—tonight's request from their private stock of not-very-PC lullabies), kissed her good night, and Squirrel as well. Remnants of their nighttime ritual in the old adored-grandmother days, all of which Jane, frighteningly docile now after the spanking, merely endured. Nan's heart ached, for Jane, for (Be honest!) herself. She thought, We are both lost.

She turned on the night-light, pulled the closet door half shut. Then she returned to the rickety kitchen table, a last cigarette, brandy, worry, grief.

Four

Val threw open the door and stood aside for Nan to precede him. "Please! Enter!"

The loft was large and very clean. A Christmasy smell testified to the recent use of disinfectant on the bare scrubbed floorboards. In front of a wall of tall windows was a daybed laden with bright embroidered pillows. Val led Nan over to it. Breathless and a little dizzy (four flights of stairs! how long since she'd done anything like that?), she sank gratefully into its various softnesses. Val snapped on a pink-shaded lamp.

"One hundred and three square meters," he said proudly. "Also, is studio." He gestured to a half-open door behind him. Nan could see rows of canvases stacked face to the wall; the bracing smell of turpentine drifted past. "Ceiling, five and one-half meters."

Nan looked up. The high ceiling was laced with pipes and ducts of various sizes, all painted a deep blue. Many-paned windows stretched from the ceiling almost to the floor. Nan liked the muted view of sky and brick through the wavy glass. The city noises, too, were muted, less insistent than at the Fred. The room's warmth and rosy light enveloped her. She leaned back luxuriously among the cushions, then reminded herself of her mission. She'd accepted Val's invitation to dinner with an ulterior motive: to find out how Deenie had died.

The door opened and a young woman entered, bringing with her a cloud of cold. There was a doily of fresh snow on her dark hair, a trembling bunch of yellow mimosa in one mittened hand. *I should have brought flowers,* thought Nan, struggling to her feet, the way we did in Bucharest, in Warsaw.

Val said, "My wife, Mel. Mel, I present you Mrs. Tice."

To Nan's surprise, the young woman's cheek grazed hers, a brush of mimosa-scented cold. "Hey!" she said. "Sorry I'm late. I didn't mean to blow you off." Her voice was downright—Midwestern. Another surprise: Nan had assumed that Val's wife would be Russian.

Mel and Val: their names, Nan noted, were as alike as they were—dark, curly hair; dark eyes; tall. Not a promising couple, Tod would have said: look-alikes don't last. While Mel unwound her scarf and took off her black leather bomber jacket, Val became suddenly voluble. Mrs. Tice, he told his wife, was greatly recovering her injured knee; Mrs. Tice's *vnuchka*, Jane, could not come tonight; Mrs. Tice had had no tea yet. Frowning, Mel bent over to shake the snow from her hair. The collarless black shirt she wore made her long white neck look longer, almost fragile—Alex-like, thought Nan. Then she noticed the many earrings (some of them little dangling skulls) along the edges of Mel's ears, the brace of tattooed snakes heading for her collarbone. Nan dropped her eyes, lest her interest be read as old-lady horror.

Mel said to Nan, "How're you feeling? Your leg, I mean, your knee—does it hurt?"

"It's fine," Nan said. In fact, Janeless for the first evening in almost a week, she was feeling like herself again—whatever that now was. Val's appearance at the Fred this afternoon to invite her to Sunday dinner had been like a door opening onto a sunny garden. And tonight, leaving a contented Jane watching *SpongeBob SquarePants* with Consuelo, she'd stepped into Val's taxi as if into Cinderella's coach.

Mel said, "I married a bunbrain! Val—the least you could do is give Mrs. Tice something to put her leg up on." She hauled a large wicker trunk across the room and set it in front of Nan, who protested, "Honestly, I'm fine."

"Did you get a shot? Like, for tetanus?" Mel sat down on the daybed next to Nan and began prying off her boots. Her short black skirt pulled up to reveal a tattooed thigh, a dark pattern of what looked like ferns, under fishnet stockings. Nan foresaw an evening of successive revelations in the realm of body ornament.

"So practical, my Melochka." Val stood looming over the two women, raking his already upstanding hair with paint-stained fingers.

"Oh, I've had all my shots," Nan lied. "Anyway, it's nothing. Val took good care of me." She touched the bandage, a smaller one now, under her Hidden Assets.

"Further," said Val, "I carry her in my taxi. So!"

Mel stood up. "Val made all this really cool stuff to eat. And I bought some vodka. You two hang. I'll be right back." She padded down the long room and disappeared behind a bright-printed fabric screen.

Now, thought Nan. Ask about Deenie.

But a sound started up behind the studio door, a sort of hollow crying, like someone imitating a baby. Val turned and crossed the room. When he opened the door, a black cat shot across the floor and landed among the cushions next to Nan. Its yellow eyes accused her.

"Clio!" said Val. "*Iti syuda!* Come!"

"I don't mind. I like cats." Nan put out a hand and received a look of weary disdain. "Why do you call her Clio? That's not the muse of painting, is it?" She stroked the indifferent cat, whose thick black fur was pure delight.

"*Nyet!* Is muse of history. That is what a painter must need. Did you not had a classical education? But Americans have not."

"Can I see your paintings? Will you show them to me?"

"*Nyet.* Another time, perhaps. At this moment I am out of love. My eyes are having *mozoli*—calluses?—at my lousy stuff."

"Val is bonkers," said Mel, coming into the room with a huge tray, which she set down on the wicker trunk next to Nan's feet. She rolled up the sleeves of her shirt, revealing sturdy, unexpectedly muscular arms. "Last year he burned all his paintings—I mean all of them—and put the ashes in a jar. Then he baked pirozhki with the ashes, and ate them."

She handed Nan a thimble-sized glass of vodka.

"Like this mythologous bird, you know?" Val said. "This *fennis.*"

"Phoenix," Mel supplied, handing a thimble to Val.

"Drink!" he urged.

He raised his glass, and the two women raised theirs. They drank. The vodka's warmth snaked through Nan. She held out her glass for more. "Wouldn't the paint be poison?"

"I made him heave, right after," said Mel. "Scarf and barf."

"Was ceremony of reborn. After, I become surrealist and study English. Only after can I do this things. My Melochka, so practical—she does not understand."

Val pulled up a chair for Mel, then sat down next to Nan on the daybed. They all served themselves, balancing plates on their laps. After more vodka came marinated mushrooms sprinkled with bright-green chives, pancakes rolled around a salty jellied filling, translucent wafers of red onion and radishes. They ate off thick, cheap china under the remote gaze of Clio. They drank kvass, chill and sour-sweet, a beer Val brewed himself. After a week of Burger King, the food and drink seemed heavenly to Nan. But she could feel a tension in the room, a net that held and shivered, entangling her yet buoying her up, like the tension at a family gathering. Val and Mel seemed to be watching her.

In new situations, *HOWDY* had advised, break the ice by asking questions. Nan asked the one happy couples like best.

They'd met two years before, in Moscow, where Mel was attending an international tattoo art convention for which Val was an official taxi driver; they'd married on the strength of six days' acquaintance; it had taken another year to get Val out; Mel made her living doing body art—tattooing and piercing, "No scarring, I'm not into that" (*Scarring?* thought Nan)—and she and Val supplemented their income by house-sitting. This was how they'd met Mrs. Horsfal.

Of course, Nan thought, Deenie would have instantly adopted these two.

She seized the opening. "I met her when I was thirteen," she said. "We've been best friends ever since."

Mel looked surprised. Her eyes met Val's for a second, but she said nothing.

Nan pushed on. She told them about that first day in homeroom, two gangly scholarship girls whose uniforms hadn't been made by the right tailor. They listened, rapt. She told them how, in freshman English, that first terrifyingly strange autumn, she and Deenie had had to memorize poems about Courageous Youths. The Spartan boy who soundlessly let a fox *gnaw his vitals* (a phrase that chilled Nan to this day) rather than ... but she could no longer remember what outcome his stoicism had avoided. The Dutch boy—were all Courageous Youths boys?—who, walking along the dikes at dawn, had seen a hole. Unable to summon help, he stuck his finger into it, then (as the hole widened) his hand, then his arm, to keep the sea from swallowing the town. Still no one heard his cries. Finally he had to plug the hole with his body, and he drowned. The town was saved. Nan had raised her hand and asked, Why didn't the boy put himself into the hole feetfirst? He would've made just as good a cork, and he wouldn't've died. Sister Alma Gertrude had given her detention for being disrespectful, and Deenie, too, for laughing.

Mel passed a plate of tiny crescent-shaped pies that Nan recognized as pirozhki. Hand outstretched to take one, she paused.

Mel laughed, a wide-open laugh, revealing a tiny gold ball nesting on the tip of her tongue. "These're okay. No ashes!"

The moment felt right, or at any rate, Nan thought, would not feel righter. Time to pop her question. "There's something I've been wanting to ask you. About Deenie—Mrs. Horsfal." She took a deep breath. "How did she die, exactly?"

Val's eyes met Mel's. Almost imperceptibly, she shook her head.

"The hospital wouldn't tell me," Nan said. "They only give out information to relatives."

Mel looked surprised. "But aren't you—I thought you *were* a relative."

Nan had forgotten, for a moment, her alias. Improvising hastily, she said, "By marriage. That, um, that wasn't enough."

"Oh, by marriage. So, like, you're not related to Mrs. Horsfal's cousin?"

"Cousin? Oh . . . no. The one in—where is it? Africa?"

"He is living now in Maine," Val said. "Is mending now from, how it is said?" He looked at Mel.

"Surgery. Like, gall bladder, or something."

A shiver slid down Nan's spine. Had her whimsical choice of alias created another fault line in the Plan? She tried to sound natural. "I thought he worked abroad somewhere. What's his name? I've forgotten."

"Walker Tice," Val said, and Mel added, "He's an old guy. At least, he sounded old. We haven't met him. He's gonna come down here and pack up Mrs. Horsfal's stuff as soon as he recovers."

Here was yet another danger. The Aged Cousin. Shaken, Nan sank back among the sofa cushions. There was a long pause in which no one spoke. The warm air held the fragrance of tarragon and garlic, the lamplight throbbed gently. Mel and Val were looking at her, their faces oddly intent. Nan leaned back, nearly closing her eyes, trying to seem as if she were merely savoring the pleasures of the meal. The mystery surrounding Deenie's death had deepened; but it was not, after all, the right time to pursue the question that had brought her here. She assessed the silence. Again that tension, magnified now, as if something big had been left unsettled, some hurdle uncleared. Through her half-closed eyes, she saw Val and Mel look at each other. *You go. No, you.*

Finally Val said, "Mrs. Tice—"

"Nan. Please."

"Nan." It came out sounding like "none." "Mel and I, we have the idea to, well, to help Jane and you—"

"It's epic!"

"—for where to live."

"A really phat idea!"

"Here in this our building—"

"This guy, he's a doofus, but his place is cool—"

"We are sitting house for Mr. Nibbrig, he is *bukhgal'ter*—"

"—an accountant—"

"He wishes to, how it is said—"

"—sublet—"

"You and your Jane need not to remain longer in the Fred—"

"—and it's *cheap*."

|

Why are these strangers so kind? I should be asking myself that.

It was dawn. The radiators, clanking insanely, had woken Nan. She yanked off her sweat-soaked nightgown and went to stand at the open window of the little kitchenette. When she pulled the shade down it snapped, rattling, to the top. Sunrise stained the sky and the piles of snow, like unwashed laundry, that lay along the edges of the sidewalk. The three floors above the darkened Food Basket were lined with the windows that stared blankly at her. Windows of rooms like Nan's.

Last night, leaving Val and Mel's place with its warmth and light and heartening smells, she'd told them she needed to think about their offer. Yet, really, what could she do but accept? Looking out onto the street, she tried not to remember the garden of her apartment in West Seattle. Her calm and beautiful refuge. Gone now.

Behind her, in the closet off the living room, Jane stirred and sighed. Why so kind?

Nan didn't feel she was a good judge of character. Tod used to say, Good judgment comes from experience; experience comes from bad judgment. Nan's married life had offered little opportunity for bad judgment (apart from the lovers—and there, except for the Last Lover, she seemed to have been lucky). The State Department had made her decisions for her. Twenty-two years in the undistinguished middle ranks of civil servants ("simple serpents," Tod had joked in the early years, before they realized he'd made himself too useful ever to be promoted) had left Nan unprepared for ordinary life. For nearly a quarter of a century she had not once had to find an apartment, deal with landlords, move her own furniture, care for her own child. Those years had not left her experienced, or even cosmopolitan. They'd lived in embassy "compounds," "fraternization" with the locals ("indigenous populations") was frowned on, "team spirit" (a code word, as in Nan's schooldays, for conformity) was the order of the day. Wherever they went, they took the USA with them. She had traveled, but never quite arrived.

Val and Mel. Their kindness was offered in exchange for something, Nan told herself as the sun grew brighter above the Food Basket. Something they wanted from her. Though it could well be (she tried for optimism) something benign. And there was the Aged Cousin. A wild card. Bound to surface eventually, whenever he recovered from whatever ailment he'd been suffering from up there in Maine—

Suddenly she realized there was a naked man in one of the windows opposite. No shock, just: a window lit, a window dark, a naked body, another window; then, *Oh!* Gray on gray in the oblique early light, one hand holding back the curtain. She must have been looking at him for several minutes without registering it. No face—his head was cut off by half-lowered, half-closed blinds—just a torso from chin to knees, broken by the triangle of dark fleece at the crotch. As she watched, a hand delved into it. Looking down, Nan saw with dismay her own naked body, weakly gilded now by the first fingers of sun. Quickly she pulled down the shade.

He knows where I live.

Her own terror terrified her. In the hot, stuffy room, she felt encased in ice. Her skin burned with cold; her nipples were so tight they hurt. She went to her purse and took out her cell phone and held it in her hand. But who could she call? She had no friends here, no one who knew her. Fugitive that she was, she couldn't even call the police. She had never, in all her life, felt so alone.

My God. I can't do this.

Going to the back of the door to pull her robe off its hook, she heard with gratitude the chirp of Consuelo's cleaning trolley's wheels.

The kindness of strangers. What alternative was there?

The next afternoon Val came to get them in his taxi. Though they'd been there only five days, Jane burst into tears at the idea of leaving the Fred and Consuelo. While Nan packed their few belongings, Jane wept, her sobs escalating as Nan zipped up her scarlet parka, her howls filling the little elevator as they descended. In the lobby she flung herself to the floor on her stomach. Her back arched and her blue-jeaned bottom rose into the air, her small body a tent of grief. Consuelo, on her knees on the dingy olive tiles, held her and rocked her back and forth. *"Pobrecita! Ay, querida!"*

I should be doing that, Nan realized. But when she knelt down beside her, Jane turned away, clinging to Consuelo. Sadness flooded Nan—where was the little girl who so loved her Nana?—but she found herself saying brusquely, "Let's go, Jane. Val is double-parked." When Consuelo looked up, a tear glittered in the downy dark hairs along her upper lip.

There was another bad moment when Val's taxi stalled in the middle of the construction along the river. But the shouted curses and frenzied honking of the drivers behind them, so different from phlegmatic Seattleites, were somehow invigorating, like the rush of carbon-scented winter air when Val cranked down his window to shout back. *"Chort!"* he cried. *"K chortu!"* Snow began sifting down as they drove along the river, despite the sun, a giant orange-red sourball behind the cranes and backhoes. The water was a dull green, still as jelly. A lone figure stood looking down on it from the unfinished footbridge where the construction ended. They swung onto Westminster Street with a seagull, wings spread wide, gliding ahead of the car. The setting sun struck the windows of the Fleet Building and turned them into a grid of burning gold.

On the third floor of the old factory building on Elbow Street they passed scarred doors holding at bay the sounds and smells of other lives. Val carried their two suitcases; Nan, the large green garbage bag full of Jane's recent acquisitions. Jane scuffed along behind them, dragging Squirrel across the dirty cement floor. Recovering from the stairs, Nan concentrated on moving normally, on breathing. What had she been thinking of, not to have looked at the apartment beforehand? The hallway offered peeling turnip-colored walls; an impression of general neglect (in the building's entryway she'd glimpsed the quick clipped shadow of a rat); years of accumulated odors coalescing into a smell as dense and dark as fruitcake.

When they were ensconced in their new quarters, Nan set herself to build a context, to make the unfamiliar familiar, a policy arrived at in the years with Tod (though she'd married him, at twenty, out of a deep longing for her own life to be foreign to her). Now, as then, she gathered the strands of herself that strained to fly apart—was this what they meant by "pull yourself together"?—that threatened to unravel into *there/here, then/now, them/me*. Only now she did not have HOWDY to advise her; she did not have the bottomless resources of the Foreign Service to come to her aid.

After all, she thought, it's only temporary. Only a week now until the twenty-first, until the first message from Alex.

Never a list-maker, more what Pop used to call a seat-of-the-pants navigator, Nan made one now.

(1) Make apartment habitable

Mr. Nibbrig, the owner of Nan's loft, was unfortunately not as anal as Mel had promised. His place was a mess. One huge high-ceilinged room, it was crammed full of plants, some of them trees taller than Nan, in pots and tubs. They were shabby, sooty, the larger ones bending and twisting to search out the light. The furniture that lurked in this jungle consisted of two lumpy overstuffed chairs, an ancient, ugly brown sofa covered with a molting zebra skin, a worktable, a bureau, a bed. There was also a large locked metal footlocker, presumably guarding Mr. Nibbrig's private life. A grimy U-shaped kitchen area contained the bare minimum of equipment.

Val came with a ladder and washed the tall windows. Mel took Nan and Jane to the Slater Screen Print factory in Pawtucket, where Jane chose a fabric with huge yellow bumblebees attacking poppies the size of dinner plates, which Mel stretched on four six-foot frames hinged together. This screened off a triangle of space for Jane's bed, bought at Goodwill. Nan's own bed she set against the one windowless wall; the worktable went across the far end of the room, where two French doors opened onto nothing. Under Val's direction the jungle was regrouped into a room divider, a sort of arbor for the sofa. ("My shorty!" Mel said, one muscular arm around his shoulders in a hug that made him wince. "He is *deep*.") The mysterious footlocker, covered with Nan's lavender silk scarf, became a coffee table.

For the first two days Nan, at the still center of all this magic, forgot to bemoan the fact that by now she should have been in the Fine-Tuning stage of life. In fact, she forgot to feel sorry for herself at all. When she finally got up the nerve to ask Val why he and Mel were doing all this, he said simply that Mrs. Horsfal would have wished it. Nan realized that they were adopting her and Jane as Deenie had adopted them.

(2) Arrange essentials: food, transport, money, other (?)

Food. The building's nonworking elevator was a problem; Nan tried to group errands so that she had to deal with the stairs only once a day. Luckily, the Food Basket delivered. There was even a five percent discount for senior citizens on Tuesdays—but Nan couldn't show her driver's license, with the name on it that she no longer called herself.

Transport. Same problem. No point in buying a car (not that she had the money), because she couldn't get a driver's license in her new name, and it would be just her luck, if she drove without one, to be stopped. Better a pair of, yes, sensible shoes—ones recommended by Mel called Doc Martens, heavy and black as nuns' shoes—and a bus pass. RIPTA—Rhode Island Public Transportation Authority, known, according to Mel, as RIPTOFF—required no ID, so long as Nan relinquished the idea of a senior discount. And for emergencies there was Val's taxi.

Money. She was already down to about three thousand. But with the tiny rent she would pay for Mr. Nibbrig's once and future home (*see (1) above*), they should be all right for two months or so. Longer than they would need, surely—Alex had said it might take six weeks. What had Nan been thinking of, agreeing to a plan that assigned her the role of what Deenie used to call Little Red Waitinghood? (The chief female activities of the fifties—dating, courtship, pregnancy—had held no charm for Deenie.) Nan could only sit and wait—at the mercy, she saw now, of Alex—for the two dates each month on which the *Pee-Eye* might contain a message. This was the stuff of which paranoia was made.

Other—oh, other. Other, Nan thought (for she could not overcome a lifetime of civil-service kept-womanhood overnight), would have to take care of itself.

(3) (Most imp't & hardest) Make peace with Jane

A neat little kitten, black with a tuxedo front, alleged by Val to be Clio's offspring and therefore death to rats, helped. More, really, than the Serious Talk the day after the spanking, in which Nan said stupid things about how someone can love you but still hurt you, about how sometimes the lies you have to tell people can be truer than truth (pronouncements met by Jane's justifiably disdainful gaze). The secondhand television that Mel hung from the loft ceiling on long iron chains helped, too. The sound of kids' TV programs—cheerful, cheering, inane—now accompanied Nan's every move. Jane mostly hung around Val and Mel, "helping" as they scrubbed and hammered and moved furniture, but she wouldn't let Nan turn off the TV. It did seem to offer some comfort. Nan could see her growing more animated, less watchful, her sharp little chin less evident, her face rosy. Even so, she refused to name the kitten.

On their third night in the new place Nan awakened to find Jane stretched out at the bottom of the bed as if to make sure Nan could not get up and leave her. Faint ruffly snores told Nan she was asleep. Oh, sweetie, she thought, you'll catch cold. Shifting carefully, she slid her legs out from under Jane's weight. Jane stirred but did not wake. Nan got out of bed, the cold floor shocking her soles, and half lifted, half dragged Jane's sleep-heavy body upward toward the pillows. Then she climbed back in bed and pulled the down comforter over the two of them and wrapped her arms around Jane. She smelled like sleep and stale milk and the Teddy Bear soap Mel had given her that afternoon. Nan's feet prickled with pain—they'd fallen asleep under Jane's weight. Tomorrow, was her last waking thought. Tomorrow I'll talk to her. It's high time.

Morning was gray, cold, a leaden sky promising more snow. The new kitten, already constructing its own rituals, curled in Jane's lap at the kitchen table. Over two bowls of Honey Nut Cheerios Nan opened the hardest conversation of her life so far.

"Jane, honey," she began; but Jane's eyes were fixed on the TV that hung in the center of the loft, where Mister Rogers was interrogating a large blue kangaroo. Nan seized the remote, and the television, winking, went blank.

"Hey!" Jane protested.

Nan tried to recall what tactics Alex used to get Jane to listen. Finally, she just plunged in. "Sweetpea, do you know why we came here, to Providence? Did your mama tell you?"

"I want Mister Rogers."

How on earth does Alex do this?

"Sweetpea. I need you to listen. It's important."

Jane's spoon clattered onto the table. She put her hands over her ears and began chanting, "Mister Rogers! Mister Rogers!"

"Stop that right now." Nan surprised herself. Where had this calm mother-voice come from? She reached over and gently pried Jane's hands from her ears. Jane stared down at her cereal, her face red with fury.

"Listen! You can have Mister Rogers back as soon as you listen."

Jane bent her head until the ends of her hair fell into her bowl.

"Your daddy . . . your daddy had to go to Guatemala. To the clinic for sick kids, you know, like he did last summer. He had an Emergency." A doctor's daughter, Jane already understood the preemptive nature of Emergencies. "And your mama . . . your mama went with him this time, because he needs her help. She hates to be away from you, but she has to help your daddy."

Jane lifted her head.

"Your mama loves you dearly. *Dearly.* That's why she sent you here with me. So you'd be safe." How lame the carefully rehearsed words sounded now that Jane's eyes were on her. Nan, who until now had prided herself on never lying to her granddaughter, went on. "She'll come and get you as soon as she can. I promise."

Jane's eyes stayed on hers. Nan reached out to hug her, this angry granddaughter whose care she had not asked for. Jane didn't hug her back; but she endured it. Nan saw in the bronzy-green eyes the wish to believe. Gently she tucked Jane's hair behind her ears: the ends were wet with milk.

"How will Santa Claus know where to find me?"

"Your mama will tell him exactly where you are, Grape Eyes," Nan said in her new calm mother-voice. She flicked the remote, and Mister Rogers's loony optimism filled the loft once more.

That afternoon Jane forgot not to laugh at Nan's jokes. ("Me Tarzan, you Jane," when they watered the jungle of plants, pinched dead leaves off the devil's ivy, dusted the long fingers of the scheffleras.) That afternoon she named the kitten Zipper Cupcake Zipper.

Not peace, but a truce. Enough to go on with.

|

By the end of the first week, the new place no longer so scaldingly new, Nan's nights had assumed a pattern. Jane in her cozy alcove, sleeping; the faint chime of the radiators; Nan reading Mel's *Complete Works of Chekhov* and chewing nicotine gum. (She couldn't smoke, she'd decided, with Jane in the same room, however large that room was.) By the end of the week, she felt calm enough, strong enough, to turn on her cell phone. Sure enough, there was the little MESSAGE icon pulsing urgently.

She hesitated. *Ye shall know the truth, and the truth shall make you free,* said Dorothea's long-ago voice in her head. She pushed "1" and tapped out her password, and there was Gabriel.

"Nan. Gabe here. Where are you? Is Jane with you? Please call me." And a second message, more imperative, in Gabe's forceful doctor voice: "Nan! Please call me. I don't know what Alex told you, but I need to talk to you. It's urgent." The third message was pure anguish: "Nan, please. I'm going out of my mind here. Just let me know she's all right. *Please.*"

Delete.

Delete.

Delete.

Nan punched the OFF button and let the phone fall to the floor. When she looked up, she saw her own face painted blurrily onto the dark window by the light from her lamp. Her own frightened, pitying face.

|

A little over a year before, on the terrace of the Queen Anne house, on a cobalt autumn evening, Nan and Gabriel had sat in companionable silence. It was the end of September, but the long, lovely day had been so beguiling, the mountains printed so clearly on the cloudless sky, that they'd forgotten the true season. High above their heads, under the eaves of the gracious old house, Jane lay wrapped in a blurry down comforter. At three and a half she still wouldn't go to sleep without one of her parents lying beside her. So here, without Alex, were Nan and Gabriel. Fireflies; the scent of wisteria and sweet woodruff; Gabriel's fingers tapping on the metal arm of his chair. Nan wondered if he was thinking of yesterday, of the Vietnamese boy who'd died during surgery.

Men are much more vulnerable, physiologically, than women, Gabriel said. He sat with his back to the darkened house, across a wide teakwood table from Nan. His voice was low, tentative. He added, Right from conception. Did you know that?

Yes, lied Nan. She didn't feel like talking. Warm, fed, a little drowsy, she wanted to savor all these things. She lifted her face to the mild, moonless night.

At every age, men are more likely to be defective, Gabriel went on. Heart. Lungs. After middle age, if they make it that far, they start shrinking. They get smaller and more fragile every year. Old men are more like women than old women are.

Physiologically, murmured Nan.

She looked up at the night sky, thickly salted with stars. A romantic sky, a sky for lovers, if only she still had one. All those old songs. Stars Fell on Alabama. Stairway to the Stars. Stardust. *Sometimes I wonder why I spend the lonely nights / Dreaming of a song.* Stardust, she thought: the dust of stars. It would burn, it would annihilate, surely?

. . . died, said Gabriel.

What? Sorry—I didn't hear you.

My mother died. Last week.

I'm so sorry, Nan said automatically.

So it wasn't the Vietnamese boy, after all. For God's sake, she thought, why didn't Alex say something? How stupid I must seem.

She heard Gabriel take a breath. Her face must be, to him, as his was to her, a milky blur in the starlight, like the priest's three-quarter profile through the dark grille. She didn't want to hear whatever her son-in-law had to confess: guilt, anger, lack of grief. Women complained that their husbands never talked about their feelings; this deficiency, in Nan's view, was one of the many wonderful things about men. It would never have occurred to Tod to "share" his feelings with her. (She had forgotten, for the moment, his many eloquent varieties of silence.)

She was sixty-one, Gabriel said.

A pause. Then a violent movement. His glass shattered on the flag-stones over by the cedar fence.

Startled, Nan shrank back into her chair, gripped its metal arms, though the glass hadn't been thrown in her direction.

She must have been very young when you were born, she ventured.

Sixteen. My father was seventeen. He took off when I was two. I never saw him again.

It's hard when the last parent dies. I remember. That feeling of being, I don't know, promoted. Sent to the front lines.

I hated her, Gabriel said softly. She never gave me one second of affection that didn't come with a hundred hours of pain.

Then you will never stop missing her, Nan thought. But she said only, I'm so sorry, Gabe.

Perhaps he imagined Nan resisting, because he continued, in a chill-ingly matter-of-fact voice: She used to walk around the house with this long leather belt looped around her neck, so that the strap hung down. Handy for discipline. Ice on the sore spots, afterwards. Then she'd cry. Drunk, of course.

Nan could hardly breathe. It dawned on her that Gabriel hadn't told Alex about this death. She took a sip of watery scotch.

The next afternoon I'd be waiting at the edge of the road for her to come home from the cannery, he said. I'd jump on the running board of the pickup and she'd pull me in through the window and hug me.

Nan thought of her son-in-law's tenderness with Jane, his refusal ever to punish her, leaving Alex (she complained) to be the Bad Cop. Repair for the damage done to the little boy clinging to the running board? Repossession, in a way, of what was taken from him?

There was an odd sound, a soft rhythmic creaking, which she identified after a second as the sound of Gabriel's chair. He was weeping, soundlessly. She could just make out the shuddering of his shoulders. Instinctively, feeling only that she must not stay, Nan got to her feet. She moved around the table toward his chair—she had to pass it to go inside.

I'm cold, she said. I think I'll—

Gabriel's arm shot out, his hand gripped her bare arm above the elbow. She was forced to stand next to his chair, facing away from him, off balance, her weight on her right foot, the left raised in a step toward the house. He held on, rocking with those soundless sobs; he leaned his hot forehead against her upper arm. His grief, like the night shadows, widened to embrace them both, filled the dark garden. Awkwardly Nan set her foot down and twisted around to find her balance, the edge of Gabriel's chair pressing into her side. How long since anyone had needed her? Surprised, she felt the itch of tears under her eyelids. How long since she had cried?

She laid her free hand on Gabriel's shoulder. His grip on her arm loosened a little. His other hand found her wrist, his fingers followed its curve. Tears dropped off her chin into his hair and were trapped in its wiry curls, whole and glinting. The smell of leaves, of earth—of autumn—filled her nostrils.

|

Wishing devoutly for a cigarette, Nan rose and opened the window. Her reflection slid away as cold night air struck her face.

Remember the Plan. Alex would leave—would already by now have left?—Gabe. She would file—would already by now have filed?—for custody of Jane. Possessory rights. Once she got them, Nan and Jane would be safe.

Would Gabe wait till then? He'd try first to pacify Alex, then to persuade her. When he tired of that, would whatever Alex had on him be enough to prevent him from taking action?

Nan took a deep breath of head-clearing winter air, then stood looking into the darkness. Outside were clouds and sea-smelling wind and the first real snow. Inside, the yellow light from the desk lamp held the two of them, Nan and Jane, in a warm suspension, and the shadows in the room beat softly, keeping time with the pulse of their own blood. *Sparrow nights,* Chekhov called them. This broody peace: the world *outside* and she and Jane safe within. Nan's eyes rested on the single locust in the courtyard three stories below, which held on to a few flickering leaves. Looking down, she could just make out its hopeful shape against the shine of the freshly fallen snow.

Five

"I think we're related."

The voice on the other end of the phone felt too close to Nan's ear, as if its force had somehow widened the holes in the earpiece. An instant of heart-bending horror; then: Don't panic, Nan told herself. Tice—he asked for Mrs. Tice. It's not *you* he thinks he's talking to.

She glanced at Jane, who sat cross-legged in the middle of the floor looking up at the television, absorbed in *Mister Rogers' Neighborhood*, both arms around the struggling kitten. It looked like the two of them would spend another day marooned together: snow had begun to fill the loft's long windows. The morning smell of burned toast hung in the room.

"I'm sorry," Nan said. "You have the wrong—"

"Wait! Please. Geraldine Tice Horsfal was my cousin."

Ah! The Aged Cousin.

"I'm sorry—"

The voice barreled on. "Thing is, I'm her executor. I have to find the people she left bequests to, or else the lawyers do, and you know what *they* charge. The Peshkovs gave me your number. You could help."

Nan shifted from one foot to the other. Her back hurt from a night on Nibbrig's mattress. How to get rid of him? He definitely wasn't buying the idea of a wrong number.

"Who is it?" Jane asked. "Zipper, stop it right now!"

Nan put a hand over the mouthpiece. "Nobody. Someone for Mr. Nibbrig."

"Hello? Mrs. Tice?"

Into the mouthpiece she said, "My husband was a, a distant cousin of Deen—of Geraldine's. I didn't really know her."

Jane was at her elbow, grabbing for the phone. "I wanna talk!"

Nan held the receiver up out of reach. Jane shouted, "Mama! Mama!"

Nan put her free arm around Jane's shoulders and squeezed. "Be quiet! It's not your mother."

Above their heads a tiny voice said, "Mrs. Tice? Mrs. Tice?"

Jane squirmed, flailed, kicked Nan's ankle hard. Reflexively, Nan let go. Jane retreated, on her face a look of pure rage.

A beautiful day in the neighborhood, Mr. Rogers crooned.

"Any rate, some of these people seem to be from Geraldine's childhood. Your husband might've mentioned them—"

"I can't help you. I'm sorry. Good-bye." Nan hung up more heavily than she'd meant to.

A wonderful day for neighbors! Will you be mine?

She crossed the room and knelt down, knees creaking, beside her granddaughter. "Listen, Grape Eyes," she began.

Jane turned away, her eyes on the TV. Two fingers rubbed her forehead in that anxious Alex-gesture.

"Sweetpea. That wasn't your mama. Remember what we talked about? Your mama loves you dearly. But she can't be with you right now. She wants you to be here, in Providence, with me. So that you'll be safe."

A sharp movement of Jane's shoulders under her not-very-clean turtleneck said, Nothing doing.

"Just for now. She'll call us as soon as she can. I promise!"

Over her shoulder Jane shot a look at Nan—her anger replaced by a weary, unchildlike skepticism—then turned her gaze back to the television.

The telephone began to ring.

"Come on, sweetie!" Nan cried, falsely gay. "Let's go shopping!"

Another Barbie doll (Fashion Fever Barbie had recently been mentioned) might just turn Jane's mood around. When in doubt, bribe. Nan got up and went to the coat tree for Jane's parka and tossed it across the room to her. The ringing of the phone showered around them, clear and chill and insistent.

|

A new experience for Nan Mulholland: the tedium-laced-with-fury that hours on end with small children evoked. The squabbles, tears, snack-time, bathtime, bedtime—the sheer *labor* of it. The wakeful nights, the nights of watching, the fears. How did Alex do it, day after day? Nan had always told herself that even the worst of parents gave a great, great gift. Now, half dragging her daughter's daughter along the snow-swept length of Weybosset Street, she wondered: without the State Department's assistance—the long procession of The Nannies—what kind of mother would she have been? What kind of mother *had* she been? Not, she feared, much of one. Yet who else was there, then or now?

|

On December 21—one of the two days each month when Alex would leave Nan a message in the *Pee-Eye*'s Personals—Nan dragged a protesting Jane down icy city streets from one newsstand to another.

Red's All-Season News, News of the World, Barnes & Noble—none of them carried the *Pee-Eye*. The large woman behind the counter at Red's said, sounding incredulous, "Seattle, *Washington*?" She wore a sky-blue sweatshirt that said, SINGLE WOMEN CAN'T FART . . . THEY DON'T HAVE AN ASSHOLE UNTIL THEY'RE MARRIED. The rich smell of cigars in the little shop made Nan, for an instant, see Gabriel, his concerned forehead, his silvery eyes. Jane crossed to the other side of the shop to gaze into a flat glass-topped case. "Try the library over at Brown," CAN'T FART said. "The one they named after that rich guy, what's-his-face." Jane folded back the glass lid and began to touch the cigars lightly, delicately. "Only, you gotta have a Brown ID to get in."

Two days later, armed with a faculty card procured for her by Val, Nan left Jane happily making s'mores with Mel and took a bus to the university. Wearing—in order to look scholarly—the glasses usually reserved for furtive snatches of clear-sightedness, she slid the card through the Rockefeller Library's scanner. The nimblest imagination could not have found much likeness between her and Victoria Uglow (FAC). But she needn't have worried. The dreadlocked young woman in the entrance booth didn't even glance up from her book.

In the Reference Room a thin, dark, intense-looking man—Ben Kingsley as Gandhi—showed Nan how to use the computer to search for the *Pee-Eye* in a database called Lexis or Nexus, like a pornographic novel by Henry Miller. When she got stuck, which was almost immediately, a peach-faced Asian girl at the next machine helped her. They found the *Pee-Eye,* the December 21 issue, the Personals. "OLD FLAME FIND-ERS: Give us a call and find that lost love." "MOTHER PEARL: Removes evil, bad luck. Helps business, lost nature, falling hair. Results 10 hours." Several minutes of mega-scrolling, as her helper, Seung-Won, called it, yielded, at last, a message from Alex.

> POOKIE: Everything going according to plan.
> Kiss her for me. HIPPIE

Deaf to the shuffling and sniffling and whispering of the students all around her, Nan sat gazing at the screen as if the tiny glimmering words could be made to yield up more. Yield up Alex herself. The message was meant to reassure Nan; yet somehow it made her feel worse. Because it pulled her out of the life, so new and so fragile, that she'd begun to construct for herself and Jane? Made her remember that that life was a stopgap, a step in someone else's dream?

Hope you're okay would have been nice, she told the glowing monitor. *Thank you* would have been nice. Still, the foolish nicknames—Pookie, Hippie—warmed her, and she felt her lips curve into a grudging smile.

She fished in her purse and pulled out the Time Line. Her cell phone came with it, falling onto the desk with a clatter. Nan unfolded the paper, which by now had the softness of an old diaper, and spread it out in front of her. Two weeks since she and Jane had left Seattle. That night, after they'd gone, Alex would have faked a phone call from Nan, then told Gabriel that his daughter was staying overnight with her grandmother. The next day—the ninth, twelve days ago now—she'd have waited till Gabriel went to the hospital, then packed a bag and left. Nan didn't know where, because Alex had insisted on neither of them knowing the other's whereabouts. Once Alex was safe, she'd have phoned to tell Gabriel that Jane was all right, but not where she was. What would Gabe do then?

On her way out of the library, Nan's cell phone rang. At first she didn't recognize the sound and looked around to see where it was coming from. When she realized, fear flashed over her. She scrabbled in her purse for the phone and pulled it out. The little window said, "Unavailable." It gave one last ring and stopped; the window went blank.

Quickly she pushed OFF. Falling out of her purse earlier must have turned it on. She knew that a cell phone—even turned on, even ringing—could not physically be traced. But still, she'd been careful to keep it turned off. Now she felt, irrationally, that it might somehow give away her whereabouts. Hadn't Alex forbidden her to take it with her? Feeling hounded, she walked down College Street toward the river, holding the phone out in front of her like something contaminated. She didn't want it. But how could she get rid of it? If she threw it away, someone might find it, and use it. What if then it *could* be traced?

HOWDY's words of wisdom came back to her. *Should you find yourself in a compromised position, be certain you do not have on your person any incriminating documents. Burn them, or in circumstances where this is not feasible, swallow or otherwise irrecoverably dispose of them.*

At the bottom of the hill, where it met the river, the street turned into one of the little arched Venetian bridges. The breeze off the river touched Nan's face with welcome cold. She breathed deep: the fishy smell of the unseen ocean, the sooty smell of approaching snow. Heartening, both. She held the phone down by her side and walked close to the low stone wall overlooking the water. When she was sure no one was looking, she stretched out her arm and let the phone fall, pausing just long enough to hear the splash.

|

"You're next!"

Mel waved the glue gun at Nan. They were almost finished reupholstering the accountant's sofa. Back: pinto-print velveteen; arms: canary-yellow corduroy (right), American flag (left); seat cushions: a demure blue-and-green plaid that Mel called "Catholic Schoolgirl." It was their Christmas gift, hers and Val's, to Nan and Jane.

Mel aimed the gun and reglued a stubborn corner of the flag, then ducked back under the branches of a fig tree to survey her work. "This is truly kiss-ass!"

"Mr. Nibbrig—"

"Oh, crap sandwich! It was ugly, it was ancient, and it was *brown*. Major sludge. Anyway, Niblets won't be back for a year. Maybe never—maybe he'll get eaten by llamas, or something."

"There aren't any llamas in the Himalayas."

"Whatever. Then you and Jane can stay here for good. Wouldn't that be great, Janey?"

Jane shrugged. She was sitting on her bed—the poppy-printed screen was folded back during the day—leafing listlessly through an oversized book called *What Do People Do All Day?* Now and then she raised her head to look up at the blue spruce that stood in front of the tall windows, its hastily bought ornaments polished by the genial winter sunshine pouring through the loft. It was the day before Christmas.

"Hold this down, right here," Mel said to Nan. "That's it." The glue gun made little spitting sounds. The smell of hot glue, like baked beans burning, filled Nan's nostrils.

"Seriously, though," Mel went on, squeezing the trigger, squinting, smoothing, her fingers turning the raw edge of the flag under as she went. "*Your* look could use an update. No offense."

Nan said nothing. Her new life didn't have the space in it for self-scrutiny that her old one had had. There seemed to be no reason to consult a mirror—in fact, there was no mirror. Unless you counted the dim door of the medicine cabinet or the shoulders-to-ankle mirror eccentrically affixed to the refrigerator. How odd: her apartment in West Seattle, as Alex had once pointed out, averaged two mirrors per room.

"To start with, you could quit baking your hair."

It was true that Nan's hair, too long now and out of shape, drooped like spaniel ears against her cheeks. Mel's own hair, since Nan had seen her last, had sprouted neon-green bangs, which she kept brushing out of her eyes with one muscular forearm.

"I'm *so* glad I had this fabric." Mel stroked the lumpy white-stars-on-blue. "Hold it down right there. No, *there*. It's wicked hard to find good stuff now. This'll last for, like, decades."

It looked as if it already had: the blue was faded in irregular patches, the points of the stars dulled as if by generations of thumbs.

"Where did you get it?" Nan asked. Why did I agree to it? she thought.

"Had it since I was a kid. My second foster mother gave it to me when I left. Her husband was killed in Vietnam, and they gave her this for his coffin. Hand me those straight pins, will you?"

"You grew up in foster homes?"

"All my life," Mel said cheerfully through a mouthful of pins. "My real mom was on heroin, she OD'ed when I was two. They told me all this—the caseworkers, in Beloit. Cheeseballs! They think they have to warn you, you know? That you have these *genes*."

Did this account, Nan wondered, for Mel's peculiar combination of fragility and strength? Striving conscientiously to bridge the gap between youth and age (Age! thought Nan incredulously, when did that happen?), she said, "That must have been hard."

"People think, oh, Wisconsin, heartland, cows, corn. Beloit! The only town whose name sounds like a fart in a bathtub."

There was a silence, broken only by the brisk little explosions of the glue gun, the slap of Jane's page turning. "There were just always too many of us, that was the thing. People take more children than they can handle. You get the same amount of money for each child, and after a point another kid more doesn't really cost anything. That's how I got my name. You can take your finger off now. This side's done."

Gratefully Nan fell back onto her haunches, then sat. She brushed away the fronds of a date palm. Her knees seemed to have turned to cinders. "I just assumed 'Mel' was short for Melissa."

Mel laughed her Marlene Dietrich laugh. No, it seemed her third foster mother had christened her "Mellow"—this child who understood by then that everything depended on not making waves—and it had stuck. By the time she'd come east, on a full scholarship to the Rhode Island School of Design, she no longer knew herself by her real name.

Moved that Mel would confide all this, Nan knew she should be grateful that she didn't seem to expect any revelations in return. Yet for a moment she wished she could make them, wished they were being demanded. How isolating it was to keep a secret. How lonely.

Recognizing in Mel's confiding mood an opportunity that might not come again, Nan said, "You and Mrs. Horsfal, you were close?"

"She was, like, my role model. But you two—you were really tight, huh?"

"She was my best friend in the world." Nan took a breath. "How did she die, exactly?"

"Peacefully, I think."

"No, I meant, what of?"

Suddenly Mel was busy filling her mouth with pins, sighting down the glue gun. "Um . . . pneumonia. Yeah, that's it—pneumonia. Let's do the other arm. Where'd I put that corduroy?" Though it lay on the floor, neatly folded, between them. Nan shook it out and handed it to Mel, then stood up, knees creaking. They moved to the other end of the sofa.

"Pneumonia? Mel, are you sure? Hardly anybody dies of pneumonia these days."

Mel mumbled through her pins, "This cloth'll really stand up."

"So you said."

Something strange, then, about Deenie's death. No use trying to get the truth out of Mel: clearly, her own secrets were the only ones she was prepared to confide. *Did* people die of pneumonia now? Nan had guessed some kind of cancer, like Tod; had pictured Deenie suffering and waiting, like Tod. And all without Nan. Why hadn't Deenie *told* her?

If only she could have a cigarette! Kneeling down again, a little painfully, in a pool of sunlight that gilded Mel's busy hands and threw the shadow of the Christmas tree across her face, Nan felt chilled. Too many secrets. Secrets within secrets.

"Hey, Janey!" Mel said over her shoulder. "Whaddaya think?"

In her voice was a hunger Nan had heard before. Now, after Mel's revelations, she understood it: a feeling of fellowship with motherless, transient Jane. She felt a flash of anger that anyone should see Jane's situation that way. *I'm* with her, she thought; Jane has *me*.

Jane shrugged without looking up. It was one of her silent, sullen days. They seemed to alternate with days of hair-trigger touchiness and still other days of eerily cheerful, grown-up composure. Reminded of Alex's teenage years, Nan had fallen back on the same strategy (if you could call it that) that she'd used then: give up trying to predict, much less improve, these moods, and just try to weather them.

The phone rang.

Mel said, "Answer that, Janey, will you? I need your grandma's fingers. So, Nan, I'm serious. We could do you next. Pinch it, right there. No—both hands. Update your hair. Maybe do a small tattoo. On your shoulder, or the back of your hand. A rose, maybe. No—too many of those around. Something more, like, *stately*."

Nan wasn't listening. *Yeah*, Jane was saying, *uh-huh . . . Yeah, we are . . . Okay!* When she hung up from this litany of affirmation, Nan said, fear clogging her throat, "Who was that, Grape Eyes?"

"Hold still, Nan!" Mel said. "Don't fade on me."

"A long, um, a lost-along relative," Jane said. She climbed back onto her bed and disappeared behind her book.

"Who? What was their name? Jane!"

"I forget. He said he'll be over in a Jeffrey."

"He's coming *here*?"

Mel said, "I didn't know you guys had relatives in Rhode Island. There! We're done. Gimme five!" She picked up Nan's hand and turned it over and slapped her palm, then stood up. No surveying her handiwork; she was already pulling on her jacket.

"We'll go with you," Nan said, thinking, Be over in a jiffy? We'll see about that.

She hauled herself to her feet. Mere seconds later, clattering down the stairs with their coats under her arm and Jane by the resisting hand, she thought, That does it! Preschool for you, my little chickadee. And freedom, freedom for me.

|

Somehow they got through Christmas. Nan, who'd never made much of holidays—they'd always seemed, in foreign places, irrelevant—did her best. A stocking hung from Nibbrig's tallest fig tree. Gifts under the blue spruce for Jane, who cried that night but would not say why, would not say she missed her mama—or her daddy. A Russian New Year's feast at Val and Mel's. Flashback to a New Year's night in Bonn—Tod's first posting—the narrow house filled with the smells of silver fir and cedar and newly papered walls, the new baby upstairs in the nursery, Nan moving among her guests, feeling them catch and hold her happiness, one by one, like candles lighting.

|

The January thaw came early. On the seventh Nan woke feeling sure today's message from Alex would say that she'd gotten custody, that she was coming for Jane—maybe even name the day.

She walked up the steps of what she'd learned, from the students, to call "the Rock," under bare branches that dripped icy water onto her hatless head, her shoulders. In the Reference Room she sat down without unbuttoning her coat. She didn't have much time: Mel could only keep Jane till eleven. Behind the semicircular desk Ben Kingsley smiled and nodded. Nan clicked her way into Lexis/Nexus unaided. The *Pee-Eye* offered stories about an eight-year-old boy with leukemia who ran away from home rather than face more chemotherapy; about Mexico City's plan to use giant fans to solve the pollution problem; about the Washington State Supreme Court's refusal to force a man to let his ex-wife be impregnated with their frozen embryo. Nan raced through them to the Personals. But no amount of mega-scrolling yielded a message from Alex.

Sounds were suddenly magnified: a pencil dropping, boot heels on the marble floor, the juicy coughs of students. Nan felt as if she couldn't get her breath. As if the wide, windowless room were narrowing, the ranks of computers crowding in on her. She looked wildly around at the lighted monitors, like blind, bland faces.

Get out. Get air.

Outside in the weirdly warm morning, she sat down on a wooden bench embraced by a tangle of dripping branches like huge black parentheses.

Remember the Plan.

Nan pulled the Time Line out of her pocket. When she opened it, she had to hold it together where it gaped along the fold lines. One month since she and Jane had left Seattle. According to her first message, the one she'd sent on December 21, Alex had already moved out of the beautiful old house on Queen Anne Hill, had filed the petition for temporary custody of Jane. By now she should have seen her lawyer and filed for divorce; by now the motion for temporary custody should have been granted.

Had something gone wrong? Alex had seemed sure that Gabriel would not file a countermotion. But what if he had? That would drag things out—but this long? Or had the legal stuff been delayed because of the holidays? Was Alex all right? Had Gabriel somehow prevented her from sending a message? Or even persuaded her to abandon the Plan? Because he would certainly try. Could Alex hold out against him—intelligent, compelling, formidable Gabriel?

He'd been forty when Nan met him, thirteen years older than Alex, fourteen years younger than Nan. Never married. A reconstructive surgeon who worked with burned children. Primed by Alex with his sterling résumé (burned *children*? pro bono one afternoon a week at a rundown hospital in the Central District? summer vacations donated to a clinic in the highlands of Guatemala?), Nan had expected to meet a man with a Public Conscience, a man who wasn't interested in people, not one at a time, not close up. Early June, six years ago, six months before Tod died. One of the long, light-filled evenings just before the solstice. Nan was late, held up at the hospital waiting to talk to Tod's radiologist. Hesitating inside the restaurant entrance, she didn't see Alex until the man with her stood up and waved. Seated, Alex leaned toward him as if caught in his magnetic field, a list that Nan recognized at once. Before she was even close enough to perceive her daughter's radiance, she knew. *This* was the man her daughter would marry. Shaking his hand, she felt an echo of the old itchy excitement, the buzz that always used to accompany encounters with attractive men. The intensity of his gaze, even at that first meeting, made her feel completely seen. Tall, silver-haired, silver-eyed. Should a mother be so drawn to her daughter's suitor? Motherless Nan didn't know.

At the end of the meal Gabriel ordered Calvados and clementines, and they sat peeling the small plump globes with their fingers. The fragrance mingled with the odor of Gabriel's cigar, which no one came to ask him to put out. Alex sat smiling, her eyes roaming the restaurant, unaware of her companions—unaware of Gabriel. As if drawn by her inattention, he turned to her. The horizontal groove in his forehead deepened, giving him the look of tender inquiry that Nan would come to know well. She thought, So that's how it is. If he's afraid he might have lost you, even for a moment, he's yours. He'll move heaven and earth to repossess you. Does Alex know that? A waiter had come just then and lit the candles in the wall sconce behind them. A shadow had fallen across the table with its litter of bright curving peels and cigar ash and half-full wineglasses: Gabriel's shadow with Alex's diminishing into it.

Nan sat and smoked. There was still half an hour before she had to pick up Jane. The sky was a bright, bottomless blue. High above, a silver plane moved across it, leaving a vapor trail like a white zipper. Nan watched it loosen and dissolve. Wasn't it possible that the legal system—as pokey and ponderous as she knew it to be—could take a month to decide the temporary fate of one small child? Surely Gabe wouldn't risk jeopardizing the outcome. He would simply call on his many influential connections and wait for the courts to decide in his favor. *Possessory rights:* the very phrase sounded like Gabriel. He would bide his time. He'd wait.

All around her, wet branches clicked in the warm wind, which moved hesitatingly across her face, through her hair. The rhythmic sound of the bare branches did something to time, slowed it, like the ticking of an old-fashioned pendulum clock. She, Nan, would also wait—but trust in the opposite outcome. What choice did she have?

A regular preschool, Nan knew, wouldn't take Jane without some sort of ID, would maybe even demand a parent's authorization. She couldn't risk it. Anyway, home care was cheaper, and not having heard from Alex had made Nan's store of cash look alarmingly small. She found Mikki from an ad on the Food Basket's bulletin board. Unlicensed, Mikki took more children than the state allowed, but she had a helper, another moon-faced Japanese woman who spoke no English, as far as Nan could tell. Mikki, herself a grandmother, seemed kind. Her rambling apartment over the Hope Street Deli was reassuringly messy. She showed Nan the indoor jungle gym, the many-colored inflatable tent, the Lego city under construction. "My grandson, they too old now," she said. "So I take children, fill up space all day." The children—three girls and two boys, all younger than Jane, and a baby asleep in a red canvas swing—seemed happy. Mikki introduced them by name, even the baby, and they greeted Nan and Jane politely.

The girl nearest Jane's age tossed tight blond pigtails over her shoulders and grabbed Jane's hand. Jane followed her to a corner filled with dolls and stuffed animals.

If only I knew what to look for, Nan thought. The Nannies had all been chosen (*vetted,* a word that made her picture them as sheepdogs) by the Foreign Service. Nan had had veto power, exercised only once (hairy, perfume-drenched Monika, in Bucharest). She'd never had to go out and look for Alex's caretakers, and Alex had always been cared for at home, more or less under Nan's eye.

There was a playground two blocks away, on Rochambeau Avenue, Mikki told Nan. And in the summertime, the chestnuts—she gestured to the bare branches crowding the windows—shaded the apartment "like in countryside, like in the mountain."

Mikki gave Nan a cup of green tea and some cookies that tasted of anise, and they sat in the little kitchen while she explained hours, fees, rules ("No biting! No hitting! Second time happen, child leave my house"), naps, snacks, occasional excursions. They agreed that Nan would bring Jane back the following day and, if that worked out, every weekday from ten to three. (Five whole hours, thought Nan: bliss!) A small boy, sepia-skinned, perhaps a year and a half old, toddled into the kitchen and up to Nan. The way he held on to the leg of her pants, two fistfuls, suggested he was new to walking. "Hi, there." Nan smiled down at him. "Whose special boy are you?" He considered this question in silence, weighing it.

Nan gave Mikki four twenty-dollar bills, half a week's fee. When she went to the doll corner to say that it was time to go, Jane cried. A good sign—this, at least, she knew from the years of The Nannies. A good beginning. She left with the distinct sense that Jane was on probation; but still. A good beginning.

|

Most mornings Nan went to the library after she'd left Jane with Mikki. Descending Mikki's carefully shoveled steps, she was surprised each time to feel a quick, sharp pang of loss. The number 42 bus took her down Thayer Street to the edge of campus. At Peaberry's Café (where else could she go and be warm, entertained, and unnoticed?), she smoked a single cigarette and warmed her hands around a cup of coffee, then cut across the Quad to the library. She took comfort from its brightness, its smells of paper and decaying leather and dust, the dim hum of fluorescent lights, the sweatshirted backs of students bent in concentration. The first morning she sat in the sunny, many-windowed Periodicals Room reading old copies of *Vogue* and *Harper's Bazaar* (a university library, who would have thought it?), limp from the palms of strangers. This palled sooner than it might once have done. Looking around at students and faculty perusing things like *Mind* and the *Journal of English Linguistics*, Nan felt the prod of conscience. What was she doing pondering ads for expensively unironed clothes in colors like "balsam" and "tusk"? Here she was in a major research library; and here was her own granddaughter crying out, as much as any child ever had, for major research. On the second morning she went to the Information Desk, where Ben Kingsley directed her to a section on B Floor.

|

The woman on trial for abduction because she'd taken her small daughter to Mexico after becoming convinced that her ex-husband was molesting her.

The woman who died of lung cancer because she was afraid to seek medical help while she and her children were in hiding from their father.

The woman who spent two years in jail in contempt of court for refusing to say where she'd hidden her three-year-old son.

The woman whose ex-husband, after a judge denied him custody, put their four-year-old daughter in the car, fastened their seat belts, and drove off the Aurora Bridge into Lake Washington.

It's not what might happen to *you*, Nan reminded herself; it's what happened (or didn't?) to Jane.

Seven Signs of Child Sexual Abuse:

  •*sexually suggestive language*
  •*touching body parts of self & others*
  •*acting out sex or sexual positions with dolls*
  •*nightmares*
  •*initiating sex games with other children*
  •*vaginal infections/discharge*
  •*hemorrhoids*

Nan put her face in her hands. How could anyone—*anyone*— She thought of Gabriel's mother, the beatings, the tears, the glad little boy running to meet the pickup truck.

In the carrel behind her, two young men spoke in urgent whispers.

"I got beet red. Hadda hide behind a magazine when she walked by."

"Just 'cause you come into the Periodicals Room doesn't mean she has some innate obligation to sit there till you get it up to ask her to dinner."

"She said, 'See you around.' That's what I said to *her* the time before."

"So . . . she was alluding to the last time you were together. That's a good sign."

What pretty problems to have, thought Nan, how lovely to be young. But then, *Jane* was young.

Every afternoon at three o'clock she picked Jane up from Mikki's, and every afternoon, zipping her into her scarlet parka, she whispered into her ear, "A runcible cat!" Some days, Jane whispered back, "With crimson whiskers!" In good weather they walked to Newport Creamery and then to Bajnotti Fountain. Some days, Jane allowed Nan to put an arm around her shoulders. Some days, she leaned against Nan's chest. They sat on the fountain's lip with their feet dangling over the edge, companionably licking their cones, and watched the chickadees, tiny black-masked bandits, forage through the leaf mold in the fountain's stone basin.

More clothes, was what Nan had in mind—*clean* clothes. She hated the spider-thronged laundry room in the basement of their building, the rubbery smell of rats, the many stairs back and forth, and had allowed their small stock of clothing to get dingier and dingier. On Friday of Jane's second week at day care, Nan picked her up as usual, paid Mikki in carefully counted bills, then headed down Hope Street. The January thaw still held. In the strange, bright, wintry gloom—clouds with a sense of the sun behind them—the wet streets were a blur of rain-blown figures. A girl in a purple slicker scudded toward them, laughing, in the wind-filled block between Mikki's building and Rochambeau Avenue.

"Nana," Jane said, "were you alive when the world was black and white?"

Nan looked down at her small heart-shaped face, wet bangs pasted to her forehead in a row of question marks. "What do you mean, honey?"

"You know, like on TV. Like Shirley Temple."

Nan laughed. "No. I mean, the world was the same colors when I was your age as it is now. It's just, there was only black-and-white film to make movies with. Like newspapers."

Jane looked disappointed. "You're hurting my *fingers*," she said.

Nan loosened her grip, but only slightly. The wind was like a hand on her back, pushing her forward.

The store on Hope Street, Small Change, had been recommended by Mikki—good cheap secondhand children's clothing and toys. Nan bought recklessly. Surely Alex's message, when it appeared on Monday, would provide her and Jane with the agreed-upon plenty of money? Jane's eyes shone at the bright turtlenecks and the angora cardigan with a rose appliquéd to the pocket and the hot-pink overalls—She takes after me, thought Nan, with the old quick thrill of pride—not to mention several children's books and a metal loom with a dozen skeins of colored yarn. Farther down the street was a women's consignment shop called Act II, the name a good sign, Nan felt. Coming into its well-lit warmth, she was met by the musty, *human* smell of used clothing. For an instant she was back in her grandmother's secondhand store, where she'd spent every afternoon after school; was back at Jane's age, or a bit older, a little girl reading book after book, sitting in a child-size rocking chair between rows of garments. She could still recall the racks of evening dresses in tissue-thin silk, chiffon, buttery velvet; rhinestones and sequins; white kid gloves the texture of gardenias. The gleam and glamour of those clothes! Dorothea (she'd refused to answer to "Gran" or "Grandma") would have been about fifty then, near the end of World War II. The store had been a comedown for her—she'd been a pilot in the years after World War I, testing searchlight defenses and towing targets for gunnery practice—but someone had to care for motherless Nan.

"Nana!" Jane hung on Nan's arm, pulling her out of her reverie. "I'm hungry. And I have to pee." Choosing quickly, Nan bought a number of serviceable garments—pants, shirts, a thick woolen sweater—in colors that verged on dirt. The kind of clothing worn by The Nannies.

After lunch at Burger King, where by now Nan actually had a favorite meal, they caught the bus back downtown. They sat in the front seat (Jane's choice) and watched the wipers caress the big windows while their wet coats steamed in the warmth. At Kennedy Plaza four men in Santa Claus suits sat down across from them. What in the world could they be doing now, nearly three weeks after Christmas? One opened a newspaper and another, a black man, sat ruminatively twanging the elastic of his beard. Jane watched, frowning. As far as Nan knew, she still believed in Santa. Jane's head lifted, and Nan followed her gaze. Above the four Santas' heads an ad advised, "Child Support Is Every Child's Right. Call 1-800-FIND DAD." Maybe she *could* read? "Dad" was the simplest of words. Nan sighed. In their six weeks of exile there had been no sign from Jane that would have indicated, one way or the other, whether Gabriel had interfered (the nuns' word, long ago) with her. In fact, since her angry outburst in front of Consuelo, when they were leaving the Fred, Jane had not once mentioned her father. This seemed, to Nan, the most ominous thing.

Ask her. At least give her a chance to talk about him—if she wants to.

Afraid, uncertain, she looked out the window where Jane had rubbed a clear spot like a porthole in the steam. The bus turned along the river, or rather, along the construction that was in the process of uncovering the river. Raw cement roadbed lay broken, wetly gleaming. Nan watched a worker apply a gunlike instrument to a row of iron spikes, one after another: a blue-diamond burst of flame, a shower of golden sparks. The figure straightened, turning toward the bus windows, and raised its face guard. Nan saw with surprise that it was a woman.

Could I do that? But I'll never have to. Alex will arrange about money—she will. And anyway, this whole trip—this *exile*—won't be for long.

The woman met Nan's eyes, then wiped her face on the sleeve of her green padded jacket. With a jerk, the bus started again.

Nan hadn't, so far, seen any of the Seven Signs in Jane. But one article had said that about one-third of abused children never showed any symptoms. One-third! She remembered how Deenie's father used to come and stand behind her on the pretext of helping her on with her coat; how he'd rest his palms on her shoulders, holding her still until she could feel his erection in the small of her back. But she'd been thirteen, fourteen. Old enough to laugh it off; to feel, even, a little proud of her power.

The black Santa removed his red tasseled cap and shook it so that drops of rain flew off and struck Nan.

The way he touches her, Mama. The way he looks at her. He'd been putting her to bed— His bathrobe was untied—

Alex's distress, her pain: there had been no possibility of doubting her. Yet what, really, had she seen? A father putting his daughter to sleep. She, Nan, didn't know what Gabriel had done, only what Alex believed he had done. So easy to slip, one small step at a time, from kissing the plump little elbows to— Nan didn't know how many unthinkable steps Gabriel might have slid, slipped, slithered. Alex herself didn't know. Not *know.*

At Westminster Street the four Santa Clauses disembarked. Jane leaned against Nan, who put her arm around her, but lightly. As if to reward her, Jane crept closer, finally snuggled.

Nan hesitated; then she said, "Those Santa Clauses were funny, weren't they?"

Jane said nothing, but Nan could feel her listening. The articles she'd read at the Rock had recommended an oblique approach. They warned about whole nurseries full of children making false accusations to please adult questioners. *Don't ask leading questions. Don't suggest particular events. Don't criticize a child's response.*

The bus continued its majestic progress down Point Street. Each time the doors opened, the smell of leaf mold and wet cinders swept in on a wedge of cold air.

Nan said, "That one on the aisle looked a little like your daddy." He'd been tall and silver-haired.

Jane stiffened.

Gently; gently. "You miss your daddy? I do."

Did Jane's head tilt toward Nan?

Open-ended questions, the articles recommended, to guard against the possibility of making a wound out of what had been merely an event. *The abused child may not realize what has been done to him or her, or may not feel it as an injury at all.*

"My daddy stuck my milk money in Larry Boy's super-suction ear, and then he shaked him upside down."

"He did? And then what happened?"

"Then Mama cried. It's not nice to tease people."

"What did your daddy do then?"

Jane pulled away, sliding along the seat until no part of her was touching Nan. She began to blow a bubble with her gum. The bright pink globe widened and thinned, wobbled alarmingly between her lips. Looking sideways at Nan, she puffed. The bubble burst. Sticky pale webbing covered her nose and mouth; in her eyes, very green now and fixed on Nan, there gleamed some kind of warning.

Nan was afraid to press further. Afraid of hurting Jane, afraid (Be honest!) of driving Jane away. Coward! she accused herself. But she couldn't risk it. She'd come to understand, in a baffled, muffled way, that she needed Jane as much as Jane needed her. Was this how other women felt about their kids? Was this what she, Nan, had missed, with her own child? And how, exactly, did you need them? What had the buffer of unlimited child care, the inescapable and (Be honest!) welcome parade of Nannies, deprived her of?

But here was their stop.

Nan went down the steps first, wind and rain like a cool palm laid against her face after the steamy closeness of the bus. Her legs ached; she was tired. She turned around to help Jane, who shook her head, then jumped with both feet down each of the bus steps and into the rubbishy torrent of the gutter. Water splashed over Nan. Soaked, shivering, she stumbled onto the curb.

I'm too old for this—for all of it.

The following Monday, crossing the Quad (now briefly, falsely green and smelling of damp earth and tree bark), Nan felt a vague itchy feeling, recognizable as one she'd had often when she and Tod were living behind the Iron Curtain. The early-morning air was fizzy and tickling. City birds, misled by mildness, clotted the tops of the elms, their clicking and twittering amplified by the humid air. A gaggle of students came toward her, laughing, hatless and coatless.

What she felt was followed. Tailed.

She looked around for Val, could almost hear his "Fancy to meet *you* here!"

There *was* someone. A figure that melted quickly into the long indigo shadow of a dormitory.

Gabriel! Nan thought. Her heart slipped.

She kept walking. Long-forgotten advice from the Iron Curtain edition of *HOWDY* filled her head. *If you suspect you are being followed, keep moving; otherwise, your pursuer will know he has been spotted.* She fumbled in her shoulder bag for her compact, thumbed it open. In the little round mirror she saw a man walking behind her. Dusty-looking brown leather jacket; dark cap pulled low over his forehead, shadowing his face; tall enough to be Gabriel. Walking faster, still looking into the mirror, she bumped into a boy with a Snugli strapped to his chest; inside was a tiny striped kitten. In the collision Nan dropped the mirror, heard it crack, had to let it lie.

What should she do now? She hadn't lost him.

For the same reason, do not speed up; instead, take the first practical means of concealment that presents itself.

She ducked into the stone archway under Faunce House. Sweat tickled her forehead, the cleft between her breasts. Breathing fast, she flattened herself against the glass of the long notice board and waited. Viewed from the shadows under the arch, the Quad in the bright morning light was like a stage set, and the noisy, laughing students were actors in a play about to begin. She watched, waiting for her pursuer to pass. A walk-on, she hoped. In her chest was the familiar feeling, not quite pain, as if a balloon were slowly expanding, pushing her ribs outward. Did she dare look for her pills? Where was he? *Who* was he? The sudden thought came to her, making her shiver, that Alex might in desperation have claimed that Nan had simply kidnapped Jane. Gabriel would come looking for them; Gabriel would not rest until he had his daughter back. Could he have found them so soon?

If you cannot lose your pursuer by concealment, try to reverse direction.

She eased along the glass notice board to the other end of the archway, then turned and went quickly, almost running now, down Waterman Street in the direction from which she'd come. Her open coat flapped around her. Her knees ached. Faster. The feeling in her chest intensified, but she kept moving, as if the balloon inside propelled her. When she turned, she saw him again. He seemed to be keeping a steady distance behind her.

Up the steps and into Faunce House. Down a corridor, jostling students. Down a flight of steps. Basement, branching, three long halls lined with mailboxes. Choose!

Pushing, stumbling, a little yappy dog, more students. Smell of winter bodies: onions and wet wool. Talking, shouting, rap music on someone's boom box. Breathe. Move.

The narrow corridor turned, and she turned with it. Find a ladies' room! He couldn't follow her there. The balloon, bigger now, urged her forward.

Dead end. Empty. No students; no one.

Frantic, breathless, Nan scanned the walls of mailboxes for an opening, a doorway. When, finally, she turned back the way she'd come, there he was.

"Mrs. Tice?"

Suddenly, her chest widening, she was dizzy. Her head felt like a bowling ball on the thin stem of her neck. The man put one hand under her elbow. Stumbling backward, she slid down a row of mailboxes to the floor. She fumbled in her purse, grasped the little plastic vial. She couldn't open it.

He took it from her and crouched down beside her.

"One? Two?"

She managed to shake her head.

"One, then."

His voice seemed far away. Without looking at him, she took the pill and put it under her tongue. She leaned back against the wall and closed her eyes. The knobs of several mailboxes bit into her spine. The nitro began to work. Her breath slowed. The pressure inside her began to ease, the balloon slowly deflating. Her head stilled.

|

They sat at one of the tippy little tables in the student café at the top of Faunce House. Sunlight fell across them in long, calming stripes. At the next table a young man sat cracking his knuckles, a bright sound in the morning quiet, while he read the newspaper. Walker Tice, pulling off his black wool hat, revealed a bald head as perfectly shaped as a darning egg. Here he was—the Aged Cousin, in the flesh. Nan searched his face for some resemblance to Deenie, but in vain. As Deenie herself would have said, he wasn't young, and he wasn't pretty. Older than Deenie: late sixties, at a guess. His neck fell in a pale wattle from chin to clavicle; he took no pains to hide it. Instead he wore, tucked neatly into faded jeans, a black T-shirt with white Gothic lettering that said, OLD AGE AND TREACHERY WILL OVERCOME YOUTH AND SKILL. He was slender and fit (which was probably how he'd managed to keep up with her—all right, to catch her) and so clean Nan decided he must be a retired dentist.

He seemed kind. He'd seated her in a quiet corner overlooking the Quad, brought her a large coffee, carefully sugared. But it was more than his kindness. She felt at ease with him: there was something about him that was familiar. Orange-scented steam from his tea, spiraling up between them, made her think suddenly of Morocco, where she and Tod had spent a belated honeymoon.

He hadn't meant to scare her, Walker Tice said, apologizing for the third time. He *had* been following her, but only to make her acquaintance. Val Peshkov had pointed her out to him that morning as she and . . . her daughter, was it? . . . left the building on Elbow Street, where he, Walker, had stopped by to collect the keys to his cousin's place. He'd been just too late to catch her. Nan, relaxing now, felt silly. The chase, which had seemed so long, had lasted only a few minutes. But she'd been terrified. Had living on the run, in hiding, already changed her into someone fearful, someone easily thrown?

The hell with *that*, she thought. She could take care of herself. *Intrepid* had been Pop's word for her from the time she was ten. Intrepid, he used to say, like your grandma. Nan's contempt for the others—the ones who allowed fear to cheat them of experience, of life—she'd never let Pop, never let anyone but Deenie, see. Courage was the quality she'd valued most in Tod. She'd loved him for the very thing that let him stay untouched by her.

"—left me her apartment," Walker Tice was saying. "Her condo, I mean. We weren't that close, but the thing is, everybody else is dead."

Nan nodded encouragingly.

"It was just gonna be till this will thing gets straightened out. But I like it here. After ten years in Blue Hill, Providence feels like the big city. I don't have any ties up in Maine anymore. So I might just— But you don't want to hear all this."

He'd turned rosy above the wattle, charmingly abashed. Nan saw that he was not immune to her. And how lovely it was, basking in male regard after such a long time without. Not quite admitting to herself that she was flirting, Nan made little sounds of encouragement. He told her more. Revealed himself as retired—though when Nan asked from what, he appeared not to hear the question. He'd been widowed "a good few years." When he asked about Nan's deceased husband, she murmured something vague, the Missouri branch of the family, third cousins on Deenie's father's side. A tangled web, indeed. Walker Tice's very certain, very blue eyes looked as if they would miss nothing; but he seemed satisfied. As he listened—Tice rhymes with Nice, Deenie used to say—Nan thought, Harmless? Better than harmless: he can be used. She'd tried, that first week in Providence, to go back to Deenie's, but Val had claimed he'd mailed the keys to the cousin in Maine.

"Anyway, all I seem to do up there's go to funerals. You want some more coffee?"

Nan shook her head. "No, but thanks."

The little café, nearly empty when they came in, had begun to fill with students, backpacks flapping, a few professorial types recognizable by their dusty duffle coats (men) and trench coats with trailing belts (women). Above the silky sound of newspapers turning, the clink of spoons on china, Walker confided, "Birds—that's my passion. That's why I stayed up north after Christy passed on. Your lesser-known birds don't congregate in cities. You don't have the flora, you don't get the fauna."

A family obsession? Nan thought of the cages in Deenie's living room. Why was he telling her all this? Tod used to warn her that people rarely said what they intended to say, let alone what they meant. Walker Tice sounded like a real ornithologist—but how would she know? Like the

Last Lover when he spoke of volcanos, Walker, talking on about birds, gathered force and became at once vibrant and didactic. Words Nan hadn't the dimmest apprehension of—species-specific aberration, avocets, *lamellae*—glimmered in the space between them. He was especially interested in cranes. Siberian cranes, Inca terns, blue-billed African somethings.

"You sound like you've traveled a lot. What was it you said you did? Before you retired?"

"Little of this, little of that. Engineering, mostly."

So he didn't want to talk about his work. Unusual man! But why not? This kind, concerned man—could his profession be private detective? HOWDY: *Appearances CAN be deceiving! Be most on guard when everything seems completely normal.* But his connection with Deenie—surely that couldn't be faked.

Test him. Ask him something about her.

Nan rummaged in her purse for her Marlboros, taking her time, sifting through old crumbled tobacco and shredded Kleenex and an abandoned lollipop of Jane's. Then it came to her. Something Deenie'd told Nan and Nan alone, in those heady early days when each of them had arrived at the blessed realization that she'd found someone she could admit things to. She pulled out the mashed half-empty pack of cigarettes and a pack of matches.

"So," she said, as casually as she could, "it sounds like you managed to escape the family curse. Deenie used to talk about it. She used to say . . . What was it you all called it?"

Walker reached across the table and took the matches. His hand, when it grazed hers, was cool, with clean, smooth nails. Without the least hurry he lit one of the matches and held it to the tip of her cigarette.

"The Blood of the Elk," he said, his tone equally casual. But his eyes met hers, and stayed there.

She looked down at the flame held steadily toward her, sucked in, let the smoke stream out through her nostrils. The Blood of the Elk. Unless he was on the up-and-up, he couldn't possibly have known. And besides, there was the mysterious sense of ease that she felt with him.

"Damn!" Walker gave an abrupt shake of his hand. The match, which he'd neglected to blow out while looking so intently at Nan, had burned his fingers. She hadn't had this kind of effect in years.

A scrubbed young man in a ponytail came over to point out the NO

SMOKING sign. Walker rose—he was taller than she'd realized, a head taller than the young man—and took him by the arm and walked him between the tables to the entrance, where they stood talking for a few seconds. Then, ponytail flapping, the young man vanished down the stairs.

"What did you say to him?" Nan asked when Walker returned to their table. Smoke from her abandoned cigarette rose between them. She dropped it into the remains of her coffee.

"I told him smoking bans are unconstitutional."

"But why did he take off like that?"

"I told him I was the dean of the faculty and you were a lawyer for the ACLU."

Nan laughed; then Walker did, too. They couldn't seem to stop. She tried to, looked at Walker through the tears in her eyes, and that set her off again. Pent-up tension from the chase through the catacombs of Faunce House, she would tell herself later; latent hysteria. But at that moment, laughing, she felt only a sudden lightness—an *ascension*—as if the two of them, she and this stranger, were borne aloft on some mysterious current of air, above the bowed heads of the other patrons, up through the magically yawning roof of Faunce House.

Six

In mid-January the cold returned, snapping down on Providence like a glass bell. Nan had forgotten, during the years in Seattle, the brilliance of sunshine in a world of snow, the light without warmth, the cold that colonized your bones. She invaded her shrinking store of cash to buy herself a warmer coat at the winter sales.

January 21 found her once again in front of one of the Rock's computers, watching the *Pee-Eye* unfurl. EIGHTH-GRADE STUDENTS IN LOVE SUICIDE; EGG-SWAPPING AT BIRTH CLINIC; GIRL, 14, SHOOTS FATHER. Alex's message appeared immediately beneath an ad for WIFE-IN-LAW ("Your ex-husband married her. Your present husband divorced her. Better read this!"); Nan had scrolled past it before she realized. Her heart bumped and restarted. She fumbled with the mouse, lost the cursor, backed up.

POOKIE: Not yet. Minor snags. Kiss her for me. HIPPIE

Nan begged a pencil and a piece of paper from the boy next to her and copied out the message with a shaking hand.

Outside the library, in the bright blustery morning, she walked and walked. At last she sat down in the noon sun on the stone lip of Bajnotti Fountain, feet dangling over into emptiness, and unfolded the piece of paper. She reread it without putting on her glasses since by now she knew it by heart. Looking up at the empty fountain, the stilled mouths of Neptune and his mermaids filled with deep bruise-colored shadows instead of water, she remembered a phrase from the Baltimore Catechism, chanted aloud year after year in catechism class. *The sins against* HOPE *are* PRESUMP*tion and* DES*PAIR.*

She lit a cigarette and, throwing her head back, let the fragrant, stinging smoke stream out of her nostrils into the milky air. She could no longer close her mind to the thought that Alex, once (still?) so much in love with her husband, might have been too weak to leave him as she'd planned. Anger and helplessness knotted in a hard lump just under her diaphragm. Should she phone Alex? Demand to know what was happening, when she and Jane could come home? But calling was dangerous, could lead to discovery. More important, she had promised not to. All the broken promises in the past she could do nothing now to mend; but *this* one—

The wind tugged at the piece of paper in her hand. She thought, I will take Alex's message to mean exactly what it said. *Not yet:* soon, just not now. *Minor snags:* those could be anything. Bogle and Grant (best lawyers in the state of Washington) might have had a full calendar for custody hearings this month, for instance; or there could be some red-tape formalities with family court. Nan would not let the cool tone or the cryptic brevity of Alex's message worry her. Hadn't they agreed that her messages should be brief and vague? She, Nan, could wait. It wasn't so hard, now: there were Val and Mel, strangers turned friends; there was Mikki. The five hours a day Jane spent at day care restored Nan and gave her back some of the joy of grandmotherhood. She could wait.

Nan felt something pressing into her thigh. She looked down. A child's chin rested just above her wool-clad knees. It was the toddler from Mikki's day care. Nan twisted around, looking for his mother. There was no one in sight but a young black boy in a green Celtics jacket, kicking at the ornamented rim of the fountain, his eyes on Nan and the child. Suddenly the wind gave a ferocious tug on the scrap of paper and, gloved hands clumsy, she lost her hold on it. It soared out over the fountain and spiraled away. The child, watching, laughed in delight. He caught his lower lip between teeth as small as rosary beads and gazed up at her.

Nan had saved a life once. Probably saved it. At the time she didn't think of it in those terms at all: more like putting something back where it belonged. She and Tod were driving their little two-cylinder Polski Fiat back to Warsaw from Zakopane, where they'd spent Christmas in the Tatra Mountains. They were on the highway north of Sosnowiec. Twilight burned in the flat, snowy fields on either side, turning them to smoke and lavender, softening the black bare-as-crucifixes trees that punctured the horizon. Up ahead, at the side of the road, was a small smudged figure. Drawing level with it, they saw that it was not, as Tod had guessed, one of the stray dogs that roamed the roads, but a child. Very young, in a padded jacket too big for it, tangled yellow hair glowing in the car's headlights. Of course they stopped. In the crowded front seat, the little girl, placed on Nan's lap, turned on her a look of pure terror. Slowly, almost formally, she bent her head to the tender skin of Nan's wrist between her glove and the sleeve of her sheepskin coat. Her teeth sank in. They took her to the Politsia in the next village, and when they got back to Warsaw Nan got a tetanus shot from the British doctor. "No good deed goes unpunished," he said, his whiskey-scented breath warming her ear. For weeks the flesh of her inner wrist had borne a slowly fading crescent of red. Tod had tried, but he was never able to find out what became of the child. Officially she had never, it seemed, existed.

Wind wrapped itself around Nan like cold bedsheets, pressed an icy pillow to her face. She looked down at the little boy clutching her pant leg. A triangle of mucus gleamed on his upper lip.

"Hey, sweetie," she began, but his small face broke suddenly into radiance, his eyes on something behind her.

She turned. It was the black boy in the Celtics jacket.

"Hey, Bug!" he said to the child. "You buggin' this lady?" He held out his arms. The little boy, already scrambling around Nan, leapt at him, climbed his blue-jeaned legs. The older boy was even less warmly dressed, in a thin nylon jacket and sneakers. He picked up the child and Nan saw that the two of them had the same head of tight, shiny black curls. They came closer, and Nan could smell an oddly chemical smell, like ether, like the glue Tod had used for his ship models. Above them the bare branches of a sycamore sparred in the bitter wind.

"It's getting colder," Nan said. "You ought to take your brother home now."

"Brother? This my *son*." The older boy gave the child a shake. "Ain't you, Buggy-Bug? Deciolaria, that's his mama, she got busted. He *love* it here, it is his hard-core place."

"His nose is running."

"Not the safest spot, though. That's what I come over to tell you. I seen you here before, you and your little girl. You gotta be, like, *cautious* around this area. Last week some dumb-ass kid, Fatmir Somethin', he got slashed right here. Sliced his hand right off. And that's with two cop cars doin' a sixty-nine a block away."

"Here," Nan said. "Here's a Kleenex."

The boy ignored her outstretched hand. Bug was struggling to get down. "He think he *rule* you. You know? Deciolaria gonna have her hands full when she gets outta the ACI. He gonna humble her ass." Bug's flailing feet connected with the boy-father's groin. "Fuck!" Then, shouting over Bug's joyous squeals, "Deciolaria got no idea!"

They went off, the small boy wrapped around the big one. Nan watched them cross the snowy plaza beyond the fountain and vanish around the corner of the Upchurch Building, filled with a sense of loss she could not explain.

The wind blew all that night and all the next day and night, recalling the wind in Warsaw in January, filling the loft with its steady, disquieting fervor. Both nights Jane woke, long after midnight, screaming, "Mama! Mama!" Nan held her small, warm, quaking body. Nightmares, she remembered, were one of the Seven Signs of the Abused Child. Looking out at the night sky through the No-Theft grille that guarded all of Nibbrig's windows, she sang the non-lullabies she'd sung to Jane since babyhood. "Zombie Jamboree," "Salty Dog," "Hernando's Hideaway." The nearly full moon threw over them a shawl of light patterned with skewed diamonds from the window grille. Just when Nan thought she'd fallen sleep, Jane said, "Nana!" with the special note she used for questions other grown-ups had refused to answer, the note that recalled their pact, Nan's and Jane's, that Nan would never lie.

"What, Grape Eyes?"

"Did you know that all animals and people die?"

"Yes. That's true."

"So *you're* gonna die?"

Nan hesitated, then said, "Yes."

"Well, doesn't that worry you?"

Nan bit back a laugh. "No, Sweetpea. Because it won't happen for a long, long time. You'll be all grown up."

Jane gave a satisfied sigh—children, Nan believed, always knew the truth when they heard it—and wriggled closer to lay her head on Nan's chest. Nan's arms, tired from a day's worth of lifting, holding, wiping, fastening, ached with her weight. She said, very softly, "You miss your mama, don't you, Sweetpea?"

Jane's head, nose in Nan's armpit, moved slightly. A nod?

"She misses you, too. She doesn't want to be away from you, but she has to. Did she tell you that?"

The small body, humid with sleep, stiffened. "Secret," Jane murmured.

"It's just temporary. Just for a little while."

The hard little nose burrowed deeper into Nan's armpit. "We don't tell. Secrets. Ever." A small expiring breath. Then sleep.

Zipper leapt onto the bed and curled in the curve of Jane's belly. Nan thought of the little boy at Bajnotti Fountain—the radiance in his face when he looked at the older boy who was his father. She rubbed her cheek across the top of Jane's head, feeling the silky dampness of her hair.

|

When Walker put up the shades, dust shot out, peppering them both. "Good Christ! Afraid I'm not much of a housekeeper."

Nan was relieved to hear it. She found his cleanness, which had held steady through three meetings now, unnerving. The Last Lover had been unfastidious—generally, if she heeded her instincts, a good omen for sex. But why was she even thinking about that now? The sex chapter of her life was closed.

From Deenie's—now Walker's—windows, the sky above the State House was pale and paved with small thick clouds like cobblestones. The weather had turned cold again. The late-afternoon air outside, as they'd walked down Benefit Street, had tasted of iron. It had taken almost no effort to get herself invited to Deenie's apartment. But how, Nan wondered, could she broach the subject of Deenie's death?

"Christy, the way she was, it made it impossible. Housekeeping, I mean." Walker seemed intent on completing the portrait of his dead wife begun earlier on their walk. "She liked to walk the two miles to Stop and Shop and bring home a grocery cart. One time—this was way before she died—I came back from a couple weeks in Nairobi and there were five of them in the living room. Christy looked around and said, 'Hon, would you take me home?' I had to tell her, You *are* home. She wouldn't believe me. All those carts around, it had to be the Stop and Shop. Stubborn?" His voice grew fond. "Why, if she'd drowned in the Kennebec, I'd've looked for the body upstream of where she fell in."

They stood side by side gazing out through the dirty windows. In Seattle this would have qualified as a territorial view. Alex and Gabriel, in the six years of their marriage, had progressed from no view to territorial view to a view of the water. Nan started to tell Walker this, then remembered she was supposed to be from Missouri. She looked out at the dome of the State House, like a huge egg in an eggcup. Hadn't she promised herself, for the sake of security, to keep her two lives separate, her *then* and her *now*?

"Any rate." Walker clapped dust off his hands and turned away. The scolding of Deenie's birds was like a dozen tiny hacksaws. "Any rate, life with Christy was never dull. Why, if she saw a heavyset guy on the street, she'd go right up to him and smile and say, 'Aren't we *fat*?'" He chuckled bleakly.

Poor man. Was he uxorious, or just compelled to put a cheerful face on things? Nan watched while he quieted Deenie's birds, stopping at each cage in turn. No pity, she reminded herself; pity is dangerous. This man was concealing something—that had been clear from their very first meeting—no matter how many fond marital stories he told. In fact, the very smoothness of his stories, the ease with which they unreeled, was something her Foreign Service years had taught her to recognize as a sign of concealment.

Walker offered wine, which Nan refused in favor of green tea. He went into the kitchen—Deenie's kitchen—and Nan sat down on the sofa. She could see him puttering comfortably among her dead friend's crockery. The long leather strip of sleigh bells, Deenie's great-grandfather's, hung beside the refrigerator just as they had in Deenie's kitchen in Chicago. Walker paused to give them a playful tug. Deenie used to jingle them when either of them said anything she thought was bullshit.

"Smoke if you like," he said, coming back from the kitchen with a gently steaming mug in the shape of a flamingo, its long, inquiring pink neck the handle, which he placed on the low table in front of the sofa. Deenie's favorite mug. Walker settled beside her with a bottle of ale. Eyes on the bright, implausible pink of the flamingo's plumage, blinking back unexpected tears, Nan found she didn't want a cigarette after all.

"So, listen." Walker pulled a sheaf of papers off the coffee table and began flipping through them. "You said you'd help. Most of these people I've already found, or the lawyers have. Or they found the lawyers, more like. People can be pretty quick about wills. But there are two left, nobody seems to know who they are. Peter Yerkes. Annette Boyce Mulholland. You know either of them?"

Nan felt the blood leave her face at the sound of her name, unheard for weeks. There was a pounding in her temples. MulHOLland. MulHOLland. One TWO three.

"No," she said faintly. She picked up her mug to take a sip of tea, but her hand shook so badly that she had to put it down again. She stroked the flamingo's bowed head with her thumb. She felt Walker looking at her, composed her face, and turned to him.

"I'm sorry. Those names aren't familiar at all."

"Your husband never mentioned them? Either of them?"

"Not that I remember." Nan fought the urge to get up and walk past her host into the kitchen and pull on the worn leather strap, hard, until the bright sound of sleigh bells filled the apartment. She gave him a smile—Dazzler No. 5, Deenie used to call it. "I wish I could help."

Do I dare ask what Deenie left this Annette Boyce Mulholland?

She looked over Walker's arm, but without her glasses the long, curling sheets might as well have been Sanskrit.

"Can I use your bathroom?" Would *you* use it, so I can get a look at that will?

"Sure. It's the second door on your right."

Good thing he said that. She'd have betrayed her knowledge of the apartment by going straight to it.

The little bathroom smelled bracingly of toothpaste and shoe polish. Sitting on the toilet where Val had treated her injured knee all those weeks ago, she wondered, Did he tell Walker about finding me here? If so, why hadn't Walker mentioned it? Was he suspicious of Nan?

A penciled yellow Post-it note on the medicine cabinet said, "It's not the heat—it's the stupidity." She opened the door and checked its contents. Halcyon with Deenie's name on the prescription label; for Walker, blood pressure medication (the same as Tod's) and, aha!, Viagra. She closed the door and fluffed her hair in the mirror, trying in vain to make the spaniel ears lift back from her cheeks. Did Walker believe her story? That was the question. Because her story was becoming more and more complicated.

Always tell the truth, Dorothea used to say. It's so much easier to keep your story straight.

With Tod Nan had always tried not to lie outright—just refrain from specifying. Of course, she'd had Tod's willing collusion. He'd wanted so deeply not to know about the lovers.

On her way back to the living room she passed the bedroom door. She eased it open a crack and peered in. No metal box on top of the wardrobe—or anywhere in sight.

"Thing is," Walker said, when she returned to the living room, "do you like movies?"

"Yes."

"What kind? I mean, do you mind if they have subtitles?"

Mind? Oh, of course—Christy. Nan imagined homey scotch-plaid aprons with oven mitts to match. "No," she said. "I like them."

There was, it transpired, such a film at the Avon Cinema on Thayer Street, on Saturday. Would she (this came out in an endearing rush) do him the honor?

Yes, she said, provided Val and Mel could babysit. Walker looked so pleased that, over a second cup of tea—having waited a few minutes to blur any feeling of quid pro quo—she nerved herself to ask, almost casually, "What did Cousin Geraldine die of?"

Walker set down his bottle carefully on the coffee table, then sat looking at it. BLIND FAITH ALE, said the label in letters arching over the head of a blue moose.

"AIDS," he said finally. "She died of AIDS."

"AIDS?"

"I know. People our age."

"But— Why didn't she—" She stopped. From Walker's point of view there would have been no reason for Deenie to tell Nan.

"She never told me," Walker said heavily. He stared out through the filmy windows at the darkening winter sky. "That must've been why she moved to Providence—nobody knew her. She made me promise not to tell a soul she was here. Wouldn't say why. I didn't know she was sick until after she was dead. When they told me, I just lay up there in Augusta, in the hospital—it was right after my hernia—feeling like shit because she didn't trust me enough to tell me."

"Oh," Nan said, and in comforting Walker comforted herself, "oh, no! It wouldn't've been that. Probably it was to, to *save* you. She felt— might've felt, *must've* felt—why make people you love suffer along with you?"

Walker looked skeptical.

"Besides, if you didn't know, that made it easier for *her* to forget about it. When she was with you, or talking to you. So, you see, you *did* help her. By not knowing."

Oh, Mother! (Alex's voice) *I swear you can rationalize anything.* But Walker brightened. Watching him turn toward her, a plant seeking sun, she understood that this was something he'd needed, probably for a long time. Conversations with a Soft Woman, as Darwin put it in his journal, totting up the reasons to marry. Before this could make her warm to him, Nan rose, brushing imaginary lint from her gray wool pants. Outside the tall windows, evening had set in. The pale lights of houses and cars pricked holes in the deepening darkness.

"I have to go. Mel'll have picked up Jane by now." Then, because she wanted to come back, look for the metal box, find out about her legacy, she added, "I'll think about it. Those people you mentioned. Maybe something will occur to me."

"Great! Now you're cookin' with gas!"

As he helped her on with her coat, deftly steering the sleeves over her arms, a smell came to her, familiar but elusive, suddenly strong in the close air of the foyer. It wasn't until she was out on the street in the cold blue dusk—she insisted on walking to the bus stop by herself, and Walker reluctantly gave in—that she recognized it. The mingled smell of mildew and mothballs. A musty, *old man* smell.

|

On February 7 there was another message from Alex.

POOKIE: In temporary possession of our treasure. See you soon. HIPPIE

Temporary possession—that must mean custody? *Possessory rights,* which meant that Alex could send Jane wherever she wanted, which meant Gabe wouldn't be able to bring a charge of kidnapping against Nan? The most he could do would be to petition the court for visitation.

Relief flooded through her. She had to lean back in her chair and put her hands on the edge of the table for balance. This was the first unambiguously positive message. Yet Nan found, to her surprise, that she did not feel unambiguously glad. Seeing Alex soon meant handing over Jane, meant the end of this strange, scary, cobbled-together life in Providence. A good thing, surely? Then why this odd tickle of loss? She lifted her eyes from the glowing screen and looked around at the diligently scrolling students, as if their hunched forms might provide an answer. Outside, against the long windows, snow swirled upward, fine and dry as smoke.

|

"Some blunt?" Mel passed the end of the joint to Nan, who thought, Oh, why not? She took a deep toke, held it prickling in her chest, then slowly let it go.

"It's great, huh?" Mel giggled. "Really dope dope."

Nan passed the pinched remains to Val, who burned his fingers as he inhaled. "*Chort!*" The word came out in a ragged puff of smoke. Mel began to roll a fresh joint, bent lovingly over her task. Her neon-green forelock fell across her face and she kept stopping to brush it back.

All three sat shoeless and cross-legged on the floor of Val and Mel's loft. Behind the painted screen at the far end of the room, Jane slept in Val and Mel's bed. Around them were strewn the remains of their dinner, takeout from the Thai restaurant on Federal Hill. They were celebrating Mel's good luck—a gig as tattoo consultant for a documentary on South County bikers—with stuff much more potent than the last Nan could remember having—when was it?—oh, nearly three years ago, with the Last Lover. A celebration for Mel; for Nan, an escape.

Val passed the lemongrass chicken one more time, then the pad thai, urging, "Treat yourself!"

Nan shook her head, which felt deliciously light. The floor, which had seemed so unyielding when they all sat down—she'd disdained the cushion offered by Mel—began to soften. The light from the rosy-shaded lamp grew pinker and more tender.

Val cut open the pomegranates Nan had brought for dessert. (What they were doing in the Food Basket, she couldn't imagine; she'd felt, that afternoon, as if she were rescuing them.) Their bright many-chambered hearts always made her think of desire; they were what desire would be if it were—what was the word? The fresh joint came to her and she took a long, reckless puff. *Incarnate*—that was it. The sumptuous seeded flesh of the pomegranate glowed incarnate on her tongue. Persephone brought pomegranates back from the Underworld. Persephone was the daughter of . . . Nope, can't remember. Alex is *my* daughter. Nan felt herself becoming lighter and lighter; her head felt borrowed. At last she understood everything. She said, "Alex is in the Underworld. The Nannies have stolen her."

Then suddenly someone was shaking her. "Nan. Nan! Wake up!"

Nan opened her eyes. How had she come to be lying down with a blanket over her and a pillow beneath her head? She threw off the blanket, which itched, and sat up.

"You were dreaming," Mel said. "Here. This one's yours." She handed Nan a crisp little yellow pod. Examining it dutifully, she recognized a fortune cookie. She looked around. The joint and the ashtray had disappeared. Someone had opened a window, and a cold stream of air hit her, clearing her head, at least a little.

Mel snapped her pod in two and pulled out a strip of paper. "'Now is the time to try something new.'" She looked appealingly at Val, who was studying the toe of his sock.

"You go," Mel told Nan.

Obediently Nan cracked open her cookie. Without her glasses the tiny purple words might as well have been mouse tracks. Mel took it from her and read, "'Imagination is more important than knowledge.'"

Val spread his fortune out on his knee. "'You are never selfish with your advice.' This, I believe to belong with Melochka." He handed it to her, laughing.

Mel flung herself backward so that her head hit the floor with a thump that made Nan wince. She lay on her back with her legs still crossed and closed her eyes. "Blunted. Blurred. Baked," she crooned.

Nan remembered what she'd been meaning to ask Val, and did. Had he told Walker he'd found Nan in Deenie's apartment?

No. It had not seemed need to say.

"I'd rather he didn't know," Nan said.

Val nodded, unsurprised. "The world is narrow," he said, in a quoting voice. Another Russian proverb?

Mel said, opening her eyes, "So how about it, Nan? Next week, when I get back from South County, we do you over."

"Oh, I don't think . . ."

The dark eyes, shiny as coal, studied her. "You a wuss, or what? I dare you!"

Dare you! Deenie used to say. The frog in Sister Emmanuel's desk drawer; their first cigarettes, out in back of the gym; going to the upper school mixer at Christian Brothers without any underwear. Nan, always trying to measure up to older, faster, smarter Deenie, could never resist. *Now is the time to try something new.*

"Deenie died of AIDS," Nan said. Her tone, under the emboldening influence of marijuana, was unintentionally accusing.

Mel, not meeting Nan's eyes, said, "We promised Mrs. Horsfal we wouldn't tell."

She looked so unhappy that Nan couldn't bring herself to pursue the subject. What did it matter now? Deenie was dead. Val and Mel had honored her wishes; she, Nan, would do the same.

"I've got to go," she said. "See you tomorrow?"

Val went and gathered up the sleeping Jane, to carry her downstairs. When Nan turned to say good night, she surprised Mel in the doorway, looking after Jane with that hungry half-wistful expression on her face.

|

How did you get it, Deen? For love? For sex? Or could it have been drugs? Was it (could it, could anything be) worth it? Or did its value lie in this: that it flung you up against the last dare, the one nobody is allowed to refuse?

Why didn't you tell me?

|

Despite the cold, which deepened all through February, Nan found herself walking the city with Deenie's cousin. It softened the isolation of life alone with a young child. She dropped Jane off at Mikki's every morning at ten. The minute they entered, Jane would sit down happily on the floor and struggle with her red rubber boots, the light from Mikki's rice-paper globe gilding her bent head. "*Gospodi!*" she'd mutter to herself, one of Val's lesser oaths ("Oh, Lord," according to Mel, was the equivalent). Finally she'd let Nan come and kneel beside her and tug on the bottom of each boot until it released the foot inside. When they were done, Jane would pull off her anklets as well—"Because bears don't wear socks," she said once, incomprehensibly—and run into the playroom to join the other children. Letting herself out through Mikki's front door, Nan could hear her laughing, that husky laugh deeper and longer than the laughter of the others. (*Barefoot . . . bear foot,* Nan realized, making her way down the stairs; and then, Why doesn't she ever laugh like that with me anymore?

Sometimes they walked in the late morning, after Nan's stint at the Rock, fortified with sandwiches made by Walker, or chocolate and oranges. Walker was a tireless and, she had to admit, interesting companion. What he liked was to read, then put his newly acquired information to use—a true autodidact. So they walked along Benefit Street from one end to the other, with Walker pointing out the first Baptist church ever built in America, the Jeremiah Tillinghast house, the Caleb Ormsbee house, the Providence Athenaeum (where Edgar Allan Poe fell in love). They walked all over the East Side, while Walker lectured on Providence as a haven for maverick architects through the centuries and pointed out dadoes, mansard roofs, a corbeled arch. They saw the spot on Summit Avenue where Lafayette's men camped during the Revolutionary War, the spot along the river where Roger Williams first stepped ashore, the spot on Prospect Terrace where he was buried. Not unexpectedly, Walker knew many facts—such as that the balding marble dome of the State House was the seventh-largest unsupported dome in the world—that Nan could happily have lived in ignorance of. Their walks often ended along the canal-like ribbon of the Providence River. Walker liked watching the progress of the construction and savored the absurdity of paving and then unpaving a river. He speculated about where the money had come from for so frivolous an undertaking. Did the Mafia (Providence, he informed Nan, was their farm team) require it, for some nefarious reason of their own? Nan told him what her cabbie had said, the night she arrived in Providence: the Venice of the Northeast. Maybe that was it, Walker mused. Nostalgia for the Old Country.

Sometimes they walked in the afternoon, picking up Jane at Mikki's and striding down Hope Street in the swiftly falling dusk. Jane, who liked Walker almost as much as she liked Val (like the little girls in the case histories Nan unearthed at the Rock, she preferred men, was almost vampy around them), would trot along uncomplainingly for a mile or more, then ask to be hoisted to his shoulders. She rode with her head at a queenly slant, tossing her mane of hair and chanting words that Val had taught her. *Sobachka! Byelka!* Walker brought along some poster paints, and on the slope above the university playing field they made snow paintings, pouring out the shiny red and yellow and blue, watching the three streams course across the smooth snow, merging and changing, producing now orange, now green, now purple. Another time they rented skates and Val drove them to Barrington Beach and they skated, all four of them, on the ice-coated sand.

Gradually it became clear to Nan that she felt better than she had in years. Without admitting to herself that Walker's disapproval had anything to do with it, she cut down to two cigarettes a day. Her lungs no longer protested the stairs to the third-floor loft. A good thing, because of course she and Jane had fallen into the great slough of the uninsured. No Medicare for the fictitious Nan Tice; no way to use Jane's Blue Cross without becoming traceable.

The thought of a romantic, or even an erotic, agenda behind their walks occurred to her. She couldn't afford it, she told herself; she wasn't interested. If Walker was, that would have to be his own private joy and sorrow. Alex would have accused Nan of using him. If so, he was clearly happy to be used.

|

February 21. No message from Alex.

Beyond the cool blue glow of the computer screen everything seemed to flicker and grow dim: the high overhead lights, the morning sun slanting through the long windows, the students quietly clicking away. Fear made Nan's fingers tremble on the keys as she scrolled fruitlessly back and forth. What on earth was happening back home? She searched through the rest of the paper for some clue, something that might explain Alex's silence. BARRINGTON GIRL MISSING; or something worse. WIFE OF PROMINENT SURGEON DISAPPEARS. Oh, stop! Nan thought. Stop! She must have spoken out loud, because Ben Kingsley hastened around the Information Desk and started toward her, looking alarmed. She grabbed her parka off the back of her chair and ran.

That afternoon, on their usual walk, Jane lost her spacer—the tiny false tooth, attached to a pink plastic palate hooking onto the teeth on either side, that replaced a front tooth dislodged in a fall the summer before. The three of them retraced their steps, scanning the icy sidewalk and the graying snow along its edges. Nan could see Jane's tongue exploring the delightful new emptiness behind her upper lip. "*Nyet,*" she murmured to herself. "Not yet." White on white: it was hopeless.

When they'd gone all the way back to the river, Nan sat down on one of the benches placed to give a view of the construction. Jane came and stood with her hand on Nan's knee, rubbing her forehead with two fingers, Alex's gesture. "Are you *so* tired, Nana?" Those green, green eyes fixed on Nan's, sure of a welcome. But Nan, hating her own meanness, said, "Why couldn't you be more careful?" and turned away.

A backhoe idled on the esplanade below them, its bumper sticker in the cloudy winter light seeming to say BABIES KILLS until Nan made out, in smaller letters underneath, VACCINATE YOUR PET. How were they to get a replacement? Apart from the money, questions would be asked: how did so young a child come to lose a tooth? For all Nan knew, any dentist they saw would be obliged to report them to child welfare.

Walker sat down beside her and put one arm around her slumped shoulders. He said, "She didn't *mean* to lose it."

Nan pulled away. What did *he* know about it? It wasn't his place to intervene.

But she was ashamed of taking out her anxiety on Jane. No message this morning: what did it mean? Good: having gotten temporary custody, Alex was busy making arrangements to retrieve Jane—so busy she couldn't find time to send a message. Bad: the custody decision had provoked Gabriel, made him angry and, maybe, reckless. What might he do, in that case?

Nan shivered. If only she could talk to someone—Walker, for instance—about all this. Dorothea used to say, *A joy shared is a joy doubled; a sorrow shared is a sorrow halved.*

As if to underscore Nan's aloneness, Walker turned away to comfort Jane. "Hey," he said, "you know what they say. You can pick your friends, but you can't pick your nose."

Jane laughed. Pointedly detouring around Nan, she sat down next to Walker. The three of them sat there on the bench in the chill of approaching dusk and watched the construction workers. Walker and Jane were both infatuated with the machines that loomed like prehistoric creatures. One had a huge claw for picking things up: a long-necked brachiosaurus; another was squat with a sort of shovel-horn: a triceratops. (Jane knew her dinosaurs.) Above the sound of the machines came the mewing of seagulls, the only thing in Providence that reminded Nan of Seattle. It was strange to see them against the backdrop of city buildings, with no ocean in sight.

As if reading her thoughts, Walker said, "They're out of place, but they don't know it. That's the thing."

Nan watched them blurring the air—hundreds of them, their testy cries blending with the noise of the machines—above the bare black trees. Their bodies were the same gray-white as the capitol dome against the smoke-colored sky. For an instant Nan had the vertiginous illusion of a world without color. She looked down quickly at Jane's scarlet parka.

"There are seagulls over the Great Lakes now," Walker said.

"I'm not givin' you CPR, buddy!" the dump-truck driver shouted to a welder standing too near the edge of the river. "Don't even think about me givin' you mouth-to-mouth!"

Odd: usually there was so much noise here, along the river, that such an exchange would have been inaudible. Why had the machines stopped?

Walker was complaining to Jane about his next-door neighbors, a couple from Michigan named Tulk. *He* insisted on referring to himself as a Michigander, which made *her*, Walker maintained, a Michigoose (giggles from Jane). *He* owned every power tool known to man, which even in the dead of winter *she* found some use for. "Seven thirty on a Sunday morning, they're out there currying the sidewalk. A person can't hear the birds!" Above the upturned collar of his pea jacket his wattle quivered with indignation.

Nan said, "Look! Something's happening."

There were now several workmen (or workwomen—it was hard to tell) standing on the ledge above the river. They were looking down into the water, studiously, not far from the spot where Nan had thrown in her cell phone. A blue rubber raft appeared, and three divers in wet suits slipped over the side into the water. Floodlights on either side of the narrow river snapped on. Nan fished her glasses out of her purse. The workers were joined by two meter maids who stood checking their watches. A small crowd began to collect around the bench where Walker and Nan and Jane sat. On the half-finished pedestrian bridge a little downstream a crane appeared. Someone inside flung down chains that hit the water with loud spanking sounds. The divers seized them and disappeared. Jane reached across Walker and grabbed Nan's arm. She *does* need me! flashed through Nan as she put her gloved hand over Jane's mittened one. A second boat appeared, a sort of wooden dory, filled with bright orange life preservers. One of the workmen, his yellow hard hat shining in the floodlit dusk, walked out along a rusting iron girder that served as a plank to the other side of the river; he was angrily waved back by the two policemen on the dory. There was a pause, while the crowd pressing, now, around Nan murmured and coughed and stamped booted feet on the snow-crusted ground. The aromatic fragrance of a cigar somewhere behind her made Nan think of Gabriel. She turned, heart pounding, to scan the crowd. He wasn't there. Of course he wasn't. As so often when she thought of him, the memory returned to her of Gabe on the night he'd told her about his mother's death, Gabe shuddering with silent tears. Sad Gabriel. Moving, pitiable Gabriel. Could Alex hold out against *that*?

Walker nudged her. "Look! They've found something."

Divers' black-sheathed heads, like vipers, broke the surface of the water one by one. The last one up made a sign with his arm, and the crane reared back. The heavy chains began to rise. The crowd fell silent. Nan could hear, above the steady grinding of the crane, water falling from the chains like garbled bells. The air seemed suddenly colder, and she shivered. At the bottom of the chains an automobile appeared, upside down, covered with black-green slime. In the light of the floodlights it looked like a car made of moss. Water poured off it as it was lifted clear.

Walker was on his feet, hoisting Jane to his shoulders, holding both her hands in one of his while he held out the other to Nan. Half a dozen policemen were suddenly among the crowd, herding people up the snowy slope away from the water. Nan and Walker—with Jane protesting loudly, "What is it? I wanna see!"—turned to follow, their boots punching through the crust of snow.

The ten o'clock news had some footage of the event, though Nan didn't remember seeing any TV cameras. Jane, who should have been in bed, watched avidly for a glimpse of herself while a newscaster's voice explained. The car had apparently gone into the river a year ago and had immediately been covered by the concrete poured for a temporary footbridge. Removal of the concrete, which had been going on all week, had revealed the presence of "something unexpected" in the water below. And inside the car? As Nan got up to turn it off, thinking, Jane mustn't see this, her own image appeared on the screen.

Jane yelled, "Nana!"

Nan sat down again. She waited for the room to come to a stop. The camera lingered—not, she realized, interested in her but in the mayor, who stood behind her, bright-eyed beneath his toupee, looking like the cheerful gangster he was. He removed the cigar from his mouth and smiled.

"Where'm I?" Jane cried. "They didn't show *me*!"

After several seconds Nan's face gave way to footage of the car, right side up, the doors being pried open. Quickly she put her palm on Jane's nape and pressed Jane's face against her breasts. With her free hand she jabbed at the remote, but not before she'd seen, inside the dripping, algae-covered car, the shadow of something human.

|

"You're cherry!" Mel said. "I love that."

"What?"

They were in the studio Mel shared with Val, Nan on a comfortably padded examining table, Mel on a wheeled stool. "You know—a tattoo virgin. I get a lot of them 'cause I'm gentle. I have a reputation for that. Okay, what are we gonna do, and where are we gonna do it?"

"I don't know." Why in the world had she agreed to this? "How about a heart with 'Mother' inside it?"

"Sarcasm is the lowest form of irony, did you know that? Here. Look through this while I get things ready."

Today's tattoo was the last step in Mel's makeover of Nan, providing her with the new look that Channel 10 News had now made a necessity. Nan began leafing dutifully through *Tattoo International*. It was mostly color photographs of men and women, not all of them young, many of them nude. Tattoos occupied much larger portions of their bodies than Nan would have imagined: the length of an arm or a thigh; whole backs; two or three men in what at first looked like long-sleeved paisley bodysuits. Many of these people had pierced noses and/or eyebrows as well. Feeling queasy, Nan turned the pages faster. Archangels, demons, Indian chiefs; the head of Rasputin; nipples turned into flowers or stars. Mel assured her that whatever she liked could be duplicated on her, Nan's, body. It was like sitting in a yarn shop paging through knitting pattern books, except for the feeling of seasickness.

Mel slid the magazine gently out of Nan's hands. "Some people, when they get the urge to hurt themselves—you know, like those teenage girls who cut their arms and legs with razor blades?—they get a tattoo instead." Nan knew without being told that she was talking about herself, and felt a quick stitch of pity. "How about a small fleur-de-lis? Tasteful."

"A scorpion?" Nan suggested. "That's my sign."

"Zodiac signs're cheesy. Let's see . . . Maybe one of these tribal things from New Zealand? Maori? No? Look at these Chinese characters. I've been wanting to try one of these for, like, forever."

The characters were graceful and mysterious. Nan nodded.

"Long life? Or happiness?" Mel asked.

Oh, happiness, definitely. What good would the other be without it?

Mel's question reminded Nan of a joke, which she told while Mel xeroxed the symbol onto transfer paper, applied it to Nan's shoulder and peeled it away, tore open packets of needles ("See? Sterile!") and began fitting them into a pen-shaped metal holder. A joke from Bucharest days. Haso says to Mujo: Which would you rather be—beautiful, or stupid? Mujo (after thinking deeply): Stupid. Because beauty doesn't last.

"Just lie back, now. I think the shoulder. In front, right here. Okay? Lie back." Mel pushed down with her foot. A noise like a dentist's drill filled the space between them. Mel lifted her foot, and the noise stopped. "Perfect!"

I'm going through with this, Deenie. *Dare you!*

Nan lay on her back. At the far end of her body loomed her new shoes, bulbous, black, and ugly. ("Plats or kickers?" Mel had wondered aloud to the incurious saleswoman. "Better be kickers. Platforms'll be too hard to walk in. Too bad you can't get steel toes anymore—they've been declared concealed weapons.") Mel pulled on a smoky plastic visor, then began stroking surgical gloves over her hands. This end of the loft, Mel's end, was dominated by a large poster advertising the San Francisco Tattoo Museum ("Ancient as Time, Modern as Tomorrow"); next to it hung a laminated blowup of Mel's business card, with "INKSLINGER . . . Ink-credible!" in spiny Gothic letters. There were framed certificates from the Rhode Island Department of Health and a wooden plaque that said, "Cheap Tattooing Is Not Good; Good Tattooing Is Not Cheap."

Mel scooted around on her stool, its wheels squeaking on the wood floor, snapped on a blinding overhead light and moved it closer to Nan. Nan closed her eyes. She felt Mel unbutton her shirt and ease it past her right shoulder. There was more scooting, then the smell of deodorant soap, a coolness spreading across her shoulder.

"I'm gonna outline, then do a little whipshading," Mel said.

The pain was hot, sour, constant—a dull razor blade being drawn over and over across her skin. Nan did her Lamaze breathing, as she would have at the dentist or the gynecologist, and tried to put her mind on other things. Yesterday Mel had done her hair. It was now a bright teal blue ("Really dope with your fair skin!") and cut in a sort of long crew cut, close to her head at the back and sides and standing up longer in front like a cockatiel's feathers. A little dated, had been Mel's opinion when she'd finished; but better, she thought, to go with an established look. ("'Be not the first by which the new is tried, / Nor yet the last to lay the old aside,'" Nan quoted. "Huh?" Mel said.) It had been a shock to look in the mirror this morning: she certainly was not herself. Not the all-too-recognizable Nan Mulholland who'd appeared on Channel 10 News. *God has given you one face,* Attila the Nun used to say, *and you make yourselves another.* Yes: exactly. Suppose the pulling of a car—an unhappily occupied one—out of the Providence River made the national news. The mayor *was* a convicted felon, after all; and besides that there was the Mafia presence in Providence. Nan had been watching TV and checking the papers, especially the *New York Times* (Gabriel's favorite newspaper) in the three days since she'd appeared on Channel 10. Meanwhile she'd found a book at the Rock, *Methods of Disguise,* and absorbed its principles. Hairstyle (check!) and Color (check!); Weight Loss (check!); Mustache, Beard, and Assorted Facial Fuzz (n/a); Eyeglasses (never!). These were listed among "Natural Means of Disguise." "Artificial Means"—Aging Lines (absolutely not!), Cheek Inserts, Nose Putty, Scars, Prostheses (ugh!), Voice-Altering Devices—she'd begun a careful list of, for later. But there was so much to write down that, in the end, she'd stolen the book. Afraid to risk using Victoria Uglow's card—she now had absolutely no resemblance to the photo on it—she'd peeled the bar code sticker off the book and hidden it under her parka. Fittingly, its back cover boasted, "As Seen on *America's Most Wanted*!!!"

Every now and then came a blessed pause while Mel dipped her needles in ink or sprayed Nan's shoulder with cool water and gently wiped it off. "There's a little blood. Don't look." The drill emitted a hot-metal smell, like a car engine that had been running too long. Nan had imagined Mel would confide in her while she worked, confidences that might pave the way to pumping Mel about Jane. Instead, Nan learned that Janis Joplin had had tattoos; that Bert Grimm was the greatest tattoo artist who'd ever lived; that tattooing was the first preventive medicine: tattooed warriors survived wounds better because of their revved-up immune systems. Surfing the pain, Nan let her thoughts wander.

Yesterday afternoon Mel had taken her shopping, because of course the new hair had looked wildly wrong with what Nan thought of as her Nanniewear, all those tan and gray and brown garments. "Geriatric!" Mel dismissed them. At the Gap they bought a bright-yellow parka and black velvet leggings and two long sweaters—one white, one fuchsia— that looked baggy until you put them on. In the dressing room, happily surprised by her own reflection, Nan remembered excursions to Strawbridge and Clothier's with Deenie, in high school, trying on things they couldn't possibly buy. They'd been in love with their own arms and legs, with their whole bodies, striking poses in the mirror while a saleslady with large white teeth smiled grimly.

"So Monday this old guy comes in, I mean really old, sixty at least, he wants a heart with a banner that says 'Vinny.' I couldn't get him to see how lame that'd be. Geriatric dipshit! *And* he had a bad case of plumber's butt." Mel stopped to dip her needles in ink, and the haze of pain lifted.

"How much longer?"

"Maybe twenty minutes. Okay, you ready?"

At Strawbridge's, in their junior year, Deenie had shoplifted two garter belts. Satin, one for each of them, along with two pairs of the sheerest nylon stockings, still a luxury then, in 1955. No one they knew even had any. Ugly flesh-colored lisle stockings, held up by girdles, were required with their school uniforms. Oh, the delicious strappy lightness under her skirt, continuously admitting the reality of her crotch! Her thighs, when she crossed her legs, silkily greeting each other. Could people tell? Freedom—but something more. Something both light and dark. The beginning of things.

Outside the heavy glass doors of the Gap, Nan had stood still and laughed, feeling free and light: legginged legs, fuchsia sweater, puffy yellow parka. Mel had gazed at her, squinting against the late-afternoon sun. "You look totally bad-ass! Nobody'd know you."

Exactly.

Mel stopped the drill. Nan, as the sudden absence of pain made her light-headed, thought, This is my chance.

"Mel. Has Jane ever mentioned her parents to you?"

The drill paused in midair. "She told me her mom was home crying.

And once she said her dad was on a trip to Watermelon—I think she meant Guatemala?—and that he's coming to get her soon." Mel brushed the damp curls off her forehead with one muscular forearm. "He isn't, is he? You and Janey're gonna stay here in Providence, right?"

"How did she sound? Did she say anything else?"

"The next time she came over, she clammed up. Stonewalled me, totally. But why are you—"

"So here you are, talking into blue streaks," Val said. He came in and stood leaning against the Tattoo Museum poster, a bulky black Leica hanging from one shoulder. He'd recently stopped painting in favor of photography—what Mel called "drive-by shootings," pictures snapped holding the camera out the window with one hand while he drove. "How it goes? Okay, yes?"

When Nan turned toward him, dislodging her shirt, which Mel had unbuttoned and pulled down from her shoulders, he turned away. Gentlemanly. But Nan thought wistfully of the old days, when a man would have moved to where he could see more.

Mel re-draped Nan's shirt. "Take a look."

Val stepped closer to inspect the tattoo, which Nan didn't yet dare to look at. He smelled of cold winter air and gasoline.

"*Prekrasno!*" he said; then, looking at Nan's averted face, "Console! Console! Soon it ends and you are beautiful." He patted her clenched hand.

Mel, her penful of needles poised like a conductor's baton, waited.

"I am destructing you? Okay, I go. Good-bye, my loveds!" He vanished around the corner of the screen.

Mel swabbed Nan's shoulder gently, then started up the drill. "Last time."

Breathe. Count. Breathe.

When Nan opened her eyes, Mel's face was inches from hers, tongue protruding between closed lips as she inspected her work. The tiny gold stud winked in the light. At last she drew back.

"Yes!" she said, laying down her pen, and grabbed Nan's limp, unresisting hand to give her a high five.

Seven

It must have been while she was at the gym that the burglary happened.

Mel had guided Nan through the noisy, neon-lit spaces of East Providence Fitness Plus, having provided her with a pair of black leggings and a T-shirt that said, MY OTHER CAR IS A BROOM. She took Nan through various machines garnished with black leather that looked as if they belonged in an S&M parlor, tersely stating the purpose ("Tits!" "Buns!" "Abs!") of each. They spent half an hour on adjoining treadmills, Nan trudging along considerably more slowly than Mel. The music that issued from speakers all over the huge, many-mirrored room made conversation impossible, which suited Nan fine. In the locker room Mel had teased her about getting the bod in shape for Walker ("He's buff— no Buddha-belly!"), making it plain she thought Nan was being less than honest with herself. The treadmill on Nan's other side held a large biscuit-colored man in swimming goggles who ran faster and faster. The goggles gave him a sinister, basilisk look. She wondered: Was he planning to sweat that much? If so, his sweat would certainly land on her. Could you get AIDS from sweat? Don't be an idiot.

In the sauna Nan and Mel, wrapped in soft white towels, reclined on the wooden benches. Clouds of steam swooned around them, scented with the prosy smells of cedar and cement and their own sweat. Mel's towel was knotted below small breasts with surprisingly dark nipples; black curly hair grew under her arms. Nan kept her own towel high, just under her collarbone. Her tattoo stung a little from the heat. She began to feel a delicious ease. Val had volunteered to pick up Jane from Mikki's;

the whole afternoon was hers. Mel closed her eyes, and Nan did too. Above them two women gossiped lazily.

"You know, like in the movie *Alien,* like at the end? All those people with big eyes? She went to a Catholic priest to get herself exorcised."

"She should've gone to the gym."

"She told me some people's spirits turn into mailboxes or, or ketchup bottles."

The warmth, the sinuous half-concealing steam, the languor of a body well used, made Nan feel happy, not in her mind (or heart, or wherever it is that happiness usually flares) so much as in her cells. Like, now that she came to think of it, sex. Good thing Mel couldn't read her thoughts—she'd have been in for a merciless ribbing of the kind that Deenie used to provide. Something that, like the friendship it grew out of, had been missing from Nan's West Coast life. She and Mel, she realized dreamily, were friends. Girlfriends. She could feel the blood hum through her body, radiating pleasure, until her skin tightened all over like a perfectly inflated balloon.

One of the women on the bench above swung down a leg dotted with wiry black hairs. "The what?" she said to her friend. "The wedlock law?"

"The gridlock law. Gridlock, not wedlock."

|

The feeling held, a sort of vibrant undertow, through the cold walk from the bus stop down Weybosset to Elbow Street. There was pleasure in every movement, in the calm contraction and expansion of her lungs, in the quick obedience of her arms and legs. Nan and Mel walked with arms linked, like schoolgirls, to help each other over the corrugated surface of ice and gravel and frozen dog turds. They made fun of passersby. A pompous young man walking a Doberman ("Big dog, small dick," murmured Mel); a fur-coated woman who tried to elbow them off the sidewalk into a pile of old snow. Mel told a joke: "What's the definition of paranoia?" "I don't know. What?" "Putting a condom on your vibrator." It was something Deenie might have said. They were still laughing when Nan pushed open the door to her apartment and stood staring, key in the lock, hand frozen on the key.

"Nan?" Mel, behind her, couldn't see what Nan saw. Her voice rode a last ripple of laughter.

Nan thought: Gabriel. He's found us.

She made herself take a step forward, then another. Plants and trees lay on their sides, pots shattered, dirt all over the floor. A shard from one of the pots rattled and broke as Nan stepped on it. The yellow chains that had held the TV hung empty. Mr. Nibbrig's footlocker, its lid wrenched off, spewed papers and manila folders. She felt Mel grab her arm.

"Don't!" she whispered in Nan's ear. She yanked her backward into the hall. "They might still be in there."

They moved toward the stairs, still backing up. Nan's arm ached from Mel's grip. Below them the outer door slammed. Jane's voice echoed in the stairwell, to the sound of her hands clapping.

They flew so high, high, high
That they touched the sky, sky, sky
And they never came back, back, back—

"Val!" Mel shouted. Her voice bounced off the cinder-block walls. "Val! Get up here, quick!"

The beat of boots on the stairs, like gunfire; Jane's voice, plaintive. "Hey! Wait for me!"

Val appeared. "The mollies is terrible today! Everywhere is tickets—" At the sight of their faces, he stopped.

Mel put a hand on his arm. "Nan's place. Somebody broke in."

Val pushed past them. They followed his long strides down the hall. Over Mel's protests, he pushed the apartment door wide. "*K chortu!*" he muttered.

Mel wanted to wait for the police. Nan burst out, before she could stop herself, "No! No police!" Val did not seem to find this strange. He pulled his arm from Mel's grip and went inside. Nan and Mel watched from the doorway while he looked behind Jane's screen and then disappeared, checking the little bathroom.

Jane, panting, crashed into Mel. "What *happened?*" she cried in an aggrieved voice. "Hey—where's the TV?"

Before Nan could stop her, she ducked under Mel's arm and ran into the apartment. "Zipper!" she shouted. "Zipper-Kitty! Here, kitty, kitty."

Mel ran in after her. Nan followed.

Inside, Jane darted around, long horsetail hair flying, behind her screen, into the kitchen area, into the bathroom (colliding with Val, coming out), shouting, "Zipper-Kitty! Here, kitty! It's *oh-kay.*"

Val held out his hands, palms up, to signify that whoever had been there was gone. Nan stepped into the room, pot shards crunching underfoot, the smell of spilled earth oddly springlike. The light, without the filtering green of the plants, was hard and white. Geraniums lay scattered, bright as blood, across the floor. This had happened once in Warsaw—a break-in, their belongings rifled, broken, strewn, they never knew by whom. Only personal things, luckily. (*Never, under any circumstances, keep official State Department documents, whether restricted or not, in your place of residence,* HOWDY had warned. But everyone did, of course—even Tod.)

Nan trembled with the same helpless fury she'd felt then, the same sense of having been violated. Stepping over the debris, she picked her way across the room. Her hands shook as she slid out the top drawer of Nibbrig's dresser. She felt underneath the top until she found the envelope, pulled it loose, opened it. The money, half her remaining cash— thank you, God—was inside. Still trembling, she sat down on the bed (sheets yanked off, mattress slit open and spewing gray cotton stuffing)— and there, in a jumble of other underwear, lay her Hidden Assets.

She fingered one of the half-slip's pockets, torn so that it hung down empty. There had been nearly a thousand dollars in it, for the rent (due tomorrow) and Mikki (ditto) and the Russian émigré dentist who'd agreed to make Jane a new spacer. Her money had been dwindling at an alarming rate: there was enough in the envelope to replace the thousand, but not much more. Nan felt the other pockets. Her passport was there, and the vial of nitroglycerin.

An ordinary thief, then. Not someone sent by Gabriel. It was only money he'd been after. Relief poured through her.

Val, coming from the kitchen with a tumbler of water, looked surprised to find her smiling. He held out the glass, and she took it and drank. She noticed the coppery taste of blood, realized she'd bitten the inside of her cheek.

"Is like house of Ukrainians," Val said, gazing around the room. "Or Uzbeki." He saw the torn slip in Nan's hands. "This *vor*—this robber—he is perhaps pervert?"

"Perhaps." Impossible to explain to Val why she sat with her hands full of underwear.

"Americans don't be comprehended. You are fearfree, isn't it?"

Jane came in. She climbed up on the bed and thrust her head into Nan's lap. "I can't find Zipper," she said, and began to cry.

Nan stroked her head helplessly. "He'll turn up," she said, not believing her own inadequate words. "He's just hiding." Jane scrambled away and sat up. She stuck her finger into a slit in the mattress and began pulling out stuffing and flinging it in Nan's direction.

Nan drank the rest of the water, wishing it were bourbon. "I'm as cowardly as the next person," she told Val. "More." Stuffing flew in all directions. "Jane!" she said warningly.

"Then it must to be that you are brave. Console! Brave is opposite of fearfree. Brave is far more to admire."

Mel came in then. "Janey—what're you doing?"

Nan said, "Stop that."

"Bullshit!" Jane shouted. "You're not my mother! I don't *have* any mother!" She got down off the bed and ran out of the room.

Mel bent down and pried the torn half-slip from Nan's clenched fingers. "You look totally weirded out. Should I go get your cigarettes?"

Nan knew Mel wanted to follow Jane, to put her arms around her, reaching into the past to comfort little Mel. She thought tiredly, Jane doesn't want *me*; let her at least have Mel. She said, "Actually, I'd like to be by myself for a while," then surprised herself by adding, "Would you call Walker? His number's on the fridge, 351-something."

Val declared that he himself would carry Walker in his taxi, and followed Mel out of the room.

Alone, Nan sat in the wash of late-afternoon light from the tall windows. A bowl of water stood on the radiator beneath, to send moisture into the dry winter air, the way Dorothea had always done. The water's stale smell, like ashes, made her think of her grandmother's secondhand store. Closing her eyes, Nan saw not Dorothea's face but her body, strong and certain, always in motion. Raising Nan at the cost of her own wellearned late-life freedom, she'd somehow managed to avoid becoming bitter. She had not encouraged Nan to feel resentment and call it virtue, had not taught her self-sacrifice. Courage—yes, she'd taught her that. But not compassion. She hadn't been any better at comforting little girls than Nan was now.

Outside the window a red winter sun was slipping down between snow-quilted roofs where the freeway poured out a thickening stream of lights. Its low, unceasing hum came to Nan through the glass. She heard herself sigh. She'd seen things—oh, she had. A young man bitten by a viper on a trip—one of the excursions discouraged by the State Department—to the ancient cliff towns of the Cinque Terre. He'd died before the makeshift litter in the Jeep's backseat reached Genoa; in the heat, his hazel eyes, which no one thought to close, slowly turned opaque, like yellow soap. (Tod's second posting; Nan's first death. *HOWDY* had offered no helpful tips for watching people die.) On the road to Timisoara, a Rumanian girl no more than eight or nine, carrying a rust-stained bundle of clothing that turned out to be the body of her baby brother. Crossing the border from Poland into East Berlin, the morning after Reagan was elected, East German guards with dogs searching the train, pulling up seat cushions and grinning. How do you like your president now? they laughed. Later Nan had seen them dragging a man and a woman, in jackets too thin for November, along the platform, leg irons clanking in the clear morning air.

Other people's suffering—never my own.

Mel appeared in the doorway. "Walker's on his way," she said. "Jane and Val are looking for Zipper. Mind if I sit with you?"

Nan shook her head.

They sat in a silence broken by Jane's occasional grief-edged cry of "Zipper! Zipper-Kitty!" Mel took Nan's hand and held it, resting it on one blue-jeaned leg. There was a ragged hole in the denim through which her pale knee gleamed.

"You and Janey—you're on the run, huh?" Mel said softly. "You're in trouble?"

Nan felt hot, then cold. Sweat sprang between their two palms.

Mel regarded her in silence. Then she said, "C'mon—chill! I won't say anything. I haven't even told Val. He's probably figured it out, though. He's no bunbrain."

"It's not what you think." What *does* she think?

"Hey! None of my business. Only—if you need anything. You and Janey. Val and I'd be really bummed if you didn't let us know. That'd be *bitter.*"

|

Until she saw Walker's face Nan had forgotten all about her recent transformation. Even then it took her a second to interpret the look that slid, quick as an arpeggio, from shock through amusement to acceptance. Those sure blue eyes. One could lean on this man.

He located Jane's cat in the twilight behind the refrigerator and coaxed it out with (Nan would never have dreamed of this) two raw hot dogs cut into mouse-sized lengths. He'd brought along a toy he'd bought the day before for Jane—a stuffed yellow creature with a pointed head and the stunted limbs of a thalidomide baby, dressed in what looked like a prison uniform. When you squeezed its fingerless yellow hand, it sang:

Bananas in pajamas
Are chasing teddybears,
'Cause on this day their stares
Can catch them unawares

A toy too young for a four-year-old, but neither Walker nor Jane seemed to notice this. Jane, holding fast to a wildly purring Zipper, smiled and smiled. The gap where her front tooth should have been, and her hair, pulled back into two tight looped braids, gave her the comical face of a rag doll. Must be Val's work, Nan thought. She looked like a Russian schoolgirl.

"I shot a mollie," Jane said to Walker. "Val let me shoot."

For a second Nan was taken aback. Jane shot a meter maid? Then: Oh—the *camera*.

Walker said to Nan, "How about a walk? You've got your coat on."

Nan looked at Jane, now happily ensconced on the sofa next to Mel, a headlock each on Zipper and Bananas.

Mel, Val, Walker, Mikki—any of them can offer Jane more than I can, right now.

"Okay," she said; and Walker went to the door and held it open for her, bowing and doffing an imaginary hat.

Rescue; rescue.

On Elbow Street in the chilly dusk, they turned, without needing to consult each other, toward the river. Walker put his hand under Nan's elbow, an old-fashioned gesture he hadn't ventured before. Courtly (he took care to walk between her and the curb) and kind. Staid attributes, which, in a lover (the Last Lover, for instance), she would once have scorned. Despite the fog, thicker as they neared the river, she was glad to be outside. Glad that Walker had suggested it. The feeling of violation she'd had in the apartment—a tightness across her chest, as if the available air had been already breathed and expelled by someone else—began to ease, dispersing into the darkness.

It was so cold—that austere New England cold that wrapped around your bones—that there were few pedestrians. The ones there were hurried along, heads down, unspeaking. Nan and Walker reached the river and turned south along the narrow wooden walkway where the construction began. Once or twice they bumped awkwardly, hip to hip. Walker whistled under his breath, an old Beatles song.

If there's anything that you want
If there's anything I can do

Nan glanced sideways at him. Above the lumpy purple muffler (touchingly hand-knit: Christy?) his profile made her think of a pelican. His wattle, like a pelican's expanding crop; his thin beak of a nose. The pelican, she remembered, was an ancient symbol for nurturing. For tending, as kind and courtly Walker tended Nan.

"Sunset. Twilight. Dusk," he said. "That's the order they come in. Twilight—that means between light and darkness. Dusk is almost dark. But not quite."

"Walker, thank you." Nan pressed his arm. "For everything. Jane felt better the minute you came through the door."

I felt better.

He held out a hand to help her squeeze past the metal barrier with its dented, graffiti-sprayed KEEP OUT sign, and they walked slowly along the arched pedestrian bridge. Its surface was ice-coated rocks, not yet paved, and no railings stood between them and the water. Walker kept a grip on Nan's arm so firm she could feel his fingers through her sleeve. Ice edged the river. Mist rising off it twirled slowly in a chill, damp breeze that smelled of fish. An east wind off the unseen ocean. Nan said as much, and Walker nodded. "Nor'easter's on its way. Might blow out to sea before it gets here, though." A watercolor landscape, wet on wet: bare black trees and the stark shapes of machinery dwindling into the mist, like the Chinese paintings that Tod had, in a small way, collected. The paintings that had supported her since his death—or rather, that had supported Nan Mulholland. This thought threw her into furious calculation: what was left in the bank account (not quite a thousand dollars); what bills were urgent (rent, food, Jane's day care); how long until Alex's next message (today was the first of March, so, six days). Adding and subtracting made her head ache.

As if he'd read her mind, Walker said cheerfully, "A fool and his mother are soon parted. Don't look so glum! It's only money. Thing is, you could've been there when he broke in. You and Jane. Good Christ! Some crazed druggie with a hammer, no telling what he might've done."

Once again Nan had the contradictory sense that Walker was both familiar and hidden. She was at ease with him in a way that continued to surprise her—that mysterious sense of being in tune with someone quite unlike you that the Italians called *sintonia*. More at ease than might be accounted for by his relationship to Deenie. Yet alongside this deep feeling of comfort—interwoven with it, even—was the sense that Walker was concealing something. Where did *that* feeling come from? The way he held himself, the way he looked at her? What was it HOWDY had said? *The most ordinary-appearing person, often offering help of some kind, may present a security risk.* But she didn't feel, about Walker, that he was a danger in some way—not at all. The opposite, in fact.

The hell with it—*K chortu.* Everyone our age has something to hide.

And who was she, after all, to cast the first stone? She pulled the hood of Mel's double-thick Champion sweatshirt closer around her newly bare neck.

Walker said, "How about tomorrow morning, minute the stores open?"

"What?"

"For the dead bolt. And I think you ought to have a Yale lock, as well. The guy must've just slid your door open with a credit card. Any rate, Val agrees with me. Says he has the owner's okay for that kind of thing."

"Oh. If *Val* agrees. Who am I, a mere woman, to say the two of you nay?"

Walker didn't laugh. He stopped dead in the middle of the bridge and turned to Nan. She thought, Why, he's worried about me. *Worried.* It had been a very long time since a man had been that. Tod had been too sick, in those last years, had moved onto another plane entirely; and the Last Lover was never one to let the worry-light shine in his eyes.

Walker put both hands on her shoulders, and she thought he was going to shake her—his face beneath the dark wool cap looked grim—but then it came too near for her to see his expression, and then he kissed her. His lips were cool, then warm. The taste of salt, the oceany mist from the river trapped between their two mouths. His clean smell, like pencil shavings. The faint grittiness of his chin. Surprised, she felt an answering tug, somewhere at the center of her.

When she opened her eyes, the world seemed to have dissolved into fog. The two of them were all that was left, standing on the arch of the empty bridge. She blinked. Streetlamps at the far end of the bridge bled light onto the snow, like windows left uncurtained in the violet dusk. Her mouth buzzed lightly, as if the muzzle of a gun had pressed against it; her underpants (oh, blessed little blue estrogen pills!) clung to her crotch, damp with desire. Somewhere a dog barked with bell-like regularity, and there was the sound of buoys from the unseen ocean.

Walker took the edges of her sweatshirt hood and tugged it gently over her bare head. His fingers smoothed the sprigs of hair at her temples.

"You're cold," he said. "We'll head on back."

|

She wasn't cold. Had never been cold, despite the myth that beautiful women are. Her lovers had often seemed surprised at her eagerness. If they'd believed the myth, why had they pursued her? Though, come to think of it, maybe that *was* why.

Nan stood at the window of Nibbrig's darkened living room watching the fog roll in and thinking of the past.

How engrossing—what a lifework—it had been. Chasing the moment of escape from yourself. Different every time, old yet new, the way each orgasm was different from all others. Impossible to make any man understand this: theirs must be pretty uniform. Different colors, textures, shapes—different music—impossible, anyway, to find words for it. The pleasures of surprise, of not-yet-knowing, of discovery, beckoned at least as strongly as the predictable pleasure of the act itself. Which was never just itself anyway, but was taste and sound and smell and touch. Was the ring of the muezzin beyond the shutters, the fragrance of Siberian lilac floating through an open window, light reflected off snow, cool sheets, warm bodies . . . oh, bodies! The smell and taste and feel of them. Skin, simple skin. Pale, freckled, blue-black, olive; like apples, salt, bread; like silk and linen and coarse curly wool. Sex had always made Nan think of a hymn from her high school days:

O everlasting streams
And oceans of delight

It had taken the proverbial seven years for Nan to discover adultery. She'd married up, as the saying goes. (Up and away, Pop had said, sorrowing.) On yet another scholarship, this one at Douglass College—the state of New Jersey's women's school, a pale imitation of the Seven Sisters—she'd met Tod Mulholland, who was finishing a master's degree in political science at Princeton. Who was tall, shy, angular, awkward—and speedily smitten with Nan. She'd loved his loving her. Had tried, in gratitude, to be a good wife. Tod hadn't understood how the lovely, buffered life of State Department wives (oddly like the life of nuns) could fail to be desirable. Could, in fact, drive a woman bonkers. After several years there was Alex. But The Nannies claimed her, as they claimed the house, the meals, the marketing. Studying the other Foreign Service wives showed Nan a narrow choice of remedies. Alcohol; Valium; cocaine; sex. Like the other drugs, adultery led to more adultery. Resistance became not merely difficult, but unthinkable; remorse, easier to endure than temptation. A quick study but a slow learner, Nan did not see that what served as an escape from her life also kept her from living it. She did not see—not until Tod began dying—the irreversible distance that adultery had imposed between her and Tod. *Not scatterbrained—scatterhearted*, he had called her once, in anger. Yet by ignoring her affairs he'd seemed almost to encourage them, as, in the first years of their marriage, he'd seemed to like the idea of her previous lovers (she had been a wild young girl), had liked her to murmur their names when they made love.

They never talked about any of this. A diplomat, Tod used to say, is a person who thinks twice before saying nothing.

All of it—the new, uncharted bodies, the florid meetings in hotel rooms, the yearning—stopped when Tod was diagnosed with lung cancer. Nan was fifty-two, arguably past the age for lovers, but in practice, not. She gave them up—*she* gave *them* up—in the simple, believing way a child gives up candy for Lent. For the duration, which turned out in Tod's case to be nearly three years. A thousand mornings: waking, those first precious seconds of forgetting, then the need to decide, all over again, every single day, to stay. Looking back, Nan saw that time as a sleep-deprived blur of bodily fluids.

Piss
Shit
Blood
Spit
Snot

She matched this list with a list of her lovers. Jack (Genoa, 1968); Anton Waldfisch (Warsaw, 1972); Matthew Prout (Washington, 1976); Daniel Hess (Bucharest, 1980). The two lists made a litany she recited to herself when shoving sheets into the washer at three in the morning; or swilling Clorox around a plastic urinal (breathe it in, bless the rankness that cancels all other smells); or driving behind the ambulance before sunrise, eyes gritty with unslept sleep, thinking, *This time he stays; I can't keep on doing this.* But of course she brought him home, he always came home, he died as he wanted to die, at home, with Nan asleep on the cot next to his high bed, one hand on the long cool worm of his oxygen tubing. Waking, she knew immediately that he was dead: she'd slept through the night for the first time in almost a year.

Reparation. That was what, dry-eyed at the funeral (because her tears would have been not for Tod but for Nan), she called those years. Reparation: to repair. One of the conditions for forgiveness. Number of lovers; number of gallons of bodily fluids. Sleepless, Nan counted them instead of sheep, over and over, night after night. If only she knew the correct ratio! Did she need to suffer more, even now that he was dead, or could her grief be just grief? She got out her old Baltimore Catechism and read and reread it obsessively, until Alex took it away from her and threw it out.

It was Deenie who saved her. Deenie who persuaded her to come to Chicago, to stay on there for weeks. Deenie who made her laugh. (*Why can't Santa Claus have babies? Because he only comes once a year, and then it's down the chimney.*) Gradually, during that monthlong visit, Nan's lunatic calculations ceased. In Deenie's wide pearwood bed she slept and slept. The terrible weariness unwound itself from around her bones and slid away into the thin blue air over Lake Michigan.

Why had she ever gone back to Seattle? The place Tod had chosen for their declining years: clean and new and complacent. The place where the major metropolitan newspaper would say, "In addiction to his wife, Mr. Mulholland is survived by a daughter." The obituary next to Tod's was "Victor Dorman, 80, Altered the Packaging of Cheese Slices"; below it ran the headline SCIENTISTS SUCCEED IN GIVING ALZHEIMER'S TO MICE.

Alex had written an angry letter to the editor of the *Pee-Eye* protesting both her father's obituary and the company it kept. To be near her dying father, she'd gotten herself transferred—she worked for the VA then—from Denver to Seattle. If Tod hadn't chosen Seattle to retire in, if he hadn't gotten cancer, Alex would never have met Gabriel. Jane would not have existed. Nan would not, at this very moment, be standing at a window looking out over foggy Providence, the new moon at midnight a silver suggestion above the State House dome.

Such thinking made her dizzy—that tiresome butterfly beats its wings in Guatemala, and off the coast of Maine a hurricane strikes—and she turned away. She stumbled over something. Wearily, she bent to pick up a Barbie doll. The chill air seemed full of ghosts. She imagined the women—of course they would have been women—who'd once worked in this building, in this very room, their heads in hairnets bent over the creaking conveyor belts, their large-knuckled hands flying. Those women would have been the same generation as Dorothea. Would they have had her courage? Fear rose in Nan's throat. What would she do now? With no money and no way to get any? No recourse, really, but to wait for Alex's next message? The wooden floor burned with cold beneath her bare feet. She dropped Pet Doctor Barbie and left it where it fell. Planless, she went to bed.

Eight

Scrolling through the *Pee-Eye* for March 7, Nan learned that Congress had given itself an exemption from the federal law against sexual harassment; that a nine-year-old Tacoma boy had backed the family car over his mother; that a whale had swum seventy-five miles up the Columbia River to linger just south of Portland, Oregon. More to the point was a small article on an inside page. A judge on the Washington State Supreme Court had overturned a conviction of child molesting on the grounds that the accused's six-year-old niece was too young to understand the significance of an oath and so could not testify.

When she finally found Alex's message, Nan copied it out with a hand that shook.

POOKIE: Gone underground for a while. More soon.
Kiss her for me. **HIPPIE**

Her breath came quickly, shallow sips of the mentholated air coughed out by the students on either side. She scanned the rest of the paper for some clue as to why Alex had gone underground. Nothing illuminating emerged, though there was plenty to horrify. A five-week-old baby in Issaquah bitten fifty times in the chest by a pet ferret; a father in Renton awarded custody of his small son three years after his ex-wife had kidnapped him and taken him back to Puerto Rico.

Nan pushed back her chair with a harsh, refusing sound. An infuriating tear of self-pity burned in the corner of each eye. She grabbed her parka off the back of the chair and went out, almost running, through the Rock's marble lobby.

At home—she no longer thought of the place as Mr. Nibbrig's, some-how the burglary had made it hers—she barely paused to take off her parka. The contents of Nibbrig's footlocker (rifled a second time by Jane, who couldn't believe there wasn't something more interesting in there than income tax records) lay strewn across the living room floor. When she yanked off her parka, Alex's Time Line fell out of the pocket. She picked it up and tore it down the middle. Pookie! Hippie! She flung the pieces on top of Nibbrig's messy papers and strode into the kitchen. The mirror on the refrigerator showed her own headless torso in a fuch-sia sweater and leggings; its gaiety mocked her. She seized the phone, punched in Alex's number.

Fuck our agreement. Fuck the Plan. Fuck everything.

The continent-crossing rings seemed to drill into her breastbone. Her breath matched their rhythm, cut-off, stoppered. With her free hand she dug into her sweater pocket for the nitro, thumbed it open. The ringing paused. She waited, pill tucked under her tongue, for Alex's voice on the message recorder. Why hadn't she done this sooner? She could leave! Leave all this, all of it—the makeshift, the mess, the relentless daily rou-tine—and go home.

The number you have reached is not in service.

But where *was* home?

No further information is available at this time.

She punched in the number for Seattle Information. A voice with a Southern accent informed her that there was no number for an Alexan-dra Verdi or an A. Verdi or (Nan's inspiration) an A. Mulholland. There was a Gabriel Verdi, M.D. Would she like that number?

She would not.

The pill began to take effect. A pleasant dizziness invaded Nan's de-spair and she leaned, light-headed, against the counter. The phone slipped from her grasp. She watched it dangle, swaying, from its curly cord while an ant-sized voice begged her to please hang up and dial again.

|

Nan had only an hour to indulge her anger and (Be honest!) her fear. Then she had to go pick up Jane at Mikki's. Gradually her turmoil eased, soothed by the evening routine, the eat-at-least-three-bites, where-are-your-pajamas, only-one-bedtime-story, one-more-drink-of-water-and-that's-*it* that had come to be an essential part of her day.

But when she'd sung the last of their unconventional lullabies, and Jane was relaxing into sleep, Nan felt a sudden urgent need to get things clear, once and for all. If Alex had abandoned them, if she and Jane were on their own, she needed to know why. To know—really know—what she was dealing with. She ventured, "Your daddy always put you to bed, didn't he?"

Jane stiffened. Watching her face, Nan went on, softly, "I bet you miss that."

Two fingers came up to rub the space between her brows. Eyes on Nan, she still said nothing.

"What did you do with him? Did he sing to you?"

The arm clutching Bananas-in-Pajamas came up to shield Jane's face. She began rubbing the creature across it. Beneath the blue quilt her small body shuddered lightly. Nan waited a minute, watching, then gently laid her hand on the mound of Jane's belly. She flinched. She turned on her side, away from Nan, and pulled the quilt up over her head.

I can't, Nan thought. I can't do this to her.

The realization swept through her that the reason she'd been questioning Jane—interrogating her, really—these last few weeks was so that they could go home. If Jane said the right thing—the thing, whatever that was, that would convince Nan no sexual abuse had occurred—then Nan could take her home. Could go home herself. Could be free.

She sat on the edge of Jane's bed, trembling.

After several minutes Jane murmured, "Nana?"

"I'm here."

Very gently Nan laid a hand on Jane's shoulder underneath the quilt. Her head stayed covered, but her small body seemed to relax. Nan sat on, afraid to move or speak. She thought of those long-ago nights in Italy, when she'd sat by Alex's bed, one hand on her shoulder, the other on the rough, cool plaster of her cast. After a while the sound of Jane's breathing deepened and slowed. The little alcove filled with Jane's sleep-smell, like strawberries. Nan folded the quilt back from her face. She put her lips to one small damp ear, flushed with rosy heat, turned off the lamp, and left.

|

"Gone underground"—what did that mean? How long would "for a while" last? Suppose it was months.

Nan sat on Nibbrig's sofa in the dark, smoking. Moonlight fell in skewed diamonds across the floor and cast soft shadows over her through the leaves of Nibbrig's trees. It looked warm but felt cold. She blew smoke into the chill air, trying for the smoke rings Pop had taught her to make. (Sharing a cigar with a child! What had he been thinking?)

Mothers give up their children, Pop used to say; that's how that love affair has to end. But he hadn't meant give them up the way Nan's mother had, by dying before her only child turned five; or the way (Be honest!) Nan herself had, by keeping her distance, by letting other hands perform the hundred daily tasks that would have bound her to Alex. And he certainly hadn't meant what Alex was doing now.

Nan watched another failed smoke ring unravel upward into a patch of moonlight. Her brain felt buttery from the two glasses of brandy she'd needed in order to go back through her child abuse research. She looked for a passage she'd copied out at the Rock during the morning's research.

Frequently the non-abusive parent—usually, but not always, the mother—resists awareness that abuse has occurred. When she does acknowledge it, overwhelming feelings of shame and guilt may come flooding in. However unwittingly, she has allowed the abuse to occur.

Nan stopped. She thought of Alex sitting on her sofa on that mild December morning, heard Alex's voice, cramped with sadness: *Somehow I let this happen.*

She stubbed out her cigarette, lit another. Alex had always struck people as steady, calm, and rational, like her father. The least histrionic of women. But there was another side to her, a side that Nan had glimpsed from time to time. A side that called up vivid flashes of Dorothea. Alex as a baby, almost frightening in her determination, striving in Nan's arms. Alex at six, hurling Poetry Frisbees—paper plates inscribed with rhymes she'd made up, all by herself—into the blue air above Zakopane. Alex at twelve, hobbling around Washington on unneeded crutches, accepting the homage paid by kneeling buses. *That* Alex had stayed alive inside responsible-organized-CPA Alex all these years. Nan splashed more brandy into her glass. She made herself read the rest of the passage.

The guilt feelings of the non-abusive parent cannot be underestimated. She has failed, on the most elementary level, to protect her child. Shame and horror may lead the non-abusive parent to feel unfit to care for the child, or may even lead her to view herself as a danger to the child.

If Alex believed that—really believed it—if she felt that whatever Gabriel had done was something that she, Alex, was responsible for—

What if Alex abandoned Jane for good?.

Nan took a large swallow of brandy and let it burn its way down her throat. The gift is always larger than you mean to give—Tod was right, saying that, all those years ago. Moonlight then, too (the moon a small bright button above the snowy peaks of the Tatras). Cold, then, too.

I can't raise her. I'm too old; I might not even live long enough to see a four-year-old to adulthood; I want my life. (Here the thought of Walker surfaced briefly, uninvited.) I *deserve* my life.

The checkered swath of moonlight had narrowed and was receding down the room. The bell in some far-off church tower began tolling faintly. One . . . two . . . How late it was! She'd be useless in the morning, the three-more-spoonfuls, where-are-your-snow-boots, yes-all-right-*bring*-Squirrel morning.

I can't raise her.

Nan put a hand on either side and pushed herself up off the sofa. Her ankles wobbled from sitting so long.

I can't. I won't.

|

Once the wall of security has been breached, it is only a matter of time before it falls. (HOWDY)

Contrary to her promise on the day of the burglary, Mel told Val what she'd guessed. Val knocked on Nan's door with the offer of a fake Social Security card. "A created card," was his term. Nan didn't ask where such a thing might come from; nor, in the demoralized state that followed her attempt to reach Alex, could she deny her need for it—or for any other help, legal or illegal, that might be offered. Mel made it easy. Matching Nan confession for confession, crime for crime, she said that Deenie had asked Val to get morphine for her. He'd done so through a Russian acquaintance who'd since been deported. She should have guessed, Nan thought: the box on top of Deenie's wardrobe. Why had they been willing to take such a risk, she wondered aloud, especially when Val wasn't yet a citizen? Because Mrs. Horsfal had been so kind to them. She'd paid for Val's taxi medallion. Then, when Nan had suddenly appeared, they had to find out how much she knew. That was why they'd befriended her at first; but only at first. Now, it was because Nan and Jane— Because Jane— At this point Mel, tough, cocky Mel, began to cry.

Nan touched her hand, then put an arm around her. Making reparation was something she understood.

So it was that Nan found herself, the next evening, in a strategy session with Val and Mel. Mel's revelation about Deenie had created a new sense of ease among the three of them. They were fellow miscreants now. "Think!" Mel commanded. "Start braining!" The three of them scanned the *Providence Journal*'s Help Wanted section, sipping vodka from tiny painted cups while Jane sat cross-legged on the floor and doled out lumps of sour-smelling Russian cheese to Clio. Quite a few of the jobs advertised were ruled out by Nan's New Look. Val was for entering the Ms. Senior America contest—Mrs. Horsfal had won, why shouldn't Nan?—until Mel pointed out the publicity that that would entail. In her corner Jane admonished Clio, "*Nyet*—not yet." They settled, finally, on four jobs that seemed either weird enough or boring enough for the employers not to be too choosy.

Neither Val nor Mel had asked why Nan and Jane were on the run. Though Mel, while Jane was in the bathroom, did murmur, "Beatings?" Val made a shooing motion. "Melochka! Is not our affair."

Putting off Walker, who sounded hurt at the abrupt cessation of their daily walks, Nan got herself in gear, as Mel put it. The first ad she answered was for the Food Basket (part-time, flexible, no experience necessary), where Claire, the seventyish owner, interviewed her right there at the checkout, in a baby-blue pinafore with SHEILA stitched across the breast pocket.

"Where you from?" was the first thing she wanted to know. Chicago, Nan lied, brushing snow from her stiff new hair.

"I'm from Hackensack, myself," Claire confided. "How I ended up in this place, I have no idea. I'm a *head* person, you know? No good with my hands at all."

She rang up the purchases of a tottering, sweet-faced old man whose scalp gleamed through dandelion hair: four quart bottles of cooking sherry, a carton of eggs, a grapefruit. "You got any experience, hon?"

"Yes." What a fluent liar she'd become. "But your ad said no experience necessary."

"Naturally. But nobody *means* that. It's just, we don't want these empowered types in here, know what I mean? Won't dirty their hands sweeping up after closing, or give the restroom a quick once-over." Leaning closer (the sherry man was still counting his change), Claire whispered, "We gotta have a restroom. All these old folks comin' in. Some of 'em, their aim ain't what it used to be."

Ugh, Nan thought, and said brightly, "I'm willing to dirty my hands. *Happy* to dirty them. Really."

At the pay phone in the corner beside the glass doors, a man began loudly haranguing someone in Spanish.

Claire said, "Plus, these feminists. They're always on the edge of the ledge, know what I mean? Customer lays a little hand on 'em, a little old fart's pat, they're yelling for the cops."

"*Yo te amo!*" the man shouted into the phone. "*Te amo!*"

It was ten in the morning and the Food Basket was filling up with customers. Claire took the rest of Nan's particulars and said she didn't know, she'd see. The man slammed down the receiver. He began punching the wall next to the phone. Claire locked her register and went off to deal with him.

Next stop: a gun shop on Atwells Avenue. Its sign, in Gothic lettering, at first glance appeared to say ARQUEBUS DUNG & AMMO. Inside, guns of every shape and size hung behind locked glass doors, and boxes of cartridges waited in demure rows beneath the spotless glass counter. Bob Swinehart turned Nan down right away—"People don't buy guns from broads"—then spent ten minutes explaining the peculiar hardships of the job. Illiterates, for instance: they always claimed to have forgotten their glasses (one had had them sticking up out of his shirt pocket at the time) and said, Will you fill out the paperwork for me? Then, where it said "Signature," they *drew* their names.

A middle-aged black man in overalls came in and bought a .357 Magnum. Bob Swinehart laid his change on the counter next to the ordinary brown paper bag containing the gun. The man said, "You give me my money in my hand, like I gave it to you."

Complying, with the slightest roll of his eyes, Bob Swinehart said to the departing Nan, "Hang in there! You know how many guns I cleaned before I cleaned one right?"

At Rent-to-Kill Plant Service a heavy girl with a face like restaurant china told Nan the job was filled.

The woman behind the cash register at Ray's Touchless Car Wash took her information down carefully. "Will vacume," Nan read, upside down. "Strickley day time." Through the long windows Nan watched the hoses, the leaping sparkling spray, the huge round brushes.

"This is the best job I ever had," the woman said. "I look out those windows and wish *I* could run through, just once." She looked at Nan more closely. "You live in the neighborhood?"

"No. Why?"

"Nothing. Just, I feel like I seen you somewheres before. Only maybe your hair was different?"

And that was how Nan found out that the car pulled from the river had been in the news again. The body had finally been identified. It was the governor's niece.

March 21 came and went without a message from Alex. Instead of getting angry, Nan found herself oddly relieved. She went outside and sat down on the wooden bench in front of the Rock, to think. The branches surrounding it had sprouted tiny green buds since she'd been here two weeks before. By the time she came back again, two weeks from now, they'd be exploding into exuberant yellow rockets of forsythia.

Will I still be here?

Gone underground, Alex's last message, a month ago now, had said. All right, then: Nan had to believe that that was where her daughter remained. With friends? But Alex didn't seem to have any; her friends from the HMO had drifted away after she'd quit working, replaced by mothers with preschool children, none of whom seemed to appeal to her. Somewhere anonymous, then. But sheltered, hidden, safe. And Gabe had taken no action, apparently. That might mean that he was guilty of abusing Jane; or it might simply be that whatever Alex had on him was strong enough to keep him at bay. Strong enough to buy her time—time in which she would come to see that, no matter what had happened, her place was with Jane.

If we can just stay hidden, everything will be all right.

Nan started buying the *New York Times* every morning, scanning for the small item that might report new developments in the case, praying for no photographs of the car's resurrection and the surrounding crowd. She should be doing more than watching and praying, she knew that. But what? She considered asking Val for advice—he undoubtedly knew quite a bit about disguise and evasion—but she feared his hotheaded

Slavic impulsiveness. He would have no qualms about acting outside the law. Or she could ask Walker. But that would mean confiding in him—entrusting him not only with her safety but with Jane's—and she thought, I just don't know him well enough.

She'd have to wait and see. One thing: it was no longer the kindness of strangers that Nan had to rely on. The kindness of strangers had turned, in the past three months, into the kindness of friends.

Meanwhile, no job. She would level with Nan, Claire of the Food Basket said over the phone. They wanted someone over sixty-five—a lot of employers did, these days—it saved on health insurance if you already had Medicare. Oh, crap sandwich! Nan, who'd shaved six years off her age on Val's forged Social Security card in order to look more employable, hung up from this, the last rejection, utterly disheartened.

And that was how she came to be standing, at eight o'clock on a cold April night, in a sixth-floor studio in the Waterman Building, naked.

|

Artists' models didn't need Social Security cards, green cards, or any other kind of cards. Groups of artists like the one Mel belonged to chipped in to hire a model for weekly sessions. It was all done under the table, "*Na levo*," Val noted approvingly. "It's a crazy idea," Nan said; but even as she spoke she saw that it wasn't. It was either this, or cleaning houses. Even babysitting jobs, given her New Look, were going to be few; in any case, they'd never pay the twenty dollars an hour that modeling paid.

Mel had spent that morning, while Jane was at Mikki's, coaching Nan. It turned out to be far more complicated to lounge around in the buff than Nan would ever have imagined. "First off," Mel said, "it's not about sex." Then, teasingly, "So don't even let Walker cross your mind. Modeling is an art form in itself." A good model *designed* her pose, mindful of negative space ("the place where you aren't") and foreshortening and intersecting masses. Mel showed Nan how to assume a position—standing or reclining, mostly—that looked interesting but distributed her weight evenly, so that she could maintain it. They did one-minute and five-minute poses, working their (Nan's) way up to twenty. Mel demonstrated stretches to do between poses for the stiffening in her muscles, and a way of massaging arms or legs that had fallen asleep. Think apples, melons, pears, Mel advised. Be sensuous and flowing. They leafed through *Art through the Ages* and *Twentieth-Century Nudes* for ideas. (Nan drew the line at Egon Schiele's women, legs sprawling. "No way. I'm not show-ing anyone my clitoris.") By the end of the afternoon she had lost all sense of awkwardness in front of Mel. Her body seemed to her, at least at moments, more *itself* without clothes than with. When Mel said, "Good thing you don't shave your pubic hair. They hate that," Nan had nodded, as if it were the hair on her head they were discussing.

Now, though, standing in the third of a set of one-minute poses—this one with one foot perpendicular to the other, like fifth position in ballet, hands clasped behind her back to support her lower spine—Nan felt not merely naked but flayed. As if in taking off her clothing she'd removed her skin as well. Under the flicking scrutiny of twelve pairs of eyes, the *stark* of *stark naked* took on real meaning. Standing up here, utterly with-out defenses, waiting to be liked. The old familiar first-time feeling—only with a dozen lovers at once. The humiliation of adolescent dreams in which you find yourself naked in homeroom, with all your classmates looking at you. Nan made herself look back, eyes skimming over the sketchers. Mel, head poking around her easel in the far corner, mouthed, *Pears! Pears!* She heard the collective rasp of charcoal on paper. She was sweating, but her nipples (Don't look down!) pricked with cold.

Some five-minute poses, still standing. One was a sort of lunge, in which Nan had to allow her limbs to be arranged by a rodent-faced woman who seemed to be the group's unofficial leader. Her elbow grazed Nan's pubis; the impersonality of this touch made Nan feel inanimate. She might as well have been one of the wooden easels, or the clock on the wall at the back of the room. It was better that way: she stayed where she was put, like any inanimate object, unseeing, unhearing, simply *there.*

Then, during a thirty-minute pose seated backward on a chilly metal chair, she made the mistake of looking down. There, despite the regular visits to Mel's gym, were her thighs: jellied consommé trembling on a plate. She thought of the pleasure, the reassurance, she had once received from this body—not only from using it, but from beholding it. Entering a room full of strangers in its company, knowing she could count on it, this body, not to abandon her. It had not made life simpler, of course. The punishment for being a beautiful woman is the same as the reward. She thought of all the people who had helped themselves to this body. The old Italian tailor on South Street who'd made her school uniform when she was thirteen, squeezing her tender new breasts through the hot gabardine while she watched, desperately, a pigeon's progress along the dusty windowsill. The eye doctor scooting around on his little stool and pressing his crotch to her bare knees. The crackpot pinching dermatologist who'd treated her for shingles in sophomore year. Staring, that time, at the sign above the examining table—«A beautiful young body is an accident of Nature, a beautiful old body is a work of art»—words she couldn't imagine ever applying to her.

Rain tapped on the skylight. The floodlights beaming down from the high ceiling warmed Nan's back. She regarded her feet, slender, still shapely. Good legs, except for the pale ladder along one thigh, where they'd taken the artery for her bypass.

She remembered browsing through the Old Testament with Deenie on one of their many afternoons in detention, where only morally uplifting reading matter was allowed. Deenie, who wasn't beautiful but had the luckier gift of looking like exactly who she was, had lingered over the image of Judith holding up the head of Holofernes. Nan had been more taken with unblemished Esther. So beautiful she'd captured a living king; so beautiful she could afford to take prisoners. The lavatory mirror had revealed twenty-six moles, uncounted freckles, and a coffee-colored birthmark in the shape of a teapot; nevertheless, it was Esther Nan longed to be.

A twenty-minute pose, mercifully reclining: elbows resting on a pillow, head on one hand. Then a break.

The difference between naked and nude—maybe no more than a state of mind, but essential—made itself clear. The minute everyone laid down their charcoal, Nan went from nude to naked. Too embarrassed to look at any of the drawings, she pulled on the embroidered apple green kimono lent to her by Mel and padded out to phone home. The dim brown reaches of the corridor smelled of turpentine and oil paint, the scent of childhood failure: cows that looked like Pekingese, dull little lollipop flowers. Nan's left knee ached, and her arm, reaching up to fit two quarters into the slot, felt as if it had been twisted. Assured that Jane was asleep, no need to worry ("Console! Console!" Val advised), she limped back down the hall and stood outside the studio and lit a cigarette. Mel found her leaning against the rough plaster wall.

"Hey! Why're you looking so down? You're great!"

"They hated me." Nan heard herself sounding absurdly like an actress on opening night. "*You* couldn't see their faces. Frowning. Gnashing their teeth."

Mel laughed. "It was their drawings they were frowning at. Not you. We're never satisfied with the first couple of things we do working from a new body. It takes a while to warm up. To, like, *learn* a model."

Nan dragged on her cigarette and felt her lungs widen, her head begin to clear.

The second half was easier. Her aches receded for minutes at a time. She was able to look around, when her pose permitted, and take in the artists. The woman with the bright little rodent face, who shifted a wad of gum from cheek to cheek as she drew. A younger woman who looked like Nixon, right down to the caterpillar eyebrows; a man whose skin was very pink, giving him a sort of newborn, scalded look; a large girl whose body got larger as it descended, in tiers like a wedding cake, from her neck to her thighs. Balloon Butt, Mel had called her. Most drew silently, listening to jazz from the public radio station, except for Rat Woman, who seemed to double as a self-appointed lecturer. Go easier, less detail—she advised Balloon Butt, who didn't look particularly grateful—the human eye completes an incomplete line. At the end of the session, when each person in the class displayed his or her best drawing, Nan in her kimono walked from easel to easel. The images—all in charcoal, dark masses and sinuous sweeping lines, depending on the artist's skill—weren't her, Nan. At most she was, she saw, a sort of medium, a go-between who linked the artists with the physical world. She was surprised to receive congratulatory smiles from one or two as they snapped their paint boxes shut and dragged their easels against the wall.

A good drawing, Mel explained in the echoey tiled ladies' room while Nan put on her clothes, was always to some degree a gift from the model. Nan pulled Mel's red velvet beret over her turquoise hair. Greeting her image in the freckled mirror, she saw a cross between an exotic dancer and a teacher's aide. Mel's image appeared beside it, hands on her breast and eyes crossed, miming delighted vanity. Nan stuck her tongue out at her in the mirror, feeling suddenly fifteen again, in the girls' lavatory with Deenie. Her heart rose. She'd done it! She was a bona fide—or at least, a paid—artists' model.

"You can go ahead and think about Walker now," Mel said, and smirked.

The best, the most beautiful, of surprises was how little she'd forgotten. Everything was new, was old: the sweet shock of alien flesh along the length of her whole body; the salted-almond smell of sex; the sensation, when she came (and she did come, but quietly, because surely—the first time, at her age, and three years without a partner—she shouldn't have been able to?) of light flung down.

"Beautiful!" Walker murmured into her ear. He didn't seem to care that he'd been unable to come himself. "We're golden."

Afterward, in the luxury of lying skin to skin, she returned, bones slowly settling, to specific things. Walker's smell, different now—a vegetable smell, like deer-tongue grass; the way his remaining hair was curlier at the temples than anywhere else. Deenie's sagging mattress tipped them toward each other. The bright sounds of the parakeets came clearly from the living room; out in the street a truck trundled by.

Walker's hand traced the renegade pubic hairs on Nan's thighs, the rosy flush, like measles, fading from her breasts, her neck. He didn't seem to notice her scars. No stroking of her lumpy breastbone with a tender finger, for which she was deeply grateful. Yellow light from the bedside lamp showed her a hand freckled with brown, knuckles over which the shiny mottled skin stretched tight. It didn't look old so much as finished, complete. He stroked the Chinese symbol tattooed on her shoulder. "Happiness," he noted. He laid his head, smooth as polished wood, on the soft inner flesh of her arm. She could feel the pulse ticking in his temple. His fingers had her smell, their smell; it was on the skin around his mouth when he kissed her. He did not speak; he did not need to. Their bodies (Wise bodies! thought Nan) had left nothing to be said. *That* was not old, not familiar—had not happened to her in many years. Not since Jack. *Chemistry,* they said. *Physical attraction.* Cold, dry words that let the reality slip right through. The words *mere* and *passing,* generally (in Nan's memory) attached to them, seemed equally wrong. This felt as weighty and enduring as mountains.

It had been so long.

Dressing, she met her body differently. The shape of it felt graceful; her muscles chimed. Walker watched her pull on her underpants, fasten her bra. She didn't mind being looked at, felt, not the blinkered unselfconsciousness she'd learned from modeling for Mel's group, but true ease.

Light spilled onto the bed, onto the shuffled white sheets where their bodies had been. Walker's back when he bent to look for his pants was broad, creased at the waist like ruching on a dress, the chained knobs of his spine visible through freckled flesh. He was as matter-of-fact about dressing as he'd been about undressing, about leading her by the hand (after they'd been necking on the sofa for an hour, like teenagers) into Deenie's bedroom. Friendly: a friendly lover. His underwear wasn't what she'd expected: blue boxers printed with snowmen. He looked up to find her watching, and grinned. The loose halves of his belt buckle applauded. He shrugged into a red-checked shirt and strode out exuberantly, buttoning, into the hall.

Midnight. Peaceful flesh. Time for a beer and a snack. (Mel was with Jane. She'd brought over her income tax records to sort through, along with a box of designer condoms that resembled sea anemones—neon colors, waving fronds—for Nan.) Walker's contentment showed itself freely, radiating from him as he moved in and out of the kitchen. Nan remembered other times afterward, when sex had been especially good: the man's withdrawal, sometimes drawn-out and wintry, sometimes abrupt, bright, back-to-business. Half waiting for it now, she wandered around Deenie's living room, looked at Walker's books in the bookcase, at the photographs propped on the mantel. A pleasant, round-faced woman slowly getting older; Walker beside her, ditto; no children. There was a large black-and-white photo of Walker thirty or so years younger, dancing with cranes. They were nearly as tall as he was, their long question-mark necks ending in tiny heads crested like Nan's. From the kitchen came sounds of cracking and scraping and the smell of eggs being cooked in butter. Quietly, Nan slid open the drawers of Deenie's desk. They were empty. No sign of the will. Deenie's black-and-white checkerboard floor was piled with cartons and austere objects that Nan didn't recognize. Camera parts? Too big, surely; and Walker hadn't ever mentioned photography. Some kind of ham radio setup? But why would he have such a thing? He'd never mentioned radios, either. A black leather briefcase tucked behind the largest carton caught her eye. She could hear Walker in the kitchen, whistling, shuffling plates and silverware. She walked over to the briefcase and grasped its handle, meaning to pull it out of its hiding place. As she lifted it up, she felt her palm press down on a button of some kind. A small oblong plate in the side of the briefcase slid back to reveal a hole about the size of a calling card. There was a click, like a camera shutter closing; then the plate slid back into place. Hastily Nan let go of the briefcase.

Walker came up behind her. She pretended to be examining an open carton of books. His arms circled her waist. He pulled her away.

"Come and sit," he said.

Nan arranged her face in a look of bland incuriosity. Walker led her across the room to the sofa. Two glasses of beer and two plates of scrambled eggs were arranged on the coffee table. They sat down, and he handed her a glass. She closed her eyes and inhaled the yeasty smell.

"Butterflies have their sense of smell in their feet," Walker told her. "How about that?"

His way of saying, I know who you are. You don't know the half of it, thought Nan; but she was comforted, nevertheless.

He began to talk about cranes. Siberian cranes, African crested cranes (the ones dancing with him in the photograph, in Zimbabwe), demoiselle cranes (looked like Bartleby the Scrivener), sandhill cranes. Dozens of species, ancient, unchanged since the age of the dinosaurs. Nan, rolling her glass between her palms, thought, You don't really know this man. You don't know his profession, or what he was really doing in all those exotic places, or why he would own a briefcase that contains a hidden camera. Yet there it was again, unshakeable: that deep, mysterious familiarity. That *sintonia*. They sat for half an hour eating eggs and drinking beer, looking out at the bright little knob of a moon that hung just above the State House, Walker with one finger hooked companionably under Nan's bra strap. Then he walked her home through the cold, clear, tingly night.

|

Time doesn't pass; time grows. This was the one thing Nan had learned from loss. Time doesn't slip docilely behind you, vanishing like the wake of a boat, water into water. It accumulates. Piles up somewhere, and waits for you to find it again. Nan sometimes thought death might be simply that: being reunited with the whole of one's experience.

In what sense, then, did you ever get over anything?

|

Of course he was younger. The Last Lover.

They met at a weekend workshop on Loss and Grief. In her first year as a widow, Nan, who hadn't had time to make friends in Seattle before Tod began dying, hardly saw anyone except her increasingly worried daughter. She hardly spoke to anyone except Deenie, who phoned three or four times a week and made Nan stay on the line. Tod had been dead eleven months—long enough for his clothes in the closet to lose their frank male smell, but not long enough for Nan to feel ready to part with them. There was a sports jacket she'd particularly loved—silvery-blue tweed with bone buttons—and when, one slovenly dark winter day, Alex found Nan drawing her tongue along its roughness, she announced that things had to change. Nan, ground down not so much by grief as by remorse, agreed. Alex signed her up for what Deenie referred to as the Dead Ducks Convention.

They met laughing—she and the Last Lover. Never, in the nearly two years they lasted, did they laugh longer or harder than in those moments before they knew each other's names. It was the pompously pious lecturer—a young man who looked like Robin Williams—that set them off. Both of them had to leave the conference hall precipitously, coughing to disguise their laughter. Hands up to shield their mouths, like errant children, they collided at the drinking fountain in the glass-walled corridor. He looked like a black Lenin: bony, ascetic face; neat mustache; pointed beard. They exchanged apologies.

Laurence ("with a 'u'") Meagher. A volcanologist. Lived in Vancouver, Washington, just north of the Oregon border. Pinpoints of water glittered in his curly beard as he told her all this. His mother had died in November. Nan introduced herself, traded Tod's death for Mrs. Meagher's. This exchange should have sobered them; but "Denial, Anger, Bargaining, Grief, Acceptance," he murmured, and that set them off all over again. They stood, quaking, and looked out the streaming glass walls at the drenched fronds of hemlock and cedar, the green hills of Tacoma blurred as if with tears. *Time to plant tears* popped into Nan's mind, a line from a long-forgotten poem. It made her feel preposterously cheerful.

Alarm. Delight. She'd never expected to fall in love again, much less to be fallen in love with.

Because Vancouver (handily near Mount Saint Helens) was two hundred miles from Seattle, they saw each other, from the first, at planned intervals—a stately pavane of meeting and parting. As often as Nan reminded herself that desire, like irony, occurs in the gap between beholder and beheld, she never quite accepted the arrangement. Laurence thrived on it. He was best at the middle distance: his graduate students loved him. Involvement in worthy causes had the advantage of requiring him to travel constantly. Committees on behalf of his black brothers, the Third World, the environment; boards of trustees of charitable foundations; lectures on the imperiled ecosystem to student audiences wreathed in the fragrance of marijuana. He was as busy, as scheduled, as the CEO of General Motors—except that (Deenie pointed out) *he* would have had a secretary who sent Nan flowers. When they were together—for a weekend at most, usually just a night or even an afternoon—Nan found herself doing things like scrubbing Laurence's back in the bathtub or kneading the tight muscles in his neck and shoulders. Acts of light, Pop used to call them: things you did for others that really you longed to have done to you. Things you did so that at least they would be happening somewhere, to someone.

His dark glowing skin, like the definition of skin. His *otherness.*

Intermittent as he was, Laurence nevertheless saved her. She no longer woke before dawn to a world withdrawn into grayness and grief like a fishhook in her heart. The fragments of old songs, the ghosts of old photographs, the no-longer-clearly-remembered smell and feel of Tod—these things ceased to pursue her. Grief was driven out by longing. Memory was replaced by desire. It was almost like the old days in Italy, with Jack. She felt, inside, as if she were thirty again and just beginning. At times she was seized by a sort of celestial restlessness—such a burning, fizzing sensation in her midriff that she thought she would levitate. For God's sake, Mother, act your age, Alex said. But which one?

There were signs. Nan ignored them. If you observe too carefully, previous love affairs had taught her, you find out beforehand exactly how you will be hurt. There was Laurence's swift style of leave-taking, an emotional economy he seemed to expect her to admire. (It did not escape her notice that he sometimes, while they embraced at parting, looked at his watch behind her head.) There was the avuncular cheerfulness he adopted when comforting her for the lack of himself. Meagher by name, meager by nature, was how Deenie characterized him.

Once they were at the Other Place, Seattle's trendiest restaurant. At the end of dinner, while they lingered over decaf cappuccino, a short, dark man (Gypsy? Indian?) strolled from table to table, his arms full of quivering dark-red roses like beating hearts. Nan caught his glance and he came toward her; but when he arrived at their table Laurence, without a break in his speech about global warming, waved him away. Nan felt shamed. She had told the Gypsy with her eyes that she was the kind of woman men bought flowers for. Laurence's peremptory arm said not.

At last she tired of being the one who loved most. She picked fights with Laurence, because in the sweet aftermath of making up she felt pursued again. They fought about the Italian goatskin gloves he had specially made, like a prima ballerina's toe shoes, to preserve his smooth, dark hands. They fought about whether to have salmon for dinner, standing with their bare feet—two white, two black—in the clear cold fish-smelling Pacific and watching the sun sink far out in the water. Nan never knew whether the Last Fight was simply that—one too many—or whether she'd chosen the one unbroachable issue that everyone has. It was the first and only fight in which Laurence lost his usual Apollonian calm, stopped lobbing facts at her and simply shouted. The image she retained, after all these years, was of the two of them in her bedroom, naked in a widening white swirl of feathers like the snowstorm inside an old-fashioned paperweight turned upside down.

You have no idea who I am! Laurence is shouting. You don't see what my work *means*. No—it's worse. You do see. (An expression of complete and utter horror crosses his face.) And you want me to abandon it, for you. For *you*.

It's a soap opera speech. She flings another pillow at him. It breaks, like the first one. More feathers swarm between them, thousands of them, iridescent in the moonlight, blown here and there by a warm summer wind through the open windows. Around them, between them, the air is full of a spiraling storm of white, like snow so wild it seems to come at once from the sky and from the ground.

Which is sadder—to stop being loved, or to stop loving? Which is the greater loss?

Goddamn him! Nan said out loud, night after night, alone with a glass of forbidden brandy in the room where, now and then, a stray feather floated up from under the bureau. Goddamn fucking black bastard!

After some months of this, she came to see that she'd endowed Laurence with virtues there was no reason to suppose he had, and then gotten angry because he didn't have them. And not only that. Really what she missed was not Laurence but the woman she had been with him.

Had she reached that age, then? When the mere rising up of feeling is so greatly to be prized, that it doesn't matter whether the feeling is pleasure or pain? To feel—just to feel. Not to not feel.

Deenie sent her a book called *Men Are Just Desserts.* Gabe and Alex took her to see cheerful Italian movies in which matriarchy triumphed. Gradually it became, first undeniable, then acceptable, that Laurence had been the last of her lovers. And finally there she was, still essentially Nan, her heart not broken, though certainly bent. Denial, Anger, Bargaining, Grief, Acceptance.

|

Now she realized, pacing down Benefit Street in the cold night, Walker's arm a lovely weight across her shoulders: Laurence wasn't, after all, the Last Lover.

Nine

POPE AND YELTSIN CHAT OF MULCH

No—that was *MUCH*. April 7. At the Rock, in a cloud of warm, flesh-filled air (it was midterms), Nan scrolled rapidly through the *Pee-Eye* to the Personals. No message from Alex. She was surprised to find herself digesting this disappointment with a minimum of pain and rage, or at any rate, a quickness of them.

Emerging into the April morning, the smoky air of early spring, she realized that she hadn't really expected a message. In fact, she no longer waited for one. It had been a month now since the terse message that Alex had gone underground. A month! Nan thought. She crossed the street and walked along the gravel path across the Quad, nearly crashing into a girl on a bicycle as lost in thought, apparently, as Nan.

Striding down Waterman Street past Faunce House, toward the bus stop, she took great gulps of sweet, champagne-tasting spring air. It tickled her throat and made her head as light, suddenly, as her step. The scent of growing things, of buds about to burst. *Are flower and seed the same?* At some point, but very recently, she'd joined up with spring. At some point, without her noticing, her life had become a seesaw of joys and problems so absorbing that she forgot to blame Alex for thrusting her into it. At some point, her life had become *hers*.

There was her new profession, if that was the word, at which she seemed to be more or less succeeding: a second group, sculptors this time, had hired her, on Rat Woman's recommendation, for Mondays. There was Walker, and sex with Walker—sex *at all*, something she hadn't realized she missed, hadn't allowed herself to miss. And there was Jane.

She was happier, lighter—more at ease. Sometimes now, playing Go Fish with Nan in the evenings or eating pizza at Val and Mel's, she became almost chatty, talking about Mikki's and the other children there, about helping Val with his drive-by shootings.

Nan was—she realized, ascending the steps of the bus, choosing a seat by an open window—no longer living according to Alex's Plan. She was following her own seat-of-the-pants navigational instinct. More of a Divining Rod than a Plan.

The bus gathered itself, heaved, and turned right. They descended into the gloom of the tunnel that led to South Main Street and the river.

The problems? As whose didn't, Nan's boiled down to two things: money and time. At the gym—her next stop after the Rock—pacing to nowhere on the treadmill next to a man whose sweat-stained stomach supporter had NORM embroidered on it, Nan added and subtracted. Five hundred and sixty-two dollars left in the envelope taped inside Nibbrig's dresser. Two hundred and fifty untaxed dollars coming in every week from modeling, soon to be increased by another hundred (Mel had found another group that wanted someone "different"). Two hundred to Val's ask-no-questions dentist for Jane's new spacer. Four seventy-five a month for the loft (but Val was willing to defer that, or rather, had volunteered Mr. Nibbrig to do so). One sixty a week to Mikki for day care. Food, seventy a week, if she was careful. So, then (pacing faster, upping the glowing orange numerals on the treadmill's console in some foolish compulsion to keep pace with Norm): twelve fifty a month coming in. Thirteen sixty-five going out.

In the studio every Tuesday and Thursday night, Nan found plenty of time to ponder this shortfall. The bottoms of her feet ached. If I were a waitress, she thought, I could at least wear orthopedic shoes. Leaning on one leg to create a fluid line while discreetly resting the other, she pursued her calculations. Really, the only expendable item was day care. But things were going so well now between her and Jane; she didn't know how crucial to that harmony their daily apartness might be. She didn't want to jeopardize that; and (Be honest!) that time was the only time that was Nan's, the only time she had to spend with Walker.

Circling Deenie's bedroom in the early April afternoons while Walker made lunch in the kitchen, Nan felt surprised at herself. How far off her past life seemed! How much she preferred the life she was living now, problems and all. Open, not closed; alive, not settled; full of questions. However imprudent it might be (for shouldn't someone in her circumstances be feeling fear, doubt, dread?), what she was was happy.

|

Late-life love. Shouldn't it be prudent, temperate? (The Four Cardinal Virtues, Deenie's version: Prudence, Justice, Fortitude, and Boredom.) The old in one another's arms. Love among the ruins. Shouldn't it be hedged about with suspicion and hesitancy and *partialness*?

Walker to Nan: "I would close my eyes and fall backward into your arms."

|

April unfolded. The lurching, uncertain New England spring steadied and took hold. The days grew longer. Days of increasing vegetation, increasingly green. In place of their winter walks, Walker took Nan and Jane for drives in his ancient mouse-colored Volvo. They didn't sight-see, just took in the green. Little Compton; Jamestown; Westerly. On days when Nan wasn't modeling, they stayed out till dusk. Violet sky, McDonald's, games of padiddle with Jane.

When they broke clear of the city, passing into the wooded stretch of South County, Walker would burst into song. (Oh, no! Nan thought, the first time it happened. He's one of *those*.)

When I left my boyhood home to go to college
There was one thing I hoped to attain
It was not a perfect philosophic knowledge
Nor a pure mathematical brain.

Gradually Jane picked up the words—Walker's repertory wasn't large— and sometimes she joined in. They traveled down the highway in a car full of song.

'Twas to wear upon my breast the badge of SIG! MA! PHI!
With the pride that the Sigs only know

In self-defense Nan began logging bumper stickers in a notebook she found in the glove compartment.

WHO PUT A STOP PAYMENT ON MY REALITY CHECK?

IF YOU'RE PSYCHIC, THINK "HONK"!

ASSASSINS DO IT FROM BEHIND

|

April 21. No message from Alex.

|

The last night of April was the first night Nan and Walker spent together. In the early-morning light they woke and turned to each other. Walker was like a boy in his suddenness, eagerness. Now that they'd been lovers long enough to know each other's bodies, familiarity seemed to heighten desire rather than dim it. This was a mystery to Nan. But then, she thought (Walker's cock warm and burrowing against her belly), it was mysterious how, at their age, they could do this at all.

I don't understand it. But, as Dorothea so often said, understanding is the booby prize.

Darkness was receding from the room, layer by layer—ultramarine, indigo, navy—lifting and floating away. Soon she'd have to leave, to go and retrieve Jane from Mel and Val's, where she'd spent (Bless them!) the night. She could see Walker's eyes, pebble gray, and the pale gleam of his wattle as he turned his head. Gratitude in his face. Walker's breath circled her throat, pooled in the hollow above her clavicle. Deenie's bed was wide, the mattress deep and firm. Nan reached up and pulled a pillow under her hips. The bed frame chimed with their movements. Walker's not-at-all-tentative hands on her made her aware of skin, skin. All-over skin; not being *in* a skin (a soul imprisoned inside a body), but *being* skin.

Afterward—after, as didn't always happen, they both had come—she said as much. Walker told her that, of all animals, the mole is the most sensitive to touch. "I wish you were a mole. Then anywhere I touched you would be an instant erogenous zone." His fingers traced the silvery stretch marks along her thighs, around her belly. Her whole body was still ticking gently, as if it housed a very gradually slowing pendulum.

The window by Nan's head was open. In the early-morning stillness— even the birds had barely begun—came the sound of a piano played, haltingly, somewhere close by, doling out a melody note by note. A child, probably.

Row, row, row . . . your boat
Gently . . . down the . . . stream

Walker gave a replete sigh, which, his lips having just relinquished her earlobe, stirred in the chamber of her ear.

"I never thought I'd get to this point in my life and have my body answered like—just like this," he said softly. "After we're dead, our bodies will remember us."

She knew he meant (Walker, more scientist than poet) that molecules had memory. That *their* molecules, scattered and absorbed into other configurations throughout the universe, would carry some imprint, some sensory residue, of each other. Walker's, she thought, smiling up into the eaves, would be very *clean* molecules, smelling of pencil shavings and deer-tongue grass.

Merrily
Merrily
Merrily
Merrily

Nan moved her feet, tangled with Walker's underneath the red-striped woolen blankets and starched sheets. She laid one leg across his groin, curving her foot so that her instep fitted against his thigh. She loved the firmness of his thighs. She lay watching the first light finger the slanting ceiling of their room, where joy seemed to have collected in the eaves. She thought, Even if it never happens so perfectly again, we have had this.

Life is
Life is but
Life is but a

"It's May Day," Walker said. "Let's celebrate. Let's go get Jane and have a picnic."

The darkening sky emptied. Walker threw the remains of their picnic into the basket while Nan bundled up the rain-soaked blanket. They hurried back to the car in a violent rain squall, gusts of wind against which Jane could barely stay upright. Walker carried her, one arm around Nan as well. When the storm ended, as suddenly as it began, they drove home through evening air that was soft and smoky toward a smudged horizon, clouds lit from beneath by the setting sun. Walker sang, "Far down the highway wet and black." Nan took the Bumper Sticker notebook out of the glove compartment and began to watch for good ones. The damp, loamy smell of freshly turned earth poured in through the open windows.

OF ALL THE THINGS I'VE LOST,
I MISS MY MIND THE MOST

"Look, Nana!" Jane cried from the backseat. "The sun is eating up the dark."

Immediately Nan remembered—heard, really, across a quarter of a century—Alex's voice. *Look, Mama! The moon is eating up the sky.* Heard Alex's laugh, the same husky Dietrich sound that Jane was making now.

IN GODDESS WE TRUST

WE HAVE ENOUGH YOUTH—
HOW ABOUT A FOUNTAIN OF SMART?

Nan felt Jane's arms come around her neck from behind, one sharp little elbow digging into her collarbone. She reached up and clasped the small linked hands in one of her own—warm hands, still wet with rain—before she said, "Fasten your seat belt, Sweetpea."

Beside her Walker glanced over and smiled.

It was true, what he was thinking. Jane had grown steadily happier these last few weeks. Winter Jane—sullen, silent—had departed with the last blackened lumps of snow. Each day of April had seen her rosier, looser-limbed, more loquacious. Now, as they swung north onto I-95, Summer Jane's face grazed the back of Nan's neck; her rain-damp hair tickled. She hummed into Nan's collarbone, low and tuneless, a sound Walker called the Vacuum Cleaner Song.

"Seat belt!" Nan and Walker said, in unison.

Though the sun had set, the sky glowed blue as noon. Twilight, Walker explained. "It skews the color balance. The Purkinje effect. Twilight increases the intensity of blue at the expense of all other colors." The air had begun to turn cold. Nan pulled down the sleeves of her sweater and reached to crank up the window.

"Nana, don't! The wind is nice. It feels like ice cream."

Who could resist? Nan let go of the handle.

"Knock, knock," Jane said.

"Who's there?" said Walker.

"Poop."

"Poop who?"

"You said a bad word!" Jane dissolved in giggles.

Nan remembered the joke Alex had loved most when she was Jane's age, the one she'd told over and over the first year they'd lived in Genoa. She said, "Why couldn't the sunflower ride a bicycle?"

A brief silence. Then Jane said, "Give up."

"Because it lost its petals."

Jane's and Walker's laughter, equally deep and husky, filled the car.

I made her laugh! Nan thought. She turned her head to the open window, sending her pleasure, like a prayer, out into the deepening blue-violet night.

|

That night Jane fell asleep halfway through *Goodnight Moon.* Her skin when Nan bent over her radiated heat. Fever? Nan thought, momentarily alarmed. But her cheeks and forehead felt cool. She was fine—more than fine: she was safe. Happy. Nan pulled the blanket down over one bare foot. Zipper lifted his neat little head from Jane's pillow, and her closed eyelids quivered: butterfly wings. Suddenly aware that her waiting was more hopeful than watchful—that she was willing her granddaughter to wake up and reach for her, hug her, talk to her—Nan backed away, around the corner of the screen, and put the space of the loft between them.

In the dark living room, restless, unable to sleep, Nan settled on the sofa with a glass of brandy and a cigarette. Their separate smells rose up around her like the memories of home.

Where was Alex right now? Nan imagined a furnished room on the wrong side of Capitol Hill. Moonless Seattle nights, Alex pacing in the stillness, corner to corner, her fingers interrogating the furniture as she passed, her eyes questioning her reflection in the dark windows. No—if she was hiding from Gabriel, she'd leave town. A cottage, then, on the Olympic Peninsula, damp and cold and out of season, the smell of fish and pine needles, the ocean gray with rain? Walks to the little store in La Push where a few Quillayeute Indians stared at her without interest. No; not there either. If Nan could imagine her there, so could Gabriel. Say she'd gone out of state, then. Or gone to Canada—that was better. Vancouver was only a two-hour drive from Seattle, and it was a city plenty big enough to get lost in. But where would Alex stay? How would she live? She had no friends there, no relatives—no one.

Nan dragged on her cigarette, took another swallow of brandy. Alex would be—was—all alone. Like Nan herself—but wait. Nan had Jane. Watching Alex with Jane—that had been Nan's belated introduction to the art of mothering. When had she ever stood yearning by Alex's bed as she'd stood just now beside Jane's?

A shock of pain flashed through Nan's fingers. Her cigarette, unregarded, had burned down to the filter. She dropped it onto the rug, which immediately began to smolder. Without thinking, she poured the last of her brandy over the spot. A bitter smell rose up. Sucking her burned fingers, too weary to get up and go into the kitchen and hold them under cold water, Nan sat on. Outside, the freeway traffic had ceased; inside, the dark and silence grew denser. The remote control for the new TV Walker had given her lay beside her on the sofa, where Jane had left it. She picked it up, flicked it on, found the eleven o'clock news.

"A government-sponsored SEX RING has turned out to be DEADLY in the nation's SMALLest state!" a joyful voice announced.

And there on the screen, once again, were the shiny black-suited divers, the algae-covered car being pulled from the water, the mayor of Providence—and Nan.

|

Rat Woman clapped twice, her signal for a change of pose.

Nan got off her tall stool and lay down on the platform, its pine planks warmed by the spotlights, in what she thought of as her Little Mermaid pose: knees, hips, elbows all comfortably deployed. Oh, she'd become brazen, all right (the nuns' word, long ago: Catholic for *chutzpah,* Deenie used to say). Her breasts as she leaned on one elbow swung sideways, more like eggplants than pears; but her gym-enhanced stomach folded only once. For the first half of each evening, she tried to surprise the group, to challenge them. (In their training session Mel had quoted Robert Henri: "Have you not seen many pictures that bowled you over at first sight, staggered you on the next, and did not stir you thereafter?") The second half of the evening usually found both Nan and the artists too tired for such considerations. Rat Woman had mentioned, in a previous session, the legendary model Charlie Moccio, who could maintain a handstand for twenty minutes. *K chortu!* thought Nan. Forget it.

Brazen woman that she was—"The Dame That Shame Forgot," Mel called her—she rarely felt naked anymore. Just nude. Mermaiding left her thoughts too free; they turned to last night's TV news. Fear crept in goose bumps down her gracefully curved spine. Last week, May 7 had brought no message from Alex. Two months now without any word. Nan had had to let go of her anxiety for her daughter. Worry over Alex's safety was too much, added to worry over Jane's, worry over (Be honest!) her own. She could only hope, now, that Alex's silence meant she was successfully lying low. Unlike Nan and Jane. The new developments in what the tabloids had christened the Deathmobile Drowning had made this morning's *New York Times*. Murder, politicians, and sex—the media weren't going to let go of an amalgam like that anytime soon. Earlier tonight, at dinner, Val had considered grimly and at Slavic length the chances of discovery. Suppose the *Times* decided to run the photo of the crowd watching the Deathmobile rise up out of the river—the mayor chomping on his cigar and, right behind him, Nan? The old Nan, with the cocker-spaniel hair; but still. The old *recognizable* Nan?

Gabriel read the *Times* every morning.

She tried to distract herself by looking at the sketchers. Balloon Butt kept yawning. From Nan's angle her chin seemed to melt into her collarbone without benefit of neck. She'd brought someone new with her, an older man with a nose like a Bartlett pear—a drinker's nose—and small black eyes. Nan could easily imagine him as a prison guard. "Draw the feet," Rat Woman advised him. "Get the feet right, and the rest will draw itself."

"—sour cream, hard-boiled eggs, and scallions," Prison Guard was saying to Balloon Butt. "You put it in the fridge overnight. Serve it with—of all things!—a boiled potato."

"Ugh!" from Mel.

Three claps signaled the end of the evening. Nan stretched, put on her kimono, massaged her calves. Then she went down the hall to the restroom to get dressed.

She and Mel left together, as usual. In the lobby of the Waterman Building a large red-and-yellow poster invited entries for a juried exhibition to celebrate Women's History Month. OPEN SEASON FOR WOMEN ARTISTS! it said. Underneath, someone had written in large black letters, KILL ALL YOU WANT!

Mel stalked over and tore the poster off the wall and flung it, a crumpled ball, into a corner. "Dumb-ass dickheads!"

She hooked her arm through Nan's and pushed open the heavy glass door onto Steeple Street. A cool wind off the river wrapped around them. "Nan," she said, "what're you gonna do?"

|

What *could* she do? That night, staring into the darkness of the midnight loft, its rough brick walls striped with moonlight, Nan made up her mind. Then she turned her face to the pillow, and slept.

|

"Nan—of course I'll help. Only thing is, let's level with each other."

They were lying head to foot in Deenie's wide bed, in the sweet slow aftermath. Walker's hand grasped Nan's foot and moved it so that it lay against his cheek. He put his lips to the arch. "Annette," he said. "Annette Boyce Mulholland."

She caught her breath. Her foot jerked, but he held it firmly. She felt the faint scratchiness of his day-old beard on her sole. "How did you know?"

"Deenie's photograph album. You were all over it. You two and your tucked-in schoolgirl smiles and your little starched round collars. What are you on the run from? You and Jane."

Play for time. "And *you* aren't really an engineer, are you?"

Walker's grip on her foot tightened. She turned her head away. The long windows had filled with twilight, a blue so intense it seemed to squeeze her heart.

Please. Tell me something I can believe.

"CIA. Retired."

Thank you, God.

"Why didn't you tell me?"

"It's not exactly America's best-loved occupation." He turned his head. Lips against her toes, he said, "I thought you wouldn't sleep with me if you knew."

No wonder she'd felt comfortable with him immediately, that first time over coffee in Faunce House. His familiarity didn't come from some buried resemblance to Deenie, but from being a type Nan had met over and over again in those years in the Foreign Service. How had she failed to put the clues together? His physique (trained—*honed*—for chasing and being chased); the briefcase concealing what Nan was now sure was a camera; the travel to exotic lands. Even his passion for ornithology—a good cover for someone who turned up in out-of-the-way places.

But there was, unshakable, that something else that shimmered between them—that *sintonia*.

Nan took a breath. "I kidnapped Jane."

She told him the whole story. He listened, motionless, one hand still grasping her ankle. When she finished, he closed his eyes.

Nan felt free and light, literally unburdened, for the first time in nearly six months. Even not knowing what Walker's silence meant. From her perspective, squinting down the length of their naked bodies in the fading afternoon light, he looked pained. Maybe he disapproved. She had no idea what his religious beliefs were, if any; or his morals, when it came to something like this, to lawbreaking. Maybe just knowing Nan made him an accomplice, put him in violation of some CIA equivalent of the Hippocratic oath.

She needn't have worried.

That night Walker showed Nan his tools. (Some giggling, like errant children, over the word *tool*.) Besides the briefcase that concealed a camera, there was a signet ring that could hold a microdot; a wallet of lock-picking tools ("surreptitious entry kit," Walker called it); a buffalo nickel with a hidden curved blade; a fountain pen that contained a microdot viewer. Some of these things—the lock-picking set, the coin—were museum pieces, he told her, issued forty-odd years before, when he'd first joined the Farm. One hand fiddled with a miniature wrench, sliding it in and out of its pocket in the lock-picking wallet.

Did he have a gun?

You bet.

Goose bumps of horrified interest pricked Nan's bare arms. Where was it?

In a safe place.

And no pious invocation of the danger of guns around small children would pry it out of him.

They went out into the small backyard. They had a rare whole night with each other. Jane was spending the night with Mel and Val, to give Nan a break, Mel had said—though really it was as much for Mel as for Nan. It was a warm night, the calm, voluptuous darkness pocked with fireflies. Lightning bugs, Walker called them. The air was full of the sound of crickets. They lay on their backs in the soft, fragrant new grass. He told her the two stories of his life with guns.

The first story was also the story of how he came to be a CIA agent. Drafted right after college, at the height of the "Police Action" in Korea, he found himself in OCS. He was sent, he never knew why, to ordnance school. "No aptitude test was involved. No *aptitude* was involved." During lectures on the color codes of ammunition, he read, under his desk, J. K. Wright's *Encyclopedia of Ornithology*; during lectures on how to set up an ordnance company in the field, he read *The Origin of Species*. He failed four out of the six exams. Each time, he had to write a letter to his CO explaining his failure and ending, "It will never happen again." The army didn't send incompetents into battle, in accordance, Walker said dryly, with the National Gene Pool Reduction Act. Walker was transferred to Intelligence. He went to Germany instead of Korea.

"So that's how guns saved my life."

The night sky, as Nan's eyes adjusted to the dark, filled with stars. They seemed to crowd the sky, to jostle each other. She'd read somewhere that the stars were moving infinitesimally closer together all the time.

"Some as large as goose eggs, some as small as hemp seed," Walker said softly.

"You know that? I didn't know you read Chekhov." Her heart lifted with delight.

"You love me," Walker said, in the same soft voice.

She stiffened. "The usual thing is to say, *I love you.*"

"But you already know that."

He did not touch her, or even reach for her hand, which lay in the cool, prickly grass inches from his own. She said nothing. The ringing of the crickets seemed to grow louder, like the ringing of a thousand tiny bells. After a while Walker resumed their previous conversation.

The second story was about death.

"Christy always set out spring bulbs in autumn. Said it helped her to be able to think across winter."

Ah, Christy. Dogs instead of children; Christy had been the child, Nan divined.

"She was shot in our own backyard. By a hunter who mistook her for a deer. It wasn't even hunting season yet; he was up from New York, poaching. Christy had these orange mittens. Fluorescent orange. She wouldn't wear hats. Her brain couldn't breathe in them, she said; they trapped the bad thoughts inside. But that day she didn't have the mittens on, either. October fourteenth—it was too early."

"What happened?" Better this subject than love.

"She died in the ambulance. Good Christ! They wouldn't let me ride with her. We'd had a fight that morning. Sometimes I'd forget that she wasn't all there, that you couldn't expect— The hell of it was, there were times she *did* mean what she said. Just, you couldn't be sure. That morning she made me so mad I broke the toaster oven. I lost command of myself."

Well, of course you did; she was bonkers, Nan wanted to say. Chivalry! Why were men always drawn to the unstable ones, the ones who glittered? The dangerous—or at least, the uncertain.

Me?

"I'm sorry, Walker," she said; and she was. Sorry for more than he knew, but certainly sorry for this death, so grim, so gratuitous. She felt him withdraw. He didn't want her pity. There was a long silence in which love and death seemed to hang in the night sky. Then they got up and went inside, leaving the stars to their slow collision course, the sweet smell of new grass, the clamoring crickets.

In Walker Warren Tice's former line of work there was no such thing as a résumé. If there had been, his would have read something like this.

1953: B.S. in Biology, Colby College, Waterville, ME
1953–56: Underling [very far under] at the National Science Foundation, Washington, DC

1956: Applied [out of a combination of boredom and irony] to the CIA

1957: "The Farm," Camp Peary, Virginia: Training in covert action, self-defense, and murder with and without a weapon

1958–60: Field agent: Assigned first to Bonn, then to West Berlin [known at the time as "Spy City"]

Cover: Deputy Agricultural Attaché, specializing in ornithological ecology

1961: Loved: Danuta Freiborg, an East German actress

Married: Claire Christine Atkins, a secretary at the Embassy in Budapest. [Marriage to an "indigene" would have ended his career]

1960s: Remained in West Berlin [young man on the rise]: Highly successful operative; Prague uprising; first kill

1972–73: Langley AFB: Trained young field agents

1974: Angola: Assistant to the Political Attaché

1978: South Africa: Political Attaché

1983: Langley

1984: Afghanistan

1987: Langley: Permanent Training Staff at the Farm

1994: Retired to Blue Hill, ME [back to boredom and irony]

All this Nan pieced together over the next few days, amazed at how often, over the years, her life and Walker's might have intersected. (Had he and she passed each other on the snowy Kurfürstendamm in 1961? Crossed at the same light on Pennsylvania Avenue under the blossoming cherry trees in 1973?) Walker had been a man of action, intrepid, resourceful. Now his experience—all the things he knew and could do and had been for years unhappily unable to use—was once again needed. A man in need of a mission had met a woman in need of rescue. *You see, girls*—Attila the Nun—*See how God provides.*

|

In Swan Point Cemetery the afternoon light was warm on their three faces. Walker and Nan and Jane strolled along winding gravel paths past headstones green with age, the occasional looming marble angel, newer graves garlanded with May blossoms. A clump of hazelnuts littered the ground with bright yellow catkins. Nan took deep breaths of spring-scented air. They passed two lovers with their hands in the back pockets of each other's jeans, a white-haired man on Rollerblades, three little girls carrying bunches of buttercups. Walker pointed out the notched tail of a barn swallow, sitting on a large marble monument to ABNER DAGGETT, KILLED BY LIGHTNING, 1937.

They came to a space without gravestones. Grass dotted with buttercups spread downhill to a small pond. Pushing through a glittery mesh of gnats, they laid out a quilt under some magnolia trees. Jane clutched a stuffed lion—"Lion *King*," she corrected Nan—which, whenever she squeezed it, seemed to fart. Walker had bought it for her on their way up Hope Street. He'd also bought her slippers in the shape of fire engines; when pressed, they made a noise like sirens. Are there no *silent* toys anymore? wondered Nan.

It was only eleven thirty; no one was hungry. Jane fitted herself between Nan and Walker and leaned back, comfortable, proprietary. They sat in silence for a while. To the other visitors—few, on a Sunday morning—they would have looked (from a distance, anyway) like a family. A little family of three, their quilt a small blue raft afloat on a sea of yellow buttercups.

The day Nan's mother, dead of a heart attack at thirty-six, was buried, leaves had covered the ground, leaves everywhere, yellow and darker yellow and gold. The night's rain made their colors sing, and the autumn sun, reflecting off them, turned the whole world saffron. Their smell was rich and wormy; their yellow light shone upward, like a thousand buttercups held under your chin. How had Nan gotten the idea of putting letters into the ground? The letters laid inside the coffin, was that it? Dorothea's idea: she and Pop and Nan had each written a good-bye, to be buried with the woman who had been daughter-in-law, wife, mother. Four-year-old Nan had had to dictate hers. Afterward, every October, Dorothea took her to the grave, where she wrote to her dead mother about the year just ended and tamped the folded paper into the soft earth under the yellow leaves. ANNETTE FREIHOFER BOYCE, WIFE AND MOTHER DEEPLY LOVED, 1914–1943. "*Where your treasure lies, there shall your heart be also.*" Nan would put her ear to the ground and listen, feeling, even as a teenager, a presence. Something trying to speak.

"Look!" Walker said. A heron stood in a clump of reeds at the far end of the pond. A tall, scholarly-looking bird: long neck, long legs, long pointed bill. Walker erupted in a little lecture about heronry, the family Ardeidae, the diet of freshwater birds (minnows and frogs). Jane listened with an air of indulgence. A boring bird, Nan thought; and then: If only we could stay this way for always. They watched the heron amble away along the shallows.

Walker said, "Janey, why don't you go see what those kids are doing? See them jumping, over there, under the trees? Looks like there might be a trampoline."

Jane dawdled down to the little pond and wandered along its rim. Nan could hear the Lion King farting. The sound mingled with the voices of unseen children, the call of blue jays from the willows at the pond's edge.

Walker said, "There's a guy. He's up in Boston now, but he used to operate out of Georgia. The CIA used him a lot back in the seventies. We used to call him Our Man in Savannah, back when I was at the Farm. He arranges things for people who need to get out of the country."

Nan picked up a tiny white-feathered triangle—the air was full of them, twirling and drifting by—and sat turning it over between her fingers. Winged, pointed, on its way to propagate. Spring, she thought, really *is* all about sex. "You think we should leave."

"It's only a matter of time before you're spotted." Walker's eyes rested on the top of her head. "Cockatiel crest and all."

"But Alex said—"

"You can't depend on Alex. One, she's gone into hiding, you don't know why. *Something's* gone wrong with her plan. Two, you can't reach her, thanks to her cockamamie message setup."

Walker's scorn was clear, and Nan felt a stab of annoyance. He's a man who needs a mission, she reminded herself. But she remembered how Deenie had despised the idea of being rescued. *D in D!* she used to cry, scornfully. Damsel in Distress.

"This man. He'll work for you? Even though you're retired?"

"Of course, Nan. That's the whole point. We were in the field together. In Berlin. If it wasn't for me, Sam would've bought it back in sixty-four."

It was the first time he'd ever sounded impatient with her. She'd forgotten that saviors tend to feel they own whoever they save. She reached for a clump of buttercups. They came up unresisting, earth clinging to the shallow roots.

Walker said, "Look, it's hard to leave here. I know that. But Janey's not safe. She needs—"

"I know what Jane needs."

"Sam can set up everything. Visas, passports—"

"*False* passports."

"They'll be watching the airports, Nan. You can't use your own names."

Nan remained silent, grinding the buttercups between her palms. If she wasn't careful, they would find themselves having their first quarrel here among all this green, all this bright spring promise. What she really wanted, she realized, was for Walker to say *we*. For Walker to come with them. The thought shook her. She clapped her palms together to brush off the buttercups' sticky golden dust.

"What do you think I should do?" she asked.

"You and Janey move in with me. Right now, this afternoon. If—"

"I can't do that. I can't move her again, not now, not when she's finally happy."

"You've got to, Nan. Happy doesn't make you safe. If I can figure out who you are, others can, too."

"But—"

"Sam'll need time to make the passports and visas. Credit cards; driver's licenses. Say, three or four days. Then you can go."

"Where?"

"Wherever you want." So she *was* a partner in her own destiny. "I'd suggest New Zealand. No extradition for custody cases. No language problem. Easier for Jane, with school and all. Any rate, if you don't like it, you can always go somewhere else from there. Bali, say," he added with unexpected whimsy, and smiled.

Nan mentioned money, her lack thereof. She could pay him back eventually, she told him, having no idea how. Not necessary, he said, looking uncomfortable. Sunlight through the flowering branches above them splashed his face, making it look somehow naked. Nan looked away. She should not accept all this from someone she did not love. Should not. Had to.

She found herself saying, "We could go to Europe. Jane and I, I mean. We could go to, to Genoa."

"Genoa?" His tone was incredulous.

"Tod was stationed there. It's a place I know. A language I know."

"Nan. Thing is, if you don't want 'em to nail you, don't go where they'll predict you might go. Lines of desire, we used to call it. You look at the person—their past, mostly, because the past is the best predictor of future behavior—along with their personality, their temperament. Then you sort of graph all that, extrapolate from it. What vectors does it yield? Those are the lines they'll follow. The lines of desire. Those are the directions they're driven in, instinctively, like migrating birds. Like herds of elephants crossing the veldt—they'll charge right through a village if it's in the line of march."

Nan had had much the same thoughts about Alex, about where she might go to hide from Gabriel. She felt in her bag for a cigarette. Walker lit it for her.

What he said sounded logical. Commonsensical, as the nuns used to say. Were spies that? How could a reasonably normal person—a person whom she, Nan Mulholland, could recline next to on a blue quilt on a sunny May morning—be a spy? He sounded so confident. Too confident? She stubbed out her cigarette in the springy new grass.

Walker picked up the butt and began to fieldstrip it. "Spy biz isn't all that different from any other line of work. It just takes the usual stuff—goodwill, vigilance, a taste for the absurd. And it's a helluva lot more interesting than working for IBM." He frowned. "Where's Jane? I can't see her."

Nan looked toward the pond, shading her eyes against the buttercup brightness, the white winged seeds glittering through the air. "There she is. See? Talking to the little boy in the red overalls. You don't make it sound very exciting."

"What?"

"Spy biz."

"The more like James Bond an agent is, the less likely he is to be successful. Same principle as with gadgets. Simple is always better than complicated, because it's more dependable."

Like washing machines, thought Nan, who'd always bought bottom-of-the-line, the model with the fewest knobs.

"Nap if you want," Walker said. He must have wanted to, himself. "I'll look out for Janey."

Out on the pond the heron gave a single slap of its wings, heaved itself into the air, and was gone.

"You nap," Nan said. "I'll go check on her."

She found her granddaughter on the trampoline in the middle of a stand of poplars. Her small blue-jeaned body rose and fell among those of several other children, some even smaller than Jane. Her face, like theirs, was pink with pleasure. Nan watched, envious. Then suddenly she was hoisting herself (Thank you, Nautilus!) over the metal frame and onto the canvas.

Bounding; landing; bounding again. The sensation of being free yet impelled, in motion without effort, was surely the next best thing to flying. Jane looked astonished, then mortified. She stopped moving and stood there, balancing against the waves made by the other children. Breathless, a little dizzy, Nan kept on jumping. The other children shrieked at her and giggled; then the little boy in red overalls caromed over to jump alongside her. Nan felt strong, soaring, invincible. The little boy beside her executed a neat cannonball, then grabbed Jane's hand. Soon they were all, even Jane, bounding happily up and down. Anything seemed possible. Nan threw back her head and laughed in delight. No doubt Walker was right, about lines of desire. Yet visions of Liguria, the scent of umbrella pines and olive trees, the cool call of church bells through the late-afternoon heat, enveloped her when she closed her eyes.

Ten

On May 20, the Providence County medical examiner revealed the cause of death of the governor's niece. She hadn't drowned; she'd been smothered, probably with a plastic bag, then held under water—tap water—before being put into the car.

Of course it made the headlines, not just local but national. TV news programs reran the footage of the car being lifted from the water, the mayor with his cigar, and Nan. "Hey!" said the woman in the CAN'T FART T-shirt when Nan stopped by the little newsstand to pick up USA Today and the *New York Times*. "Ain't you that woman on Channel 10?"

On the next day, May 21, there was at last a message from Alex.

POOKIE: Location, location, location. Love you both. **HIPPIE**

Location, location, location: Alex's absurd signal for the worst eventuality. *He knows where you are.*

Only he doesn't. Thanks to Walker.

Nan's eyes kept sliding off Alex's message to the one below:

LOOK HERE WILMA. Ain't a lumpy chick on this planet gonna make me forget who is and always be my Number One.

If only she could be Wilma, lucky Wilma, scanning the Personals for lighthearted words of love. But then (her eyes escaping to the wide sun-filled windows of the Reference Room) there was love here for her. *Both,* Alex's message said. *Love you both.*

Val offered to take Janechka to his mother in Novosibirsk.

"She doesn't speak Russian," Nan said, as though this was the only possible objection to such a plan.

"*Nyet problema.*"

How good they were to her, these former strangers! Reparation for the part they might have played in Deenie's death; insurance against Nan's revealing what she knew about it. Nan saw this; but she also saw their love for Jane. In a way, Mel and Val were Deenie's gift to her, Deenie's legacy.

Gently Nan turned him down. She could not be separated from her only granddaughter, she told him, appealing to his Slavic sense of family, of blood. Then (against Walker's advice) she said that she and Jane were leaving, that Walker had offered to help them disappear.

Mel was silent during this exchange, which took place in whispers in Nan's living room while Jane slept behind her screen. Her face was— Nan realized that this was the first time she'd ever seen it so—grim. She said, "Nan! You barely know this guy. He's old. The male brain shrinks faster than the female brain with age, did you know that? You're gonna trust Janey—*Janey*—to a guy whose brain is smaller than yours? Jump back!"

Val said, "What plan you have? Where you will go?"

Nan couldn't tell him, since she didn't know. And Walker's eminent qualifications, his CIA past, were a secret that wasn't hers to tell. She let Mel abuse her further—"Bunbrain!" she shouted at one point—until she finally stomped out of the apartment. Val, with a reproachful, dark-eyed look at Nan, followed.

|

Here came that feeling again—the sense of being tailed. A presence behind you; someone on the other side of a door, a window. On the leafy streets of Providence, Nan's scalp tingled with it, as if she were still behind the Iron Curtain. *A totalitarian regime does not keep under surveillance all of its citizens all of the time; it merely makes them think it does* (*HOWDY*). Each morning, coming out of the building with Jane, she looked up and down Elbow Street; climbing the steps of the bus, she took one last look behind her; every afternoon, when she picked Jane up, she asked Mikki whether anyone had spoken to Jane, any stranger.

There was no one. No one walking behind them; no one in the shadows of a doorway; no one Mikki (with, each time, a quick assessing look at Nan) had noticed. Yet the feeling persisted.

Then on one warm, bright afternoon, walking down Hope Street on their way to meet Walker, Jane waved to a man in a plaid scarf pulled up over his chin. A wool scarf, on a bright May morning. "Oh," she said airily, in answer to Nan's question, "I saw him across the street, at Mikki's. We were making a mud man. In the yard."

Nan felt her stomach leap.

The police? Gabriel's agent? A reporter?

If the man *was* following them, he was no match for HOWDY's lose-your-pursuer tactics. Nan grabbed Jane's hand and dragged her into the little children's resale shop, then out its back door into a tree-shaded parking lot. They walked the four blocks to Elmgrove Avenue and caught a different bus downtown.

She told Walker about the incident. They were head-to-foot in Deenie's big bed, enjoying the afterglow, for what Nan feared might be the last time. Walker sat up. He swung Nan's legs over the edge of the bed so that she had to sit up, too.

"Where there's smoke, there's toast," he said. Then, "Here's what we do."

|

For that *we*, Nan very nearly loved him. It made her (giddy from relief mixed with fear) think of an old joke, Tod's favorite. The Lone Ranger and Tonto are trapped on a hill, surrounded by hostile Indians, no way to escape. "Tonto!" cries the Lone Ranger. "What are we going to do?" Tonto turns to look at him. "What do you mean 'we,' white man?"

In the hectic, difficult two days that followed, Nan treasured Walker's *we* as she treasured Alex's *both*. Two talismans against fear and doubt.

|

Morning. Hot. Sunshine and the smell of coffee woke her. The linoleum stuck to the soles of her bare feet when she walked into Deenie's kitchen, releasing them with little sucking sounds. Jane and Walker sat side by side at the scrubbed wooden table, eating Frosted Flakes. Nan poured herself a cup of coffee and sat down across from them. In her hand was the copy of *Methods of Disguise* that she'd stolen from the Rockefeller Library weeks before. Fortunately, she'd thought to tuck it into their suitcase when she and Jane had packed for the move here, to Deenie's.

Walker was silent, thinking. One hand, palm up, offered itself to Nan across the table. She grasped it gratefully. Beside him Jane turned the pages of *What Do People Do All Day?* as she ate her cereal. Zipper sat in her lap with his chin on the edge of the table, eyes following the progress of her spoon. Beyond the screen door a bird sang, one continuous burning note.

"It's on," Walker said. "We leave tomorrow."

Jane looked up from her book. "Leave? Whaddaya mean leave? We just *got* here."

"It's only a few days earlier than we planned." Walker was talking to Nan. Those sure blue eyes, though, looked not at her but at something beyond her, invisible. The eyes were serious, but his voice held a note of buried glee. How men love action! Nan thought. Still, she could lean on this man, as she'd realized back in March; she *was* leaning on him. Completely.

From nowhere Walker produced a small tablet and a pencil and began writing. *(1) Call Sam,* Nan read, upside down.

"Leave?" Jane repeated. "Whaddaya mean leave? Zipper likes it here!" She clutched the surprised cat to her chest. Birdsong came again, closer now, pure and clear through the screen door.

"Hear that, Janey?" Walker said. "That's a cardinal. He's courting his lady."

Jane leapt from her chair and ran to the door and began slapping the leather strap of Deenie's sleigh bells against it.

"I'm not leaving!" she shouted. "I'm *not*!"

Zipper struggled in her arms, clawing and spitting, broke free and streaked out of the room. Jane kept on ringing the bells, her face gleaming with tears and snot. A bright beading of blood sprang up along her bare arm from Zipper's claws.

Looking at it, Nan felt her head go light. She pushed back her chair and bent over until her chin rested on her knees. The sound of the bells, oddly festive, beat at her ears.

Walker got up and in two strides had his arms around Jane. "Stop it!" he shouted—the first time he'd ever shouted at her. "Stop that damn racket!" There was a slap, followed by wild, hiccupy sobbing. Then Nan heard Jane's bare feet running out of the room.

When she looked up, Walker stood in the middle of the kitchen with a hand cupped over one eye. His face wore an expression of mixed anger, pity, and pain. "She hit me," he said.

"Leave her alone for a while," Nan said. Her head had cleared. Stupid to be this way about a little blood, at her age. "I'll go to her in a minute." In the space of two days Jane had had to leave Mikki and the other children, leave the loft, leave Val and Mel. Too much leaving, Nan thought, her stomach clenched in sympathy.

Walker got on the phone, spoke a few clipped phrases. "Got 'em? Okay. Okay. Eleven." He hung up and turned to Nan. "Get her now. We're going out. Sam wants all three of us."

"Why? Why can't just you go, and pick up the stuff? He's got our photographs already."

"Nan." Weighty tone of male patience. "Sam is doing this as a personal favor. It's off-the-charts illegal, what he's doing for us. He has one rule—he never makes docs for people he hasn't met."

"Do we really have to leave the country? What if we all looked completely different?" She held out *Methods of Disguise*. Walker glanced at it and snorted.

"Good Christ, Nan! Have you lost your marbles?" Then, seeing her face, seeing the way her outstretched hand, holding the lurid yellow book, trembled, "Aw, come on."

He walked around behind her chair and put one palm across her forehead in an oddly soothing gesture.

"Come on. Everything'll be okay. You're with me."

|

"Sketchy. Sketchy."

Our Man in Savannah had reservations about Walker's escape route. Nan sat on the sofa (a genuine Biedermeier, she could swear) beside Jane, each of them holding a lightly sweating glass of cold lemonade. A warm breeze plied this, the wrong side of Boston, with the rank smell of uncollected garbage from the street below. She tried not to stare at this man who, one cold December night by the Wannsee—Walker had told her on the drive up here—had killed the East German agent chasing

Walker. ("S-T-R-A-N-G-L-E-D," he'd spelled out, because of Jane.) The house was shabby, peeling, with a falling-down porch along one side; but the room, with its velvet-covered furniture, blazed with flowers in pots and vases. A contradiction, like its owner.

"Not from where I sit," Walker was saying. "From where I sit, we're cookin' with gas. Fly to Chicago, scuff up our trail there, then go Minneapolis/San Francisco/Auckland. Plan's so sweet it could give you pimples."

Sam shook his head. He looked like a retired professor of philosophy. Bald in the center, a monk's tonsure surrounded by a seraphic froth of silvery hair; forehead grooved with inquiry; wire-rimmed glasses. When they came into the living room, he'd snapped off the stereo, *La Bohème,* cutting short Mimi's declaration of love.

For heaven's sake, Nan said to herself, what did you expect? A face like a pit bull? Someone ignorant, dark, and looming?

Sam held up one hand. "For starters, how're you-all gonna get the little girl out of the country?" His voice, with its gentle Southern accent, suggested years of patient explanations to undergraduates.

Walker gestured toward the table by Sam's armchair. "With that passport, which you just made."

"You can't take a child out of the country without a notarized letter from the parents. I gave all three of you the same last name, but there's no way you two'll pass for the parents of little Lee here."

"Jane," said Jane, the first word she'd uttered since they got there.

"Not anymore, missy."

"Look, Sam, we've got to leave tomorrow." Walker explained about the TV footage of Nan. On the way over he'd picked up a copy of USA *Today,* and there under National News was an item, LITTLE STATE, BIG SCANDAL.

Sam looked grave. "Good night, nurse! You didn't see fit to mention this?"

"It just happened yesterday. Any rate, Nan on TV doesn't look anything like the way she looks now. Nobody'd know her."

"You always were a sanguine son of a bitch. You got to watch out for that, Walker. That optimism. Everybody has one thing—Achilles heel, tragic flaw, whatever you want to call it—you know that. The human factor. Remember Kreuzberg?"

"This isn't your kind of gig, Sam. Good Christ! This is strategy, not crowbar stuff. Once you grab your gun," he added, to Nan, "intelligence stops."

"Within the problem lies the solution," Sam said in a quoting sort of voice. "Here's my thought." He leaned forward, pushed his glasses farther up on his nose. "We make the child a boy. That way—"

"No!" Jane shouted. "No boy! I'm not a boy!"

They had to hold her down. Or rather, Walker did. The three of them filled the little bathroom, Jane screaming and thrashing, Nan terrified she would cut her granddaughter's ear off with the scissors. In the end Jane had a crew cut shorter than Nan's and a red scratch along the tender nape of her neck where the scissors had bitten. Emerging, they found Sam arranging pink and yellow tulips in a brass pitcher, thin scholarly fingers placing each stem just where it had to be. Watching those hands—tender, deft, inescapable—Nan felt a chill of foreboding. Silly, she chided herself. *We* aren't using him to kill anybody. But the feeling stayed with her, an animal tension, a darkness.

A new picture was taken of Jane. Sam disappeared into the back of the house to develop it.

Jane, curled in a ball of refusal at one end of the sofa, now and then gave a violent squeeze to the Lion King, which farted sadly. Misgivings filled Nan. What they were doing was irreversible. They had no way (Walker had roundly criticized Nan and Alex's primitive method of communication) to let Alex know, let alone ask her approval. By the date—eleven days away—of Alex's next message, they'd be in New Zealand.

Sam returned with Jane's photograph and glued it into her new passport.

"I've thrown in a birth certificate, just to be on the safe side. That plus the notarized letter I cooked up should do it. Had to make up names for Lee's parents. Good night, nurse!"

All three passport photos had the spectral look of dime-store photobooth pictures. Nan, her teal-blue crest now faded and half grown out, resembled Andy Warhol; Jane was a scowling little boy with a snail track of tears down one cheek; Walker's calm baldness made him look like a Buddhist monk. The documents—passports, credit cards, driver's licenses, birth certificate, letter, plane tickets—were placed in a manila envelope and handed ceremoniously to Walker. Then Sam opened a bottle of chilled champagne and offered a toast. "Fair seas and prosperous voyage." He and Walker clicked glasses. Noon sun lay in bright lozenges on the Persian carpet. Jane sobbed in her corner of the sofa, shorn head concealed under a crewelwork pillow. Nan lit a cigarette, not asking permission. Over the rim of his wineglass Sam regarded the three of them with, Nan realized fearfully, compassion.

"Beautiful!" Walker said. "We're golden."

|

In the dark Nan stood alone in Deenie's tiny backyard. Above the capitol dome was a sky full of stars, a nearly full moon like a pale, pitted stone. The fragrance of resin from nearby pines and the sweeter smell of some flowering tree filled the night air. Ferns brushed Nan's ankles; she imagined the movement of their roots in the warm earth. Wherever Alex was now, did she have anything like this? She imagined Alex alone, afraid. She'd already been in hiding for a month and a half now; so how had she found out that Gabriel knew where Jane was? Had he caught Alex, threatened her, dragged her back to Seattle? But no—she must still be free, or she couldn't have sent that last message. *Location, location, location.* What did that really mean? Walker was right. Silly—their whole code had been silly, their whole system of communicating.

I can't do anything to save Alex now, or even help her. Now there's only Jane.

Inside, in the kitchen, Walker was whistling softly. He'd carried the sleeping Jane, exhausted from weeping, inside from the car and tucked her beneath a quilt on Deenie's sofa. Now he was making a shrimp-and-cheese omelet for their dinner.

Location location location, Nan thought, feeling the warm, sweet breeze on her bare neck. Poor Jane! Of course she doesn't want to leave here. I don't want to leave here either.

Behind her the screen door sighed as it swung open. Walker's arms wrapped around her; he kissed the back of her neck. She stood in his embrace and looked up at the night through tears of—what? Fear? Regret? Grief for the lost life of Nan Mulholland?

But she wasn't Nan Mulholland any longer. Would never, if their escape plan worked, be Nan Mulholland again.

There was a rustling of wings, some night bird, in the hedge alongside them. Walker's arms tightened and he leaned into her. His warm breath stirred in her ear. "Feathers evolved long before flight. Did you know that? Some dinosaurs had feathers, head to tail."

Yes, Nan thought. Yes—but they couldn't fly.

|

Mel stood on the sidewalk with Zipper in her arms. She was crying silently. Her nose was running; she ignored it. Nan felt responsible for her suffering. She looked around, out of habit, to see if their little group was attracting attention. Sunlight and a soft breeze and the exhilaration of departure didn't dispel her sense of someone, somewhere, watching.

Jane refused Val's hug and threw herself down on the sidewalk. Nan heard her knees hit the pavement; then her small body arched into its tent of grief. Appalled—Jane hadn't done this for months now—Nan said, "Sweetpea! We need to go. The toy store, remember? The picnic?" She moved toward her; but Walker was quicker. He lifted her up, wincing as she kicked him, and carried her to the car.

Nan hugged Val, who kissed her on each cheek. His face was slightly scratchy, his skin warm. Mel, arms tight around Zipper, turned her face away from Nan. Her eyes were on Jane's huddled figure inside the car. Feeling Mel's sadness, her anger, Nan accepted the weight of both. Her own sadness, Nan realized, was partly grief for Deenie: in losing Mel, she lost Deenie all over again. The terse cries of the gulls wheeling above Elbow Street were the sound her heart would have liked to make. She took a breath. The morning air was clear and warm and painfully sweet in her throat. She could not bring herself to say good-bye.

Val stepped back, pulling Mel up onto the curb. "We meet again. I am knowing it."

Nan got into the car. Walker already had the engine running—the old Volvo looked as if its engine would knock and rattle, but it didn't—and the inside smelled of upholstery shampoo. Nan cranked down her window in time to see Val and Mel slide away. Behind her Jane wept—hopelessly, stormily. Afraid she might choke on the sobs that tore through her, Nan twisted around in her seat and stretched out one arm, clumsily. The quaking of her small shoulders underneath Nan's hand brought a sudden, sharp memory of Gabriel in the garden in the September twilight. (So long ago, now!—though not even two years had gone by.) Of Gabriel's whole body shuddering under Nan's touch, as his daughter's did now. *Who saves one person saves the world.* One of the many Russian proverbs that she'd always suspected Val of inventing. As the Volvo turned smoothly onto South Main Street, she wondered: does saving one person even save the person?

|

The new bribe, Native American Barbie—what could be less suitable for the tough little boy Jane now was?—was administered at Uncle Sig's Toy Shop on their way to Swan Point Cemetery. Refusing both Nan's hand and Walker's, Jane shuffled morosely along the gravel path. They held each other's hands instead. Walker carried the Last Picnic—sandwiches, oranges, wine, and Gatorade—in an old wicker basket of Deenie's.

Nan looked around. No one behind them. It was still early: midmorning sun slanted along the path and down the sloping lawn. Trees newly in leaf threw tender shadows across the bright young grass. On the other side of the iron palings a peacock, pacing alone, stopped and suddenly spread its tail.

"Look, Janey!" Walker cried. "You won't see that everywhere." He explained to Jane's indifferent back how people in the Middle Ages saw in the peacock's tail the stars and planets, the layout of the heavens.

Nan wondered whether it was years of spy biz that enabled Walker to picnic in the midst of peril, or the reckless optimism that Sam had warned against. Granted, Jane had been nearly hysterical when they'd packed the car at Deenie's; granted, the promise of a picnic was the only thing that calmed her. But they were on the run. Gabriel was looking for them. Nan kept remembering something Tod used to say: there is no greater misfortune than to underestimate your enemy. She'd tried, while Jane was out of earshot in the toy store, to give Walker a sense of how formidable an antagonist Gabriel was. She'd asked about Sam's cryptic "Remember Kreuzberg." "That was two decades ago," Walker had evaded. "The guy's retired now. He's writing a *book,* for Chrissake. What really corks him is he's not in the field anymore."

They found a spot in the tender new shade of some flowering trees—a stretch of sun-warmed grass, the domain of Susannah Oglethorpe, 1802–1853, presided over by a marble swan with arched neck and outstretched wings. Walker shook out the blue quilt, which he'd been carrying under one arm. The three of them sat down, Jane a little apart, with her small stiff back to Nan and Walker. Birds called in the trees overhead. White flecks of dandelion seed floated past. Nan took off her denim jacket and

Walker rolled up the sleeves of his work shirt. Susannah's headstone, which seemed at Nan's first glance to have been erected by "Her Loving Bother William," made a comfortable enough backrest. Walker leaned back with her and took a deep breath of the fragrant, sun-warmed air. He said, "It's always a beautiful day when you leave town."

It was nice to be out, Nan had to admit. It had felt as if they were under house arrest at Deenie's these last two days. And the promise of one last picnic did seem to have calmed Jane. Their suitcases were safely stowed in the Volvo's trunk; as soon as they'd had lunch they would drive straight to T.F. Green Airport. Walker handed out peanut-butter-and-banana sandwiches and oranges, a bottle of Gatorade for Jane. He poured wine into two plastic cups and gave one to Nan. They ate—even Jane, hunger winning out over anger, though she still refused to turn around—as if they had nothing weightier on their minds than spring. Looking around as she chewed (where on earth had Walker gotten the idea that peanut butter went with bananas?—oh, of course: Christy), Nan saw that they were not the only picnickers. On the other side of the gravel path, an elderly man in baggy trousers held up by red suspenders had set up a card table. As Nan watched, he shook out a white lace tablecloth and let it settle, then began to lay out silverware and china.

"Hey!" Walker said. "Am I talking to myself here?"

"What? Sorry."

"I was thinking about that song. Was it Johnny Mercer? You . . . something . . . and the angels sing."

"'You speak, and the angels sing.'"

"Sing it for me," Walker said, and Nan obliged, in a low voice. Jane threw a look over her shoulder, embarrassment elbowing scorn.

"Good song for this place," Walker observed.

Nan watched Jane's small straight back in the boy's yellow T-shirt and overalls. Her silence was like her old silences, the way she'd been on the flight east and during their first few days in Providence. Nan got to her feet. Crouching down next to her, she put an arm lightly around her shoulders. Jane shrugged it loose but didn't move away.

"Grape Eyes—how about an orange?" She held out two neatly sliced halves.

"Zipper's coming with us, right?" Jane kept her back to Nan. One arm clutched the Lion King; the other, Native American Barbie.

Nan hesitated.

"Is he? Or not? Because I need to know right now."

How like her mother she sounded. Her voice held a quaver inside the harshness; it was too old a voice for a child. Too many leave-takings, thought Nan.

Jane turned to look at her. Her eyes—green, so green—were her mother's eyes, full of reproach. Without her long, abundant brown hair, her face looked thinner, her chin more determined than ever. With difficulty, Nan kept her own gaze steady.

"Yes," she said.

Intake of breath from Walker. He'd explained New Zealand quarantine laws to Nan the evening before. Not to mention the risk: it was much harder to travel discreetly with an animal in tow.

Nan waited, heart high in her chest; but Walker said nothing. Her arm tightened around Jane, and Jane, though her thin shoulders hunched grudgingly, let it stay. Screw the risk, Nan thought. She watched Jane stick her tongue into the heart of the orange. One thing was clear to her, sitting with her granddaughter's warm flesh under her fingers, the sky beginning to fill with milky clouds, an unseen bird calling in the tree above them: there were other kinds of safety besides physical.

The man in the red suspenders set a large cake with chocolate frosting in the middle of his table and began sticking candles into the top. A birthday cake, Nan realized. In a cemetery.

Walker left the quilt and went to sit with his back against a tree. Jane curled on her side and slept. The sun went in; the dappled shade around them deepened to a uniform blue-green dimness. A breeze lifted Nan's collar against her neck.

"Pardon me, ma'am?"

Here was Red Suspenders standing at the edge of their quilt. "Can I trouble you for some water? Forgot it completely. Imagine that!"

Walker spoke curtly from his tree trunk. "We don't have any."

Nan opened her mouth to protest his rudeness, then realized. Of course: even a harmless-looking, picnic-possessing old man could be a Tail. Must get into a more Iron Curtain frame of mind. She glanced down at Jane, who slept on, cropped head pillowed on Lion King: a little boy, except for— Discreetly (she hoped), Nan maneuvered Native American Barbie under her outspread skirt.

Red Suspenders had taken in Nan's hair, her tattoo, visible where her scoop-necked dress had slid down one shoulder. "You from RISD?"

She shook her head.

"I seen you *some*place before."

Nan froze. The TV clip, she thought.

He sat down cross-legged on the grass, oblivious to Walker's "Hey!" of protest. "You mighta seen me, too. I been on TV. Imagine that! 'Count of my grandson. You know?"

If he'd remembered seeing her on TV, he would have said, *too. I've been on TV, too.* Relieved, she smiled at him. Slightly crazy people had always been drawn to her, usually on means of transport. On planes, especially, with their feel of the confessional, the confinement and invisibility of those high-backed seats, she'd listened to many a wintry monologue.

"Your grandson?" she said.

"My boy's boy. Billy. Little boy in a swing? You'd'a seen him on the commercials for Drunk Drivin'. He was killed by a drunk driver in 1994. That's him over there." He gestured toward his lace-covered picnic table.

"I'm so sorry," Nan said. One suspender, she saw now, bore a button that said, M.A.D.D.

"Billy's face. They show you his face real close, him swinging toward you. Feels like he's gonna pop right outta your TV. My boy took that movie at Billy's last birthday party. Five. He was five. You seen him?"

"I—I think— Yes, I have."

Walker snorted. Two lies in half an hour. Nan threw him a quelling look.

"He's a beautiful boy," she told Suspenders. Oh, shit. "Was."

Suspenders sighed, looked down at the ground, looked up above Nan's head. "I work with animals now. No people. I'm the night man down at the animal shelter on Bassett. That *your* boy?" His head nodded at the sleeping Jane.

"My . . . grandson." Did he notice her hesitation?

"What's his name?"

Did he look at her suspiciously?

"Uh, Lee. His name is Lee."

"Looks about Billy's age. You raising him, are you? Lotta folks doin' that, these days—bringin' up their kids' kids. What happened to his mama?"

"She died." Nan didn't dare look at Walker.

"This here's a good spot to sit and reminisce, ain't it? That's a redbud tree, the one your husband's sitting under. Some call it ironwood. No idea why."

He said this as if giving Nan a gift. Then he bowed and turned away. Nan watched him walk back across the grass to his little laden table. He struck a match and a ring of light bloomed on the cake.

"You shouldn't talk to strangers, Nan." Walker left his spot under the redbud tree and came to sit beside her. "No matter how harmless they look. Promise me, from now on."

Nan was silent. She did not like to be rebuked, especially by men, especially if they were her lovers. More than one of whom had, in the past, brought about the end of the affair in just that way.

"Nan? It's important. A closed mouth gathers no feet."

The attempt at lightness, with its little accompanying *heh-heh,* an *old* person's laugh, infuriated her.

"For how long? How long am I supposed to be full of suspicion and withdrawal? Just while we're traveling, or after we get to"—would they really, ever?—"New Zealand?"

"This is no time for sarcasm, Nan. We can't afford it."

His voice made Nan look at him, really look, for the first time in days. Maybe he wasn't as calm as she'd thought. His cleanliness seemed to be wearing thin. The OLD AGE AND TREACHERY T-shirt looked gray at the edges, and his eye, where Jane had hit him yesterday morning, had begun to swell, the skin around it puffy and bright.

You twit. This man is helping you—you and Jane. *He* doesn't need to flee the country. And what's more (oh, coals of fire), he'll never point that out. Never say (like the Last Lover), *I feel like you drove a truck through my life.*

Nan sighed for the backward nature of things. If the Last Lover had been like Walker, how that would have delighted her. Or then again, if things with Walker had been allowed to unfold naturally— First we elope, she thought, later we'll be courting. "Sorry," she said—coughed, really. A hard little pellet of a word, a word (Alex had often pointed out) rarely uttered by Nan.

While they were talking, the afternoon had turned gloomy, brightness fallen from the air, the birds silent. Nan watched Red Suspenders blow out the candles and cut the cake. When he'd served it, he turned his picnic basket upside down and sat on it. As he ate, he talked, gesturing with his fork to the empty place opposite.

Walker moved closer to Nan. His thumb stroked her anklebone. He said—his own oblique apology—"Butterflies have their sense of smell in their feet. Did you know that?"

"You told me, in March. The first time we made love."

Abashed, he pulled up a blade of grass and twirled it between his fingers.

As she was vowing internally to be better, nicer—for how could this whole plan possibly work, otherwise?—he said, "Actually, I have a confession to make. As they say."

He paused; Nan waited.

"Thing is, I was afraid you—that if you had plenty of money, you wouldn't need me."

"Walker. What are you talking about?"

"Like I told you, Deenie mentioned you in her will. Thing is, it was more than just a mention."

Nan arranged her face in an expression of nonjudgmental encouragement, a look she'd often worn for the Last Lover.

"She left her estate to be divided equally between me and you. That's, well, it's roughly four hundred thousand. Each."

Walker's sigh of unburdenedness, of relief, made Nan catch her breath in outrage. "You *lied* to me?" she said loudly. Walker made shushing motions. "All this time?"

The first drops of rain fell. Jane woke, stretching luxuriously, then remembered she was mad, and frowned.

"Nan!" Walker said urgently. "Look—I'm sorry. But you couldn't have collected the money, anyway—not without revealing who you are."

"So what happened to it? When you couldn't find me?"

Walker looked uncomfortable again; his wattle turned red. "It, uh, it reverts to me."

That does it.

Trembling with fury, Nan stood up. One foot had gone to sleep and she stumbled, which made her even more furious. She turned her back to Walker. "Time to go, Sweetpea!"

Jane shook her head. "I wanna write a letter," she whined. "Like you did, Nana. And dig it in the ground."

"Who to?" Nan began gathering the remains of their picnic and hurling them into the basket, then thought, Fuck it. She grabbed her jacket and thrust her arms into it, then picked up Jane's.

"To Daddy."

Nan went cold all over, the skin on her bare neck prickling, and not with rain. She'd forgotten that she'd told Jane about writing letters to her dead mother. It must have been weeks ago. Why in the world had she mentioned it? She held out Jane's jacket.

"We don't have time. Look how dark the sky is. It's going to pour. Come on, Sweetpea, let's—"

"I want to!" Jane cried. She stamped one foot, then the other, then both, jumping up and down on the grass. "I *want* to! I *have* to!"

Nan looked around nervously. Red Suspenders, who sat on at his lace-covered table oblivious to the rain, was watching them with interest. On the gravel path a young mother holding a newspaper over the head of her baby stopped to stare.

"Good Christ!" Walker said. He reached for Jane, but she leapt away. By now it was raining in earnest, fat drops that exploded softly as they hit the ground. The wind had shifted, bringing the seaweed smell of the ocean to mingle with the odors of damp earth and grass.

"I wanna write a letter to Daddy!"

Walker and Jane stood, frozen for an endless second, on opposite sides of the blue quilt. Jane's face was red and angry and she was coughing, a tight, clanky cough, like a cowbell. We'll be drenched by the time we get back to the car, Nan thought. She longed to rub Jane's hair dry with a linen towel, the way Dorothea used to do when Nan got caught in the rain, then give her hot milk and honey, to ward off a chill.

Walker hesitated, she saw, because of the people watching. Red Suspenders hooked a pair of spectacles over his ears and stared through them; a little knot, now, of mothers with young children stood on the cinder path in the rain.

"You said we were gonna have a nice picnic. But it's not. It's *not*!" Gusty sobs; more of that clanky cough.

Too many good-byes, Nan thought. She said, "Jane—come over here. Look! I've got"—patting her fanny pack—"some paper. We'll write a—"

Walker's hand encircled Nan's arm. He said in a loud, carrying, calmly parental voice, "Lee! Time to go home! Let's pack up!"

"I'm not Lee! I'm Jane!" Screaming, now. Beyond her granddaughter Nan saw Suspenders rummage in his picnic basket, pull out something small and black—a camera?—no, a cell phone. He punched in a number, then held it to his ear.

Walker saw it, too. He crossed the quilt and seized Jane by the shoulders.

Nan became aware of pain, a grim radiance in the center of her midriff. Like nausea, only not. She felt in her fanny pack for the little plastic vial, opened it, stood there with the nitro in her palm, gauging the pain, willing it to leave. Rain slid down her bare arms, warm as blood.

Jane writhed and twisted in Walker's grasp. He looked around at the spectators, but held on. She kicked him in the shins. Wincing, he threw one arm across her chest. Jane bent her head and opened her mouth wide. Nan saw the shine of her teeth as they closed around flesh.

With a wordless shout, Walker let go. Jane ran.

"Go to the car! Wait there!" Walker called to Nan. He was too upset to see her distress or notice the vial of pills in her hand. He took off after Jane, a flash of yellow T-shirt that disappeared behind a stone mausoleum.

Nan sank to the ground. She was still clutching the pill. The drenched grass clung to her bare legs and rain soaked her skirt.

"You in trouble?"

Red Suspenders, beside her, was barely audible over the sudden baying of dogs, a racket Nan realized must be inside her own head. "Help is on the way. Just rest, and don't move. That boy of yours. Where'd he get to?"

For a second Nan couldn't think who he was talking about. The imaginary dogs were so loud. "He—he ran after his cat."

He crouched down beside her. He pulled a handkerchief out of his pocket and began to pat her face gently, wiping away the rain. "What's his name, again? You take it easy now. Just rest."

"Zipper."

"No. Your boy."

Odd line of questioning. Then she remembered the grandson—in the swing. Billy. Dead Billy. If only she could lift her hand. Why was the pill so heavy?

"I—" she managed, over the plaintive voices of the dogs. "His name is . . ."

She had forgotten Jane's alias.

Suspenders' face loomed close to hers, suspicion in his eyes. She felt his hand on her shoulder. The hand wore a wristwatch. She could hear it ticking. Drops of water slid off the hand and darkened the denim of her jacket just over her breast. It seemed as if she'd been waiting all her life for this hand—so inescapable, so firm. So heavy, as if freighted with the transgressions of a lifetime.

The pain widened. The dog choir swelled. Nan shut her eyes. *Breathe.* Scent of grass; bitter odor of wet leaves.

"Nan Mulholland?"

Eleven

Cage. Cage of pain. Rib cage.

"I always put out my lawn deer at the first sign a spring."

"I mean, they're the, the hob . . ."

"Harbinger."

"Uh-huh. The hobbinger of spring. Shit! Where'd I put that catheter?"

A shroud of light, like a ship's sail. A square of darkness: glass. Window glass.

"Then, the week after, I put out the chipmunks— Hey! She's comin' around. Get the doc, would you, hon?"

Hands. Smells. Where is this? Hospital. Tod? Tod is dead. Oh—*that* old sorrow, waking and stretching inside. Grasping the bars of the cage.

"There's a God," someone said, and someone else said, "Where?"

Good question.

"Out in the hall. I said, you can just wait out there till we're done, it's too crowded in here."

God in the hall? I'm dying, then?

More hands. Injunctions to open her eyes, which she did.

Of course. This was the Emergency Room. Not the one where they always took Tod. Somewhere else, somewhere back East, Providence, yes, that was it. New England voices. But it might as well have been Seattle. The same canvas enclosure, the same hard light pouring down, the window dark and misted with cold, a cold she could feel, cold as a duck's foot. No—that was the stethoscope, wielded by a twelve-year-old in a white lab coat. The adolescent staff of Emergency Rooms, is that why the vending machines are full of different kinds of potato chips? Plain, sour cream, salsa. Other kinds, too. What are the others? The others! I need to find— Find—

"Mrs. Mullen, you're gonna be okay. Atrial fibrillation. Syncope—uh—you fainted. But in all probability, no heart attack. You're fine."

Fine?

|

Sometime later. Nan knew it was later, because the square of darkness had been replaced by one of luminous pink. Sunrise. A blessed absence of human voices. She could hear the beep of heart monitors, hers and one in the next cubicle, competing. Somewhere beyond the canvas curtain an ice machine produced occasional eruptions. She remembered the sound from all those nights with Tod: a huge steel stomach in distress. There was a smell, sulfur, like rotten eggs. Like Dorothea's hair when she gave herself a permanent. A dark-blue figure sat in one corner of the cubicle. Solid, motherly. *Dorothea sat by my bed, long ago. Am I hallucinating?*

A flurry of excited noise, an unseen gurney wheeled into the cubicle on Nan's other side, bulges in the canvas, someone muttering, "Shit!" and then, more loudly, "Can't nobody tell a patient from a corpse out there? Fuck Admitting! That's twice this week."

On the wall a yellow chart said, PAIN INTENSITY RATING SCALE CONVERSION TOOL. It seemed important to decipher this. *Pain, okay: I understand pain.* (Not so much now, though, she noted, interrogating the region of her diaphragm.) *Intensity rating: in my case,* LOW. *Then the question of what one might convert pain* to—now, that was something she'd been wondering about for years. *Offer it up,* the nuns used to say. Nan had offered up visits to the dentist for the pagan babies in Africa: the hot metallic smell of Dr. Diefenbach's drill, the odor of her own sweat, the pain. *Novocain cost extra.*

The blue figure rose from its corner and went out. There was some hissing and shushing. Then the woman—it *was* a woman, wide, upholstered, with the reassuring solidity of a dressmaker's dummy—returned and sat down. She didn't look in Nan's direction. The waltz of the heart monitors was audible again in the silence, eerily gay.

Mail carrier? Flight attendant? One of the Three Fates? No, of course not: it was a policewoman. Remembering everything—the last picnic, the sudden rainstorm, Red Suspenders—Nan came abruptly into possession of herself, and as quickly thought, Mustn't let them know. She turned her head away from the seated figure.

"Why am I always the one that has to take their rings off them?" the voice from the next cubicle complained. "Shit! This one's fuckin' stuck."

"That's a job for the funeral parlor," another voice said. "Everybody dies. You're *born* to die."

"Takes some getting used to."

Nan laughed out loud. Instantly the blue figure was up and leaning over her. Not grandmotherly at all. The face inches from Nan's had cold doll-like blue eyes.

"Mrs. Mullen?" Her voice was too loud. "I'm Officer O'Farrell. I'm your god."

|

Questions. Waking again, in a different room, a room whose windows were full of shining green leaves, Nan emerged to a world of questions.

Can you understand me, Mrs. Mullen? Are you feeling well enough to follow? Do you have an attorney?

Mornin', Miz Mullen. Can you stick this under your tongue?

Mrs. Mulholland? Captain Abernathy, Providence police. Can you tell us the whereabouts of Jane Elizabeth Verdi?

Mine was completely prefforated. You ever had a prefforated ulcer? Nice to have a roomie again. What're you in for?

Reason being that, folks who don't have a lawyer, the court'll appoint one. You just let me or Officer O'Farrell know, okay? Ma'am?

Afternoon, Miz Mullen. No poop in the pooper? Think you better have an enema?

DOCTOR PING? DOCTOR WALTER PING?

. . . charge of Kidnapping. We can make it hard for you, or we can make it easy. Where is the child?

Gene Riccio, Providence Journal. What a story! If you tell it honestly, which I can already see you wouldn't be able to do any other way. So—it is true you kidnapped your granddaughter?

Those dittoheads at the Public Defender put you on my schedule this morning and nobody let me know. You been arraigned yet? No? All-righty. You understand that I'm your court-appointed counsel?

DOCTOR PING. THIRD PAGE. DOCTOR WALTER PING. WHERE THE HELL IS THE FUCKER? SHIT! IT'S STILL ON?

Hi, Miz Mullen. I'm David? I'll be your nurse tonight?

|

"Mulholland!" Nan shouted at the hapless phlebotomist, who was so astonished that she jerked her needle painfully out of Nan's forearm. "Mulholland! Mulholland!"

|

So—Red Suspenders had turned her in. By the afternoon of her first full day in Methfessel Memorial Hospital Nan was lucid enough to start piecing things together. Officer O'Farrell, the police god (goddess, rather, thought Nan), confirmed it. She brought her folding chair inside the room and sat at the foot of the bed, the way Nan used to do with Tod. Her hands held flashing silver needles attached to a long shapeless yellow something; she knitted and nodded, knitted and nodded. Yes, a charge of Kidnapping had been brought against Nan in Washington State. Yes, the Providence police had been informed of her presence in Rhode Island, which made her a Fugitive from Justice. An anonymous phone call had led them to Swan Point Cemetery. The police had arrived there just ahead of the ambulance; Nan had fainted; they'd found the nitroglycerin on her, assumed a heart attack, and brought her here. Best hospital in Providence County.

One question Officer O'Farrell couldn't answer. Why had Gabriel decided to bring charges against Nan? Why (Nan of course didn't ask her this) hadn't whatever Alex had on him stopped him—as it had, presumably, all these months since December?

More teenagers in lab coats. More blood (Nan looked hastily away) drawn, stethoscopes wielded, bedpans inflicted.

The papal "we"; the royal "we"; the medical "we."

"What would we like today?" Cheerful, motherly, a gray-haired woman in a striped pinafore entered Nan's room without knocking. "*Ladies' Home Journal? Woman's Day?*" Patting her perfect hair, she regarded

Nan's now ragged head; then her eyes moved downward to take in the tattoo visible above the neckline of her hospital Johnny. "Um . . . *Road & Track*?"

"We'd like a pack of Camels," Nan said.

"Oh, we don't have *cigarettes*, Mrs., uh, Mmmm. This is a nonsmoking facility."

"An orgasm, then."

The neat gray head withdrew in alarm.

That afternoon, Nan finally saw a doctor out of his teens. Not the much-maligned Doctor Ping; someone called Milani. Stifling a yawn (tired? bored?), he pronounced her fit to be arraigned. "Not quite in the pink," was how he put it, "but not in the red, either. Heh, heh." She hadn't had a heart attack, after all—only an "incident." In the other bed, behind a drawn curtain, the woman Nan had begun to think of as Roomie coughed—a cough she seemed to have acquired that morning in Radiology. It sounded like "Clio! Clio!" "Need I say, take this as a warning?" Milani said, withdrawing the cold coin of his stethoscope from Nan's cleavage. A magistrate would come to arraign her later, he added. After that, she'd stay in the hospital another day, day and a half, until they'd collected three days' worth of her blood; then she'd be released into the waiting arms of the Law. "Good luck to you," Milani said, and left.

The police came, again, along with the assistant state's attorney for Providence County, a tall, frowning man in a suit too big for him. Captain Abernathy—the same man she'd seen the day before, courtly and calm-eyed, with a luxuriant mustache—introduced everyone, as if they were all at a business meeting. Nan failed to hear any of their names. She was too busy bracing herself against the questions she knew were coming. She felt their evident concern for Jane; there was even a little kindness toward Nan herself. "Mrs. Mulholland, your position is grave," Captain Abernathy said. "I can help you. Just tell us where the child is."

For the fourth time Nan said, quite honestly, that she didn't know. Of course she was not believed.

|

That evening, after dinner, the magistrate arrived. She sailed in, a plump fiftyish woman, in a violet track suit and running shoes, attended by an extremely thin young woman carrying a computer case and the tall, frowning assistant state's attorney in the too-big suit. Captain Abernathy brought up the rear. "Good evening, Mrs. Mulholland," he said. His face, like his voice, was unexpectedly kind. Stroking his mustache, he performed the introductions: Judge Pertl, Miss Carcieri (a court stenographer), and Big Suit, whose name Nan once again didn't catch.

The skinny stenographer sat down in the visitor's chair in the corner and opened her computer and set it on her lap. Big Suit arranged himself against the doorframe. Judge Pertl and Captain Abernathy came and stood on either side of Nan's bed. (Conveniently, her roommate had just been wheeled out, on her way to Urodynamics.) Cranked up into a sitting position, Nan could see, through the leaves outside her window, the sun low in the sky, bleeding rose and saffron into banked purple clouds.

She was asked to give her name, address, date of birth. The stenographer began tapping at her keyboard.

"I understand you've waived the right to counsel," Judge Pertl said. Captain Abernathy looked startled. The judge regarded Nan over the top of her glasses. "Someone from the public defender has been to see you?"

Nan said yes, she'd dismissed a Mr. Dupee, a fat young man wearing someone else's hair. Captain Abernathy opened his mouth to say something, then didn't. The judge gave Nan a we-are-not-amused look, then began to read the charges. *State of Rhode Island . . . Violation of Section 729 of the Penal Code . . . Fugitive from justice . . .* The stenographer typed soundlessly in her corner. The Latinate phrases filled Nan with a sense of displacement, of looking on. As if she were a watcher, peeking in perhaps from the sunset world outside the window, the pleasant prospect to which her eyes (the eyes of the Accused) kept returning. *Court order . . . Gabriel Atkinson Verdi,* MD *. . . State of Washington . . . Kidnapping . . . Bound over for trial . . . Extradition . . .*

There was a pause. Nan looked away from the window to find their collective gaze upon her, waiting, expectant.

The judge said, "Those are your choices."

"My choices?"

"Refuse extradition. Or waive."

"Wave?"

"*Waive.*" Judge Pertl's purple bosom rose and fell in an audible sigh. "That means you agree to be extradited."

The hospital loudspeaker clicked on. "DOCTOR WALTER PING! PLEASE REPORT TO THE O.R.!"

"I'll explain again," Judge Pertl said. "You can waive—that is, accept—extradition. In that case, the State of Washington assumes jurisdiction and you'll be tried there. Alternatively, you have the right to refuse extradition if you so choose. In that case, you're entitled to a hearing."

"A hearing?" Nan said.

The judge heaved another sigh. "To contest your extradition."

"Contest?"

"Ask your attorney! Now, do you waive extradition or not?"

Extradition, okay, that meant going back to Seattle. Gabriel was in Seattle.

Nan pulled a voice from somewhere outside herself, from beyond the IV pole, the three pairs of waiting eyes, the sun-filled window. "I want to stay here," she said.

The judge looked grave. "You refuse extradition? Did you understand the question, Mrs. Mulholland?"

"I don't have to go back to Seattle, if I don't want to?"

"The State of Rhode Island got you first," Judge Pertl said dryly. "Our mayor has a thirst for justice."

Captain Abernathy cleared his throat. The judge frowned at him.

"DOCTOR PING! DOCTOR PING TO THE O.R. STAT!"

"I don't want to be extradited," Nan said. "I don't want to go back to Seattle." Ever, she added silently.

"Another trial that'll be run by the media," Judge Pertl said to Captain Abernathy. "I don't know why they don't just put a reporter on the bench."

She went back to reading from the paper in her hand. The skinny stenographer tapped away. Big Suit, who so far hadn't said a word—Did that, Nan wondered, mean things were going his way?—listened silently, his back against the doorjamb as if he were Velcro'ed to it. Only Captain Abernathy's eyes were on Nan. His face wore an expression of—Could it be?—sympathy.

"This arraignment is concluded," Judge Pertl intoned. "Good evening."

She turned and billowed out the door. Big Suit flattened himself against the doorjamb for her to pass, then followed, still without having uttered a word. The skinny stenographer closed her computer, put it in its case, and left.

Captain Abernathy remained at the side of Nan's bed, stroking his mustache. He looked nervous, Nan thought, though she couldn't imagine why.

"What happens now?" she asked him.

A lot of waiting, apparently. Wait to be released from the hospital. Wait for the police to escort her back to Providence. Wait for her extradition hearing. (Little Red Waitinghood, with a vengeance: Deenie would have been outraged.) Meanwhile, as of this evening, she, Nan Mulholland, Fugitive from Justice, had been handed over (Who giveth this woman?) to the State of Rhode Island.

"Look, Mrs. Mulholland," Captain Abernathy said. "It's none of my business. But you should have representation." He hesitated, stroking his mustache. "I shouldn't be telling you this. But there's a lot of interest in your case. Interest at the highest level. See what I mean? You need a lawyer." Then, as Nan was silent, he sighed. "Good luck," he said. He reached for her hand and shook it.

Sunset light filled the room, striking off the heart monitor and gilding the TV stand and Roomie's IV pole. Even Officer O'Farrell had gone: now that Nan had been arraigned, Captain Abernathy had decided no police guard was necessary. For the first moment since the picnic—was it really only yesterday?—Nan was alone. Soon the little night nurse with the ears that stuck out would come in with night meds, and Roomie would return from Urodynamics; but right now, there was peace. Right now, Nan could think.

She found she didn't want to. Couldn't afford to. Long-forgotten lines from a poem that she and Deenie had loved came back to her:

If the Sun & Moon should doubt
They'd immediately go out

She couldn't afford doubt. Jane was with Walker; Walker was to be trusted; therefore Jane was safe. She couldn't afford doubt, no more than she could afford a lawyer. It wasn't a question of money; it was a question of questions. A lawyer—even a nincompoop like the one from the Public Defender—would want to know where Jane was. Right now, Nan couldn't tell him that, because she didn't know. But eventually, when she *did* know? She couldn't risk it. Couldn't let anyone be in a position to turn Jane over to Gabriel.

No. She would have to go through this—jail, trial, whatever—alone.

A quick, noiseless storm of sobs shook her. She lay there, shuddering, while the spangled light slowly departed. She felt as if someone had dropped her down a well.

What have I done? What in the world have I done?

|

Mama.

The word woke her. A word from a dream? No—real. A real sound. Whispered.

"Mama!"

A hand gripped her shoulder and shook it. Opening her eyes, Nan saw, against the nighttime dimness, a head close to her own. Coarse, thick hair brushed her cheek.

"Alex?" Surely she was dreaming. The sleeping pill they'd given her—

"Shhh!"

In the dark Nan heard the curtain travel on its track around her bed. Then a light snapped on—the tiniest of flashlights. She struggled for consciousness. *My bed; my window; my hospital room.* Her visitor dragged a chair close and sat down. The flashlight turned upward, showing Nan her daughter's face.

Oh, God! She's come for Jane. My daughter wants her daughter, and I don't know where she is.

"Mama—you look awful! What happened to your hair? No—forget about that. Just tell me, how's Jane?"

Nan gazed at her daughter, whose face was still illuminated by the narrow upward beam of the flashlight. Thinner—shadows under the eyes, cheekbones more pronounced. Her brows (dark, straight, Tod's) drawn together; her determined chin, so like Jane's.

I always forget how beautiful she is.

"Mama! *Is Jane okay?*"

Every whispered word felt precious, a talisman. Like listening, in the long dark Bucharest evenings, to Radio Free Europe.

"She's fine." Nan tried not to let her voice waver. *If the Sun & Moon should doubt.*

The flashlight beam darted around the small curtained space, then fastened on Nan. She turned her head away. On the other side of the curtain Roomie coughed in her sleep: *Clio! Clio!*

Alex lowered the flashlight and leaned forward. One hand grasped

Nan's arm below the sleeve of her hospital johnny. "Don't tell me where she is."

Nan wasn't thinking clearly, she knew that, the sleeping pill made everything smoky and vague, but surely—

Alex said, "If I don't know, I can't tell anyone. No matter what they do to me."

"But you— Haven't you come for her? For Jane?"

The narrow beam of light trembled between them. Alex snapped it off. After a pause, she said, "I want you to keep her."

"*Keep* her?"

"I'm no good for her now. I haven't been, for a long time." Her whispered voice faltered. "A long time."

Wake up, Nan told herself. Think. Without the flashlight she couldn't see Alex's face. Did she mean it? In the dark there was only her voice, her smell—the way animals apprehended each other—to go by. Her desperation, her sadness—those were real; but there was something off. Something false.

Clio! Clio! Roomie coughed again.

"Alex. Sweetpea. Jane can't stay with me. I'm going to jail."

"You'll get out on bail. Then you can take her somewhere far away. Somewhere he'll never find her."

"Sweetie, Jane needs you. She misses you."

"She's better off without me."

The sadness in her daughter's voice ran so deep Nan felt as though she herself might drown in it. Nevertheless: "Alex—for God's sake. I *can't.*"

"You have to. There isn't anybody else." *And you owe me,* her tone added.

Obstacles had always strengthened her resolve; pleas had only made her hold tighter. In that, too, she was like Tod. Yet her voice held something else, a wavering-then-hardening, the way she used to sound as a child, a teenager, when she lied.

Alex moved restlessly. Nan smelled the odor of clothes worn too long and unwashed hair and sweat. She reached out and laid her hand lightly on her daughter's blue-jeaned knee. Oh! she thought, I've missed— I want—

"I'm waiting," Alex said.

"How did you find us?"

"I hired a detective. Mama, promise me you'll take Jane away."

Red Suspenders! Hired not by Gabriel, but by Alex? Astonishment cleared Nan's head like a whiff of ammonia. Questions came rushing in. "And Gabriel? How did *he* find us? How did he know Jane was with me?"

Clio! Clio!

She felt Alex fold her arms across her chest. "He had detectives, too. They followed *me*."

"Followed you here?"

"Of course, here. Now listen, Mama! Gabriel is on his way east right now. He'd've been here already, only he had an emergency. He's got a court order. Promise me you'll take Jane. Promise me you'll get her away from here."

"How long have you been here? In Providence?"

A quick, dismissive movement. "A couple of weeks. Mama—"

"But you, where have you, you've been *following* us? Watching us?"

"For God's sake, Mama! I had to see Jane. I had to be sure she was all right. Now, listen. Are you listening? Take her out of the country."

"Out of the country?"

"Mama! Get her away from here. Away from Gabe."

"Where?"

"Wherever you want. As long as Gabe can't get the authorities there to send her back."

"For how long?" Nan heard the stinginess of her own question, but not until it was already out of her mouth, already asked. She felt Alex draw back. Her hand fell away from her daughter's knee into empty air.

Alex rose, a darker blur against the window's blue darkness. "You've never really loved *anybody*, have you, Mother? Daddy was right."

Clio! Clio!

"Kiss her for me. Tell her I—" Alex's voice broke. The canvas curtain rustled. "This time, hide her better." And she was gone.

|

Pop used to say, The first child is for the father; the second is the mother's. Only there'd never been a second. Yes: Tod had loved Alex, and not only because they were so alike. Was it because she did not ask for love that Tod had loved her? Alex, always so judging, so severe, beginning on that long-ago afternoon in Genoa. Alex, whose steady brown eyes ceaselessly communicated the shortfall between what she wanted from

Nan and what she got. Alex had survived. But, Nan asked, gazing into the darkness, at what cost? And to whom?

|

This wedding—what was the hurry? More to the point, whose?

A hundred times in the two months after her first dinner with Gabriel, Nan wondered why Alex—practical, sensible, methodical Alex—wanted to wed in such haste. Of course her daughter stonewalled Nan's delicately tendered questions.

Talk to her, for God's sake, tell her straight up, Deenie advised in their weekly heart-to-heart. Tell her the guy's an adirondack.

A what? Nan said.

An adirondack. You know—high on himself.

But Nan's worries were more complicated. Men like Gabriel didn't make good husbands. He knew that, or he wouldn't have stayed single. Why marry now? There was, of course, Alex's beauty, which none of her previous suitors had seemed up to, or at least, hadn't wanted enough. (But didn't men like Gabriel, if they married at all, usually choose a wren, a mate of lesser plumage?) And there was Alex's self-reliance, her deep reserve, which made her mysterious and hard to win. Oh, the dangers Nan longed to mention. Better not have children, she wanted to say. This man will take all the energy, care, vigilance—all the *wiles*—you can muster; and anyway, children and mystery don't mix. But the weeks went by, and she said nothing. Reasoning: since Alex turned thirteen, Nan's advice had unfailingly been enough to send her in the opposite direction. Reasoning: if Alex told Gabriel that Nan opposed the marriage, it would just make him want her more. Reasoning: when the wedding did go through, battle lines would have been drawn. Nan would have made things harden.

On Alex's wedding day, the fifth day of a mid-August heat wave almost unknown in the Northwest, Nan awoke at dawn to a ringing telephone. Beside her Tod stirred, groaned, then returned to his morphine dreams. She uncoiled the long, cool tube of his oxygen tank, which had somehow wrapped itself around her wrist as she slept, and picked up the phone.

Mama! Can you come? I need to talk to you.

The wedding was at noon. She'd pack her makeup in the bag with her dress and put it on later. That way there would still be time to come back and get Tod, feed him, help him dress, get the wheelchair out to the kneeling van she'd rented for the occasion.

The door to Alex's apartment was slightly ajar, something Nan had repeatedly begged her not to do, not even for five minutes. Nan locked it behind her and followed an uncharacteristic trail of underwear down the little hall to the bathroom. Alex, in hot rollers and a pistachio-colored mud mask, sat on the edge of the bathtub. She looked like a Martian. A beautiful, vulnerable Martian: the thick scarlet towel wrapped like a sarong left her slender arms and shoulders bare.

Nan closed the toilet and sat down on the lid. Her *Hi, Sweetpea!* sounded inane. But what, under the circumstances, *should* she say? Or, for that matter, do? Mother of the Bride: yet another role for which motherless Nan had no model.

Alex looked at her, opened her mouth to speak. Her green-coated face broke in a web of fine cracks like the skin of the very old, and she began to cry. Nan reached out and took both her hands. They squirmed in hers like small, moist, bony fish.

Tod is the one who should be here; Tod is the one she wants. Do what he would do.

So she sat and listened to her daughter's—what? Fear? Apprehension? Simple wedding jitters? Sobs echoed off the porcelain. From the bedroom across the hall an air-conditioner hurled streamers of chill air.

Finally Nan had to speak. What is it, Sweetpea? she said. What's the matter?

Alex stiffened, withdrew her hands. She hiked the scarlet towel higher.

Alex? Honey?

Gulping, no longer sobbing, Alex rubbed the back of her wrist across her nose. Tears had cut vertical channels through the green mud. She did not look at Nan.

Speak? Don't speak? Nan took a deep breath of almond-scented steam. She said, Alex—sweetie—why not wait? You can always get married.

The wedding, at Gabriel's insistence, was to be a city-clerk, immediate-family-only affair. And not Gabriel's family, either. He was an only child, his father long dead, his mother never mentioned. Not hard to call off such a wedding, Nan unwisely pointed out.

Suddenly (Alex's anger had always been sudden) she leaned away from Nan, shouting, That's what you'd like, isn't it? That's what you really want. What you came for! Just because *you* can't hang on to a man—

The towel slipped, revealing one shining breast, one rose-pink nipple. Grabbing at the edge of the towel, furiously trying to yank it up, Alex toppled backward. She fell with a resounding thud into the bathtub. For a shocked instant she was stuck there, glaring at Nan as if she had pushed her. Nan looked down at her green-faced daughter, sprawled across the chipped porcelain, legs waving like an overturned beetle, and out of sheer helplessness she did the one unforgivable thing.

She laughed.

|

That was, Nan realized now, the only other time, besides the December morning nearly six months ago, that her daughter had asked for help. Had let Nan see her need. Two dawn phone calls; in a whole lifetime, only two pleas (okay, demands) for help.

And tonight. Tonight makes the third.

There was hardly any hospital bustle beyond the closed door: it must have been two or three in the morning. But Nan was wide awake. Blood racing, muscles jumping, brain alive with wild, impossible images. Charged with a welter of contradictory emotions—pity, fear, anger, grief. Weirdly, it made her think of the Easter vigils of her girlhood, when she and Deenie, sharer of those vigils, had savored the gritty grown-up feel of sleeplessness. The pranks they'd played, sneaking through the connecting door to the convent at midnight while the nuns and the other girls knelt spartanly, occasionally fainting, in the chapel. Nan could still remember the heavy carved door resisting their combined strength, could still hear the reproachful sound the hinges made as it closed behind them. Even now, anxious and angry as she was, listing those long-ago deeds made her smile to herself in the dark.

- throwing crotchless black lace panties down the nuns' laundry chute
- wedging colored Fizzies tablets in the showerheads
- stretching Saran Wrap across the toilets, underneath the seats, so that when the nuns peed, it would bounce

Preparation for a life of crime? Paving the way—the Slippery Slope, Attila the Nun used to call it—to where Nan was right now?

She's better off without me, Alex had said—the most terrible thing for a mother to say, and the saddest.

For the first time Nan saw, truly saw, the depth of her predicament. Like it or not (and I *don't* like it, she thought, I didn't ask for it), she was now responsible for Jane.

And as if that weren't enough, I don't even know where she is.

Suddenly furious—at Alex, who'd left her no choice; at Walker, whose overconfidence had landed her here—Nan shifted restlessly in the high hard bed, a cross between a pool table and a coffin. Beneath the hospital smells she could detect the smoky animal odor of her own sweat.

God, if only I had a cigarette.

|

"Visitor!" caroled the day nurse at eight the next morning. Nan braced herself, gripped the edge of her breakfast tray. But it wasn't Gabriel who appeared in the doorway.

"Val!" she breathed. "What are you— How did you—"

He was beside her bed in two strides, stooping to give her a bumpy, bumbling hug, to kiss her on each cheek. He laid a bunch of yellow roses across the foot of her bed, then pulled up a chair and sat down, smiling. "The world is narrow."

Roomie was in the bathroom, where she spent an audibly striving half hour each morning after breakfast. Val leaned forward. He took Nan's hand between his two large ones. Warmth communicated itself from his palms to her fingers. She felt it, a shining current, up her arm and through her whole body. Relief—here was someone who knew everything, from whom nothing need be hidden—made her shiver. Val squeezed her hand. He was wet, she saw now. Little gray dimes dotted his jacket sleeve. For the occasion he'd put on a dark suit that gave him a stern but nefarious look. Nan saw herself through his eyes: ragged two-tone hair, unlipsticked lips, limp hospital johnny. This is no time for vanity, she told herself. It seemed light-years since there *had* been a time; and when, if ever, would it come again?

"Is it raining?" she said.

"Nan. What I can do? You are fine? I think not."

"I'm all right. Truly. But Jane—"

Val leaned closer. His breath misted her ear, and she smelled gasoline and Juicy Fruit and the doggy odor of wet wool. He whispered, "Walker is sending this message: We are gold."

"Walker!" Nan exclaimed, and Val, looking over his shoulder, murmured, "Shhh! *Tishina!*"

Walker. Apples and pencil shavings.

"You've seen him? And Jane? You've seen Jane? Is she all right? That cough—"

"*Nyet, nyet.* He has telephoned. First Mel is speaking to him, then I. He does not tell where he is. He asks where you are, if you are unwell, if you have need. He telegraphs money. What to hell! Mel calls every hospital. So here I come."

"But you *will* see them?"

Val shook his head. "Walker is saying, too dangerous. Also, yesterday police come to our flat. They ask questions about you, about Jane. Does she stay with you of her own free will."

How good Val was! She remembered that Khrushchev used to say communism merely put into practice the teachings of the New Testament. If only Val had seen Jane. If only she could know how she looked, how she sounded. Whether she missed Nan.

In the bathroom Roomie groaned, then sighed. Val pulled a pack of Camels out of his jacket pocket and lit one, then held it out to Nan. "Treat yourself!" She shook her head, then thought, How could I be in worse trouble than I am already?

The first drag was heaven, a chorus of seraphim. Nan felt as if she might levitate. She let the smoke issue slowly from her nostrils, watched it ascend toward the ceiling. Val opened the window, then lit a cigarette for himself. Rain-wet air filled the room.

After a minute, he said, "I have also potato chips. You would like?" Nan shook her head. "Probably, police follow me here. Walker says, Best not to know where he exists, or Jane. But he wants that you hear, he has plan."

A plan. Of course Walker would have a plan.

"First of all, he is sending to you *advokat*, a lawyer—"

"No! It's too dangerous."

"A lawyer," Val repeated firmly. "I am finding one, the best. Walker says, you must have."

"But—"

There was a loud commotion beyond the closed door. *Gabriel,* Nan thought; and something inside her descended steeply.

The door opened. Captain Abernathy entered, followed by the little blond nurse, looking frightened, and a square-faced, black-browed policewoman who immediately scowled at Nan. Absurdly, her first reaction was panic at being caught smoking. She stuck her cigarette into the remains of her breakfast cereal. Val pinched the end of his between two fingers and tucked it, without hurrying, into his breast pocket. In the bathroom the toilet flushed.

Courtly Captain Abernathy said, "Good morning, Mrs. Mulholland." His calm gray eyes flicked across Val, who stood by the open window in his up-from-the-underworld suit. "This is Officer Grace Blank. Rhode Island State Police." The woman nodded, still scowling.

The jug-eared nurse stuck her head in the door. Unfazed by the assortment of people in the room, she chirped, "Have we moved our bowels today, Miz Mullen?"

"Yes," Nan lied.

"Excellent! Then we won't be needing a suppository." She withdrew.

"I'll say good-bye now," Nan said to Val in a calm voice. "I'm going to jail this morning. These good people are here to escort me."

Ignoring the two policemen, Val kissed Nan on each cheek. "In Russia we say, Beware to divide skin of bear not yet killed."

"Give my love to Mel," Nan said.

No time for more. In the doorway—by now the policewoman had him by the arm—Val stopped. The policewoman wouldn't let him turn around. Sequins of rain gleamed in his dark curly hair. He raised one hand in a quick thumbs-up; then the door shut behind him.

Almost immediately it opened again. "Small, medium, or large?" the jug-eared nurse asked.

"I didn't look," Nan said. "I just flushed."

Captain Abernathy said, "Officer Blank will help you dress. Then she'll escort you to the station."

"You'll go with us?" Nan said. Please, she thought. Don't leave me alone with *her*.

He shook his head. "I've got other business. I just came by to make sure everything was in order." He held out a hand, and Nan shook it. He left.

Roomie, emerging from the bathroom accompanied by a faint smell of shit, gave a little gasp on seeing the policewoman. Her disappointment at being asked to leave the room made Nan smile, a smile that

Officer Blank, mistaking it for insouciance, repaid with chilly hauteur. Coldly she watched the little blond nurse unhook Nan's IV and take the port out of the back of her hand, then help her stand.

One good thing. This speedy departure would save her from Gabriel.

She realized, as the little nurse untied her johnny and help her slip it off, that she still didn't know why Gabriel had come after her now, when almost six months had passed. She stood naked under the cold gaze of Officer Blank while the nurse popped her heart monitor wires from the snaps stuck to her chest. What had made Gabe file charges now? She hadn't thought, last night, to ask Alex.

Officer Blank's eyes flicked over the tattoo. "Happiness," Nan murmured defiantly; and saw Mel leaning forward, holding the coffee mug that said, WHY AM I THE ONLY ONE AWAKE AROUND HERE?, her chapped lips kissing the edge of the mug. Mel, closer now than Nan's own daughter; Nan's life in Providence more real now than the lost life in Seattle.

The little blond nurse held out Nan's underpants. Stepping creakily—how out of shape three days of enforced sloth had made her!—into them, Nan felt their now-strange civilian texture, smelled their now-unfamiliar smell, which was her own. The nurse fastened her bra, then helped her pull her cotton sundress—chosen, it now seemed, years ago—over her head. She eased Nan's arms into the sleeves of her denim jacket and straightened the collar. She held out Nan's glasses and, when she made no move to take them, stepped up close and put them on her, hooking them gently around her ears. Officer Blank produced a heavy chain wrapped in orange plastic, from which dangled a padlock and two handcuffs. The nurse backed away. Officer Blank clasped a cuff around each of Nan's wrists, pulled the chain around her waist, snapped the padlock shut. Nan's hands were pinned to her sides.

Nevertheless, on the way out she managed to snag Val's yellow roses. She thrust them into the arms of Roomie, who stood outside the door in her bathrobe, coughing.

|

The hospital lobby held the festive smell of popcorn and the sound of a hundred strings playing "Don't Cry for Me, Argentina." A big red-white-and-blue banner said MEMORIAL DAY FESTIVAL FUNDRAISER. Officer Blank unhooked a velvet rope, then refastened it behind them and towed Nan into the crowd. A clown with a bouquet of helium balloons accosted them, then stopped short when he caught sight of Nan's chains. Officer Blank hustled Nan along, pretending not to see her stumble, brushing children briskly out of the way. BITCHCRAFT STUDIOS, proclaimed a display case in the center of the lobby. Eddying around it with the other festival-goers (BIRCHCRAFT—too bad), Nan felt oddly light. No responsibility; nothing to carry; no one whose hand she needed to hold. With each step toward the revolving doors and the waiting police van, her relief increased. Illogical, but she felt as if she were leading her pursuers away from Jane. The farther she went, the less danger Jane was in. Up ahead, someone let go half a dozen white balloons. Ribbons trailing, they rose purposefully to the high peaked glass roof, like so many sperm. (Deenie's joke: Why does it take a million sperm to fertilize one egg? Because they won't stop to ask directions.)

"Nan!"

A shout, audible over the sound track from *Evita,* over the feet and voices of the crowd. Nan stopped so suddenly that Officer Blank was jerked to a standstill.

"Nan! Wait!"

Even before she turned around, she knew.

At the bend in the corridor, behind the velvet rope, stood Gabriel.

The whole length of the hospital lobby seemed to darken, all the light withdrawing upward into its high angled glass roof. Its sounds dimmed too, an outgoing tide of voices and violins and metal on metal. What was left was Gabriel, silent, in a glove of light. The set of his body: that violent humility. Too far to see his eyes, yet she felt them meet hers. She raised a hand to shield herself, but it was jerked painfully back, the steel cuff biting into her wrist.

Gabriel knocked down the velvet rope, posts and all, and thrust himself into the crowd. A woman in a green security guard's uniform caught him by the arm. Violently, he shook her off. She hit the wall and slid down it. "Stop! Stop her!" Nan could hear Gabriel shouting. Then his voice was drowned in other voices, a whistle piercing the air, a woman screaming. Gabriel dodged another guard, a big black man, feinted to the left, and began shoving his way through the crowd, toward Nan.

Officer Blank by this time was half dragging, half pushing her charge toward the revolving door, about twenty yards ahead. Outside it Nan could see the police van with its doors open, a man in uniform standing beside it. Officer Blank wasted no time on who Gabriel was, or why he was chasing them. "One side, please! One side!" she cried, breasting the crowd.

"Nan!"

Fury and—what was it? She could almost recognize it, that deeper note. Feet moving forward, head turned back (Lot's wife), Nan saw Gabriel gaining on them. Figures in uniform converged at a run behind him.

"Stop! Stop her!"

Anguish—that was it. That was what she heard.

Then Gabriel went down, slammed to the floor by two men in green uniforms. Nan felt the impact in her own body. The steel links across her belly clanked. Then they were at the revolving door, Officer Blank's arm a yoke across the back of her neck, Officer Blank's hand digging into her clavicle, the heavy glass panel sweeping them forward.

Twelve

The Providence police station—dark, with the scuffed linoleum floors and cinder-block walls of Nan's South Philly grade school—smelled of sweat and exhaustion. The walls of the elevator were covered with graffiti. AMANDA IS COOL! Nan read. JESUS WON'T FUCK ME. (An ongoing refusal, or just an impossibility?) They emerged, she and Officer Blank, into a long hallway redolent of gym shoes. Officer Blank pushed open a frosted glass door. Inside, it was terribly hot. All over the large room, desk fans whirred.

Nan was so tired she could barely stand. She refused to let Officer Blank see this. Trembling, she held on to the counter, trying not to let the chain clank at her wrists. They waited for the woman behind the desk to finish her phone call. Heavy eyes, yellow hair that stood up in slept-on shocks: Bed Head, Mel would have called her. A blue policeman's hat sat on top of the in-box by her elbow. "When you're depriving a dying person," she said into the phone. "That's outrageous. That's *hard.*"

Behind a partition someone was whistling. Nan knew the tune but couldn't remember the words. Willing her eyes not to close, she gazed at a map of the city that covered the back wall. "Downtown Larcenies," the caption read. The map was stuck with little red pins, like the chart of some World War II campaign. To distract herself Nan counted crimes on Elbow Street.

Bed Head said into the phone, "Now lemme get this clear . . . So, sometime Wednesday night . . . disturbances, okay, all right . . ." She looked up at Officer Blank and made a one-more-minute face. Behind the partition the whistling stopped. Two young policemen came in, in shorts that disclosed bare burnished knees. They studied a schedule posted on the wall next to Nan. "Sunday night," one said, "who they gotcha doubled up with?"

Just when Nan thought she would have to give in and ask to sit down, or faint, Bed Head hung up. "This the hospital transfer?" she asked Officer Blank.

"Yeah. The Fugitive."

"Lawyer's waitin' for her inside. Down-city type."

Nan opened her mouth to say, No. No lawyer. But two hours in the company of Officer Blank—two hours in handcuffs—had weakened her. Had made her wonder if she really could manage this alone.

Officer Blank's teeth made a clicking noise. Glancing sideways, Nan could see she was put out. Good, she thought; and the urge to faint disappeared.

"I s'pose they want bail," Officer Blank said in a tone of disgust. "Who's on?"

"Hold-'Em-Tight Wright."

"Giddout! This I wanna see. *He* don't turn little old *ladies* loose."

Bed Head raised her eyebrows and glanced in Nan's direction, as if to say, That *is* a little old lady. Fury erased Nan's tiredness. She straightened up, clanking, and tugged her jacket down over her hips. Her arms didn't reach high enough to smooth her hair.

Behind her someone said, "Urgent! Comin' through!" Officer Blank yanked her aside. A woman accompanied by a pretty black policewoman stood at the counter next to Nan. The woman had dark-red welts and bruises all over her cheek and neck.

"Go on in," Bed Head said to Officer Blank. She produced a sheet of paper with the outline of a female figure and began recording the woman's injuries as she recited them in a dead voice.

"You goin' to the deli?" one of the young policemen in shorts asked the other. "Get me a coffee milk, wouldya?"

"Get me an orange slush!" a voice called out from behind the partition. "It's ninety fuckin' degrees in here!"

The unseen whistler resumed, a different tune, an old song whose words Nan knew.

Once you told me I was mistaken,
That I'd awaken
With the sun

And order orange juice for one . . .
It never entered my mind

Back in the corridor, long and dim, feeling as if she were being taken to the principal's office, Nan clanked along at Officer Blank's brisk pace. She had the suspicion, from glances shot at her belly by passing policepersons, that she should by now have been unshackled, that all this hardware was required only on the outside. They stopped at a vending machine. Officer Blank shoved in some coins and a can of Coke thudded into the trough. She popped it open, took a long, shuddering swig. Thirstily Nan watched her throat pulse above her uniform collar. They continued, Nan Cokeless, down the corridor.

At the end they came to a door painted a scrofulous military gray and marked WOMEN'S DETENTION. As they approached, a face appeared in the little head-height window: pale, with lightless eyes and sagging cheeks. *Poor woman.* Then, with a lurch of recognition, Nan saw that the face was her own. The window was a mirror.

Officer Blank pressed a button on the jamb.

|

Jenny Root—that was the lawyer's improbable name. Val had hired her, she said. With money from Walker, Nan assumed. (*My* money, really. Thank you, Deenie!) Tiny, stick-thin, *young*. A twit, the Last Lover would have called her. She had Nan's hair, or what would have been Nan's hair if Nan had been able to make it to a hairdresser. A crisp, upstanding thicket, only Jenny Root's wasn't teal blue, but black. It looked strange above her stiff, dark business suit. A twit in armor.

Having a lawyer was part of Walker's plan. She would go with Walker's plan.

She sank into the chair indicated by a wave of Jenny Root's pin-striped arm. At least she didn't have to do this alone. She did not let herself think of freedom, of the fragrant summer air outside, of Nibbrig's leafy loft, now so desirable. A hospital room, a cell—what was the difference? You can manage, she told herself.

"Get those things off her! You wanna be sued? Want that on your record?" The Twit had an unexpectedly deep voice, the sound of a bassoon in the body of a clarinet.

Sullenly, Officer Blank unlocked Nan's bellyband and cuffs. Her bent head, under Nan's chin, smelled like steamed asparagus. Nan failed to repress a shudder.

"Thank you. Now I'd like a word with my client. Alone."

Officer Blank left. Nan regarded her lawyer with the beginnings of interest. A twit with clout.

"Okay, we don't have much time, so let's— How're you feeling?" Standing on the other side of the scarred wooden table, Jenny Twit seemed to dance in place, waiting for Nan's answer. Nan could see her instructing herself: Remember to show concern for the client.

"I'm all right," Nan said. "Thanks for getting me unchained."

"*Nada.*" Jenny Twit didn't sit down; Nan had to crane her neck to look up at her. "We've got a special hearing even though it's Saturday night, because of your health. Precarious, jeopardy, yadda yadda yadda. The judge'll be here in ten, so we gotta cover ground. You don't keep Overbite Wright waiting. Smoke?"

The pack of Newport Lights that came skidding across the table glittered in the harsh overhead lights. Nan's fingers trembled as she took one. Jenny Twit's match, igniting Nan's cigarette, seemed to go off in Nan's brain.

"Thank you," she breathed out, in a heady cloud of mentholated smoke.

But her lawyer was already moving on. She glanced around the room, then threw the spent match onto the floor. Nan's heart—here was a fellow rule-breaker!—tugged upward. Jenny Root sat down and opened her briefcase and pulled out a yellow legal pad and a pencil. She spoke faster than anyone Nan had ever heard; her nasal, pursed-lips Rhode Island accent took all Nan's nicotine-enhanced concentration to decipher. They would get bail, tonight. "Your pal Val gave me ten grand up front, good friends you got!— This judge is a mean SOB— Lemme do the talking, don't answer unless he asks you directly—" Jenny Root's pencil moved rapidly across her pad as she spoke. "Legally he can't bully you about your granddaughter's whereabouts, not at a bail hearing, but he may try anyway, if he does let me take care of it— Unpredictable fucker, we'll hafta play it by yeah— What? By yeah"—tugging at one pierced lobe—"you know, go with the flow."

Setting down her pencil, she reached across the table and grasped Nan's hand in her small, sweaty one. "Before we start, you gotta level with me. I mean totally. First off, why did you take your granddaughter?"

She'd never told Val and Mel exactly why she was on the lam, so they hadn't been able to tell Jenny Root. "My daughter asked me to," Nan said. She paused, looking down at their joined hands resting on the scarred table.

"Why?" Jenny Root squeezed Nan's hand, then released it.

Nan kept her eyes on the tabletop. Someone had carved into it a crude circle enclosing the words BANG HEAD HERE. She ran both hands through her hair, rubbed her neck. Her wrists hurt where the handcuffs had rubbed them.

"Why?" Jenny Root repeated.

"He was— My daughter thought, she was sure, her father was abusing her."

"Sexually?"

"Yes."

"Okay. Don't mention that when we're in there with Wright. Let me do the talking. Now, the second thing." Her eyes held Nan's. "Do you know where your granddaughter is?"

"No," Nan said.

Jenny Root looked at her.

"I know who she's with," Nan admitted. "But I don't know where they are. Truly I don't."

Another, longer look. "But you could find out."

Here it was. On this, Nan could not bend. No matter what Walker's plan was. "But I won't," she said.

Jenny Root looked at her. She opened her mouth to speak, then thought better of it. Frowning, she made another note on her pad, closed it, and put it back in her briefcase. She began rummaging around in its depths. The artificial quiet of the little room attacked like an undertow, threatening to sweep away Nan's nicotine high. Nervously she rubbed her aching wrists. "Ms. Root. I have a question of my own. Why did my son-in-law bring charges now?"

"As opposed to when?" Jenny Root was pulling small objects out of her briefcase, one after another, little plastic cases.

"Anytime in the last six months. That's how long Jane and I've been living here, in Providence."

"No idea."

Jenny Root stood up and walked around the table and set a handful of cosmetics in front of Nan. She spat into her palm, then rubbed it vigorously over Nan's hair. Nan was too surprised to protest. Still talking, Jenny Root snapped open the cosmetics cases and lined them up on the table. "This Wright's got a heart of anthracite." She dipped a finger into a pot of blue eyeshadow, ran it under Nan's eyes. "But, hey—you croak in jail awaiting trial, he's responsible, there goes his bid for appellate court judge, right down the toilet." Brownish blush went into the hollows above Nan's eyes and under her cheekbones; beige lipstick coated her lips. "That's better; pallor, you need pallor—" She stepped back to view the effect, then moved in close to run a powder puff over Nan's cheeks. "Precarious, yeah, okay, we're saying the doctors warned you in Seattle, he won't have time to check Seattle—What medical condition? Angina? Okay, sounds good, okay, immediate jeopardy, cumulative damage, yadda yadda yadda—"

Nan found herself rising, moving (*being* moved, really, by Jenny Root, by a sort of magnetism, apparently, since they weren't touching) toward the door. Knuckles poised to knock, the younger woman stopped. Gently she removed the cigarette from Nan's fingers. She dropped it onto the floor and ground it under one shiny black high-heeled shoe.

"Suck in your cheeks! Slump!" (Nan did not find this hard.) "Totter!"

Jenny Root put an arm across her shoulders, a quick bracing embrace. Nan's neck hurt, her wrists ached, she did not feel in the least hopeful. Jenny Root knocked on their side of the door. "Ready!"

|

When Alex was seven (in Bucharest, where Tod had disappointingly been posted), she'd had a pet mynah bird. One morning the Rumanian peasant girl who cleaned the apartment had left the cage door open. It must have been open the whole day. But Nan and Tod came home from a reception at the embassy to find the bird a blue-black ball still hunched on the topmost perch just under the cage's bamboo roof. One eye was cocked doubtfully down at the open door, with its terrifying invitation.

A Fugitive and a Kidnapper, but out on bail nevertheless, Nan Mulholland hesitated on the steps outside the police station. A warm fish-scented breeze, coming in off the ocean, touched her face. Seagulls circling overhead complained. She began listing the enclosures she'd passed through in the last week, barely emerging into the outside air between one and the next: Deenie's place, ambulance, hospital, police van, jail. Tears of self-pity invaded her view of an unnamed brick building, a narrow alley. She looked down the street, but Val's taxi was nowhere to be seen. She pushed her jacket sleeves up above her elbows and sat down on the steps to wait.

The deepening twilight carried the smells of summer: earth, rain, tree bark. They mingled with the city smells of cinders and car exhaust. Nan felt in her pocket for the pack of cigarettes Jenny Root had put there when they parted. She'd been late for a deposition—on a Saturday night, what a girl!—and had phoned Val to come and get Nan, after setting up a "serious meet" for Monday morning. Nan didn't have to talk to the police, no grilling about where Jane was, Jenny Root had taken care of that. *You're free now, you're exhausted, go home and crash, don't talk to anybody!*

There were matches tucked into the cellophane, thank you, Jenny Root, Jenny Twit no longer. Nan still wasn't sure how she'd done it, but somehow tiny Jenny had persuaded Judge Wright—who did indeed have an overbite, weighed a good two hundred and fifty pounds, and was black—to let Nan go. The word *precarious* had figured prominently in her plea, delivered with majestic slowness in her surprisingly deep voice. The judge, also known as All-Night Wright, had responded with a sonorous series of aphorisms. The only one Nan could remember went, *Some circumstantial evidence is very strong, such as when you find a mouse turd in your beer.* The charge of kidnapping, set forth in the Washington State warrant, was noted. The fact that Nan had waived extradition was noted. Bail was set at five thousand dollars—Jenny Root having made the point that her client, barely ambulatory, was unlikely to flee—and Nan was free.

Free.

She lit a cigarette. She sucked in, felt her rib cage widen, her heart tilt. Exhaling, she watched blue smoke spiral up into the bluer dusk. Somewhere she'd read that people who went blind usually stopped smoking, because so much of the pleasure in it was visual. Free. She'd known—everyone knew—intellectually, that freedom is frightening. Hadn't the existentialists made that clear, while muddying everything else? (Nan hadn't come of age in the fifties for nothing.) The hospital, she saw now, had felt safe. No possibilities; no choices. Had she come to rely on those constraints? To crave that safety?

What would have become of her after a few nights in jail?

Feeling suddenly much too warm, Nan stretched out her legs, lifting her face to the humid evening. City grit traveled on the light breeze, and she had to rub her eyes. When she opened them, Val's taxi was at the curb. Mel got out and crossed the sidewalk, running. Her arms were around Nan before she could rise.

|

Alone for the first time in days, Nan stood on the threshold of Nibbrig's loft. *Her* loft, was how she thought of it now. She didn't have keys to Deenie's place, but it didn't matter. She wanted to be here, in the place where she'd made a home for herself and Jane. Even the bare hallway of Elbow Street, when she'd entered it on Mel's arm, had felt welcoming. The rubbery smell of rats, the odor of other people's boiled vegetables, embraced her.

The celebration painstakingly planned by Mel had fallen flat. It was just the two of them—Val had had to work—and Nan was too tired to eat. Neither of them had much heart for the fortune cookies, or the vod-ka with a spear of buffalo grass floating upright inside, or even the mari-juana. Mel missed Jane, it was clear. She kept getting up and grabbing Zipper, who kept escaping (he was in hiding from a resentful, vengeful Clio). She showed Nan a Barbie costume she'd made—velvet and crino-line and peacock-blue taffeta glue-gunned into a gown vaguely reminis-cent of Queen Elizabeth I—and some pop-up books featuring a hippo-potamus with one gold tooth. After the joint, Mel thumbed through the books over and over, no longer speaking.

Now, as Nan moved forward, the heavy metal door closed behind her. Its firm, decisive sound was reassuring—not shutting Nan in, but shut-ting the rest of the world out. Jenny Root had raised the possibility of hiding Nan somewhere, to save her for a little while from the Press. Nan had refused. Everything in her had said, No. Had said, Home. Meaning this place.

The sound of seagulls, like the crying of terse babies. The argyle pat-tern of moonlight pouring through the No-Theft grille onto the wide wood floor. The smells of cinnamon and burned toast. Nan walked into the middle of the room and stood in the freckled shadows cast by the ar-bor of Nibbrig's trees and plants. She remembered, vividly, the first few nights she and Jane had spent here, back (so far back, it seemed now) in December: those Sparrow Nights. Across the wide expanse of floor, Jane's orange-and-yellow screen still stood, concealing all but a corner of her bed. For a moment Nan thought she heard Jane breathing. The sound was so real that she found herself moving across the loft on tiptoe. Slowly, she edged around the screen.

Moonlight striped Jane's bed, the army blanket neatly tucked in around the edges, just as Nan had left it when they'd moved in with Walker. The small space was nearly bare. Most of Jane's things had accompanied them to Walker's, then gone into the suitcases stowed in his trunk while they had their ill-starred final picnic. Jane's dresser top held only a couple of Barbie dolls—the lesser favorites—and a secondhand copy of *Treasure Island,* spurned because it didn't have enough illustrations ("I can't *hear* without pictures," Jane had whined when Nan read it to her. "The words don't *go.*")

Nan picked up Miami Getaway Barbie and straightened her pale stork legs. Suddenly trembling, she sat down on Jane's bed. Her hands, of their own accord, moved across the blanket, smoothing a patch of moonlight over and over. Pop used to say, You don't know how heavy a burden you're carrying until you put it down. And wasn't it (Be honest!) a relief to be alone, after the months of cajoling and disciplining and worrying, of brush-your-teeth-did-you-change-your-underpants-where's-your-jacket? A relief to be just Nan? To sit in the moonlight, hearing only the distant hum of the freeway, feeling the rough woolen army blanket like a penitent's hair shirt under her palms? But beneath the relief was longing. Nan ached to feel Jane's warm weight in her arms, on her lap, anchoring her. Looking down, she found she was clutching Miami Getaway Barbie so hard that its fierce little fingers bit into her palm. All the things she felt glad to be relieved of were also, in the slowly withdrawing moonlight, the things she deeply missed.

|

The next day, Sunday, was the seventh of June. Without really expecting any message from Alex—their whole scheme seemed now to belong to another life—Nan found herself once again at the Rock. It was empty now of undergraduates, hot summer sunlight falling through long windows onto Nan's bent head. Scrolling through the *Pee-Eye's* Personals, she felt her heart jerk.

POOKIE: Working on A plan, Love and Kisses, Everything all Right, stay tuned. **HIPPIE**

Surprise followed by relief followed by surprise. Such optimism was wholly unlike Alex—not to mention the love and kisses. Baffled, Nan leaned back in her chair and stared at the blue-lit screen. This message would have been composed before Alex's late-night visit to Methfessel Memorial, but after she'd come to Providence. Had she been so sure Nan would agree to take Jane away?

Then, farther down the same column, something else caught Nan's eye.

POOKIE: Safe for now. Hope you are too. Trust in God. Who else?
HIPPIE

Now Nan was even more puzzled. Why would Alex send two messages? Was the second intended to cancel the first? She copied both messages onto a piece of paper begged from Ben Kingsley.

Outside the library she found a dew-dappled bench shaded by locust trees and, throwing her unneeded sweater over the damp wood, sat down and lit a cigarette. Smoke unfurled into the sweet morning air. She smoothed out the piece of paper in her hand and read the two messages, first in order, then reversed. Something tugged at a corner of her mind. Something she couldn't quite see; something about the way the two messages had looked on the page.

Flinging her half-smoked cigarette into the wet grass, not stopping to pick up her sweater, Nan ran back up the cement ramp into the Rock. Into the Reference Room, log on, call up the *Pee-Eye*, yes, there it was. *Working on A plan, Love and Kisses, Everything all Right, stay tuned.* The "Love and Kisses" coming in the middle of the message; the odd capitalization. Having begged another piece of paper from Ben Kingsley, and a pencil as well (hers was in the pocket of her sweater), Nan copied down the words in the first message that began with capital letters. *Working, A, Love, Kisses, Everything, Right.* W, A, L, K, E, R.

The first message wasn't from Alex; it was from Walker.

Joy filled her, a ravishing lightness, the sense of her buttocks leaving the chair, the fear that she might bump her head on the high beamed ceiling of the Reference Room. Walker. Scornful as he'd been of Alex's message system, he'd remembered it, right down to the childhood nicknames. Resourceful man! Forgiving him, completely, for everything—for his deception about Deenie's will (wasn't that just the flip side of his planfulness?), for the ill-conceived Last Picnic (wasn't that the flip side of his optimism?)—Nan walked slowly out of the library and back under the locust trees to retrieve her sweater. It was the same bench, she realized, where she'd sat six months ago, despairing, after searching fruitlessly for a first message from Alex. How alone she'd felt, back then. She remembered the January thaw, the trees dripping onto the back of her neck, the false scent of spring. Now, too restless to sit still, she tied her sweater around her waist and set off down College Hill toward the river. She would walk home. She could walk, she felt now, all the way to Genoa.

The day shone clean as silk. Unseen birds in the trees along Angell Street sent spirals of sound—tuneful, hopeful—into the clear air. In the distance the river gleamed. Oh, day—thought Nan—oh, beautiful day.

At the bottom of the hill she hesitated, then turned right onto Benefit Street. Deenie's door; Walker's door. She went up the steps, expecting against all reason that, as it had that first time, the door would open. Of course, it didn't. Nan had no key—she and Walker had never gotten around to exchanging keys. She stood with one hand on the lion's head knocker, feeling the hot metal, the sun warm on the top of her head. Small birds scuffled in the laurel bushes beside the steps. She wondered, briefly, about Deenie's parakeets; but Walker—provident Walker—would have made some provision for them. As he was doing at this very moment for her, Nan.

A Damsel in Distress, for sure. *D in D* indeed. How Deenie would have scoffed!

Nan turned and began to walk back along Benefit Street to Angell and the river. Alex's actual message—the second of the two messages—surfaced in her mind. "Safe for now. Hope you are too. Trust in God. Who else?" A black cat streaked across the brick pavement in front of her and she remembered how Alex, when she was little, used to say that cats had too many legs when they ran. Alex was as much a feminist as Deenie, and then some; yet hadn't her life with Gabriel been as full of Little Red Waitinghood as lives come? Perhaps it had caused her pain, the discrepancy between what she believed and how she lived; Nan didn't know, because she'd never asked. *Trust in God.* She had no idea what that meant. As far as she knew, Alex was an atheist, as Tod had been—certainly, since the age of sixteen, a resolutely lapsed Catholic. Did her message mean that she'd given up, or that she'd reached some sort of larger understanding?

I don't really know Alex at all.

Nan paused at the apex of the arched footbridge across the river—the same bridge, completed now, where she and Walker had first kissed. Squinting sideways, she could almost see his pelican profile, feel his hip bump hers, hear him whistling.

If there's anything that you want
If there's anything I can do

He would not phone, she knew. He would think it was too dangerous. Ditto, phoning Val again. (Oh, she felt inside Walker's head now—that close to him. When had this happened? Why hadn't she noticed it before now?) He would keep to Alex's message schedule, would remember it though Nan had mentioned it only once, just as he'd remembered about Pookie and Hippie. Yes—he'd keep to Alex's schedule, the seventh and twenty-first of each month, knowing that Nan would check the *Pee-Eye*.

She leaned on the wall and looked down into the water, green like old glass, but moving. She could smell the sea. Midday strollers—lovers, children, old women in wavering pairs—passed back and forth across the bridge. The murmurous, gleaming water, the still air, the sky polished to a deep summer blue—these were what she had right now. She took the comfort they offered and went home.

|

Advice and warnings.

The next morning Nan made her way to the Blackstone Boulevard office of Jenny Root. At first glance the calligraphic sign on the bright green lawn seemed to read MCCLOSKEY, GERONIMO & TOILET. If Jenny Root was, as Val claimed, the Providence Russian underworld's attorney of choice, why didn't her name appear in gilded curls alongside those of McCloskey, Giannino, and Follett? But inside, there was no time for questions; only answers. Only advice and warnings.

Dressed in black leather, Jenny Root brought the cold in with her. The weather had turned in the night, and rain glazed the arched windows of the reception area. Chilled, Nan felt her nipples tighten inside her summer shirt, under her poncho. Jenny led her into a conference room whose walls and ceiling were decorated with intricate pastel moldings, like a wedding cake. She took off her motorcycle helmet and ran a hand over her cropped hair. Her leather jacket smelled of animal; amplified by the rain, it made Nan think of lambing time, in spring, in Rumania. She put her helmet upside down on the shining mahogany conference table, where it sat like a soup tureen.

They took their places at one end of the long table. The chairs were too big; Nan skidded from side to side on the leather seat, feeling like a little girl. The room's reverent silence was threaded with business sounds (ringing phone, fluting female voices) from beyond the paneled door. It reminded Nan of the undertaker's office, when she'd buried Tod. What was his name, something so silly she'd had to fight the urge to giggle.

Jenny Root, suited up for court ("Got a trial at ten, so let's not dick around"), was very angry. In her fury, she talked even faster than she had on Saturday night at the police station. Nan didn't interrupt with questions, just gleaned what she could. Tod's dead face kept interposing itself between her and Jenny Root, the closed eyes large and oval in their sockets, like eggs. Apparently Nan had committed crimes in both Washington and Rhode Island, but not the *same* crimes. In Washington, it was Kidnapping; in Rhode Island, Fugitive from Justice. But pressure had been brought to bear. Gabriel had influence that extended all the way across the country. Rhode Island—anxious to show that when it came to crime its heart, if not its mayor, was in the right place—had adopted the Washington State charge of Kidnapping as its own.

Jenny Root slapped the table. "Goddammit! Who *is* he, this son-in-law of yours? This *never* happens. You're just supposed to be detained here until the extradition hearing. Then, ninety-nine times out of a hundred, they ship you back to the other state."

Nan must have looked as terrified by that idea as she felt, because Jenny Root paused. She ran a hand over her short, thick hair and signed. "Okay, we got a coupla problems, we can smother 'em in the bud, let's dope out our strategy."

Our?

"Problem Number One. There's gonna be a feeding frenzy in the media. You been contacted yet? Humph. Maybe they don't know where you are, but they'll find out. A missing kid, everybody's heart bleeds. Don't talk to the press. No newspapers, no magazines, no TV. *Nada.* Got it?"

Maybe Nan looked skeptical, because Jenny Root leaned forward and said, slowly for her, "Yeah, okay, I'm young. But I'm good. First in my class at Tufts, Law Review, superior court clerkship, yadda yadda yadda. Okay?" She waited for Nan's nod. While she was speaking, her fury had shifted into a kind of joyful ferocity—because, Nan guessed, she now had an *interesting* case to deal with. She went on, "Okay. Now, we got lucky with Wright. Next time we might not be. So, Problem Number Two. The state's attorney may try to grill you. They're supposed to leave you alone once you have a lawyer, but a lot of times they don't. You've got the right to walk away. Just blow 'em off. And don't say Word One about abuse. Okay? That way, when it comes to trial, we can surprise 'em. Good. Problem Number Three. Don't talk to your son-in-law."

"Gabriel? I don't even know where he is. How could I talk to him?"

"He'll be around. Didn't he come to the hospital?"

Nan nodded.

"You think he won't come to your apartment, too? He'll try to get you alone. Try to get you to feel sorry for him. Figuring, if he can't make you cave, make you turn his daughter—Jane, right?—over to him, well, hey, maybe you'll let something drop. Some clue. Then he can figure out where she is and go get her. If he finds her, we're toast. If he's got her with him, no judge on this planet's gonna give her to *you*."

Give her to me?

Jenny Root paused, looked at Nan. "And you can *still* go to jail."

Sudden funereal hush. What *was* that undertaker's name?

"The charges'd still hold. Your son-in-law—Gabriel?—even if Gabriel dropped the charges, the State of Rhode Island has an interest in Jane's welfare now. They could still prosecute. Nan? Are we on the same page?"

In the outer office a fax machine began its low, soothing hum. In the coffin Tod's face hadn't looked like Tod, the forehead smoothed free of pain. No one had seemed to notice this but Nan.

Jenny Root put a hand under Nan's chin, made Nan's eyes meet hers. Eyes narrowed, face aglow with logic, she said, "Don't see him. You don't *need* to see him. I'll depose him, yadda yadda yadda, we'll know what he has in mind. Till then, blow him off."

Nan nodded. Nod, nod, nod. Gabriel would be visibly suffering; defiant, yet defensive. Tears in his silver eyes. (Depression is the better part of valor, Walker had said once.) What could Jenny Root—probably all of twenty-six years old—know about the tears of men?

"Problem Number Four. The biggie. How're we gonna plead?"

What do you mean *we,* white man?

"We've got three options. Guilty. Not guilty. Or nolo contendere—no contest—that's if we plead out."

"Plead out?"

"Strike a bargain. You give them Jane; they give you *you.*"

"No," Nan said.

Silence. Then a sigh from Jenny Root. "Wounded bird, right?"

"What?"

"You wanna lead them away from the nest, from where your fledgling is hidden. That's why you refused extradition, right?" Jenny Root's voice mingled exasperation with admiration. "You're willing to go to jail to keep everybody tied up here until Jane makes her getaway."

Nan stared down at her reflection in the polished mahogany surface of the conference table. When she'd refused extradition she hadn't been thinking of Jane—only of not going back to Gabriel's city. It had been her own safety, not Jane's, that she'd cared about.

Mistaking Nan's chagrin for modesty, Jenny Root put a hand on her shoulder. "You are *posh,* you know that? But it's my duty to keep you *out* of jail. You could be found guilty. You really could. I'm good—I'm fuckin' kick-ass—but, shit, it's your *life* we're talking about here. Let's not dick around."

Nan said, "I can't give Jane to Gabriel. I can't." *I can't keep her, either. What in hell am I doing?*

"If you go to jail, you won't see your granddaughter for years. She'll have to live with whoever she's with now. Okay, I don't know who that is, but do they love her the way you do? She'll be with *them.* Not with her mother, or her father, or you. *Think,* Nan. Is that really what you want? Is that really best for the child?"

Best for the child. Best for the child. Was Jenny Root advising her to give Jane up? Why? Was it because that was best for Jenny? Her best chance—maybe her only chance—to *win?* Nan felt as if she'd been catapulted back into the world of the Foreign Service: hidden motives, secrecy, lies. Where there was no one, even on your own side, that you could truly rely on. Where trust was a luxury forever beyond your means. She shook her head, to clear it. She mustn't—couldn't afford to—confuse the present with the past. It was true that Walker was no blood kin to Jane. But he did love her, and Jane loved him. Nan trusted that. *Had* to trust it.

She looked up at Jenny Root. "You're right," she said. "It's my life. Mine, not yours. I know you're doing your best for me, and I appreciate it. It's my decision."

"You won't give her up? You're sure?"

Nodding, Nan thought, Now ask me whether I'm sure I can keep her.

But Jenny Root began shuffling papers into her briefcase. "Okay, so we'll enter a plea of Not Guilty. The child's mother arranged for her to go with you, you were just being a helpful granny, yadda yadda yadda." She sounded as if she were agreeing with Nan, though Nan had suggested no plea.

Muggleton—that was the undertaker's name. A. Lincoln Muggleton. Deenie saying, Now what in the world could that "A" stand for?

Jenny Root stood up, shrugged on her jacket, put her helmet on her head and gave it a settling tap. She looked like an underage storm trooper. "One, no media; two, no Gabriel; three, take the Fifth with the state's attorney; four, Not Guilty; five, fuck, didn't get to that, gotta work on your look. Next time. Friday at, let's see, eleven. Okay? Okay. I'm outta here, I'm history."

Her hand grasped Nan's; then she was gone. The heavy carved wooden door slammed behind her. Seconds later, it opened again.

"We've been lucky so far. Don't push it. She's his daughter—don't forget that. Because *he* won't."

She disappeared.

Nan re-fastened her poncho, which there hadn't been time to take off. A sweet-faced male secretary showed her out. She started down the slate path, picking her way carefully over its rain-glazed surface. Jenny Root's motorcycle was a black spot at the end of Waterman Street.

His daughter?

For the first time, Nan understood that she no longer thought of Jane that way. Jane was her granddaughter, period. Jane was hers.

Thirteen

Now Nan Mulholland entered a period of waiting more intense and bleaker than any in her life so far. Little Red Waitinghood didn't begin to cover it.

First they had to wait for something called the pretrial hearing. A judge talked to the lawyers for both parties—Nan, the Defendant, the Accused, was one party; the other was Gabriel in conjunction with the State of Rhode Island—and decided whether the case merited a trial. If so, the judge would first try to get the parties to settle the matter without putting taxpayers to the expense of one. If they couldn't, or wouldn't, the judge would assign what Jenny Root called a Date Certain. After that, they could begin waiting for the trial itself.

Nan had always believed that she knew all about waiting. The years behind the Iron Curtain—first in Rumania, then in Poland—had been filled with waiting. Waiting in bureaucratic offices for visas; waiting in lines outside stores for bread or milk or vodka (though—Be honest!—*that* waiting had nearly always been done by servants); waiting for taxis, waiting for security clearances, waiting for the ambassador to summon her and Tod to dinner. There was the waiting, no matter where they were stationed, to see whether Tod would once again be passed over. Then the waiting to see where the downward spiral of his career would land them next. And of course the happier waiting—a pleasant buzz, like too much champagne at an embassy reception—for the current lover to call, to come to her.

Yes: Nan was practiced in the art of waiting. So she'd thought until now, in the long, lush days of June, in this down-at-heel city that had somehow become home. Always before, however long or tension-filled the wait, she had been surrounded by those who loved her. Tod; Alex; the current lover. Their closeness had been her safety.

Now there was neither closeness nor safety. Tod dead; Walker in hiding; Alex who knew where. And Jane. Nan was surprised at how much she missed her. Heartache—that old cliché, an idea Nan had always dismissed, the way she'd dismissed her lovers—was a faint but literal ache, she was discovering now. Not in the foreground, but always there, like a train in the distance going endlessly by.

They received a date for the pretrial hearing. The fourteenth of July—nearly a month away. Bastille Day. The day on which, every year, the Foreign Service postings had been announced. The day on which, in Paris shortly before Alex was born, Nan and Tod had walked hand in hand beneath huge red banners to see the fireworks above the Seine.

Mel did her best to distract Nan. They went to the gym every day, pacing adjacent treadmills in the late-afternoon light. Mel cracked jokes. *How do you get a man to do sit-ups? Put the TV remote between his toes.* She pointed out the best T-shirts: I'M JUST *BETTER* THAN YOU. I'M SHIPSHAPE—PADDLE HARDER. Afterward, in the sauna, shawled in hot, fragrant steam, she laid a towel across Nan's shoulders with little daughterly pats.

On most nights Nan had dinner with Val and Mel. The three of them sat on cushions on the floor, surrounded by take-out cartons under the rosy-shaded lamp, while outside the summer evenings lengthened, softened, filled with the smell of rain-wet earth and flowering trees. Afterward, though—no matter how late she stayed—there was always the moment when she had to enter the empty loft, with its dim checkerboard of streetlight or moonlight, its faint smell of brick dust, its absence of Jane. Jane in a corner making flowers out of Kleenex and wire, the floor around her a drift of pink and blue and yellow. Jane setting Zipper's empty bowl upside down on her head: "Now I'm an army person!" Jane unrolling a ball of yellow yarn given to her by Mel and stringing it all around the loft, from one piece of furniture to another, to make a giant spiderweb.

Then the Press found Nan.

Pretrial discovery—the collecting of statements to the police that became, to Jenny Root's disgust, a matter of public record—was what triggered it. She didn't offer to show Nan the statements made by the prosecution's witnesses, and Nan didn't ask to see them. (Fear of her own compassion for Gabriel? Or of what he might have said about her?)

What seemed to captivate the Press was the fact that the kidnapping charge in Washington State had been adopted by Rhode Island without any inquiry—the result, according to Jenny Root, of Gabriel's appearance in person before the state's attorney and of his standing in his own community. The charge of Kidnapping held a special appeal for readers, according to the nasal-voiced reporter on whom Nan hung up first. In the beginning, she kept on answering the phone, thinking it might somehow be Walker. Mel drilled her in responses to her implacable callers. *I have to hang up, my head's on fire . . . Whoops! There goes the baby off the fridge . . . I know you're a front for the White Aryan Nation.* They called, like telemarketers, at mealtimes; they called in the middle of the night. They drove Nan to stop answering the phone at all and, in the end, to unplug it with such force that she tore the jack from the wall.

After a few days of phonelessness, a reporter turned up at the entrance to Elbow Street one evening as Nan was coming out. The man was small, dark, wily. Nan's stomach leapt; her first thought was that Gabriel had sent him. Trembling, she pulled out the can of Mace Val had given her and held it pointed at his face in the blue dusk. He backed away. She ducked inside the building, pursued by shouted questions. *Is it true you kidnapped a child? Where is she now?* She'd gone from being a Fugitive from Justice to being a Fugitive from the Media.

That night, jittery, afraid to stay in the loft alone, she went down to Val and Mel's. When they'd heard the whole story, Val announced that from now on he would be driving Nan everywhere. "But I hardly ever go out," Nan said. Now that she was once again Nan Mulholland, she could use the money in her Seattle bank account and her IRA to live on; with no modeling (which, absurdly, she missed) and no Jane, she would need to leave the building only for legal stuff. Well, when she did, Val insisted, he would escort her. In vain Nan pointed out that here, unlike the former Soviet Union, the press was not a Party organ. That harassment was the price of freedom. "They are ess-holes!" Val shouted. "*K chortu!*" He'd seen, he reminded Nan, the marks left by the handcuffs on her wrists the night she got out on bail. Mel, from her cushion on the floor, silently handed him a joint. Without putting it to his lips he passed it to Nan, then got up and went into his studio. When he came back he handed her a small, bent black-and-white photograph. The young man in it, with cropped hair and a square, shadowed jaw, wore no visible clothing. Bony shoulders; clavicle. The photo cut him off just above the nipples; across one armpit was the number 2054. He looked directly at the viewer out of eyes that offered no compromise. Val left the photograph in Nan's hands and went back into his studio and closed the door.

"His grandfather," Mel said. "Died in the camps. It was right before Stalin croaked. If he just could've made it three more weeks . . ."

Val didn't return. After a long marijuana-laced silence, Mel began to talk. Janey's laugh; Janey's birthmark, like a bird's wing, on the side of her neck; the way Janey said, "*Nyet*—not yet!" The longing in Mel's voice made Nan think of the word *bereft*. Made her understand what until then she'd only dimly perceived: Jane was Mel's chance at repair. In fact, Nan realized, sitting there on Mel's floor in the rosy lamplight, Jane seemed to be everyone's chance at repair. Mel's; Gabe's; Alex's. Nan's own. How many pasts could one small child heal?

|

June 21. The solstice: the word echoed in Nan's head as she pushed open, perhaps for the last time, the heavy glass door of the Rock. The longest day of the year, the day when summer seemed eternal, a season you could never leave.

Against Jenny Root's instructions, she'd come out by herself this afternoon—she'd had to—crawling out a ground-floor window into the alley behind Fred Street, an exit that Val had showed her. She wore a black wool hat of Mel's that completely covered her hair, a pair of mirrored sunglasses, and a workman's jacket provided by Val that said NARRA-GANSETT ELECTRIC COMPANY front and back.

She found Walker's message first, sandwiched between LOOK HERE, WILMA (a persistent guy! thought Nan) and BABES, READ THIS.

POOKIE: Can carry out original plan. Await your instructions, printed here, any day. Everyone fine & walking. HIPPIE

Nan copied out the message. *Walking*: definitely a communication from Walker. But what did it mean? In the Sunday-morning hush of the Reference Room, empty except for Nan and Ben Kingsley, she pondered. *Original plan*. That must mean that Walker would take Jane to New Zealand. All Nan had to do was put a message in the *Pee-Eye* on July 7—two weeks from now—saying, Do it.

New Zealand. Nine thousand miles from here.

She was so shaken that she nearly missed Alex's message, one column over from Walker's and almost next to it.

POOKIE: *Ti prego di aspettare e non disturbarti. Ti prego di capiscere, Mama.* **HIPPIE**

Nan's hand shook so much that she could barely copy down the words. Long forgotten, still beautiful, they fell onto her yellow legal pad like the petals of a pressed flower. Slowly, uncertainly—it had been so long! almost thirty years—she translated. *Please wait, and don't worry. Please understand, Mama.*

Alex had gone to Italy.

Nan must have turned pale, because Ben Kingsley appeared at her side with a paper cone of water. Gratefully, she drank. It was cold and sweet. Alex had used the wrong word for "worry"; it should have been *preoccuparti.* She thanked the librarian, who was already retreating toward the safety of his wide, curving counter.

Italy.

New Zealand.

|

Dusk.

The darkening air held the clarity of midsummer. Walking along the river, wrapped in the blessed anonymity provided by the Narragansett Electric Company's blue jacket, Nan tried to remember what Walker had said. Sunset; twilight; dusk. Was that the order they came in? She imagined his arm linked through hers. I wouldn't be afraid, she thought, if he were here. Behind the State House a brightness the color of pomegranates lingered in the western sky, and gulls circled the white dome.

Mama: Alex had called her Mama. Alex had gone back to where, in a sense, all this had started. Back into the past, thought Nan, the way we all want to do, the way no one can. To repair? To understand? Or just headlong, instinctual flight?

Please understand, her message had said. Please accept, was what she meant. But that had been Tod's gift, not Nan's: to accept without needing to understand. A gift that had kept him a second-rank diplomat.

Nan turned onto College Street and began to walk uphill. On her right was the rosy brick building that housed the superior court, where, in three weeks, her fate would be decided. At the Pre-Trial Hearing the judge would ask where Jane was, invoking the pious phrase she'd come to hate, the words so readily twisted into the opposite of their meaning: *What's best for the child.* He would not be pleased with Nan's answer. But it wasn't only the judge she feared. There would be Gabriel, with his new haggardness, his face riven by grief. Jenny Root had warned her that the state's attorney would want him present, he made such a credible plaintiff. Suppose he showed only his sorrow. Would pity weaken her? Would she (Mel's word) cave? Don't think of him as your son-in-law, Jenny Root had said. Think of him as your enemy. Dick-nose! was Mel's assessment; Pusbag! How had it come to this? How had she, Nan, come to be what she now was: a woman in late middle age facing a criminal trial, cut off from everyone she loved, everyone who loved her?

Best for the child. Not wanting to go home, savoring her momentary freedom from reporters, Nan kept walking uphill in the direction of the university. A skateboard careened toward her, two figures on it facing each other. Nan pressed her back against a telephone pole as it swept by. The girl's legs were stretched out on top of the boy's; her bare feet clasped his buttocks. Wistfully, Nan turned to watch them. All the way down the hill, people on the sidewalk leapt out of its way. The beauty of the evening—the warm, still air, the lessening light—seemed to hold a sense of something lost. Sweat tickled Nan's forehead. She unzipped the Narragansett Electric Company's jacket. At the bottom of the hill the skateboarders melted into the long indigo shadow of the courthouse.

Best for the child. At the top of College Street Nan paused before the university's high iron fence. Her fingers curled around the bars of the Van Wickle gate. The Judge (whoever that might be) could decide Nan's fate; but only Nan could decide Jane's. She had two weeks before Walker would look for her answer in the *Pee-Eye.* Two weeks to decide. If she said Yes, Walker would go to New Zealand with Jane. If she said Wait, he would wait. Either way, Jane was her responsibility.

Nan remembered that December morning on Alex's deck, Alex's eyes dark with hope, the *Yes* that had come from Nan's own lips. She thought, I did not mean to give so great a gift.

The streetlights came on, making darkness gather around her and crowd in underneath the Van Wickle Gate's great stone arch. Overhead, gulls moved through the last of the light, weaving, over and over, the symbol for infinity. *Best! Best!* they seemed to cry.

The next day, Monday, Nan and Jenny Root met to discuss Strategy. Skinny Jenny, in a big-shouldered black linen suit that made her look as if she'd raided her mother's closet, had dark circles under her eyes, and her deep voice sounded raspy. She was pleased that Nan had heeded her previous admonitions, had not spoken to the Press or to Gabriel; but she was puzzled that Gabriel hadn't tried to contact Nan.

"Maybe when we get his deposition, we'll see. Hey, you sure stone-walled Jamison Leer. He's a real tricky dick, I told you he worked on von Bulow's defense back when he was in private practice. You were way posh!"

Leer, the state's attorney, *had* badgered Nan, as had the police, full of disconcertingly genuine concern for Jane.

Jenny Root rifled through her briefcase, came up with a sheaf of yellow paper that she fanned across the conference table. First they disposed of the matter of character witnesses. Deenie dead; friends in Seattle too far away. ("No minister? Counselor? Nobody with spine?") Morosely, Jenny Root considered Val and Mel, a non-citizen of doubtful employment and a tattoo artist. She finally agreed to audition Mel but rejected Val as too risky. ("Gnarly" was her word.) A local shrink—a counter-shrink, to balance the one the state's attorney would inevitably call—would testify to Nan's all-around mental health and stability. "But"—resignation tolled in her voice like church bells—"I'm gonna have to put you on the stand."

Talking faster than ever, she established that their (their?) defense could only be Jane's welfare, the Best Interest of the Child, but that this would have to be handled very delicately.

"You don't, *we* don't, have any proof that your son-in-law abused his daughter."

A father's bathrobe untied; nightmares; a little girl's too-intent reliance on attention from the men in her life. All this had already been mentioned, and Jenny Root had understood; but all of it was oblique. Suggestive, but not conclusive. "Right," Nan said wearily. "No proof."

The whine of the fax machine in the outer office echoed, Proof! Proof!

"So. Let's run through it one more time. When the other side deposes you, you don't get into specifics. You just say you were concerned for your granddaughter's welfare. Her mother was very worried. Her mother asked you to take her for a while, you were coming back East to visit an old friend anyway, yadda yadda yadda. You didn't know the child's father hadn't been consulted."

Nan nodded. Through the conference room windows, the bright June morning seemed like a series of paintings hung above the shelves of lawbooks.

"We don't cast any aspersions, okay? We just gotta hope that Gabriel does something or says something, makes himself look doubtful. No mudslinging. You're just a K.O.G. Kindly old granny. The more like a K.O.G. you look (remind me to talk to you about your Look), the more likely the judge'll be to bypass Gabriel and give Jane to you."

Give Jane to me.

Nan must have looked doubtful, because Jenny Root, running her fingers (nails bitten, Nan noticed, to the quick) through her porcupine hair, stopped short. "Nan. You don't have to go through with this if you don't want to. We can still plead out."

Nan said, as if this were the only obstacle, "I don't know where she is."

"But you know who she's with. That'd be enough for the police to find her. All you have to do is give them a name."

Nan was silent, looking through the windows behind Jenny Root's head, where a breeze stirred the painted-looking trees.

"You may be thinking that I want you to turn your granddaughter in." (Nan had been thinking exactly that.) "Well, I don't. Not per se. I just want you to save yourself. You're my first responsibility, Nan. Not Jane. You."

A warming tide of self-pity washed through Nan, and she had to fold her hands tightly on the polished table. Who else cared about her now? Walker was taking care of Jane. Alex had gotten Nan into this situation in the first place, and then had abandoned her. It isn't my choice, Nan thought for the hundredth time in the last two weeks. I didn't choose this.

"A name, Nan. Easy! Just a name. And you can walk out of here and never come back."

It would be easy. Easier than Jenny Root knew. Nan hadn't mentioned the possibility of reaching Walker through a message in the Pee-Eye. July 7 was only thirteen days away.

Jenny Root reached over and put a hand on her arm. "The person she's with—they wouldn't necessarily get in trouble. We could negotiate that."

Nan moved her hand away, wrapped both arms around her rib cage. What am I *thinking*? She shook her head violently. "No," she said.

Jenny Root sighed. Even her sighs were faster than other people's, quick little puffs. Nan longed to lay her head down on the cool, gleaming surface of the conference table. To fall asleep amid the drifts of yellow paper and wake up somewhere else. Somewhere far away.

". . . and you don't mention the word *sexual*," Jenny Root was saying. "You don't mention the word *abuse*. Stick to the positive. Welfare. Best interest."

The sweet-faced male secretary padded softly into the room and laid a note by Jenny Root's elbow. She read it in a single quick look.

"Okay, that's it for now, you'll be deposed on Monday, Tuesday at the latest, call and lemme know how it went, you got my cell number, my beeper? We can modify if we need to, it's not set in gold, didn't get to your look, Max'll explain what you gotta do for your look, right, Max? Okay, I'm outta here. I'm archives."

|

Plead out. Nan rejected the thought; yet it stayed with her. The Thought, she began calling it, to herself: something that hovered, throwing its shadow wherever she went, like a large, dingy dirigible low in the sky.

|

Val cranked down the driver's-side window with angry thrusts. The river smell rushed in, carrying rumors of the unseen ocean. A camera with NEWS 10 on the side glided rashly toward them.

Val stuck his head out the window. "Fucking cocksuckers!" *Cokesackers*, it came out; but close enough.

He stepped on the gas and drove up over the curb straight at the hapless cameraman, who jumped into a doorway. The camera swayed on its long legs, then toppled. It hit the pavement with a loud crash. Val's spittle slid down its side.

"Ha!" he cried. "When thunder growls, a man will cross himself!"

His own camera was out the open window. Nan could hear it clicking—more drive-by shootings—as they bumped down off the sidewalk, Val steering one-handed. She shut her eyes and clung to the back of the seat in front of her. They sped off into the hot, wet morning.

In the backseat next to Nan, Mel read aloud from a piece of paper. "HAIR: neat, not too long or short, not obviously dyed. Recommended salon: Hair and Now, 722 Hope Street." She snorted. "APPAREL: suitable for church service, non-funeral. Men: dark suit w/tie in subdued pattern. Women: skirted suit or dress in dark color; no prints, no pants; heels, low to medium; flesh-colored stockings. Ugh! Geriatric! Hat, optional. Well, *there's* a break. TO BE AVOIDED AT ALL COSTS: flashy jewelry; piercings other than ears (one hole); tattoos—you're cooked, Nan!—red lipstick (women); facial hair (men). So a Bearded Lady would be okay."

She tossed the paper—given to Nan by Max, Jenny Root's secretary, two days before—onto the floor and threw her head back against the cracked vinyl upholstery. "Crap sandwich! I can't believe I'm gonna help you do this to yourself."

A syrupy summer rain coated the city. Gradually, still muttering an occasional *Chort!*, Val slowed to ordinary speeding. They crossed the river and turned onto South Main, headed for the consignment store where they'd gone in the winter, when Nan had first come to Providence. Jane had been with her, she remembered wistfully, looking out at the gray morning. They'd been outfitting themselves for—it seemed now—an adventure.

Mel must have read her mind, because she sighed. "Janey looked so cool in that little red jacket. Super-fly. Not a true red, more of a blue-red. *Caput mortuum* red, did you know there's a color called that? 'Head of the dead,' it means. Dead-head red."

Val said, "Janechka I miss. Both two of us, Mel and me, we miss. What to hell!" The taxi hit a pothole, bounded out of it. "*Chort voz'mi!*"

Nan twisted around to look out the back window. No one seemed to be following them; for the moment, at least, they were Pressless. She retrieved Max's list from the floor and smoothed it out. The Make-Under, Mel had christened this project: a makeover that left you worse off than when you started. She'd refused to have any part in it, until Nan pointed out that it was for Jane's sake. The duller and safer she, Nan, appeared, the more likely the judge would be to believe her.

Val dropped them off on Hope Street, camera clicking as they climbed out of the car. "Good-bye, my loveds!" he said. "Tender ladies!"

As they went from place to place, the morning lightened. The rain stopped. Clouds began moving east toward the ocean; the sun appeared, wan as an invalid, and made the rain-wet pavement steam. Mel kept drawing poignant parallels with their makeover excursion in February—Four months ago! Nan thought in astonishment—when Nan had acquired the look she was now at such pains to lose. It made her feel split between the present and past, as if she were living through two mornings at once.

In the consignment store's rickety, hot little dressing room she felt suddenly dizzy. Maybe it was just from so much looking at herself in mirrors: somewhere in the last few months she'd lost the habit of self-regard (Be honest! of self-admiration) that had sustained her through a lifetime. The full-length mirror, less than a foot away, showed a woman she hardly knew. Truly terrible hair (white roots, band of faded blue, the cut grown out to a yaklike puff); unmade-up eyes; untended, dry, *old lady* skin.

Mel pounded on the door. "Let's see!"

Hastily Nan pulled on the clothes the shop owner had produced in response to Max's list. Charcoal-gray linen jacket, suitably boxy; matching skirt that fell below Nan's knees; white blouse with demure collar. Without looking in the mirror again, she opened the door and stepped out.

Mel took her in with curled lip, then clapped a hand to her forehead. "That really rocks!" she said. "That is *so* special."

Behind her hovered the shop owner, a pale woman with a large jaw and soft dark eyes, like a very pretty cow. She said, in a voice that matched her eyes, "It needs a little something."

Mel snorted. The woman went up to the front of the shop and came back with a dark-red plaid ribbon. She tied it in a neat bow around Nan's neck under her collar. Nan stood quietly under her hands, which smelled of lavender.

"There," Cow Eyes said, giving a last twitch to the bow. "Perfect!"

"Propagandistic!" crooned Mel, in a cruel parody of the woman's tone.

She didn't seem to notice. "I've got just the shoes," she said. Another trip to the front of the store, from which she returned carrying a pair of gray-and-white pumps. She stood waiting, bovinely attentive, while Nan wedged her bare feet into them.

"Of course they'll look a lot better with stockings."

"Oh, *yes*," said Mel. "Woolen ones, doncha think? A nice argyle pattern."

This time Cow Eyes got it. Looking hurt, she retreated behind the counter. "Let me know if you need further assistance," she said.

Nan threw Mel a reproachful look. "I'll take everything," she told the woman. "Thank you for your help."

Outside, walking up Hope Street in the weak sunshine while rain steamed off the pavement, Mel said, "Those shoes. Why're they two-tone? Bizarre-oh! Like fifties convertibles."

"They're called spectator pumps." Nan lifted her face to the moist air, growing warmer as they walked. "They used to be considered the height of chic. When I was, come to think of it, your age."

"Oh, chic," Mel said. "Right. Listen, while you were in the dressing room getting in touch with your Inner Rotarian, I checked out the neighborhood. How about lunch at an Indian place, before we hit the Salon for the Terminally Blue-Haired?"

So they lunched, like any two women shopping. Mother and daughter, the diminutive proprietor clearly believed them to be; and when he set down the steaming plates of chicken saag and puffy golden bread, Nan thought of Alex. How seldom they had sat over lunch (Alex used her lunch hours for meetings or to catch up on paperwork), except for the year after Tod died, when Nan had been unexpectedly glad, for a little while, of her daughter's steadiness, so like his.

You've never really loved anybody, have you, Mother?

Can't think about that. Look around. Smell coriander, garlic, rosemary. Hear the piped-in zither, nasal but pleasing. Listen to Mel. Sunlight through the plate-glass window by their shoulders gilded Mel's hair, which stuck out around her head in rain-wet spikes, like the Statue of Liberty. NAKED POTATO, said a sign behind her. No, of course not: *BAKED* POTATO. But the image stayed with Nan while Mel chattered on: potatoes smooth and clean as Walker's feet.

At the end of the meal, over cardamom tea with honey, fragrant and calming, Mel said, "So. What's gonna happen in this trial?"

"Pre-Trial Hearing—that comes first. I'm charged with Kidnapping. We're pleading Not Guilty. Then either the judge will dismiss the case, or he won't."

"And then what happens?"

"We'll probably go to trial. Then either the jury will convict me, or they won't."

Mel's large hands gripped her glass of tea. She was wearing a wrinkled black shirt with the sleeves rolled back. Nan could see the muscles in her forearms tighten above her bracelet tattoos. "I meant, with Janey. You'll get her eventually. Right?"

"Mel. I don't know what's going to happen. With Jane, or with me. Right now I just want to keep her away from her father. Keep her safe."

"But the judge'll have to give her to you, right? Her father's a scumbag, and her mother abandoned her."

Mel's voice quavered on the word "abandoned." Nan could see the equation in her too-bright eyes. But Jane's situation wasn't what Mel's had been. Surely Mel realized that Jane would only be safe out of the country, no matter how the trial turned out.

Mel didn't realize anything of the kind. "You'll stay here, in Providence. Where you've got, you know, *allies*. You two'll be together for good."

For good?

And there it was again: The Thought. *Plead out!* came its whisper in her head.

Better, Nan saw—feeling miserably Machiavellian—not to make Mel face facts. She needed Mel and Val too much to risk the truth.

"If I don't get sent to jail. We'll see."

"We'll see. We'll see. That's what *they* used to say. The foster mothers. *We'll see.*" Mel's voice was so loud that, behind his counter, the blue-turbaned chef looked their way in alarm.

Nan put a hand out, meaning to say (though how could she?), Everything will be all right. As her fingers closed around Mel's wrist, there was a sudden wet explosion. Liquid and shards of glass leapt into the air. Nan jumped back. Her head hit the top of the wooden booth and warm wetness sprayed her face. Something bounced off the table and fell into her lap. Bright and round. The bottom of Mel's tea glass: she'd gripped it so hard that it shattered. Across from her, Mel held up both hands, like someone stopping traffic. Blood, bright red, webbed her fingers. Looking at it, Nan felt the room wobble, then begin to spin.

The proprietor appeared with a rag and a bucket. "So sorry! So sorry!" he exclaimed. Nan had to look away as he began mopping the mess— blood, tea, glass—into the bucket. The blue-turbaned chef appeared with a brass box, out of which he pulled a roll of bandages and a tube of antiseptic. He, too, began to apologize. Then Nan apologized, and so did

Mel. Finally they left—Mel having been swabbed and bandaged—in a four-part chorus of diminishing regrets.

They walked up the street in sunshine punctuated by little bursts of wetness from the trees overhead, no longer Girls Together, each thinking her own thoughts. Nan's were of Mel; no doubt Mel's were of Jane. Mel was so young. What could she know about irreconcilable desires? About the logic of betrayal?

At the Hair and Now, a dark, Italian-looking young man retrofitted (as Mel put it) Nan. "Going to an Event?" he asked as he shook out a lavender smock and draped it over Nan. His warm fingers, tying it, brushed the nape of her neck.

"You could say that."

He slathered Nan's head with maroon paste, wrapped it in plastic, put her under the dryer. "Bake! Bake! Bake!" chanted Mel into her ear, holding up old issues of *Cosmopolitan* whose covers promised MOST MIND-BLOWING ORGASMS EVER! and PUSH HIS LOVE BUTTONS! Then the narrow young man shampooed, combed, snipped, dried, applying various fragrant potions along the way.

"Work and turn!" he exclaimed finally, stepping back. And there in the mirror was a Bellevue matron, eyes a resigned but brilliant blue under a cap of sleek dark hair. Behind the matron stood Mel, waving her bandaged hands like some apparition out of a fifties horror movie. "Cosmic! That Anglo-Saxon helmet look is just genius."

They were driven home by Val, who dutifully admired what Mel called Retro-Nan. The rain-washed streets shone in the midafternoon sun.

Climbing the last flight of stairs—Mel calling up from her own door, "See you for dinner, okay?"—Nan felt weariness like a mineral deposit in her calves, the small of her back. Her scalp stung from the unaccustomed attention. She was thinking of these things, and of the glass of wine that would banish them, when she saw the figure standing by her door. Black-coated back blending into the shadows of the hallway.

Her heart kicked. Without stopping to think, she said, "Alex?"

Fourteen

There had always been something in Gabriel's stance. Something held in check, behind a willed and therefore precarious gentleness. He'd often made Nan think of a child who isn't sure he's been invited to the party, who could join it or wreck it, depending.

He made her think that now. For an instant, as he turned and began to walk toward her, Nan saw a young boy. Bruised, battered, eager, loving. Running to meet his mother's pickup, down a dirt road through summer woods. She thought, incredulously, I'm glad to see him.

"Nan!"

He seemed about to embrace her. His arms in the black trench coat lifted. Without intending to, Nan took a step backward.

"I, I can't—" Breathe; breathe. "I can't talk to you, Gabriel." Her voice in her own ears was quavery, an old woman's voice.

"Nan—for God's sake. It's me. *Me.*"

His voice was—oh, it was!—like home.

He began walking toward her, but slowly. She made herself stand her ground. "We're not supposed to see each other, or talk to each other. Until the, the trial."

"That's bullshit! You know it is, Nan. We *need* to talk."

He was close enough now for her to see his silver eyes. One-way mirrors. In the dimness of the hallway they seemed the only source of light. She shivered.

"You're cold," Gabriel said. "Let's go inside. Can we? Can we sit down like two reasonable beings—two old friends, Nan, for God's sake—and talk things out?"

How tired he looks. Almost . . . old.

"I don't think that's a good idea."

"Nan. *Please.*"

The groove in his forehead deepened. She would have to be steel to get through this.

"I can't. I promised Jenny—I promised my lawyer. I shouldn't be talking to you at all. Please, Gabe. Please go."

"All right, Nan. I'll be brief." His voice became tender. "I want my daughter. Just tell me where she is. That's all you have to do."

The tenderness; the longing. Real, she knew. She did not need his earnest eyes, his stance (leaning now against the rough cinder-block wall) of violent humility, to tell her that. She felt it in her own body: missing Jane.

Gabriel took another step toward her. There was a very large, very hairy-looking centipede on the wall between them. Nan kept her eyes on it.

"How can you keep my daughter from me?" Softly, he echoed Nan's very question to herself. "What right do you have to do that? To me or to her? To *her,* Nan!"

My daughter, my wife, my house, my patients. But Jane loved her father. Nan knew that, though it was something she had (Be honest!) fought hard, for the last six months, to forget. She thought of Jane's distant, unmoving face whenever (so seldom) she'd spoken of Gabriel during their months of exile. She remembered the fierce, yearning way in which Jane had attached herself first to Val, then to Walker.

Gabriel said urgently, "Jane needs her father."

The hallway had begun to fill with the smell of someone's cooking, vegetables boiling, like wet washrags. Gabriel took a step closer. On the wall between them the centipede made a quick figure eight, then froze.

"Nan. Don't you remember how it was? Remember the time you and I took her to the Olympic Peninsula, to the rain forest? Remember the little cabin we stayed in, at the edge of the ocean? And Jane said, she was three then, what was it she said? About the water? 'This water is . . .'"

"'This water tastes like *brown*.'"

Jane had stood at the westernmost edge of the country in a raspberry corduroy jumpsuit and white socks heavy with sand. They called to her and she came and hung on to Gabriel and searched his pockets for his keys, patting each one and laughing.

She felt herself begin to waver. Jane *was* his daughter. Who was she, Nan, to separate father and daughter? *Whom God hath joined together.*

No—that's Gabriel and—

"Alex," she said. "What about Alex?"

"My wife left me, Nan. She left Jane. What rights does a mother have, if we don't even know where she is?" He looked at her closely. "Or *do* you know?"

Her heart checked, then began to thud. "No. No, I don't. But she asked me to take Jane, Gabriel. She begged me."

"Why?"

"You know why."

He took another step toward Nan. "*Why?*"

Here it was, the moment she'd dreaded, the thing that had to be said. "She said— She said you'd— Abused Jane. Sexually."

Gabriel straightened. "That's ridiculous! It's *preposterous*. It's—" His hand came up and hit the wall between them. It made a loud, flat sound. The centipede skated upward.

"Nan. You know that's not true. Don't you?"

She swallowed. "I don't know anything anymore." That at least was true.

Was Gabriel's indignation—clearly genuine, clearly heartfelt—because the charge against him was unfounded? Or simply because it had been made at all? It wasn't the first he'd heard it. That much was clear from the speed with which he regained his composure.

"Alex is disturbed," he said, in a calm, logical tone. "She's sick, Nan, she's been sick for a long time. You know that. You're her mother—you must have seen it."

"No," Nan said, faintly.

Gabriel took another step toward her. "I didn't want to have to tell you this. But Alex was having an affair. My wife was unfaithful. She betrayed me, and she betrayed Jane." Another step. "What rights does a mother like that have?"

Gabriel was standing very close now. He was pale with anger. The silver eyes, inches from her own, burned. Nan felt a scrabbling in her chest, like a tiny gerbil on a treadmill.

"It's too late for Alex. But not for Jane. Tell me where she is."

"I don't *know* where she is."

"Give me back my daughter."

My daughter, my wife, my house, my patients. But his voice held real anguish. As if he saw her see this, Gabriel stood still, his fury suddenly replaced by the old imploring look. For an instant Nan hesitated. And there it was again: The Thought. Beautiful, this time, compassionate, a hand extended to a fellow sufferer. *Plead out.* Then another thought flashed: What about *my* daughter? Alex trusted me with Jane. Wherever she is now, she's still trusting me.

"I can't, Gabe. I'm sorry."

The refusal—or was it the apology?—infuriated him. She saw rage take him, pouring through his body. His hands flew up, one of them bloody from the blow to the wall. She jumped back. He grabbed her shoulders. She smelled cigars, Calvados, the rusty odor of blood on his knuckles. The animal in her chest was pedaling furiously. Gabriel's face, so close. Gabriel's blood. She closed her eyes. His thumb dug into her clavicle and his breathing filled her ears.

Then there was another sound—a pounding—the noise of feet in the stairwell. Gabriel's grip loosened. His breath was moist in her ear.

"You know what's right," he said, low-voiced. "Do it."

"Nan? You there?"

Mel's voice. Mel's blessed voice.

When Nan opened her eyes, Gabriel was a shadow melting into other shadows at the end of the hall, under the baleful red glow of the EXIT sign. She heard the heavy metal door close. She started to shake.

And then Mel was beside her, Mel's strong, muscular arm under her own.

"You okay?"

|

"Christ!" Jenny Root boomed. "Sweet fuckin' Christ!"

"I'm sorry," Nan said meekly into the phone.

"How do you expect me to defend you if you do stuff like that? Stuff I explicitly warned you not to do?"

Defend.

"Or maybe you'd rather just be your own attorney? There's an old saying, ever hear it? The lawyer who defends himself has a fool for a client." The peremptory sound of a beeper came to Nan clearly through the receiver. "Okay. We'll just hafta wait and see what he does. Gotta go, due in superior court in ten, don't forget your deposition this afternoon, got the address? Call me after. Don't say *anything* except what we agreed."

Agreed?

"Got it? Are we on the same page?"

"Okay," Nan said. Before the second syllable had died away there was a click, and Jenny Root was archives.

|

An affair? Alex?

But even as she questioned it Nan saw that it could be true. The last time she'd seen her, that night in the hospital, Alex had been hiding something, holding something back—Nan had known it, even in the dark, even drugged. Farther back than that, even. On that December morning when Alex had asked her to take Jane away, she'd felt something. A sense of something not said, something concealed.

So that was why Gabe had finally brought charges against Nan. Whatever hold Alex had had on him—whatever dirt—was canceled out by her affair. Or Gabe thought it was. Affair plus Abandonment equals Unfit Mother—that was how he'd see it. And Alex, in her own way, must have agreed. She blamed herself for what had happened—what she believed had happened—to Jane. She'd failed to watch over her daughter because she'd been distracted (how well Nan remembered that state of distraction!) by her lover.

At first Nan, too, thought, This changes everything. Then she saw that nothing had changed. She'd never been sure—not *sure*—that her daughter had drawn the right conclusions from what she'd seen. Alex was no less reliable because she had a lover. Because she was (Nan realized, with bitter honesty) her mother's daughter.

|

GRANDMOTHER CHARGED IN ABDUCTION CASE

NUDE MODEL STEALS CHILD: INTERSTATE KIDNAPPING RING?

RHODE ISLAND NO REFUGE FOR CRIMINALS, MAYOR VOWS

"We tee off on Friday," Jenny Root told Nan. "The shit has hit the cyclotron."

She was furious. She rolled up the newspapers she'd brought with her and flung them onto Nibbrig's sofa along with her motorcycle helmet. It was late on Wednesday afternoon. She'd had to make a house call to coach Nan, because of the camera crews that converged whenever Nan tried to leave the building. Val had gone after one journalist with Mel's piercing gun, and nearly caught him. Nan, fearing that next time he'd succeed and be charged with assault and they'd both end up felons, had stopped going out at all.

The pretrial hearing had been moved up, Jenny Root announced. It would take place in two days. Apparently the mayor had brought pressure to bear.

"Five more days, five fucking days, and they would've rotated, Not-Too-Bright Wright would've been replaced as pretrial judge. But no, your son-in-law has to spill to the press. I'll get the fucker if it kills me. He's luggage!" She plopped down on the sofa beside Nan, batting away an overhanging ficus branch as if it were some part of Gabriel's anatomy.

Nan's first reaction was relief. She hadn't been out of the apartment in days. Mel brought in groceries and anything else she needed. It felt like house arrest.

But Jenny Root's other news was devastating. She hadn't wanted to tell Nan, but now, with the pretrial two days away, she had to. The prosecution's chief witness was Gabriel.

And there it was again. The Thought, seductive in its new (since Gabriel's visit) guise: compassion trimmed with fear.

Jenny Root looked closely at Nan, who had sunk back on the sofa. "You gonna barf? Put your head down." When she didn't comply, Jenny Root put her hands on the back of Nan's neck and pushed. Nose in her lap, Nan thought, I can't do this.

Nan should know, Jenny Root said, as if she'd read Nan's mind, that the prosecution would offer to drop the charges—in exchange, of course, for Jane. "We can still plead out, during the pretrial."

Trade Jane for freedom? *Trade* her?

Nan lifted her head. "No," she said.

"Okay, well, forget that for now. So, here's the deal. Don't think of him as your son-in-law. Think of him as a hostile witness. Because that's what he is."

They went over Nan's testimony—and over, and over. Nan wouldn't have suspected Jenny Root of such reservoirs of patience. She also seemed, for the first time, worried. Gabriel's lawyers had done their homework, she told Nan: nude modeling, adulterous affairs, not to mention that Alex had deserted her child. And for an adulterous affair of her own.

Following in her mother's negligent footsteps, Nan thought.

"The prosecution's thinking is, what judge'll look kindly on a woman taking off with her grandchild when she's messed up her *own* kid. Unfair, maybe, but that's how they see it. Any drugs at those modeling sessions? Wright hates druggies."

Nan assured her that there hadn't been, though how did she know? The marijuana at Val and Mel's she tried to put out of her mind completely.

Jenny Root got angry only twice: when Nan told her about Mikki not being a licensed day-care provider—Mikki was, of course, yet another witness for the prosecution—and when she admitted to not having declared the income from modeling. Anything else she should know? Jenny Root demanded sarcastically. Embezzling? Prostitution?

Nan's whole life seemed nothing but a trail of errors leading to this day. Chickens coming home to roast, Walker would have said.

"Okay," Jenny Root said finally, running both hands through her hair and leaning back. They had, Nan realized, been nearly nose to nose for an hour. "Let's just get through the next thirty-six hours. No Press. No Gabriel. Right? Right."

|

The next day, Thursday, Nan Mulholland, Accused Felon trying not to become Convicted Felon, did everything that was expected of her. She ironed her charcoal-gray suit and practiced walking in her spectator pumps. She stayed indoors, away from the windows, leaving Nibbrig's loft only to go upstairs and have dinner with Val and Mel. Pushing uneaten pirozhki and cabbage around on her plate, she listened to Val's proverbs (*Woman has a lit candle in her soul*; *If logic reigned, men would ride sidesaddle*) and laughed at Mel's jokes. About Jane they were silent, all three of them, as if a sort of collective mental breath-holding might make the pretrial hearing come out all right.

Returning from dinner, Nan felt her feet slow of their own accord as she approached Nibbrig's door. Gabriel's blood on the cinder blocks beside it, already darkening into anonymous grime, reminded her of what she had seen: Gabriel unguarded, uncareful. A furious, avenging Gabriel that she had not known existed, though perhaps she should have.

And if Alex simply saw what she wanted to see, to justify herself? If *he's innocent? Then I have done him a grave injury*—and Jane, as well.

In the moon-checkered loft Nan went from place to place, fingers grazing the furniture. Trying to recover, in the curved back of the sofa or the brittle clicking leaves of the fig tree, the presence of Jane. Where was she now? Nan's guess was, Boston. Our Man from Savannah was there, and Logan Airport, with daily flights to almost anywhere. But maybe not: if Nan could figure that out, then (Lines of Desire) so could the police. For some reason, a vision came to her of Jane and Walker on a sunny sidewalk, of Walker bending down to help Jane with the bubblegum that had wrapped itself in long sticky pink strands around her neck. There was a trick to it—he'd shown Jane. You took the rest of the gum out of your mouth and rolled it over the stuck gum, which came away easily from the tender skin beneath.

Without turning on the lights, Nan walked to the long windows and stood looking out, as she had so many times in the six months she and Jane had lived here. Below her the midnight city opened out, the river a dull gleam between dark clumped buildings, the streetlamps blurred with fog coming in off the sea. With her back to the room she could almost hear the sound of Jane's breathing, that light sleep-snuffle, from the alcove behind her. If only she could have back again the long, boring nights of their early exile! Those sparrow nights of uncertainty and peevish enclosure. Now, *then* seemed like paradise. Nan kept her eyes on the window, streaked with runnels of silver as a soft, implacable rain began to fall.

|

"Fockin' coke-sacker! What to hell!"

Val cut off a city bus with inches to spare and pulled into the alley by the back entrance to superior court, where, according to Jenny Root, the press would not expect them to go. Quickly Mel and Nan got out. Val cried, "Console! Console!" and drove off. It was still raining, a cold unsummery rain.

Mel guided Nan through the metal detector, its line of people all wearing the traveler's air of suppressed excitement, the lawyers distinguishable by their briefcases. The guard waved them past a man in stocking feet holding out his shoes for inspection.

They sat down on a bench in the vast vaulted hall to wait for Jenny Root. People milled back and forth. The walls and floor, all marble, threw back their voices. Cops duck-walked by, keys and handcuffs chiming at their belts. At a pay phone a man in a surgical collar stood shouting into the receiver. "*Quante televisioni?* Okay. I dunno. *Ancora vivo.* Okay? Awright!" A small dark woman in a sari sat down next to Nan and began reading a book she pulled out of her bag. *The Theory of Poker,* its bright yellow cover said.

"I'd really like a cigarette," Nan murmured to Mel.

Mel glanced around the hall: no one was smoking. "Better not," she said. "You'll get in trouble."

Nan looked at her. They both burst out laughing.

"You better be Da Bomb in there," Mel said. "I blew off a Prince Albert so I could come here this morning." A Prince Albert—piercing a customer's penis—was Mel's most lucrative gig. "That reminds me. What did the elephant say to the naked man?"

"I don't know. What?"

"How do you breathe through that thing?"

And so it was that Jenny Root, approaching, found her client dissolved in laughter. This was a new slowed-down Jenny Root, exuding sureness and dignity. Even her hair seemed calmer, tamed into a shiny close-fitting cap not unlike Nan's. She and Mel had met two weeks before, when Jenny Root interviewed her as a possible character witness; afterward, each woman had told Nan that the other was, like, wanky. Now Jenny Root stood holding a black leather briefcase plump with papers and taking in the sight of Mel. Eyebrows pierced with little gold barbells; earrings in the shape of crayons, one red, one yellow, which Nan found inexplicably cheering; grass-green T-shirt that said, GROW YOUR OWN DOPE . . .

"Thanks for bringing Nan here," she said smoothly. "I'll phone you when it's over. It could take all day, depends how soon we're called."

"I'm coming with Nan," Mel said.

"No one but the defendant is allowed in the courtroom."

"Crap sandwich! Okay, I'll wait out here."

They were fighting over her, vying for her. "Mel," Nan said. "Go home.

Please. I don't want you sitting here all day. Call Prince Albert, maybe you can reinstate him."

Mel looked at Nan, saw that she meant it, then hugged her, hard. "Be Da Bomb!" she murmured into Nan's ear.

Nan watched her go through the heavy glass doors into the rain. The back of her grass-green T-shirt said, . . . PLANT A MAN!

Courtroom No. 9 was flooded with blue-gray morning light from half a dozen tall arched windows, through which Nan could see the dripping trees and ivy-covered bricks of Benefit Street. An unexpectedly beautiful room, with its plaster garlands and gold leaf, its burnished wood paneling and high, high ceiling. Nan, gazing upward, half expected to see a cherub or two floating there.

They sat down on one of the pewlike oak benches. The smell of furniture wax assailed Nan. Wood-and-brass railings separated them from sideways rows of empty seats (spectators? jury?) to the left and right. At the front of the room was a long polished table with a stenographer and a clerk beside it, and beyond that, on its raised dais, the judge's bench (like an altar, thought Nan) with its flags, U.S. and Rhode Island, hanging limp. Ahead of them Nan could just make out the state's attorney, Jamison Leer, a small, pink man with Coke-bottle glasses. Was that Gabriel with him? She opened her purse to fish for her glasses. Her hand met something hard and pointed, and she pulled it out. Miami Getaway Barbie. Beside her, Jenny Root drew a sudden breath. Glancing sideways, Nan saw her frown. She thrust the doll to the bottom of her purse, found her glasses, put them on. Thank God!—the man next to Jamison Leer wasn't Gabriel.

But they were early. The room began to fill up. Nan found herself one of a crowd, standing room only, in the midst of a Dickensian scene: a man carrying an armful of two-by-fours; another, an empty birdcage. Once she was sure she saw the Boy Father in his blue windbreaker with Bug on his hip; but when she looked again, he was gone. Clearly Jenny Root had lied about people not being allowed in the courtroom: everyone seemed to have friends and relations in tow. People were talking, walking around, standing up and sitting down again.

As nine thirty approached, Jenny Root gave Nan a last-minute briefing. Judge Wright (suddenly shorn of his nicknames) was a stickler for order; he'd once had a guy jailed for contempt because he blew a bubble with his gum. She reminded Nan of her Foreign Service past, her "tact and diplomacy," her "good social control." Nan recalled endless receiving lines, her own graciously patronizing handshakes, standing, in graceful gowns, beside this or that smiling, nodding ambassador. How quickly, once Tod retired, she'd sloughed that glossy skin of *politesse*. How little it could help her now.

"Just act natural," Jenny Root ended. "You know, to thine own self be true, yadda yadda yadda."

Nan looked down at her charcoal-gray suit, her spectator pumps. Own? Self?

"All rise!"

Here he came, majestic, black-gowned, black, his long balding head very like an eggplant. "Good morning, Ladies and Gentlemen!"

Amid the thunder of obedient rising, the chorus of "Good morning, Your Honor," Nan, on her feet like the rest, found herself giving a little curtsy. It was so like mornings in homeroom, the nun entering, the girls scrambling to their feet. Jenny Root frowned a warning at her as they all sat down.

One by one the clerk called the cases scheduled for that day. The attorneys either responded "Ready, Your Honor!" (all this your-honoring made Nan feel like a peasant in a Chekhov story) or asked to postpone, offering various explanations for their unreadiness. The postponers left, and the room began to feel less crowded. There was a lot of restless moving around and talking among those waiting to be called, and periodically a policeman standing at the front of the room shouted, "Quiet! Quiet down!" The pretty, long-haired stenographer tossed her head as she typed, hennaed curls alive on her shoulders like some small animal. Bored, nervous, apprehensive, Nan studied Jamison Leer. His hair, too long and stiffened into curved wings on either side of his head, made him look rather like a stingray. She remembered the fake hair of the lawyer in the hospital (what was his name?) and glanced sideways at Jenny Root's. Am I doomed to run into lawyers who belong to the League for the Tonsorially Impaired? The clerk droned on. Nan began to tell herself all the lawyer jokes she could remember. What do you call a criminal lawyer? Redundant. What do you have when a lawyer is buried up to his neck in wet cement? Not enough cement. What's the difference between a lawyer and a bucket of cow manure? The bucket.

At last only the Readies were left—Wise Virgins who'd brought oil for their lamps, to illuminate the murky reaches of the Law. Plenty of empty seats now. Turning around, Nan saw a couple of reporters she recognized from encounters on Elbow Street, notepads poised.

And Gabriel.

She faced front again, the blood banging in her ears, but not before she'd noted his stance (that violent humility), his gaze (straight at her). She leaned close to Jenny Root, forgetting to whisper. "Gabriel— My son-in-law—"

"Quiet!" the policeman standing below the judge's dais intoned.

Jenny Root whispered, "It's okay. Just chill."

Mercifully, they hadn't long to wait. Theirs was the first case called. Jenny Root gathered her papers and disappeared, with Leer and Judge Wright, behind a door in back of the judge's dais.

Through the tall arched windows Nan watched the rain, slow and heavy. The streaming glass gave the world outside the courtroom a surreal quality, buildings runny, trees wavering. Half turning, she snatched another glimpse of Gabriel. He too gazed out at the falling rain. She had the sudden understanding that he was *making* himself look haggard. She remembered, now, that he'd sometimes been an expert witness in the Seattle courts. He'd know how to present himself, what a judge would look for.

Jenny Root came back and motioned Nan to follow her out of the room. She trembled, approaching Gabriel. He did not look at her until she was almost past; then he turned on her a glance so malevolent it traveled through her like a jolt of electricity.

They sat down on a bench in the rotunda, under the collective gaze of a dozen larger-than-life framed portraits of Judges Past. All men, all stern, all silver-haired.

". . . an offer I'd like you to consider, Nan."

Not a compassionate face among them. Not a glimmer of humor.

"Nan—are you listening?"

Not a face that looked remotely capable of the pain and longing she'd just seen on Gabriel's. She took off her glasses and put them in the pocket of her jacket.

"I need a cigarette."

Jenny Root led her around the corner, past a sign that said CLOSED TO THE PUBLIC, through a door marked both LADIES and WOMEN. Awkwardly, because of their skirts and high-heeled shoes, they sat down on the floor beneath a sign that at first glance seemed to say NO SMIRK-ING. Nan lit up. Heaven! She leaned back against the tiled wall and contemplated two sets of feet in black pumps below the stall doors. There was the hollow roar of two toilets flushing in unison, and two women in identical dark suits emerged.

"So he says to Judge Beckel, 'The pedestrian hit me and went under my car.'"

"Yeah, right. My guy claimed an invisible car came out of nowhere, struck him, and vanished."

The two women finished drying their hands, tweaked their identical hair, and left without a glance at Nan and Jenny Root. Their voices trailed back through the closing door. "So, get this, my client is *habeas*'ed in from the ACI . . ."

Jenny Root leaned close to Nan. "Okay, here's the deal. Just like I said. Leer will drop the charges if you tell him where your granddaughter is."

Smoke from Nan's cigarette twirled upward between them, aromatic, cheering. It failed to obscure the vision of Gabriel's face.

"You can walk out of here and never come back. Go where you want. *Do* what you want."

"No."

"Nan. Think a minute. If you refuse this offer, Leer'll really go after us. He's a mean mother, I told you that, and he's smart. Remember Claus von Bulow? Leer helped get him off. And whatever judge we get for the actual trial'll be prejudiced against us. Because we wasted the court's time, that's how they'll see it, if we refuse a reasonable settlement now."

We?

"Okay, look, say we go to trial. Say we win. The judge gives Jane to you. With a trial, he'll've had to order a psychiatric examination. Jane'll have to go through that. People will suggest things to her. Make accusations. There'll be publicity, stuff other kids might taunt her with, stuff she could maybe read later on, when she's older. And if Gabriel appeals—and I bet you he would—the whole thing could drag on for years. *Years,* Nan."

A young black policewoman pushed open the door, saw them, withdrew with a clanking of keys. The Thought hovered, closer now.

"Say we lose. And we could, Nan, we really could. If we turn down this offer everything'll be against us. Say the judge gives Jane to Gabriel. What's your plan?"

"I—I just won't turn her over. I won't say where she is."

"Then you'll go to jail. Up to ten years. Jane will spend those years—grade school, junior high, she'll be starting high school by the time you get out—with whoever she's with now. Someone she's not even related to. She won't be able to visit you. And she won't see her mother or her father, ever again."

Nan leaned her head back against the cold tile. There was a single small window high on the wall opposite. From her angle she saw only sky—wet, gray, empty. The emptiness pleased her. The world had narrowed to this.

"Nan—how'll you keep track of Jane if you're in prison? You could totally lose touch with her. You might never see her again."

Never see Jane again? Not *see* her?

"And what about your heart? You could die in prison. One day, all of a sudden, you're archives—what happens to Jane then? *Think, Nan!*"

Nan lit another cigarette from the burning stub of the first. Her fingers trembled. Of course she should have thought of these possible outcomes herself. But she hadn't.

Jenny Root stopped talking and put one hand over Nan's. Across the room a faucet dripped. The sound grew in the silence until it was a drumbeat. Jane. Jane. Jane.

Nan closed her eyes and let smoke stream from her nostrils. So this was they meant by the lesser of two evils. She'd believed that she'd encountered it in the past; she had not. The logistics of such a choice were bleaker than she'd ever realized. Either way, she deprived Jane: whether she gave her up—gave her back to Gabriel—or kept her whereabouts a secret.

"Would they let her see me? Could I visit her?"

"I can try to make that a condition."

A small stab of joy, quick as a pinprick. Nan opened her eyes. She looked down at the hard, grimy floor where they sat, then up at the blank gray square of sky in the wall across from them.

At last she said, her voice someone else's voice, "All right."

|

"All rise!"

Here was the judge again, and a lot of good-afternooning (lunchtime having come and gone) and your-honoring, and then the two lawyers once again disappeared with Wright into the room behind the dais. Nan pulled her glasses out of her jacket pocket and put them on. Gabriel had moved down to the front pew, with Leer. He sat with his back to Nan, head bent, shoulders slumped theatrically under the fine wool blazer. Nan opened her purse and felt around inside until her fingers found Miami Getaway Barbie and closed around it. Outside the tall arched windows it was still raining. Heavy, wet, weighing, it bent the juniper bushes to the ground in supplicant postures.

This time the two lawyers reappeared within minutes, both smiling the smiles of people who'd gotten what they wanted. Leer's expression as he looked toward Gabriel justified his name. Gabriel straightened.

Jenny Root sat down next to Nan and put an arm around her shoulders. "Everything's cool. They'll drop the charges right now. You just tell me how to get hold of Jane."

Nan's heart began thumping out a crazy waltz. "Now?"

She was still holding on to Miami Getaway Barbie; she pulled it out of her bag and sat clutching it in both hands. Somehow she'd imagined there'd be more time, a breathing space between the decision and the act.

If I do this, it's forever.

"Yeah, now. Leer and I go back, I tell Wright how to hook up with Jane, he tables the case with a note to dismiss. Pending Jane's delivery to DCYF."

"DCYF?"

"Department of Children, Youth, and Families. Officially she'll be in the custody of the State. Till determination is made."

"Why won't she just go home with Gabriel? To Seattle."

"Nan." Jenny Root's deep-voiced whisper held a note of frayed patience. "Allegations have been made that raise the question of Jane's welfare. *You* made them. The State has to assure itself of what's best for the child."

"How long will that take? Where will Jane be while it's going on?" Hope filled Nan's throat so that she could barely speak. "Will she, will they leave her with me?"

"She'll go into foster care." Jenny Root paused, then said reluctantly, "Maybe for several months. DCYF has a huge backlog. Once Jane's safely in custody, she'll have to wait her turn. There're kids ahead of her in way worse situations."

Nan didn't care about the problems of children unknown to her, she cared about Jane. Jane in a series of foster homes, living with strangers. Jane, who'd already spent the last six months being shunted from one place to another. She remembered her face as they'd pulled away from the curb the day of their last picnic, with Val and Mel standing on the sidewalk in the morning light. Remembered Mel's story of foster home after foster home.

"Nan!" Jenny Root whispered urgently. "Wright'll be ripshit. He hates to be kept waiting."

Looking up, Nan saw Gabriel, now straight-backed, nodding and smiling at Leer, who presumably was saying the same things Jenny Root was saying. Yet the tilt of Gabriel's head was . . . *happy.*

He doesn't care how long Jane has to wait. Or where. So long as it's him she ends up with. So long as he has his revenge, on his unfaithful wife, on me.

Suddenly Nan could see what she hadn't been able to see before, sitting on the ladies' room floor with Jenny Root; she could see another life for Jane. Jane hip-deep in marigolds beside a wooden fence that steamed in the sun, giving up the dampness of the night before. Jane smiling into the early-morning light, through the silver-leaved olive trees. Jane by the edge of the ocean, sniffing the salt air. The vision was so clear! It did not seem like something imagined—more like something transmitted.

"I can't," she said to Jenny Root. "I can't do it."

"Nan! For Christ's sake!"

"I'm sorry. I can't."

Jenny Root looked at Nan for a long moment. At last she said, "Okay. Yeah. I guess I knew that."

She gave Nan's shoulder a hard, painful squeeze. Then she rose and walked—slowly at first, then more purposefully—up to the front of the room. She tapped Jamison Leer on the shoulder; there was a brief whispered exchange; Leer turned to stare at Nan. Then both lawyers went up to the judge, and all three disappeared into the room behind the dais. Gabriel didn't turn around. After several hour-long minutes the judge emerged, followed by the two lawyers.

"All rise!"

When the shuffle of rising and reseating had subsided, Wright beckoned to Nan. Heart pounding, she got up, still holding Miami Getaway Barbie, and walked down the aisle to stand with the two lawyers below the dais. Jenny Root came and stood beside her, their arms just grazing each other. Wright gazed down at them. His face wore a more-in-sorrow-than-in-anger look.

"Mrs. Mulholland. You understand the offer that has been made to you?" His deep voice had an orator's ponderous tempo.

Nan nodded. At the other end of the dais, the stenographer's fingers flew, her machine paying out white paper tape like an adding machine.

"Speak up!"

"Yes."

Jenny Root elbowed her. "Your Honor," she whispered.

"Yes, Your Honor."

"The prosecution has offered to drop the charge of kidnapping if you will tell us the whereabouts of your granddaughter. It's your decision, and you have the right to a trial. Let me remind you, however, of the words of Anatole France. 'To die for an idea is to set a rather high price on conjecture.'"

"I understand—"

"Let me finish! Idealism is noble, but it is expensive. You should know that, if you are found guilty, this is a serious crime with serious consequences. You may well find yourself serving a prison—"

Sanctimonious dipshit, Mel would have said. "Your Honor, I can't let Jane—"

"I'm speaking to you! Let me finish!" He leaned forward, unhooked his gold-rimmed spectacles and folded them in one hand. His eyes were small and hard, like peanuts. "It is a generous and compassionate offer that this Court has made to you, Mrs. Mul—"

"No!" Despair made Nan's voice louder than she'd intended. "Don't you see? She's been abused enough already, she—"

"Nan!" Jenny Root seized her arm. "Be quiet!"

Jamison Leer said, "Your Honor, if—I repeat, if—there's been any abuse, it has been by the child's mother. Doctor Verdi alleges—"

"Shut up!" Nan told him. "You don't know a thing about it."

"Nan," Jenny Root moaned.

Wright's round, bald head glittered with sweat. He shouted, "I will not tolerate this behavior in my courtroom!"

Gabriel was suddenly standing on the other side of Jamison Leer. Fear stilled Nan's breath; she fought the urge to turn and run. Gabriel in the hallway outside her apartment; Gabriel's hands on her shoulders. A glance seemed to pass between him and the judge. A glance of mutual understanding. Nan felt a sweeping, plummeting sensation, like going down too fast in an elevator. Her fingers tightened around the doll in her hand. Fear turned into fury.

Who are these men? What right do they have to decide?

She said—she was shouting, too, now— "Jane's been through enough! Can't any of you see that? Don't any of you care about *Jane*?"

By now the entire courtroom was stirring and buzzing. The policeman beside the dais shouted, "Quiet! Quiet down!" Wright's gavel beat on the rostrum. The stenographer typed furiously.

Wright looked directly, malevolently, into Nan's eyes. She saw on his face the male's fury at losing control, not only of her, but of himself.

"Take her out of here!" he roared. His gavel hit the rostrum. "Criminal contempt! Six months!"

Jenny Root said, "Your Honor! My client apologizes for the disturbance."

"I do not!"

"Get this woman out of my courtroom!"

Two policemen appeared from nowhere, shoved Jenny Root aside, gripped Nan's arms. She stiffened, resisting. Jenny Root said, "Your Honor!"

"Silence! Or you'll go with her!"

The courtroom stilled. Nan found herself being half pushed, half pulled toward a door at the side of the room. She saw Gabriel, white with fury, lunge after her; saw Leer grab his arms and hold him back. She saw Jenny Root's horrified face. Then Wright shouted, "Next!" and the stenographer tore off a length of white paper tape with a crisp, confirming sound.

Fifteen

Nan woke to the sound of women's voices. Strangers' voices. Then she remembered: I'm in jail. She lay still and kept her eyes closed.

"Well, it creeps me out. Hearing somebody up there over my head in the middle of the night. In a *empty* bunk! I didn't know for sure the Lord is watching over me, I'd'a thought it was a ghost."

"You were really off the hook. Wasn't she, Ellen? They brought her in around eleven. Ellen and I, we just played possum. Didn't we, Ellen?"

"Looks like it ain't one of Ellen's talking days. Anyway, the new one sure can snore."

"She *old*, that's why. Lemme explain to you, Donna Jean. The nasal passages, see, the septum—"

"Forget it. There's the buzzer. I don't want Scantling ripped at me again today."

"We gonna wake up the Scarsdale Matron, or let her sleep? God! I hate breakfast the most."

"How many times I gotta tell you? Don't take the Lord's name in vain. God ain't up there going, *Marjorie!* every time He gets pissed at something."

"Shoulda combed your hair, Donna Jean. God don't like ugly."

The clatter of departure. A door slammed. Nan opened her eyes to an empty room. A narrow bed, hard, close to the ceiling, where early-morning gloom had collected in the corners. The upper bunk. Another bunk bed opposite hers. Three other women in this room, then? Two dark scarred wooden wardrobes with mildewed mirrors. Four footlockers. Two night tables. One bulletin board. A breeze through the open window stirred curtains of thin flowered cotton. Nan lay and listened to the morning sounds of birds: the bicycle-bell call of blue jays; the cardinals' "Weirdo! Weirdo!"; the dim sound of mourning doves. (Quick flash of Walker—but far away, as if seen through the wrong end of a telescope.) There were no bars on the window, she noticed.

"No cells here," she remembered the warden—Warden Gordon, could that really be his name?—saying proudly the night before. Shaved head, puffy lips, cheeks inflating and deflating: he looked like a large, pale fish. Walkie-talkies chattering; incomprehensible jokes; clipped laughter. Fingerprinting: ink that smelled like chloroform and clung to her fingers. Photographs. Undressing in a long cement-walled room with a shower and benches; a female body searcher with a face like a safety pin. Nan's tattoo and her breastbone scar were carefully drawn in red on a form that held the outline of a female figure, front and back. Just another modeling session, Nan told herself. Naked and trembling, her nipples pricking with cold, she read the rest of the form upside down:

INMATE NAME _____

D.O.B. _____

GANG AFFILIATION? _____

IF YES, NAME OF GANG _____

ANY ENEMY ISSUES _____

Nan's clothes, shoes, watch were noted on another form, then put into a paper bag along with Miami Getaway Barbie. Her arms were piled with beige garments folded into anonymity and smelling of starch. A shower, while the bored body searcher looked on. Beige pajamas, too big, scratchy. Back out to the counter, where a poster on the wall said, IN FOR LIFE? THERE'S NO FUTURE IN SUICIDE. Someone had crossed out the last two words in heavy dark pencil. Nan signed the inmate property record where they showed her, juggling the clothing in her arms while she held on to the pen. Then a kind-looking woman in civilian clothes led her down a dim, deserted hallway. Shuffling along in papery prison slippers, wearing her glasses ("If you need 'em, wear 'em; otherwise, we take 'em"), Nan was already beginning not to be Nan.

Now she thought, If the others have to be at breakfast, I must, too. She threw back the thin cotton blanket with its harsh smell of bleach and swung her legs over the edge of the bed. She was looking down and contemplating the drop (No ladder—how on earth did I get up here last night?) when the door burst open.

"Mulholland! Get your ass down to the dining room. One demerit!"

|

The first day, Saturday, passed in a blur of disorientation, boredom, and fear. Nan didn't know the rules or the routine, and no one bothered to explain them to her. (What did you expect, she chided herself, a Prisoner's Handbook? A formal briefing? This is not the Foreign Service.) By the end of the day she'd accumulated three demerits and the information that two more would earn her time in something called Seg.

Except for watching the never-silent TV in the little sitting area along the corridor, there was nothing, absolutely nothing, to do. Her roommates didn't return to the room. They must have been among the many women who stared at her at lunch (she missed breakfast altogether); but because she'd kept her eyes closed while they spoke that morning, Nan didn't know what they looked like. The room caught the afternoon sun and was hot but cheerful. Each neatly made bunk, except for Nan's, was covered by a bright-colored afghan, obviously homemade. Two or three stuffed animals reposed on each pillow. There were some books on the bottom shelf of one of the night tables: *A Pictorial Atlas of Skin Infections*; the Bible; *Reptiles of the Pacific World*. It seemed unwise to be caught leafing through another prisoner's books, even if they'd been more appealing. Nan left the room and wandered down the sunny corridor. Here and there electric fans pushed the warm afternoon air back and forth. At both ends there was the upright figure of a blue-uniformed guard, recalling in a strange, skewed way the hovering presence of The Nannies. A man in a dark suit and a Roman collar passed by, arms full of books, tightly buttoned face. He did not greet Nan. She went through an open wire door—a small, dark woman mopping the floor had propped it open with her bucket—and into another wing identical to her own. One demerit, happily administered by Safety Pin. Delivered back to her own wing, Nan sat down before the television to watch *Oprah*. A woman with very long, very black hair came and sat down next to her. Nan asked her why she, like all the other women Nan had seen in her wanderings so far, wore blue garments rather than Nan's beige. The woman shrugged apologetically. *"No hablo inglés, señora."* Nan's elementary

Spanish, begun a lifetime ago in Seattle, seemed to have deserted her. So that (another pretty shrug from the woman) was that.

Again at dinner—macaroni and cheese that tasted like it smelled, of library paste—no one spoke to Nan. The Scarsdale Matron, she remembered one of her unseen roommates saying. Perhaps everyone saw her that way, thanks to Jenny Root's make-under. She touched her hair, still stiff with spray from its day in court. The heads around her, like the women themselves, could not have been more different: Afros, dreadlocks, crew cuts, shags, and the hair of the Hispanic women, either long, wild curls or neat buns. They were all young, these women—younger by far than Nan. The ones at Nan's table talked among themselves, complaining about the food, gossiping. She felt the way she had the first day of high school, before she'd found Deenie. Then she'd been odd because she was poor and from the inner city; now the reason was the opposite.

But that night, in her room, everything changed. Marjorie changed it.

|

Nan couldn't, that second night, climb up into her bed. There really was no ladder. The night before, she remembered now, the young assistant warden had called a guard and together they'd heaved Nan up onto her mattress. She tried to hoist herself up, her feet on the mattress below, her hands clutching at the edges of her own.

"You oughta have a medical bottom."

The voice behind her, rich as a preacher's, surprised Nan so that she let go. She dropped to the floor, stumbled, fell onto one knee.

"Hey!" The woman pulled her up and folded her into the lower bunk. Then she sat down beside her, wide-bosomed, black, motherly. She held a stuffed panda under one arm.

"A medical bottom?" Confused, Nan pictured her own bare behind with a thermometer sticking out it.

"Yeah. You're too old for a top." The woman looked closely at Nan. A wad of chewing gum switched from cheek to cheek. "Too old to be in here at *all*. What'd you do, girl?"

"My granddaughter, Jane, she's four—almost five, now. I kidnapped her."

"Now why'd you wanna go and do a thing like that for?"

"She, her father was—molesting her." No point going into the questions, the uncertainties, the doubts Nan herself still had.

"So you *saved* her. You two hear that?" She turned to the two women who had just entered the room. The tiny redhead said, "Praise God!" and grasped Nan's hand, while the other one just smiled from beneath the long, tangled hair that nearly covered her face. A bewildered Nan found herself accepted, suddenly and completely.

Later she would understand that Jane had been her passport, the key to belonging; that to the women in this place the one thing that still mattered—the sole source of strength and resilience and hope—was their children. Now she just leaned into the shadow of the upper bunk, breathless and a little taken aback, as if a door she'd been pushing on had suddenly yielded, catapulting her inside.

Here they were, then: Nan's new family. Yet another pickup family.

Marjorie. Like so many black women, older than she looked. (Early forties, Nan judged: she mentioned leaving school at fourteen, in the late sixties, pregnant.) Skin the color of Italian plums, fitted close over broad, strong bones. Hair like coarse cotton thread, every strand alive. Curious about everything: the books on the night table were hers, except for the Bible. In for abandoning her father, who had Alzheimer's, at the grey-hound racetrack in Lincoln, with a note pinned to his sweatshirt detailing his condition and his care. ("It was him or her grandkids," Donna Jean said. "Now she don't have neither.")

Donna Jean. The tiniest woman Nan had ever seen—not just short (though she was certainly that: about four foot ten), but scaled down all over. Red hair, short and shaggy; freckles; a peculiarly intent gaze. "My Lord has shown me how to overcome my downfalls," she told Nan, who immediately understood that she herself was a target for salvation. In for bombing an abortion clinic, leaving one of the doctors in a wheelchair for life. Transferred here to Minimum Security just last month, thanks to three years of exemplary behavior and the merciful intervention of her Lord.

Ellen. Silent smiler; looked about twelve years old. She bobbed her head, conciliating but wordless, when introduced to Nan. Long hair that hid her face, except for red mournful lips. Sleeves of her blue prison sweater pulled down to hide the tips of her fingers, arms wrapped around her knees while the others explained this new world to Nan.

The room felt full of bodies, humid with sweat and the odor of un-washed hair—but comfortingly so. Marjorie and Donna Jean talked, often at once, contradicting and upbraiding each other. Ellen sat and smiled, occasionally patting the Raggedy Ann doll in the crook of her arm. A tide of information mixed with admonition washed over Nan—more, far more, than she could absorb. Warm night air from the open window brushed her cheek, the back of her neck, and she could hear the sounds of traffic from the freeway beyond the high wire fence. She listened, silent as Ellen. She understood her choices: be adopted or perish. At last Donna Jean said, "Kids' Day tomorrow, gotta get our beauty sleep," and Marjorie said, "You keep that bunk, honey, Donna Jean'll trade you," and Ellen said nothing at all. Donna Jean reached over and turned out the light. Darkness; silence.

|

On the second day, Sunday, Nan woke to far-off church bells, a sound that always (even now, in this place) said *Italy* to her. It was still early: a soft pink light filtered through the curtains. No breakfast on Sundays, the others had told Nan the night before; instead, the children came. There was a table with juice and fruit and peanut-butter-and-jelly sandwiches, out in the yard if it was nice weather, in the reception area if not. Nan slid soundlessly out of bed. Without waking the other three, she pulled on her scratchy beige cotton pants and shirt and left to roam the quiet, nearly empty corridors.

She discovered the Library, with its few volumes stacked sideways on the shelves, its smell—it was in the basement and windowless—of mildew. ("Everything is for the men," Marjorie told her later, bitter but resigned. "The women get the leftovers. You oughta see the men's Computer Room.") The Smoking Porch, with its pool table, its card tables painted with checkerboards (but no checkers), its Pepsi machine. Long and light, a place to catch the summer breezes. ("The guys have a gorgeous gym," Marjorie said, "*and* a law library. The philosophy is, women ain't likely to cause trouble, let's take care of the men.") The Crafts Room, where prisoners could make baby clothes and knit afghans. The yard (Nan peered through a square of glass in the heavy metal door at the end of the corridor, under the watchful Nanny-gaze of a guard), with its peeling wooden picnic tables, a gangly lilac in one corner, a couple of bees assaulting the pink and red impatiens planted around its trunk, as cheerful as they were anywhere.

What did you expect? Nan chided herself. Ashes, cinders, carbolic? The smells of Auschwitz? Frivolous comparison. Nan had seen Auschwitz. This was not that; this was nothing like that.

Then she noticed that the yard was encircled by high cyclone fencing topped with barbed wire. Beyond it was another building, the mirror image of Nan's own, a long colonial brick structure like a college dorm. It boasted a white-painted dome topped with a weather vane. Nan moved to one side of the mesh-covered window and craned to see down the street. Behind her the guard coughed warningly. Somehow Nan knew not to touch the glass, or the door itself. Squinting, she could make out more brick buildings, grassy spaces; the whole place resembled a shabby, down-at-heel college campus. The women's section of the ACI, according to Marjorie, had originally been built as a mental hospital in the forties. Both Minimum Security, where Nan was, and Maximum Security—the building beyond the fencing—were still called by the names they'd had back then, disarmingly collegiate: Dix Building; Gloria McDonald Building.

But there was the endless march of cyclone fencing, the evil glint of barbed wire. The ACI: Adult Correctional Institute. Every word a lie, Nan thought, as she turned from the window. The women so young, so often childlike; the idea of correction, like orthodontia for the soul; the suggestion of seminars and panel discussions.

Nan's bitter little exercise in translation was interrupted by a sound so foreign to the place that she thought she must be hallucinating. No—there it was again. Laughter, high-pitched squeals, the quick clap of feet. Of course: today was Kids' Day. If she turned again to look out the window and waited, she would see them. Instead, she began to walk back down the empty corridor, faster and faster, until she reached the stairs. She sat in the dim little basement library thumbing through a mildewed copy of *Great Expectations* until the lunch gong sounded.

The next day, Monday, was both better and worse.

Because she was classed as "A&T"—Awaiting Trial (because there hadn't been a trial, only a pretrial hearing)—Nan wasn't eligible for work detail. After breakfast, when her roommates disappeared—Marjorie and Donna Jean to the laundry, Ellen to the kitchen—Nan roamed C Wing, looking for other women in beige. (Beige, she'd discovered, was for A&Ts and "Papa Charlies," women in protective care; sentenced prisoners wore blue.) She struck up occasional conversations, usually accompanied by the sound of TV, either soaps or soul-baring talk shows. Under her arm—no pockets in prison clothing—she carried a little chintz-covered notebook Donna Jean had given her, with "My Soul's Journey" printed on it and a tiny green pencil attached to its spine by a string. She wrote down what she saw. Just a list at first; then somehow, in the course of that day, Monday, the little notebook became a record she was keeping for Alex. The Alex who'd had an affair was not the Alex Nan had always known. The Alex who'd had an affair was someone who might, in time, come to understand Nan. Neither of them had known the other. Now it seemed possible that one day they might. The little notebook was a beginning. A form of consolation, the only one available to her in this place: that her daughter could—someday, somehow—know every detail of Nan's gift to her.

Starting that day, Monday, she wrote it all down. The display case in the hall outside Warden Gordon's office, full of karate trophies with the names of the winners—inmates and staff side by side—engraved on brass plates. The closed-circuit TV divided into sixteen squares, each captioned: Laundry, Yard, Front Porch, Holding. The cameras. *Cameras everywhere, Alex. In the halls, in the common rooms, in the john, peering evilly down from the corners.* The sense of surveillance, the sense of confinement, of the locked wire doors at either end of C Wing, never left her, though she walked and walked. (Her heart doctor in Seattle, a lifetime ago, would have been pleased.) *Jail was the fate Attila the Nun foresaw for us, Alex. Deenie & me. More than forty years ago, now. When they found out who put the crotchless black lace panties down the convent laundry chute.*

More disturbing than the sense of confinement was the comfort it brought. Relief: that was what Nan felt. She was unspeakably weary, as if her outburst in court, that decision wrung from her at the last minute, had taken all her strength. Now the phrase *out of my hands* echoed in her head, in her footsteps on the vinyl floor, in the indecipherable mutterings of the walkie-talkies riding the hips of the guards as she passed by. *Out of my hands,* she wrote in the little notebook. A chant, a benediction, a prayer, it had, blessedly, replaced The Thought. Nan Mulholland was a prisoner; there was no longer any action she could take. Here, the only role going was that of Little Red Waitinghood. Everything she saw confirmed it.

The neutralization of color—like the Soviet Union, all those years ago. *Beige, brown, navy, gray* gray GRAY. The reduction of texture to vinyl, cinder block, linoleum. The impersonal smells of disinfectant, crumbling plaster, mice, dust. All of it redeemed only by the inmates' tireless knitting of things—afghans, pillow covers, stuffed animals, bureau scarves—in shouts of yellow and orange and red. *Only a few such articles can be kept; everything else has to be sent out with a visitor, or it will be confiscated.*

And the women. The women.

Mary Louise (Possession), small & sleek & deaf, dancing up to you & tugging at your sleeve. Crystal (Prostitution), telling anyone who'll listen, "I'm gonna turn my life around." Sharon (Aggravated Assault), raped by her mother's boyfriend, barely eighteen. Voncile (Dealing), stately, black, hates me for being the Media Queen, as seen on TV before I ever set foot in here. Radiant Lourdes (Prostitution), eight months pregnant, a Spanish galleon in full sail.

The woman in for Burglary, a safecracker who'd once worked for the police. The woman in for Manslaughter (reduced from Murder One) because she'd breast-fed her baby while on heroin. The woman Nan thought of as the Other Grandmother—the only other inmate near her age. She'd gone on driving after her license was pulled, until one day when she couldn't lift her foot off the accelerator and, careening through a city park, killed three young children. These last two were shunned by all the others. No one spoke to them; no one sat at their table at meals. Children had died.

|

Talking. Talking. When the women weren't working or napping, they talked.

"Made parole? That dumb bitch?"

"Colleen told me."

"*She's* a piece of work."

"And that Deciolaria—you know, over in B Wing?—sweet little madonna, she belong to—is it the Latin Queens, or Los Alitos? One a those gangs. Her boyfriend, too. You'll see him Sunday, Kids' Day, he bring their kid *every* week." Marjorie sat cross-legged on a lower bunk, the one given to Nan, her wide jelly breasts packed into a black lace bra. Warm night air poured through the open window.

Deciolaria. The mother of Bug? It must be; there couldn't be two women in the ACI named that.

"Those teardrops tattooed on Deciolaria's cheek?" Donna Jean said. "That's one for every person she killed."

"Nah," said Marjorie. "Could be for deaths in the family, too. Be fair."

"And Voncile, she's been in Seg twice for flunking her ions."

"Ions?" said Nan.

"Yeah, you know. That, like, paper they rubbed over your hands and arms when they brought you in here? They do it three-four times a month. Surprise checks—the Dolphin's big on surprise checks."

"The Dolphin?"

"Warden Gordon. Don't he look like one? Anyway, that paper they rub you with, it detects every drug known to man. Didn't they tell you that?"

"They didn't tell me anything."

"Honey! Well, you got *us* now. We will tell you everything. Won't we, Ellen?"

|

Fourth day, fourth demerit. Alex, you can't do a thing here without permission. You give up everything of your own, like entering the convent. You belong to them. Your body belongs to them. You can't move it without asking.

The demerit, for being off her wing, was worth it. Hungry for color, she'd gone to see the murals in B Wing, the Recovery Wing, where former addicts had covered the walls with bright paintings and words of exhortation. (WELCOME! THIS IS THE FIRST STOP TO THE REST OF YOUR LIFE! HOPE IS THE DESTINATION; LOVE IS THE ROAD.) The guard—small and freckled and clear-eyed—pointed Nan back in the direction of her own wing. Now only one demerit separated Nan from Seg. So what? she thought. What do I have to lose? I'm *out of my hands.*

|

Breakfast. Lunch. Dinner. By Tuesday, her fourth day, Nan could feel herself clinging to mealtimes, moving from one to the next, stepping-stones that kept her from falling into the vast anesthetic pool of the day. The big news at lunch (FRIED CALM PLATE, the blackboard above the steam table announced) was a woman on D Wing who'd gone on hunger strike. Something to do with her children; opinions differed as to what. Donna Jean said that the Dolphin had it in for the woman, whose name was Nancy, because she wouldn't sleep with him. Marjorie said no, it was the police, trying to catch Nancy's boyfriend, though how refusing to let her see her kids would accomplish that, she couldn't say.

"She's got gumption. You got to give her that."

"Gunction? What's that?"

"*Gumption,* Donna Jean. Christ! The word means ambition."

"Dear Lord, forgive your servant Marjorie her profanity, for she knows not what to do."

"They gonna put her on tomorrow's medical run, that's what I hear."

The dining room, in the basement, was lit by small, dusty windows set high in the walls. The effect was vaguely liturgical, women here and there bathed in shafts of light, like saints in Renaissance paintings. Gray-painted cinder-block walls; gray cement floor. The steel tables were round and bolted to the floor, each with six round stools attached to its base. The Other Grandmother set her tray down on a table near Nan's; immediately the two women seated there rose and went to another table.

Next to Marjorie, the safecracker said, "There's some people I know wanna boycott macaroni and cheese."

"Why?" Nan asked.

"Because, uh ... It has something to do with the cigarette companies."

Donna Jean said, "Nancy goes on the medical run, Doc Shovelton's gonna see her right. Could be she'll escape, like, what was her name?"

"Oh, Doc! He's all right. You meet him yet?" Marjorie turned to Nan, who shook her head. Her mouth was full of vegetable casserole. Carrots, turnips, onions. Roots! she thought, cellar food; and a phrase came back to her from her youth: Mortification of the Flesh. Penance for our sins.

Enthusiastically the women described how Doc Shovelton had been in jail himself, nearly seven years, back in the seventies. An accessory after the fact, because he'd given medical care to some black militants who'd bombed a military base, killing a guard.

"He's on *our* side, honey. You will love the man. Every one of us does."

Women had escaped while being taken to the hospital for treatment insisted on by Doc. Two, or was it three?

"'Course, they couldn't never pin it on him. He's too smart."

"He knows what it's like. He escaped himself, while he was A&T. Lord God Almighty! That's how come he got such a long sentence."

Dessert was bathroom sponges filled with magenta poster paint. Nan remembered JFK's Berlin Wall speech, "*Ich bin ein Berliner,*" much admired by Tod's colleagues in the embassy at Bonn, whose command of German did not include the knowledge that a Berliner was a jelly doughnut. That life—had it really happened? It seemed now not merely past, but *other,* not hers, something she'd read or heard about. The lunch-table talk returned to food. The safecracker said that the State spent $2.10 per day per inmate to feed them. Marjorie recited a recipe she'd read somewhere for Omelette Louis XV: 24 ortolans ("whatever *they* may be"), 18 pheasant eggs, 6 whole black truffles. Donna Jean said, "Bless us, O Lord, and these Thy gifts."

|

A new sign in the hall announced, JULY PROGRAMS!!!

- ADVANCED MACRAMÉ
- DOMESTIC VIOLENCE GROUP
- IDENTIFYING WILD LOVERS
- MIND OVER MOOD

No—that was WILD *FLOWERS.* Anyway, no prison programs were open to Nan, the A&T.

|

"Mulholland! You got a visitor. Move it!"

Nan, who'd begun to wonder why Val and Mel hadn't come to see her, felt a leap of joy. But when the little freckled guard led her to a cubicle off the sitting area of B Wing, the drug rehab wing, it was Jenny Root who sat staring around her at the walls covered with bright paintings and encouraging slogans.

Jane! was Nan's first thought. "They found her?" she blurted.

Startled out of her reverie, Jenny Root rose. "Nan! No—no, they haven't."

The guard motioned her to sit down again, then led Nan to the other side of the rickety card table. Nan sat, too, knees still wobbling. Through the open window the sound of a lawn mower approached and receded, approached and receded. It was a beautiful bright June day. The heat made her stiff cotton clothes itch; she rubbed her arms, shoulders, stuck a hand down the back of her shirt. Jenny Root regarded her with a mixture of exasperation and sympathy.

"You okay? You're, like, *pale.*"

Nan raised her eyebrows. "Prison pallor. Maybe you've heard of it?"

Jenny Root sighed. "Nan. I'm on *your* side."

"Really?"

The guard went around to the other side of the partition, keys jingling. The heady, tickling smell of new-mown grass filled the cubicle. Nan sneezed.

"Look. It was my duty as your attorney to present any offer that might be to your benefit. We've been through this. *You're* my client. Nobody else—not even Jane. Are we on the same page?"

Ashamed, Nan looked away. How could she tell Jenny Root that her very presence brought back what she, Nan, had been free of for four days now? It brought back Jane. Brought back the vision, quickly warded off, of all she had lost. Brought back The Thought.

Jenny Root handed her a Kleenex. "Your welfare, not Jane's. But now it appears they may not be . . . um . . . mutually exclusive." She waited, watching Nan, who had no idea what she meant. "Lemme explain our position. Sound-Bite Wright is treating this like civil contempt, which he can't do because this is a criminal charge, but he's doing it anyway. The way civil contempt works is, the prisoner holds the keys to her cell. All you have to do is show the judge you're willing to testify truthfully, and you're free."

"Let me guess," Nan said. "I tell him where Jane is, or I'll rot here."

"Right. You give him Jane, he'll lift the contempt charge, and you're out on bail. Then the state's attorney drops the Kidnapping charge, and you're a free woman. If you *don't* tell, Wright can keep you in here forever. When your six months're up, he'll just charge you all over again."

Beyond the partition came the jingle of coins, the whir and thump of the Pepsi machine. Nan waited for Jenny Root to urge her to give in, give up Jane. Instead she seized the little table in both hands and shook it till it rattled. "The fucker's blackmailing us!"

Us?

"It's like a fucking police state! Lock 'em in a room, keep up the pressure, everybody caves sooner or later. You've been imprisoned without trial. That's fucking unconstitutional. First Rhode Island takes over another state's felony charge, without even questioning it. And now this? Wright's making a mockery out of the law."

Visibly controlling herself, Jenny Root looked around at the ex-addicts' paintings, which covered the walls with sunrises and ocean waves and cheerful-looking animals. PATIENCE + PERSISTENCE = PROGRESS, the wall opposite them advised. She got up and peered around the corner of the partition, then came over to Nan's side of the table and leaned in close. She said softly, under the sound of the lawn mower, "Don't let the scumbags get away with it."

The freckled guard appeared, smelling strongly of cigarettes. Jenny Root retreated to her side of the table and sat down.

"Two minutes!" the guard said. She stood at the edge of the partition behind Jenny Root, arms folded, eyes on her prisoner.

Jenny Root crossed her eyes at Nan. "Okay," she said in her usual lawyerly tone, at her usual speed, "I'm here for two things, one, tell me what you need, two, tell me what you want me to do." Without a pause for Nan to do either of these: "Val will be here tomorrow, I got permission for him to visit you."

"Val?" Nan said, distracted by the guard's unblinking stare.

"*Val*." Jenny Root's voice held a peculiar urgency.

"One minute!"

Jenny Root rose. She would file an appeal. She would keep trying to get Nan put on house arrest with an electronic anklet. For now, at least she'd managed to keep her from being transferred to Maximum. "But be careful. Minimum doesn't take violent crimes, but there're a lotta crazies in the jails now, with the mental hospitals closing." Then came a volley of fast-forward questions—Nan's health, did she need anything, medication? books? money?—followed by a quick, hard, unexpected embrace.

Val would come to visit, Jenny Root said, hands still on Nan's shoulders and digging in hard. Again her voice was oddly emphatic. Nan should listen to *Val.*

|

Tampon Stew for dinner. Little deaf woman has adopted me. Relentlessly playful. They call me the woman who won't talk—about Jane, they mean, but she thinks it means I understand Sign. One of the COS—the guards

*here are called Correctional Officers, not jailers—went out on lunch break
& never came back.*

What does any of this matter?

|

Two things Nan didn't write down for Alex. That she'd felt relieved to see Jenny Root go. That this evening she'd refused a visit from Gabriel, as it was her right to do. The first right she'd found herself to have, in this place—but one she would not have traded for any other. One that made her feel, for the first time in more than six months, safe.

|

Wednesday night, late, long after lights-out, long after the CO had slammed the door and called good night. The curtains were tied back, and rain-washed night air coursed through the room. The moon, pared to a silver sliver, hung in the unbarred window. The women's faces were visible in the dim light from outside—not moonlight but the lights that burned all night on the guard towers. Marjorie and Donna Jean sat on either end of the lower bunk across from Nan, their feet meeting companionably in the middle. Ellen and Maria, Ellen's lover, occupied the bunk above them. Maria, who was Puerto Rican, had long black hair that rambled across her shoulders and down her plump brown arms. She did not look a like a lesbian, but then, what did Nan know about lesbians?

"When I get out, I'm gonna get some fancy heels and a fancy dress and go out dancing with my husband." (Donna Jean)

"I would even enjoy breaking a glass on my kitchen floor. Just normal things." (Maria)

"I miss belly buttons. Blowing on their belly buttons." (Marjorie)

"Guys? You blow on guys' belly buttons?"

"No, doofus. My grandkids."

"As much time as I spend sleeping in here, when I am free, *nunca mas*. I will never want to sleep no more."

They're young, Nan thought. So young they can still think, *someday*. Someday I'll get out of here. Someday I'll live in a pretty white house with my children. Someday I'll understand . . . everything.

And that was when she realized, eyes on the hard bright fingernail of moon, that she herself did not really expect to leave this place. *If the*

Sun & Moon should doubt. The open window made her uneasy, as if bars would have kept danger out, rather than prisoners in. Jenny Root had seemed to be saying, this afternoon, that there was some way out of here. Don't let the fucker get away with it, she'd said—as 'if there were some way Nan could fight him.

But I can't, I can't fight. Not anymore.

The weariness she'd felt earlier crawled over her, claiming her inch by inch, an undertow beneath the whispering women's voices.

"I get out of here, I'm just gonna get laid and *laid*," Marjorie said.

Donna Jean hooted. "By who?"

"Gonna advertise in the Personals, month before I go. 'Muscled Man of Color'—that's how it's gonna start."

"Those guys? If you saw one sitting here, he would scare you."

"They scare *themselves*."

Laughter pricked the darkness.

Maria said, "I was married once. He would beat me, kick me and stomp me. He bruise my ribs."

Ellen sat up, a quick motion of protest, or distress. Her Raggedy Ann doll fell to the floor with a soft thud. She rubbed her palms over her face. The gesture pushed her hair back from her forehead, and in the not-quite-moonlight Nan saw a band of red scars crosshatched on it.

Maria said, "He slice my hand to the point where I need stitches. That is when I make up my mind. *Nunca mas.*"

"Yeah—you can make up your mind," Marjorie said. "But how you gonna make up your heart?"

"He was a deeply troubled person," Donna Jean offered.

"He was . . ." a whispered word, in Spanish.

"A douche-bag!"

"Dick puke!"

Laughter like dry leaves.

Donna Jean said that before she found Jesus she used to want to have sex with Morrissey's voice. Marjorie said that she had a crush on Gorbachev, whom she referred to as "that bald Russian dude with the map of Alaska on his head." Nan's stock went up briefly when she said she'd met him once; then it was decided that she must be lying.

Donna Jean said, in a sleepy voice, "'Now we see through a glass, darkly; but then, face to face.' Lookin' at that moon, don't it make you *know* there is a Higher Power?"

|

Three a.m. For the first time since she'd been incarcerated, Nan woke with a clenching pain in her belly, the way she used to after Tod died: a sort of twisting inward, which she'd eventually come to recognize as loss. She lay awake in the nickel-colored light, listening to Marjorie's gusty snores, listing her losses. First Tod; then Deenie. Now Alex, Val and Mel, Walker.

Jane.

Nan rolled over, in tiny motions so as not to wake her roommates, and pulled the notebook out from under her pillow. Her fingers found the little pencil and she began to write, forming the letters slowly, by feel.

Do you remember, Alex? The moon bleeding into thin clouds over the Mediterranean; the sound of moths against the window screen?

Look, Mama! you said. The moon's a big big clam shell.

The clouds thickened & the moon disappeared. There was only dark ocean melting into darker sky.

Does it always come back? you asked.

Always, I lied.

Nan shut the notebook and tucked the little pencil into its spine. When it was safely back under her pillow—turned over now to the cool side—she closed her eyes. After a while there was rustling from the top bunk across the room, then a freighted silence. Then Ellen's small soft cries—the only sound Nan had ever heard her make—and the quickening twang of bedsprings. The smell that traveled on the damp air made Nan remember, though it was different, the smell that she and Walker made. Uniquely theirs—perhaps every couple's was different?—compounded from the tangible fluids of their separate desires.

Comforted, she fell asleep.

Sixteen

Jail dreams:

Alex walking toward her, carrying something, darkness in her eyes. What have they done to you? The path they stand on is paved with human bones. Drawing closer, the figure is suddenly not Alex but Nan's mother. In her arms a struggling fox cub twists around to gnaw her belly.

Deenie, fourteen again, in a dress made of rain.

Pop drowning squirrels in a garbage can filled with water. Like cooking lobsters. Their heads up till the last possible second, bright eyes begging.

Walker's legs alongside Nan's, their joined skin giving off light.

The garden in Genoa, the scent of late roses, a snake streaming toward her across sun-struck stones.

At the end of each sleep-glazed afternoon, the hollow sound of a train passing in the distance woke her. Waking was the worst time, as in the weeks after Tod's death: knowing something is wrong before you know what it is. Mourning doves crying *Cool! Cool!* filled the room with sound. Were they everywhere, these birds, even in the grimmest places? Walker would have known.

Dreams—even sad dreams, even terrifying dreams—were her one reliable refuge. Nan napped and napped. She did not dream of Jane.

|

Jenny Root came again, two days after her first visit, on Nan's sixth day in the ACI. Wright was resisting all her efforts. Had *Val* come to see her yet? As on her first visit, Jenny Root's tone was oddly emphatic, her gaze oddly intent. When Nan said, No, he hadn't, she looked grave. There was a pause. The guard, a new one Nan hadn't seen before, stood in one corner of the visitors' area, not taking her eyes off the two women. Frowning, Jenny Root said at last, with that same odd emphasis, that she was concerned about Nan's *health.*

Surprised, Nan said, "I'm fine."

"One minute!" the guard said.

"It's the Fourth of July weekend coming up." Jenny Root's eyes locked with Nan's. A lot of people were *on vacation,* she continued. If Nan was feeling *at all ill,* she should *ask for the doctor.*

"Time's up!"

Getting to her feet, Jenny Root said, "It's tough to be on the Wing twenty-four/seven. People get wiggy. Don't fade on us, Nan."

Like most warnings, this one came too late. Shuffling back down the corridor beside the silent guard, Nan knew that whatever Jenny Root and Val had cooked up, whatever they wanted her to do, she no longer had the energy or the will to do it. She was safe now, and so was Jane, and that was enough. That was everything.

Late-afternoon sun streamed into her room, igniting the brilliant green and purple of the afghan Donna Jean had laid across Nan's bed. Nan sat down on it to wait for the dinner gong.

Jail, like the State Department, decided everything for you. The result was a giving over first of effort, then of worry, then of will. What use was it to decide or even to desire anything? You went where you were sent, did (even the wives) what you were told. You accustomed yourself to the smell of open latrines, or olive blossoms; to the sound of church bells, or the muezzin, or horse-drawn carts at dawn laden with the bodies of the dead. It was possible, you eventually discovered, to accustom yourself to anything.

|

Donna Jean told me the scars across Ellen's forehead are the stigmata. Marjorie snorted. (Hers are the only real snorts I've ever heard.) They're from leaning against the barbed wire out in the yard on Kids' Day, she said. Looking for her little boy, who never comes, because he's dead.

Six days now, Alex. It could be six months. Or six years. I am so tired. We're both in exile, you & I.

|

Nan Mulholland had been in the ACI exactly a week when she received her first letter. Walker! she thought, when her name was called; and her heart lifted. But the return address was Gabriel's.

She stood with the smooth, buff-colored envelope trembling between her fingers, looking out the window in the little sitting area. In the yard a pair of iridescent dragonflies zigzagged through the bright July morning. The sound of the television, eternal as wallpaper, went on behind her; the mournful smell of poached eggs reached upward from the kitchen stairwell. Without looking down, Nan tore the sealed envelope across and across.

After lunch, sitting on her bunk in the empty room, she laid the pieces out on her bright green and purple afghan (a gift from Donna Jean) and sat looking at them a long time before she leaned close enough to make out Gabriel's physician's scrawl. There was no salutation, no signature.

Remember the night on my terrace when I told you that my mother had died? You are the only person I ever told about her.

Jane has been my redemption. I love my daughter more than anything in the world. I would never hurt her. In your heart you know this.

She knows this. And she needs me. If you separate us, you will regret it.

Queasiness radiated through Nan. She grabbed the wastebasket and leaned over it, away from Donna Jean's afghan.

My terrace. My daughter. Two cherished possessions—cherished *because* they were possessions. No mention of *my wife*. The charmed circle now held only Gabe and Jane. No place there for Nan. No *You can see Jane whenever you like.* No *Bygones will be bygones.*

The sound of feet scuffling made her look up. The little deaf woman, whose name Nan kept forgetting, stood in the doorway. When she caught Nan's eye, she beckoned urgently, then began moving her hands in signs. Nan shook her head to show she didn't understand. Dancing with impatience, the woman pointed to Nan, then down the hall, then to her own eyes. Nan shook her head again. The woman frowned, shrugged violently, and left.

Nan looked down again at the letter, half expecting it to have disappeared. The sun slanted in through the thin curtains, picking out the gold edging on Donna Jean's afghan. It was the mention of Gabe's mother—of repair—that moved Nan most, as he undoubtedly had known it would. But she knew that past injuries could work the other way. She remembered something Simone Weil had written, something she'd clung to years ago, when she was desperately trying to understand the sarcasm and meanness Tod had sometimes shown her, dying. "A harmful act is the transference to others of the degradation which we bear in ourselves. We commit such acts as a way of deliverance."

The prisoner holds the keys to her cell. Though she could reverse her decision at any moment—could decide to hand Jane over—it did not feel that way. It felt irrevocable. Part of a life that had ended, a story being told, in retrospect, about someone called "Nan Mulholland." Someone she once knew. Someone whose last burst of decisiveness had used her up.

Wearily, Nan got to her feet. Her knees creaked, and she thought: Old bones; and then: Bone tired. She shuffled the pieces of the letter together into a neat pile and tore them, stacked them, tore them again. Then she walked down the hall to the communal bathroom and flushed them down the toilet. Watching the sodden bits swirl and vanish in the rush of water, she felt free at last, and light.

A tug on her sleeve made her turn around. The little deaf woman pointed at the doorway and made furious beckoning motions. When Nan stood still, she punched her shoulder.

"Okay," Nan said, "I'm coming," forming the words carefully for the bright brown eyes trained on her lips. Why not? she thought. I'm done here. The woman grabbed her wrist, and Nan allowed herself to be towed out the door.

At the end of the corridor everyone crowded around the front windows. Nan's companion, still gripping her wrist, thrust her way forward through protesting prisoners—"Don't push me, bitch!" "Who you lookin' at?"—until Nan found herself at the very front, next to Donna Jean. On her other side, the little deaf woman's shoulder dug into her arm. Behind them, bodies kept pressing forward. They had to put their palms on the glass and push, to keep from being crushed against it.

A camera crew from the ubiquitous Channel 10 News waited in a white van at the curb. A prisoner tottered down the walk to a waiting police car, supported by the little freckled CO and a man Nan didn't know. "It's Nancy," Donna Jean said. "The hunger strike woman, the one from D Wing. They're taking her to the hospital. That's Doc Shovelton."

The woman's blue prison sweater hung from her hunched shoulders; her profile, lit by the slanting afternoon sun, was all nose. She had to be helped into the police car. The doctor leaned in after her for a moment, then turned and started back up the walk. The camera swiveled to follow him. His face, above a silvery biblical beard, looked tired, angry, kind.

Women behind Nan mugged for the camera and shouted rewards and invitations, some of them obscene, until two COs came to disperse them. Safety Pin, the one who'd presided over Nan's strip search that first night, shoved her roughly. "If it ain't the Media Queen," she said, and grinned. "Tryin' for another photo op?"

|

"Nanechka!"

Val greeted Nan like the beloved aunt he'd told the authorities she was. (Hadn't they noticed his accent? she wondered.) His face with its surround of black curls, its snapping black eyes, took her so much by surprise that she realized she hadn't expected to see him here, ever. She'd given him up, along with the rest of her previous life.

Nan sat down across from him. The smell of tobacco and Juicy Fruit and male sweat sent a swift current of homesickness through her. Folding her hands on the edge of the skittish card table, she found that all she could manage, all the lump in her throat allowed, was, "Val."

"How you are, Nan? You are fine?"

"I'm okay. How are you? How's Mel?"

Safety Pin, having clearly decided Nan was no risk, went to lean out the window of the visitors' cubicle, sucking on a forbidden cigarette. Early-morning air pushed in past her large bulk, cool and fresh and carrying the sound of birdsong.

"Your cousin Mel is fine like ever. They are saying, one visitor at time, therefore she stays home. She says, Forgive!"

He smiled, ravishingly. One foot tapped the floor, knee jogging the table between them, a boy's reflex. She always forgot how young he was. Absently, she rubbed her arm. Safety Pin had been peeved at having to track down a prisoner; her grip as she walked Nan along the corridor to B Wing had been painful. Val glanced at her broad back, then leaned across the table toward Nan.

"I with your friends, we have great concern for your health, Nan."

"I'm fine. Really. You shouldn't—"

"Your heart. Is danger. Can fail at any minute."

"Val—"

"You must listen!" The little table shuddered with the motion of his leg. He cast a glance in the direction of Safety Pin's back. "Walking. *Walking* is good for you."

Ah. I see where we're going.

"But you must also visit doctor. Luckily, is excellent prison doctor. Very helpful."

Nan remembered the tall, thin figure bent over the woman from D Wing. Val cast another glance at Safety Pin. Her grizzled head was all the way out the window, like a large Airedale enjoying a car ride. A tiny white square, smaller than a penny, appeared from under the cuff of Val's shirt. He slid his hand, palm down, across the table to Nan, waited for her hand to meet it. They clasped and released. The note was in her fist.

Val looked at her impatiently. *Open!* he mouthed.

Nan pried the paper apart. It was slightly damp. It said, in Mel's square dark printing:

Pretend to get sick tomorrow night. Ask for doctor. Go to hospital. Wait.

An escape. They've planned an escape. So this was what Jenny Root had meant.

A hand squeezed the stone in her chest: a wringing pain. My heart? No. It's only fear. A gust from the open window, carrying the smell of Safety Pin's cigarette, touched her cheek. With a great effort, Nan closed her fingers around the note.

Val said, "Fourth of July is Monday. Already today the city is, how you say it, is empty. Empty," he repeated, his eyes on Nan's.

Keys chimed at Safety Pin's belt as she turned to glance at her prisoner, then turned back to the July morning.

Val raised a hand to his lips and made chewing motions. When Nan, not understanding, continued to sit still, he reached across the table and pried the note from her fingers and put it in his mouth. Nan remembered the photograph of his grandfather. Val knew about prison.

He chewed, swallowed. The card table stilled. He said in a low voice, "You will do, *nyet?* Telephone me tomorrow morning. Say only, Yes, okay. It must happen tomorrow."

Don't let the fucker get away with it, Jenny Root had said. Nan hesitated, remembering Alex's face in the narrow beam from her flashlight, her imperious voice. *This time, hide her better.*

"Two minutes!" Safety Pin said in a bored voice.

Val slid a pack of Camels across the table toward Nan. Dramatically, he murmured, "Tomorrow! Telephone, then wait. A distraction occurs."

No.

"Nan! Things belong to the people who want them most. *Nado umet' khotet'.* One must know how to want."

I'm too tired. Too old.

Excuses she could not make out loud, because of the presence of Safety Pin. And arguments Val could not make—except for one.

"Jane," he said. The black eyes burned.

I'm afraid.

"Janechka."

Safety Pin turned around and came up to the table. She picked up the pack of Camels and put it in her breast pocket. "Time's up."

"*K chortu!*"

|

"This is her at three weeks . . . here she is at three months . . . eight months . . ."

Nan admired Donna Jean's daughter's passage through the stages of babyhood: Mister Magoo, Winston Churchill, Henry VIII. She was red-haired, like her mother, and feisty-looking.

"And my boys, Anthony and David, he's the baby there, on Cheryl's lap."

"Ain't they sweet, those shorties? God!" said Marjorie, who was looking over Nan's shoulder. Donna Jean gave her a quick poke, for profanity.

Nan was in the midst of murmured admiration when Donna Jean handed her a newspaper clipping. "This is her, last year." The headline said, 12-YEAR-OLD SAVES SIBLINGS; beneath the self-conscious school photo, the caption read: "Cheryl Naomi Miller's father perished when he piped car exhaust into his West Warwick living room last night."

Marjorie pushed her own photographs into Nan's other hand. "This here's my Aretha." A fierce young woman squinting into the sun, her

Afro a nimbus around her head. "And *her* girl, LaShon. My granddaughter." About Jane's age, with cornrowed hair and a face the color of new pennies, in a T-shirt that said, HAPPY TO BE NAPPY.

"Luis." Maria displayed her photographs. "He has eight years. And *la niña*, Annunciata."

Ellen's photo was mutely extended. Expecting yet another cherub, Nan pushed her glasses back up the sweaty bridge of her nose (it was a hot, hot night) and looked down. Her breath caught. The photograph showed a gravestone, in color, lavishly bedecked with roses, peonies, daisies, a tiny American flag, a plastic figure of E.T. ERIC, the stone said, 1995–1997. LOVE FOREVER.

Nan looked up. Ellen's face in the lamplight, half hidden by her tangled hair, asked for nothing; but her arms tightened around her Raggedy Ann doll, which tonight wore a long white christening dress, its embroidered hem gray with dirt. Maria moved over and put an arm around her.

An expectant silence descended. Humid night air coated Nan's skin like someone else's sweat. In the quiet she could hear, far down the corridor, doors being slammed one by one. It was nearly lights-out. Then she realized: they were waiting for *her* photographs, for pictures of Alex, of Jane, loved to limpness, offered proudly. Nan had none, and said so.

Their shocked surprise was instantly, tactfully, annealed by chatter.

"My sister, she takes Anthony to counseling. He's like, No way you're gettin' inside *my* head. I tell him, go. I messed up big-time. I don't want my kids to."

"Can't do the time, don't do the crime."

"I tell him, This is devil music. This rap stuff."

"I worry about LaShon. I think, is niggeritis kickin' in?"

"*Con permiso?*" Maria removed Nan's glasses, hooked them behind her own ears. "Shit! Where is everybody?"

Laughter.

"My Lord does not strike points off, even if I sin. I tell Anthony this poem: Woman or man, we are all in God's hand."

The door to the room next to theirs slammed. Maria slid off the bunk and rolled underneath it. Their door opened. The little freckled CO counted heads, bawled "'Night!" and slammed the door.

When the conversation rekindled, in whispers, it was about Kids' Day—tomorrow, Sunday—in tones of suppressed excitement, as if *they* were the children, looking forward to a party. Nan closed her eyes against the light from the guard towers outside. The threat of tears made her squeeze them tight. She must not think of Jane. Jane was safe; that was enough.

There was a series of soft movements from the bunk opposite. Nan opened her eyes. Ellen's figure appeared by her bed. She crouched there in silence for a moment; then Nan's blanket was drawn back and something was tucked in alongside her, against her ribs. As Ellen climbed back up to her own bed, Nan's hand met the limp, gritty lace of Raggedy Ann's christening gown.

|

If one cannot be happy, one can at least be brave. (Dorothea)
The unlived life is not worth examining. (Walker)
You've never really loved anyone, have you? (Alex)

But why should courage not be finite, just like anything else? Nan thought. Standing up to Judge Wright had taken all she had. Jane was safe—she, Nan, had made her safe—and that was all she cared about. All she could do. She was finished.

|

The communal bathroom, with its showerless tubs (for fear, it had been explained to Nan at some point, of inmates hanging themselves) and doorless toilets, smelled equally of Pine-Sol and pee. Sunday morning: the sound of church bells came faintly through the high windows. In a rare moment of aloneness, Nan stood before the tin mirror over the sinks. Her beige sweatshirt lay crumpled in the basin; her bra clung around her waist. She was examining her breasts for lumps, the monthly ritual, as if such things still mattered. Her nipples puckered tight as jujubes. It was always cold in here. The cinder-block walls exuded a constant chill, like the walls of Italian cathedrals.

The door opened. A cloud of mixed hairs scuttled along the cement floor. Marjorie came and stood at the sink next to Nan's and began washing her hands.

"What's the story, morning glory?"

Nan didn't bother to cover herself. How swift the progression had been: the relinquishing first of outrage, then of shame, then of modesty itself. Nan thought of her modeling days, of Mel's careful distinction between *naked* and *nude*. How long ago that seemed. How innocent. Her reflection in the mirror smiled bleakly, eyes like Teflon. She noted, indifferently, that she looked like hell, and remembered how, at fifteen, sixteen, Alex had been envious of her mother's beauty. It didn't get you anything, Nan had tried to explain. More guys, yes. More tickets; but the ride was the same. No one changed for you.

"Get a move on, girl!"

Nan jumped. She'd been so engrossed in memory that she'd forgotten anyone was there.

Marjorie's reflection frowned at her. "Don't you know it's Kids' Day? Gotta look good for the shorties." She began spitting on her fingers and twirling sections of her lively hair so that it stood out all around her head. Then, as Nan, leaning on the edge of the sink, said nothing, she added, "Listen! You gotta be strong with yourself. You givin' *up*, girl. I can see it in your eyes. You been here what? A week? That's about when it hits."

"I'm not," Nan said.

Marjorie wore a blue sleeveless shirt. She lifted her arms and shook them, regarding herself in the mirror, tapping the loose flesh that hung from her upper arms. "The Mobile Wads of Henry," she said. "That's what these things're called." She pulled a toothbrush out of her pants pocket and began scrubbing soapsuds into her cuticles. Without looking at Nan she said, "There's a thing called Prisoner's Malady. Where you get, you know, resigned. You get so you *like* bein' locked up. You think, That's what I deserve."

Feeling suddenly naked, Nan pulled her bra up, dived into her sweatshirt. Marjorie moved closer and put one arm across her shoulders. The smell of her armpit was aromatic, like onions—the smell, suddenly, of Nan's mother, long ago, and the light pressure of Marjorie's breast was maternal, too. Nan stood very still. A steep pain started up inside her.

Someone came in, a woman called Lina, and squatted in the furthest toilet stall. Marjorie moved away, rinsing her hands, drying them on a wad of paper towels. She looked back at Nan, seemed about to speak, shook her head, and left.

It's out of my hands, Nan told her own reflection. Don't you see that? Her mirrored eyes gazed back accusingly. Coward, her eyes said.

Stingy. You'll stay in this place for the rest of your life, to save Jane. But you won't raise her?

Nan shut her eyes. She stood by the sink with one arm tight across her rib cage, where the pain was, until the other woman left. Then she sat down on the cold tile floor and put her face in her hands, and her cupped palms filled with tears.

|

Never alone, Alex. Not for three minutes in a row. Remember what we used to say in Warsaw? Making fun of our poor neighbor, the widow Budzich. "Venn you haff a view, you are neffer alone."

Is Marjorie right? Something is happening to me. I don't miss my privacy, or even want it. My so-called freedom, ditto.

It's out of my hands now. Now I can rest.

|

Kids' Day.

Through the open windows came the high voices of children, raucous as jays, an unaccustomed, amazing sound. Standing in the sitting area of C Wing—deserted, the TV silent for once—Nan looked out at the little yard beside Dix Building. Green grass, blue sky: God had gussied up the world (Donna Jean's observation) for this day. They poured through an unbarred metal door, children of all sizes, stormed the snack table, fanned out across the grass. A flash of bright-blue denim. Nan's heart kicked.

Jane?

Nan took a step back, rocked by pain, by longing. Turning, she saw only the empty corridor. Everyone was outside—turning back again, she saw a file of women in blue prison garb begin to enter the yard from a door opposite—at least, everyone who had children. Those who didn't, or whose children would not come today, were hiding somewhere out of sight and sound of all this joy. Arms wrapped around herself, Nan began backing down the corridor. But she couldn't seem to look away from the window. Aunts, grandmothers, fathers stood around the perimeter of cyclone fencing, its crown of barbed wire glinting in the sun. They slouched self-consciously, eyeing the guards, thrusting empty hands into pockets. Nan had seen the list of what visitors might bring into the prison on Kids' Day: one wedding ring; one baby bottle (clear fluid); one diaper. Nothing more. This restriction struck her as a disorienting device. So lightly burdened, how could visitors feel like themselves? Impelled by some force she didn't understand, Nan went downstairs and through the empty dining hall, out into the blue afternoon.

The air held the smoky scent of clover. Bees circled Nan's head, their interrogative sound not quite lost in the clamor of children's voices. There were children of every size and many colors, from babies—she saw one, in the arms of a fiercely tattooed woman from B Wing, who couldn't have been more than four weeks old—to wavering first-time walkers to teenagers, opaque-eyed and wrathful. All around her, mothers and children rushed toward each other with illumined faces. She'd forgotten that headlong joy. The small bright countenance that said, *You! You, and no other.* Jane used to greet her that way, back in Seattle, before they went into exile.

Jane could be here right now, visiting me, Nan thought, if I gave her up. Then she remembered. If I gave her up, I wouldn't *be* here. She thought of Gabe's letter, Gabe's face when they stood before the judge. He would never let Jane see her, not here, not anywhere. Not in a million years.

In a far corner of the yard Donna Jean dropped to her knees and put her arms around three children at once. Her young daughter, graceful and grave, held a baby dressed in enough starched and ruffled splendor to compete with the Infant of Prague. Handed to Donna Jean, it extended its arms back toward its sister, hands swiveling like a safecracker's. (Nan's breath caught: Jane as a baby had made just that imperious gesture of desire.) Maria hugged her son, a small boy in shorts whose high voice carried over the tumultuous sounds in the yard. "*Sí, la computer! Sí!*" He broke away and began to run back and forth, trying to launch his bright-red kite into the windless sky. And there, across the green grass and coming toward Nan, was the Boy Father with Bug on his shoulders. He passed so near that their eyes met. His held no flicker of recognition.

Have I changed that much?

Marjorie came and stood in front of Nan, hand in hand with her granddaughter. "This here's LaShon. Say how-do-you-do, LaShon."

The little girl mumbled something that sounded like "Honeydew." She wore a yellow sundress and yellow socks whose lace-trimmed tops had worked their way down inside the heels of her black patent-leather shoes.

They stood and talked—or rather, Marjorie talked. LaShon was five (not even a year older than Jane, Nan thought, with a pang). LaShon was the smartest kid in Head Start. LaShon loved words. "Just feed her a new word, like 'apocalypse' or 'sandpiper'—and she happy." LaShon. LaShon.

All around Nan in the hot, bright air, children's voices sang of what she was missing.

"No, Mama, that's a baby cup. I want a *guy* cup."

"When I get back to my house, I'm gonna be lonely for you, Mommy."

"Whadda they make in Pennsylvania? Give up? PENCILS!"
Their mothers stood in sunlight or sat on the splintery benches under the lilac tree, and worshiped. They had learned the first lesson of prison: that deprivation put *enough* forever out of reach.

Maria's little boy, bare knees flashing, ran and ran, flinging his kite hopefully into the air. Beyond him stood Ellen with her back to the yard and her forehead pressed to the barbed-wire fencing, looking out. Looking for the child who would never again come running toward her with light in his eyes. Nan winced, as if the sharp bright stars of wire were cutting into her own forehead. On the other side of the yard, she saw Deciolaria, her face buried in Bug's shoulder, while the Boy Father tenderly brushed dirt off his son's teddy bear.

Like a flash, it hit her: even that child is better off than Jane. He's with the people who want him most.

Marjorie said, "Here comes the Dolphin. Five-minute warning," and Warden Gordon, at the entrance to Dix Building, began ringing a big copper cowbell. "Say good-bye to Miz Mulholland, LaShon."

The little girl stretched her arms up. Nan dropped onto one knee, and LaShon's arms went around her neck and squeezed. Ambushed by the smell of baby shampoo, Nan froze. She shut her eyes. How could Alex have relinquished this? And then, with a great wash of sadness: How could *I*?

She's better off without me, Alex had said, that night in the hospital. The saddest, most terrible thing a mother could say. Something—Nan only now realized this—that Alex had saved her, Nan, from having to say. Because Alex had turned to her. Alex had entrusted Jane to her. To *her.*

The heart-slamming truth of this made Nan's eyes snap open. Of their own will, her arms went around LaShon, enclosing the soft small bulk of her. The starched cotton of her sundress crackled in Nan's grip. She buried her face in LaShon's neck, breathed in the smells of baby shampoo, starch, sun-warmed skin. She hugged, kept hugging, couldn't seem to let go. Harder; harder.

Marjorie's hand on Nan's shoulder roused her. She let go and got slowly to her feet. LaShon was led away, loudly grieving, by her mother. Without saying a word, Marjorie hooked her arm through Nan's, and they began to walk toward the prisoners' door. They passed Lourdes, and Deciolaria, and Ellen, moving like an old woman with eyes cast down, and Donna Jean with her Bible under one arm. Marjorie's unaccustomed silence, the weight of her hand on Nan's wrist, reminded Nan of the way people walked away from a graveside, stately, stunned, exhausted. Relieved.

At the end of his life, when he'd finally begun to accept his death, Tod had talked a lot—wanderingly but with flashes of acuteness, the way people seemed to do under morphine—about the difference between guilt and regret. Guilt, he said, was in the camp of Fear; regret was in the camp of Love. *Regret,* Nan would think wistfully, wiping his wrinkled buttocks clean, wringing out his urine-soaked sheets: what a beautiful word, like the name of a flower. If only I could feel it.

The two streams of people, Visitors and Prisoners, parted, each to their respective doors. Sunlight slanting through the lilacs gilded both impartially. Turning her head, Nan watched the last of the children disappear: the small boy in baggy shorts, Maria's son, trailing his red kite. The Visitors' Door slammed shut behind him. A terrible, invigorating grief seized her. She heard Val's voice: *One must know how to want.*

When they got inside she stood still. Ahead of her, at the end of the corridor, the old metal pay phone caught the afternoon light like a great square jewel.

She thought, This will change everything. This will change my life forever. *Our* lives.

She disengaged her arm from Marjorie's. "You go ahead," she said. "I have to make a call."

Seventeen

"This one's really off the hook. Gonzo!"

"You never know. She might make it."

"Why don't I ever catch a break? Hey—Doc Shovelton told me this joke? Three vampires walk into a bar."

"Yeah?"

"The first vampire says, I'll have some blood. Second one says, Make that two. The third one says, I'll just have plasma."

"Yeah?"

"So—the bartender says—that'll be two bloods, and a blood lite."

Groans; then giggles.

"Okay, I'm done here. Osmosis, amoebas! Ciao for now!"

Nan opened her eyes.

Here she was—again. The smells alone could have told her. Lysol, starch, urine. In the other bed a woman lay weeping, small, despairing sounds that were nevertheless audible over their two heart monitors and the other woman's ventilator. (Tod had had such a machine, toward the end, before he'd persuaded Nan to take him out of the hospital so that he would not die there.) The woman's hands clasped the air in little useless gestures. She had beautiful curly pure-white hair; her face, turned toward Nan with eyes shut, registered each new wave of weeping.

They hadn't been talking about Nan, then—the nurses.

How did she get here? Oh—yes. The pay phone, in the basement of Dix Building. Standing there trembling, one hand cupped around the mouthpiece. Val greeting her "Okay, yes" with Slavic fervor. "This afternoon!" he shouted. "Will be big distraction!" She nodded, forgetting that he couldn't see her, clinging to the knowledge that had burst upon her minutes before, in the yard, holding LaShon. A buzzer sounded, and one of the COs came up behind Nan and tapped her on the shoulder. The door to the outside slammed shut.

God, she was tired—so tired—and weak. She remembered now: pretending to feel dizzy, nauseated; pretending to faint. Then the CO called Doc Shovelton. Whatever was in his syringe had made her black out, for real.

So, she thought now, Val didn't trust me to fake it. She went to wipe her mouth and felt her wrist jerked back: she was shackled to the bed frame. Her other hand, tethered to an IV whose needle pierced the back of it, was useless, too. Vinyl-coated wires tied her to the heart monitor. She tried to sit up but couldn't. The handcuff would have slid far enough up the metal railing to allow it, but one ankle was cuffed to the foot of the bed. Her head filled with the white noise of anger. She kicked and flailed until the cuffs rang on the metal bed frame.

Safety Pin, in full regalia including a gun in a shoulder holster, appeared. "Shut up!" she said, advancing toward Nan. "Shut the fuck up!"

Defiantly Nan rattled her chains. Safety Pin held up a silver cylinder and stood beside the bed with her index finger poised above the button.

"ASR. You want a hit of this? Because, trust me, I am authorized to give it to you."

Aerosol spray restraint: pepper spray. They aimed for your eyes, Marjorie'd said. Nan lay still.

Safety Pin was very close now. She leaned over Nan, emitting—all the COs had it—a smell like mimeograph ink. All that metal, maybe: badges, cuffs, keys. Guns.

"Grandma! Think you're some kinda heroine. You may be an idol to the geeks in the ACI. You may have Doc and the Dolphin wrapped around your little finger. But you don't fool me."

Nan raised a sardonic eyebrow. They couldn't spray you for your facial expression.

"That was a sweet trick you pulled. You and the Doc. Cyanotic, my ass! I done a EMT course before the Police Academy. You were no more havin' a heart attack than I was. Hadn't been that they were bringin' in the mayor right then, you'd'a never gotten away with it."

The mayor? So that was what all the commotion had been about— Val's promised distraction. Poetic justice, thought Nan, pleased with the idea. After all, it was the mayor who'd gotten her locked up in the first place. If it hadn't been for that TV news footage—

"You're smilin' now, but wait. Just wait." Nan could see Safety Pin's index finger tapping the button of the ASR can. She bent over until her face loomed inches from Nan's, pitted cheeks pale with fury, like a big angry moon. "Just wait." Her breath smelled like cinders. Nan shut her eyes. The only sounds were the cheeping of various monitors, the suck and swish of the ventilator.

"Officer! What's going on here?"

Nan opened her eyes. Doc Shovelton stood in the doorway. No white coat, no stethoscope; only an unmistakable air of authority. Safety Pin had straightened up. She thrust the ASR can into her pants pocket and reached under Nan's head to fluff her pillows.

"How's the patient?" The doctor smiled at Nan, came and sat down on the edge of her bed, grasped her free wrist between thumb and fingers. Safety Pin, suddenly the Uriah Heep of prison guards, stepped respectfully back. Shovelton's hand was cool and firm, and his concentration—eyes cast down at his watch, silver beard faintly quivering—enclosed Nan in an invisible envelope of warmth and safety. When he'd finished, he laid her hand gently on her stomach and looked up at Safety Pin. Suddenly his face was luminous with rage. "Get these cuffs off!" His anger, like his beard, was biblical; he roared. "I gave strict instructions. No restraints on this patient. Get them off! Now!"

Safety Pin scuttled—it lifted Nan's heart to see—around the bed. The heavy bracelets split, ankle and wrist, and Nan was free. She struggled to sit up. Shovelton rolled her pillow and put it behind her and she leaned back, rubbing her wrist gratefully. In the next bed the old woman, no longer weeping, filled the room with dim snores. Shovelton got out his stethoscope, warmed it in his palm, and began to listen to Nan's breathing, front and then back. Evading Safety Pin's gaze, she kept her eyes on the other bed. The old woman's sheet had pulled up, revealing her feet in blue hospital socks with the toes cut out. Nan felt an urge to tickle them. The doctor retied the strings at the neck of her johnny and gave her a quick pat on the shoulder, then motioned the now obsequious Safety Pin to follow him out of the room.

Nan drew a grateful—a *free*—breath. Her ankle hurt where the cuff had rubbed it raw. Through the window she could see a single pale star in the twilight sky. It would be dark soon. She knew what came next, but not when it would come. She turned her head to the starched coolness of her pillow, and sleep took her. She dreamed of a long-ago camping trip in the Apennines, with Jack: a sky thickly salted with stars, cypress trees like folded black umbrellas, the sound of ravens at twilight.

|

Jarred awake by light, motion, the clatter of wheels, Nan thought, *Now?*

But the wheeled gurney, the rustle of starched uniforms, the voices—these were for the woman in the next bed. A hand jerked the curtain closed around it. In the darkness the movement of figures made a furious shadow play against the canvas, accompanied by clipped commands, the clap of cardiac paddles, the squeak of rubber-soled feet. Safety Pin (Does she never sleep? Where is her replacement?) appeared in the doorway, and she and Nan watched the spectacle together. It seemed to go on and on. Nan, still dreamy from the drug in Shovelton's syringe, found herself on a road through the hills near Timisoara, a woman in a headscarf and hot-looking black stockings walking behind a horse, two coffins roped to its back, the bright new wood gleaming in the sun. At last the gurney was wheeled out of the room. The sheet covered not just the woman's body, but her face.

Safety Pin's whisper was hot against Nan's cheek. "Nobody ever escaped this way, 'less they went out like *her*."

Nan lay still. Don't give 'em the satisfaction, Pop used to say. But after Safety Pin had gone, she was filled with misgivings. In the darkness the burble and peep of various monitors (which, despite the nearly palpable emptiness in the next bed, no one had turned off) seemed to echo the long-ago words of nun after nun. *This is a fine mess you are in.* How had she ever imagined this could work? Why had she agreed to this crazy jailbreak, the details of which she did not, even now, know? Why—when she knew that Walker's tragic flaw, pointed out a month ago by Our Man in Savannah, was his optimism?

And yours? the monitors wondered.

Young, impetuous Nan Boyce. Older—oh, yes, older!—but no wiser, impetuous Nan Mulholland. Only this time she'd chosen, not just for herself, but for Jane. First, when she'd said yes to Alex all those months ago. Again, when she'd said no to Hold-'Em-Tight Wright. And a third time, standing in the little yard (was it only this afternoon?) of the ACI, with LaShon's arms tight around her neck. Yes; no; yes. Accidents speak louder than words: one of Walker's skewed sayings. Did desire speak louder than fear? Did it speak truer?

This is my reparation to Alex. Making up for all those years when I was a lover, not a mother.

Crap sandwich! from the monitors.

All right—but I *am* doing this for Jane. To save her.

From what? You don't even know for sure what happened between her and Gabriel.

I'm going to raise her, for God's sake! Sixteen years till she's through college. I'll be seventy-six.

You'll be seventy-six in sixteen years anyway.

Okay, I give up. I want her. I love Jane.

They came flooding in, then—all the remembered moments she'd evaded during her week in the Lotusland of the ACI. Jane extending her hand, offering Nan a palmful of sweaty raisins, "For energy, Nana!" Jane laughing her smoky Marlene Dietrich laugh at one of Walker's jokes. Jane on a crystalline winter day, in her puffy red parka, stamping her feet, snow boots punching through the crust of snow. "I'm not coughing. It's coughing *me!*" A fierceness swept over Nan. Love, yes; but also something more primitive—savage, even. *Things belong to the people who want them most.*

She smiled into the darkness. I'm doing now what I did then—what drove the nuns crazy. (The monitors chirped agreement.) I'm doing what I want.

|

Breakfast. Meds. The usual twelve-year-olds in lab coats demanding blood, perfunctorily overseen by Safety Pin's replacement—a man this time—who stayed in his chair outside the door reading the greyhound racing form. A brief, cursory interrogation by the lone resident on duty this holiday weekend, a young Indian whose spicy aftershave cut right through the hospital smells.

The hospital staff was less interested in Nan this time than they'd been in June—there was far less poking, prodding, bloodletting—and she wondered if that was because it was the Fourth of July or because now she was a prisoner. In any case, it was lucky, since who knew how convincing her symptoms might be. The room's one window was at eye level. All day Nan watched the progress of a sparrow (or a wren: she always, to Walker's amusement, got them confused) tending her young in a nest tucked between the window frame and the air conditioner. Unlikely place, thought Nan. And precarious: why hadn't the noise of the machine or its vibration frightened her off, or a summer storm dislodged her?

The day dragged interminably on. Back to Little Red Waitinghood again; and certainly Nan qualified as a Damsel in Distress. She was reminded of the months of waiting for Tod's life to leave him. The same giddy suspension; the same stillness laced with longing, like the contradictory motion of dreams. At the very end, Tod had been unable to speak. He'd had a tracheotomy so as not to drown in his own fluids, and his jaw, stubbled with silver (he'd always, to his satisfaction, had to shave twice a day), was slack. He refused the priest, printing slowly and shakily on his little notepad, WHY SHOULD I LISTEN TO A LOT OF IRISHMEN? His hand searched across the flowered sheet for Nan's. His lips moved; the tracheotomy tube wagged. Two words. *Thank you*, Nan had thought, at the time. Months later, it occurred to her that he might have said, *Love you*.

All day the bed next to Nan's stayed empty. In the late afternoon a nurse collected the old woman's few possessions and bundled them into a clear plastic bag, turned off the monitors, escorted the IV stand out of the room. By then, silent and purposeful, the bird outside the window had finished feeding her young. From the nest fitted neatly into the sooty crevice one black eye regarded Nan, unblinking.

Dinner arrived at last, pabulum in three colors, followed by something green and quivering called "gelatin jewels," with splinters of carrot embedded in it, bright as shards of glass, exactly like the desserts of Nan's youth; then visitors (none, of course, for Nan); then meds. The window became a square of mottled darkness through which Nan could hear the far-off popping of fireworks. Safety Pin returned to duty. She barked at the night nurse, a chipmunk-cheeked young man whose head tilted sweetly to one side. She sneered at Nan, who turned away and looked out the window, where an uncertain moon, not quite full, had risen. The wren or sparrow slept, head tucked under one wing, like a smooth gray stone in her nest. Nan could see a storm building, the sky beginning to fill with ornate tapestry clouds. A gibbous moon; a mackerel sky. Terms Walker had taught her.

She shifted in the bed until the pressure on her bladder eased. Oh, for the simple pleasure of walking to the bathroom, even dragging her IV stand along, to pee free of chains! Impossible: she was still hooked up to the heart monitor. Safety Pin, hearing Nan's movements, rose and stood in the doorway. Nan closed her eyes and lay still. Outside the half-open door the hospital sounds dimmed. She could hear rain ticking, slowly at first, then faster, against the window by her head.

|

In the kitchen the radio stays on during dinner, Perry Como, Julius LaRosa, then the news. Fire has broken out upstate; they're digging firebreaks to the north and east of Philly. A woman dishes out green Jell-O, shuffling plates across the plastic lace cloth. The seat of Nan's chair sticks to her bare legs; shifting, she makes a sucking sound. The woman goes to the refrigerator and comes back with a pewter pitcher of ice water. Nan reaches for it. "Honey, be careful—" The woman bites her lip and looks over at Pop. The pitcher, sweating coldly, is so heavy that Nan's wrists feel as if they're going to snap. Ice cubes thud into her cup, splashing her hands with cold tea. The pitcher wavers. Its handle starts to slide—

My mother, Nan thought, half waking. That was her, that was my mother. Her face, no, I couldn't see her face—but her hair, I saw that. Her bright yellow hair, the color of school pencils.

The room, the bed, seemed to unmoor themselves and float. *No restraints,* she heard Doc Shovelton say. Sleepy again, she felt her heart unclench. *No* (almost asleep now) *restraints.*

|

Warmth trembling at the threshold of her ear. Waking to the hospital half-dark, the cheep of the monitors, a dim shape looming. Safety Pin?

"Quiet. *Tishina!*" A whisper so soft it was hardly more than breathing. Smells: stale tobacco, Juicy Fruit. Val's hand hovered near her mouth— Nan could feel its warmth in the darkness—but he didn't need to use it. She was fully awake now, and silent.

There was someone with him. The other man whispered, "Quick! The gurney!"

A flashlight switched on. Nan was half pushed, half pulled from her bed onto the stretcher's hard surface. The flashlight's beam crossed Doc

Shovelton's face and settled on his hands. With quick, deft motions he unhooked the octopus of wires from Nan's chest, pulled the IV needle from the back of her hand. Stoned with weakness—this was more movement than she'd been permitted for a day and a half—she simply lay there.

D in D—that's all I am now. Oh, Deenie!

Shovelton covered her with a stiff cotton sheet. The flashlight switched off, and she felt Val tuck it into her hand under the cloth.

"Ready? Okay. What to hell!"

She heard the door open softly. The gurney began to move. She closed her eyes against the sudden rush of fear, bird leaving its cage, don't want to, can't—

"Whaddaya think you're doin'? Hold it right there!"

Nan opened her eyes. The night-dimmed corridor lights showed her Safety Pin's dark bulk, can of Mace upraised. "Get over there!" She gestured to Shovelton, at the foot of the gurney. "Stand next to him, and don't fuckin' twitch."

Moving very slowly, Shovelton began to obey. Safety Pin pulled the gun from her shoulder holster and stood at Nan's feet, eyes shifting between the doctor and Val, who stood at Nan's head. She paid no attention to Nan.

I could faint, Nan thought, I know how to do that. But how would that help? She looked up at Val, couldn't make out his face in the dim light. If only he had a gun, or a knife, or even a club. But of course he didn't. There was nothing he could do, or Shovelton, either. Then she remembered. Underneath the stiff cotton sheet her fingers tightened around the flashlight. She lifted it very slightly, feeling it slip a little in her grasp. It was heavy.

Can I?

Shovelton had moved up the length of the gurney and stood behind Nan's head, next to Val. Safety Pin sidled along the gurney toward the two men, gun raised, pulling the handcuffs off her belt. She was on Nan's left; the flashlight, in Nan's right hand. Slowly Nan maneuvered it free of the sheet. Her hand was shaking. She felt Val's fingers on the top of her head, a quick approving tap. He stepped sideways as Safety Pin approached, so that she had to turn her back to the gurney. Keeping her eyes on the two men, she bent to fasten the cuffs around Val's out-thrust wrists.

Now.

The flashlight came down on Safety Pin's nape without a sound. Nan felt the impact travel up her arm as if it were she who'd received a blow. Surprise made her dizzy. She shut her eyes. *Breathe; breathe.* Val murmured, "*Ladno!* Good job." There was a thud, a scraping. Several month-long seconds passed. When she opened her eyes, Safety Pin was gone. The door to Nan's room was shut.

Bright ceiling lights pinwheeled past. Val upside down in a white lab coat, a white surgical mask slung around his neck as if he'd just come from the OR (definitely a Walker touch, thought Nan), his face a blur, because—

"My glasses!"

"*Tishina!*" They slowed for a second, then speeded up again. "We cannot. Is not time."

The gurney's wheels made a purposeful sound. They moved swiftly along one corridor, down another. A woman's voice sang out, "Evening, Doctors!" Shovelton, walking rapidly alongside Nan, took one of her hands and held it. His bearded, indistinct profile was comforting. Darkened doorways slipped past. Voices sounded ahead of them, then beside them, then behind. "Looks like dirt!" . . . "Why, is she pregnant?" . . . "I told him, I says, I don't have a problem, I have an *attitude*." . . . "That toe-suckin' ho-bitch!"

They halted beside an elevator. Val punched a button.

Shovelton pulled his hand from Nan's. She'd been gripping it more tightly than she realized. "I can't go any farther," he said in a low voice. "If you feel faint or nauseated, take this." He put a pill into her hand and closed her fingers around it. "Good luck!"

The elevator doors parted. Deft as any orderly, Val maneuvered the gurney into it. Two nurses and a security guard moved against one side to make room. Nan felt Val stiffen. The bunch of keys at the guard's belt chimed in her ear. But the guard—big, young, shiny-eyed—was concerned only with standing as close as he could to the prettier of the two nurses. "I mean, he's not anybody's poodle," she was saying. "But he'll give you, like, the benefit of the doubt." "Totally!" the other one murmured.

They got off with everyone else. Val pushed Nan around a corner, stopped for a minute, then returned to the elevator. "Basement!" he muttered.

This time the elevator was empty. They emerged into a dim corridor, low ceiling, pipes. Nan got it: a patient being taken for tests in the middle of the night couldn't be seen going below the second floor of the hospital. Picking up speed, they whisked along, wheels growling against the cement floor. The pipes overhead arrived and departed, untangled, re-knotted. Now and then a drop of moisture fell on Nan's face. I want a cigarette, she thought passionately.

Suddenly they slowed. Val whispered, "Not to move!" The cotton sheet was flung over Nan's face.

Several seconds of a new, stately pace. Nan stayed still. Then a young male voice said, "Jay? Hey, man, what's goin' down? Hey! You're not Jay. What're you—"

A scuffling; a thump. Something heavy fell across Nan's legs. Paralyzed, heart banging, she waited.

"*K chortu!*"

The weight across her legs was rearranged. Nan put a hand out from under the sheet, intending to lift it off her face so she could see what had happened, but Val said, "Not to move!"

Then she was rolling again, fast this time. The weight across her legs made her feel oddly safe. Anchored, like the lead blanket they gave you at the dentist's to shield you from X-rays. Beneath the sheet she could see nothing. Sounds narrowed to Val's breathing above her, the sigh of the gurney wheels below.

An abrupt right turn; the sound of a door shutting. They stopped. The weight was removed. There was some shuffling and a thud, followed by "*Chort voz'mi!*" Then the sheet was lifted. Blinking, Nan found herself looking down a yellow flashlight beam at two piles of dark fabric.

"Put on these!" Val swung the flashlight toward the smaller pile. He held out a hand, Nan took it, and then, a little dizzy, she was on her feet. Val held the flashlight steady on the heap of clothing. Nan turned her back, looking away from the larger pile, which moved a little, then groaned. What am I doing? she thought, shivering as the cold cement floor met her bare feet. What in the world have I done? She slid out of the hospital johnny and began pulling on garments one by one. *Too late now*, bra, *two bodies*, underpants, sweatshirt, *that shock when the flashlight*, sweatpants, socks. Fanny pack, which she strapped on fumblingly. Her fingers discerned the square bulge of a pack of cigarettes. Bless him!

Val laid the flashlight on the floor and began dragging the larger pile into the corner. Nan looked away. *Not dead; don't be silly.* Shoes. She looked around the floor in the oblique glow of the flashlight, but could see none. He'd forgotten shoes.

Val's arm was across her shoulders. He hugged her, hard. "I will miss!"

Then he was guiding her toward the door. The flashlight snapped off, there was a moment of utter darkness, and then they emerged into the corridor. Val inserted a key into a metal door marked NO EXIT.

The bright, still hush, after rain. Remembering how, as a child, the brightness and the hush were what woke you. Without her glasses the sky was a blur, but Nan could feel it, a starry night. Val's arm urged her forward. They stepped together into the humid air. Smells surrounded her, outdoor smells, non-hospital smells: earth, cinders, some flowering shrub. Bands of color lay before her: the gassy pink of overhead flood-lights, the blue darkness of a small courtyard, the deeper darkness beyond. A drumroll of fear traveled up her spine.

Val bent down and wedged the flashlight to keep the door from closing. Straightening up, he must have felt her trembling, because his calm voice denied everything—the gurney ride, the soundless contact with the back of Safety Pin's head, the bundle left behind in a dark corner. Escaping, jailbreak—surely it couldn't be this easy? Surely something would happen, some obstacle, something to stop them? Turning, she pressed against Val's enclosing arm and stared back into the hospital darkness almost hopefully.

"Nan! This way! Is gate straight ahead. You see?"

I don't. I can't see *anything.*

"Fine, *ladno.* Gate is open. You land up in street. Taxi is waiting—my taxi. Mel is driving."

I can't.

"*Ladno.* You have only to walk, perhaps fifteen meters. Mel is driving you . . ." His voice began to fade. ". . . Boston . . . *aeroport* . . . Milan . . ."

Her legs trembled; her knees seemed to disappear. She felt the familiar coldness, nausea but not quite, buckle itself across her belly. Spirals of pain uncoiled behind her breastbone, along her left arm.

Val shook her, hard. "Nan!" He pried at her clenched fingers, his nails cutting into the soft flesh, hurting. He forced her hand open. The pill was pushed into her mouth. Automatically her tongue arched, curled, swept it under.

Val waited, both arms under her armpits, holding her up. Slowly the world stilled, her knees jelled, the clamor in her chest began to ease.

"Nan. I must go."

Her head felt light. No restraints. Must she do this?

"Nan! Think. Think to Jane."

And then Val was pushing her *Jane* and she was stepping out onto the pavement *Jane* and the cinders were biting through her wet socks and when she looked down *Jane* there were hollows where rain had gathered, cupfuls of starry darkness, and she followed them *Jane* through the pink light through the blue dark into the deep shadows under the trees.

Eighteen

Sulfur-colored sky; remnants of night; a few disheveled wandering stars. Looking up past the lighted sign for Alitalia, Nan Mulholland had to guess at these as much as see them, squinting, missing (had she ever before, in her vanity-driven life?) her glasses. She watched the taillights of Val's taxi disappear. Then, clutching ticket folder, passport (yet another false name!), driver's license, towing the wheeled suitcase Mel had provided, she entered the haze of Logan Airport's International Terminal.

She nearly asked directions from a life-sized replica of Peter Lynch, standing beside a huge, lighted sign that advised, KNOW WHAT YOU OWN. KNOW WHY YOU OWN IT. "You'll be met," was all Mel had been able to tell her. By Walker and Jane, Nan assumed she meant. In Milan, she hoped; though it could be all the way at the end of this blurred and desperate journey, in Genoa. Not until they were speeding north on I-95 had she asked Mel where they were going. Of course Walker had seen Alex's message next to his in the *Pee-Eye,* had understood where she must be. Of course Walker had a Plan. Like New Zealand (Mel informed her), Italy didn't extradite for child custody cases.

Nan walked, as directed by the genial fat man behind the Alitalia ticket counter, toward Security. Luckily, the bag Mel gave her had contained a pair of brand-new black sneakers, which she'd put on in the car. She walked fast, expecting every minute to be stopped. The drive to Boston had used her up—Mel speeding, chattering to cover her fear, *We'll visit you, you and Janey, you'll see, it'll be diesel, it'll totally rock*—and she had no energy left for optimism. No energy to resist the fear that coursed through her. Now—sneakers squeaking slightly as she strode, she hoped confidently, forward—it was a blessing not to see too far ahead. Even so, there were terrors. Blue uniforms that turned out to be business suits. A jingling that turned out to be the bells on a child's toy. A heart-stopping moment when the woman at the security checkpoint paused over her false passport, looked up, then down again. *Just get there. Just get to the gate.*

Her seat was in the bulkhead, no one in front of her. The plane, at this unpopular hour between night and morning, on a holiday weekend, was barely half full. Nan sat, quietly terrified, among her fellow passengers. If any of them watched her, if anyone regarded her with suspicion, she couldn't see it. Another blessing. Because now that she was on the plane, obediently belted into her seat, far from feeling safer, she felt utterly alone. Abandoned. Fear percolated up into her throat from the bottom of her stomach. The vial of nitro she'd found in her fanny pack lay curled in one fist.

But it's not my *physical* heart (that lump of glistening meat) that I need now.

All the years of State Department travel—of constant accommodation to new places and people and events—what were they worth to her now? She no longer knew *that* Nan—if indeed she ever had. In any case, for what would be asked of her now—to make a life for Jane, to make a childhood, to heal her—those years had given her no practice whatsoever.

Can we—can *I*—do this?

But here was the sky beginning to crack open: a band of pale green at the horizon shone like glass. Nearly sunrise. Look, Nana!—Jane had said, one winter morning—the sun is rinsing out the dark. They were in Jane's bedroom at the top of the beautiful big house on Queen Anne, in that other life. The life before that other plane trip, half a year ago.

The weight of all that had happened in the months between that trip and this suddenly descended on Nan. It was as if something terribly heavy had made contact with every part of her body. Feeling bruised all over, she leaned her forehead against the window glass. Cool, like the memory of a palm (Pop's? Dorothea's? her mother's?) on feverish skin.

Other passengers filed by: a turbaned Sikh; a fat man whose midsection, in a Hawaiian shirt, wavered from side to side like a waterbed; a woman carrying a brass lamp on one shoulder, refusing to yield it to the flight attendant, holding up a line of passengers behind her. Nan only half saw them. Then, in the seat to her left, a large blackness settled itself.

Turning her head, she saw a nun and, in the aisle seat beyond, a black leather cello case. Momentarily she wondered, Do any nuns still wear the habit, these days? Oh, of course: must be Italian. This is Alitalia, after all.

Nan turned back to the window. The heady smell of mothballs drifted over her, emanating from the voluminous black folds of her seatmate's garments. It made Nan think of church, the priest swinging the censor high above the heads of the faithful, the odor of incense. Fainting. She opened her fingers and took a quick look at the vial of pills. She mustn't faint now—not now. The nun shifted restlessly in her seat, annexed the armrest between herself and Nan. Perhaps she too was getting a whiff of her neighbor: in Nan's case, the smell of stale tobacco from the cigarettes she'd smoked in the car with Mel, one after another. And sweat. And fear. Nan longed to take off the new sneakers, which bit into the backs of her heels; but she couldn't afford to draw her seatmate's attention. Glancing sideways, she saw the nun extract from her pleated bosom a bag of bright-colored candy. NEON WORMS, the label said. The nun tore the package open with her teeth and took out a chartreuse jelly cylinder. She must have felt Nan's look, because she said, in an oddly deep voice, "Takeoff's the most frightening, don't you find? It always reminds me that the world would continue without me," and held out the bag invitingly.

Nan found herself reaching for one of the bright-colored worms. Then she saw what, before, she hadn't noticed, what none of them— Shovelton, Val, Mel—had noticed. On the back of her left hand was an X of white surgical tape, from which protruded the plastic receiver for the IV needle. Quickly she withdrew her hand.

"No, thank you, Sister."

She turned back to the window. Don't talk to *anybody*, Mel had warned as they hurtled through the Callahan Tunnel, the dark weight of the Charles River pressing (Nan imagined) on their heads. Through the scratched glass of the plane's windows sunrise was progressing. The sky, above a margin of live coals, had lightened to a pure, translucent kingfisher blue.

The nun leaned toward Nan to look out the window. She said, in that peculiarly deep voice, "It's always a beautiful day when you leave town."

Nan stiffened.

"Don't you find?"

Nan's fingers tightened around the nitro. Trembling, she forced herself to turn, to look.

The starched white coif hid the wattle; black serge veiled the bald, perfectly shaped head. But it was Walker who looked back at her, his eyes behind gold-rimmed spectacles shining. Joy rushed through Nan. She breathed in, trying for the smell of him—apples and pencil shavings—beneath the scent of mothballs. Questions crowded her throat. Where's Jane? Where have you two been hiding? Is she okay?

Before she could speak, Walker shook his head. In an absurd falsetto, he said, "A closed mouth gathers no feet."

The plane gave a preliminary shudder. Nan tensed, feeling all her organs leap into position. They began to move backward, then slowly turned. Melodious announcements, equally incomprehensible in English and Italian, offered the usual advice and warnings, but the voice was a smiling voice. Italy! thought Nan. No lugubrious, iron-faced attendants on this flight. Outside the window the airport no-man's-land began gliding past. Walker pulled a pair of glasses from his ample bosom and handed them to Nan. Did the man think of everything? She put them on and strict, dark trees sprang up along the far edge of the tarmac.

She turned to Walker. She said, careful to keep her voice low, "Just tell me she's all right."

"Look behind you."

She turned toward the window, then twisted around until she could look back through the space between her seat and the curving wall of the plane. In the seat behind her was a small boy with bright red hair cut close to his skull, in denim overalls. He clutched a stuffed doll of indeterminate species wearing black-and-yellow-striped pajamas. Gazing down at it, he raised a hand to his forehead and rubbed it with the two middle fingers. Alex's gesture.

Nan breathed, *Oh!*

Eyes the color of tarnished grapes met hers. Jane's whole face brightened. She leaned forward, rising in her seat, then, obeying a murmured command, sat still. A large adult hand closed over her small one. A woman's hand, lavishly beringed. Alex! Nan thought. But no—the skin was olive. Relinquishing all dignity, Nan put her eye to the crack. The ringed fingers curled around Jane's, which seemed to curl back. A pang of purest jealousy shot through Nan.

That hand should be mine.

She put her lips to the crack. "A runcible cat!" she whispered. No answer. She tried again, louder. "A runcible cat!" Silence. She waited, her heart beating fast. Then:

"With crimson whiskers!" Jane's voice sang.

"Shhh!" from her invisible companion.

She felt Walker nudge her and turned around. "Friend of Sam's," he said in a low voice, referring to The Hand. He held out a neon worm, a bright-red one. Nan took it. When she returned to the crack, Jane's eyes met hers, as if she'd simply kept on looking at the spot where her grandmother had been. Nan pushed the neon worm through the gap, and Jane took it. A small but unmistakable smile nudged the corners of her mouth before it opened and the worm dropped in.

The plane slowed, then stopped. Nan looked out the window. They were somewhere in the middle of a runway alongside a sparkling ribbon of ocean. Minutes passed. Farther back in the plane a man's voice groaned, "My Karma!" Nan felt her seat being kicked from behind, heard Jane's voice rising in familiar tones of protest—"I'm *not!*"—and from her companion a stern "Hush!" A pretty flight attendant with a face like a borzoi came down the aisle with cups of water. Nan fought the desire to get up and free Jane, drag her guardian from her seat and occupy it herself, an urge so fierce, so savage, that it scared her.

What if we don't make it? What if we fail?

She remembered the pause on the runway in Seattle, all those months ago—eerily parallel. Now, as then, Nan held herself rigid, so as not to disturb the precarious balance of the universe; now, as then, she felt afraid. Only this time, she realized with widening gratitude, I'm not alone.

The pretty borzoi was back, this time offering a tray of little white cardboard cups. "We have only one flower of ice cream," she said, apologetically.

Nan turned around to look through the crack again. Jane's eyes were closed and her head drooped at an angle that could only mean sleep. Even asleep she looked hunched. Weary. A child—weary! Too many secrets to keep; too many partings. Nan turned and faced the front of the plane. There will be so much to repair, she thought. *Restauro*: the word in Italian sounded beautiful, like a campanile bell tolling.

The plane began to move. Nan sat very straight, arms gripping her armrests, eyes on the window by her head. Between the ground and the horizon the band of blue widened. Above it, layers of smoky clouds with rose-tinted bellies flowed past. Walker's hand covered Nan's. It pinched the hole from the IV, but she didn't move. His palm was cool; his fingers curled around hers and held them fast. She glanced past him, wondering if anyone would notice. Then she thought: Takeoff, after all, a moment when many people seize the hands of strangers, and a nun, what could be more fitting? Anyway, the seat next to Walker, the aisle seat, held only a cello. His, of course; part of the Plan.

They were gathering speed. Ground, earth, trees flowed faster and faster, loosened, dissolved.

"Someday," said Walker into her ear, "we'll look back on all this and . . . plow into a parked car."

Nan laughed, surprising herself. How long since she'd laughed? Walker's eyes shone. He was a man needed, a man with a mission, an adventurer again at last.

As always, the precise moment when they left the ground went unmarked. There was only the visceral thud of the wheels being pulled up into the belly of the plane. Nan felt her heart lift.

"Beautiful!" Walker said. "We're golden!"

Epilogue

Nan Mulholland pauses on the Passeggiata and bends to remove a shoe and shake out the cinder that has lodged there. Out over the dappled Mediterranean—so calm for an ocean, looking this December afternoon like pale green gooseberry jelly—the sun is moving down the western sky.

It's the time of day she loves best here: the approach of dusk, melancholy but hopeful. A drawing-in. She walks here every day in the late afternoon, two miles, from Bogliasco almost to Nervi and then back, for her heart's sake. The Passeggiata—a wide, palm-lined, brick-paved path winding along the bluff above the ocean—is an old-fashioned turn-of-the-century promenade. Now, in mild December, the women wear furs (Nan has never seen so many, or such various, furs); the men stroll in pairs in checked golf caps and open coats. Children zigzag back and forth; babies ride pashalike in strollers. The sun strikes a shining path across the water from the horizon toward the promontory below. It's her favorite spot—this last stark extension of the land into the sea, the dark, ribbed rocks, like great beasts reclining. On the farthest one, two fishermen stand companionably at the edge of the world.

Nan checks her watch. Twenty minutes till she's due to meet Jane.

She can't resist. Before she knows it she's descending the steps cut into the bluff between wind-racked pines and feathery acacia. No railing: this is Italy, after all. She makes her careful, rubber-soled way out onto rocks encrusted with cream-colored bird shit, bright with moss. Around their jagged base the water, so calm and lakelike from above, shows its true nature. It foams, crashes upward, assaults the black granite.

Exhilarated, Nan breathes in the postcoital smell of the sea and gazes out along the shining path toward the sun. A light breeze molds her skirt against her legs and urges tendrils of her hair out of its knot. She feels pleasantly conspicuous and a little dramatic, like the figurehead on the prow of a ship. Nothing but water between her and Africa.

"*E' pericolosa—la bellezza!*" calls one of the fisherman. *It's dangerous, this beauty.* Slippery, he means. Only in Italy would a practical warning take the form of a philosophical statement.

If she falls, she won't drown. She's a good swimmer now, after half a year beside the Mediterranean. She won't die of hypothermia, either; the water is warm here, even in December, even when the air brushes your face with the faint fragrant chill of approaching winter. No—if she fell, she'd brain herself on the rocks sleeping beneath the surf. Beautiful, dangerous, and just right, Jane says, for mermaids. Do all five-year-old girls want to be mermaids? Jane has spent hour after hour this fall drawing blue and green scales on sheets of paper, taping them together, a long frail tube ending in a tail that invariably tears the minute she gets both legs into it. Her expression when this happens is ferocious, utterly unchild-like. Nan has learned not to approach her or try to comfort her then.

Her new contact lenses let Nan see, far out on the water, diving gannets circle above a freighter. There's a tanker that looks as if it's made entirely of rust. Closer in, a lone kayaker pinwheels past, the silver flash of his paddle like quick stabs of happiness. Small brown birds that Walker says are called turnstones pick through the pebbles below Nan's rock. No seagulls here, for which she never forgets to be grateful; their rusty, questioning cries always bring back the time in Providence. But they're busy bombing the little harbor at Nervi, with its unlovely human detritus. Nan never walks quite that far.

This little town of Bogliasco is near Genoa, where Nan, when they arrived half a year ago, felt sure Alex would be waiting. She wasn't. The weeks went by without a word from her, and Walker, who thought Gabriel might try to sue for sole custody, wanted to be prepared. They were, after all, stealing Jane. He set Our Man in Savannah to work. Eventually Sam ferreted out Gabe's secret—the one that Alex had referred to that December morning a year ago. A charge of cheating on his surgery boards, dropped because the eyewitness changed her testimony. An eyewitness who, Sam discovered, had been bribed. Gabe was warned (through what channels, Walker refused to say) that the whole matter—which could be proved, the eyewitness having been bought back by Sam—would be made public if he pursued Jane, legally or otherwise. Every now and then, Walker has told Nan, Gabriel is reminded—by a note, a phone call, the delivery (Sam has his whimsical side) of a rare orchid—that they have him in their sights. Pouring oil on troubled fires, Walker calls this cheerfully.

Nevertheless, it's best, he feels, for Nan and Jane to stay out of the country. No point tempting fate. "Nan and Jane" clearly means—without a word spoken, bless him—Nan and Jane and Walker. So here they are, approaching the anniversary of the day Nan and Jane fled Seattle, in a whitewashed terraced apartment on a hill above the ocean, under yet another assumed name, living in reasonable comfort on Deenie's legacy. *There is no greater misfortune than underestimating your enemy,* Sam warned them on that summer night (how long ago it feels!) in Boston. But it is Gabriel, after all, who has made that mistake.

I've lost a daughter—maybe, *maybe*—Nan thinks now, gazing down at the rocks, which the setting sun has turned deep lavender. I won't lose Jane.

Fifteen minutes now. She meets Jane every afternoon after school, at a little kiosk that sells postcards and cheap silver jewelry to tourists. The nanny of Jane's classmate Claudia and her brother Francesco collects all three children from school and walks them this far. Jane loves the owner's dog, a Lhasa apso with bright black eyes, one of the little, low dogs so popular here—what Walker calls "dropkick dogs." She'll shout *Ciao!* to her friends, Claudia and Francesco, farewells reluctant enough to reassure Nan that she is, really *is,* happy. Then the two of them will walk through a rain of church bells announcing five o'clock Mass, up steep cobblestone steps to the Via Aurelia, and make their way home. Like her grandmother, Jane prefers to cross the train tracks where it says VIE-TATO—Forbidden. Then: narrow streets, steep walls (laundry hanging bright against ancient stone), olive trees still holding on to their silvery leaves, with orange nets spread beneath to catch the season's last fruit. The smells of cooking mingle with the fragrance of late-blooming roses. Doorways punctuate the high stone walls; the one just before theirs bears a rosette of blue ribbon for the birth of the young couple's first baby. Then their own, with its carved head of Medusa, hair all snakes, two of them knotted like a Genovese woman's scarf around her neck, two peering down benignly from her forehead. (Happy snakes; and the woman's serene face is that of a madonna. It was this that made Nan and Walker choose the place.) In an upper window they'll see Walker watching for them, looking, in his soft checked cap, almost Italian. A lizard will flicker down the blue-painted doorjamb and disappear between two crusted stones. Jane will hold out her hand for the key, heavy as a small wrench, and (this is her daily privilege) fit it into the keyhole, and turn.

A last look at the shining path across the water, so bright and beckoning, so deceptively solid; then Nan climbs the stone steps back to the Passeggiata. The moon, a pale comma in the deepening blue sky, is the subject of conversation among her fellow strollers. How Italians love their moon! "*Guarda, Mamma!*" cries a bright-faced toddler, tugging at his mother's hand. She smiles down at him. "*Guarda la luna!*"

Sun and moon at once. It happens often on Nan's walks along the Passeggiata. In Russia, Val told her when he and Mel visited in October, this is a good omen. She doesn't remember ever seeing it before, back in what she's come to call—as she and Tod did long ago, as everyone in the Foreign Service did—the States. The breeze has strengthened; it whips tendrils of hair against Nan's neck, fills her nostrils with the tang of seaweed.

Ten minutes now. Nan turns up the collar of her jacket and begins to hurry.

Does Jane miss her mother? Her father? She never mentions them.

"We will know that she heals," says Jane's therapist, "when we haven't to ask ourselves these question. When she can miss them, and say it. When she can be angry to their loss." Natalia Fabri is a deceptively soft-looking woman who once met Jung. She has a lower front tooth missing, replaced by a gold one that Jane calls her Halloween Tooth. "We haven't to forget that separation from a loved one is a wound always. No matter how imperfect the love."

Natalia is motherly toward Nan, though she's a few years younger. (Her own mother was executed by Mussolini days before the Allies landed at Salerno.) She smells, seductively, of the cigarettes Nan has almost given up; she bites her fingernails; she never tries to make herself feel better by giving Nan advice. No soaring generalizations from Natalia. Instead, she tells stories—about her own life, about the lives of people she knows—from which it is possible, should Nan desire, to extract a little wisdom. Or maybe *compassion* would be a better word. Natalia's categorical pronouncements are few and concrete. Drink wine, never water, when you eat artichokes, or they will rust in your stomach.

Nan sidesteps a young man talking excitedly into his cell phone, his *telefonino,* as they're affectionately called here. "*Cido le mani!*" he is shouting. I'll cut off their hands.

If Gabriel were to kill himself, Nan thought when they first arrived in Italy—in those first weeks when her disgust and fury left no room for compassion—then she would *know.* It would be at once a confession of guilt and a self-administered punishment. Better still: dead, he would no longer threaten Jane (or—Be honest!—threaten Nan with the loss of Jane), even from a distance, even hypothetically. Headlines filled her dreams, those first weeks in Italy. PROMINENT SURGEON LEAPS FROM HOT-AIR BALLOON. BODY OF SEATTLE PHYSICIAN FOUND IN MOTEL. CARIBBEAN PLEASURE CRUISE PROVES FATAL. Nan is grateful not to need these headlines anymore. They were dangerous, not to Gabriel, but to Nan herself. Pop used to say, Bad luck follows the bitter heart.

About the impossibility of knowing—about the uncertainty that lies at the heart of life—Nan is only beginning to be resigned. She's long since stopped questioning Jane, but she has yet to give up looking (those mermaid tails!) for signs. She wrestles with the likelihood that she will never know for sure whether Gabriel abused his daughter. Or whether, if he did have sexual contact with her, either of them viewed that as abuse. Natalia Fabri says she has not known one child molester who did not speak of his victim with real tenderness; nor one abused child who did not go to great lengths to stay with such a parent. Aren't Nan's own feelings toward Gabriel, the son-in-law she once adored, irremediably mixed?

Nan has a picture of Gabriel that will not leave her: Gabriel scoring the soles of Jane's first pair of shoes, tiny white leather lace-ups. She sees his scalpel flash, a row of diagonals one way, another row across them, the careful diamond-shaped pattern that will keep his baby daughter from slipping. Nan hears the blade bite, over and over, into the smooth new unresisting leather, and Gabriel whistling a song from her youth.

We won't say goodbye until the last minute
I'll hold out my hand
And my heart will be in it

Five minutes now. She reaches the little kiosk, with its sign that says IL PIT-STOP, and sits down on a wooden bench facing the sea to smoke her one cigarette of the day. The owner's Lhasa apso sidles over to sniff her ankles and gaze up at her with, Nan could swear, a question in its eyes. Where's Jane? Giannetta, she's called here. *Dov'è Giannetta?* A small boy is kicking a blue ball back and forth. The sun, sinking toward the horizon, has stained the path to it a brilliant crimson. Evening comes early now, so near the solstice. People passing greet each other with "*Buona sera! . . . 'Sera!*" Families walk in groups, mothers and fathers and children, interrupting each other, gesturing, laughing.

As far as Nan can tell, Jane believes her explanation that her father and mother have had to stay in Guatemala, helping sick children. At any rate, she's accepted it, and doesn't ask about them, or about home. Home is here now. Her nightmares have almost stopped. Repair happens slowly, Natalia reminds her often; it comes *alla spicciolata.* Speck by speck. When Nan despairs (seldom now, but at first it happened with alarming frequency)—when she worries that Jane has been damaged forever, if not by abuse, then by the separation from her parents—Natalia helps her count the *spiccioli* of their life together. Nan teaching Jane to shout "*Salami!*" at careless motorcyclists who come too close. Walker and Jane spotting a stork's nest in a cypress tree. Jane arguing in Italian with her friend Francesco, first shouting, then laughing. Jane emerging from the sea in her yellow bathing suit, water shining on round brown limbs, wild wet hair so like her mother's.

Alla spicciolata. Alex will know where to find them when she's ready. Didn't she find them in Providence? A notice appears in the *Pee-Eye* on the seventh and twenty-first of every month, only from Hippie to Pookie instead of the other way round, with a *poste restante* address in Genoa. Walker checks their box there once a week when he takes the train into the city to teach a course in ornithology at the technical college. Returning, so far—to Nan's relief and his—empty-handed, he reminds her that things belong to the people who want them most. But it's more than that—more than Nan's own wish to keep Jane. It's also that Alex entrusted Jane to her. Natalia has made real to Nan, via stories about the niece of a friend, the shame and horror and torment a mother feels whose child has been abused. A mother who has let this happen. "*Allora,* you see, your daughter has quite problems." Natalia does not point out the extension backward of the chain, daughter to mother, daughter to mother,

Jane to Alex to Nan. Crying, "Enough of all this broken-hearting!" she takes them both, Nan and Jane, to the corner *gelateria* for pistachio ice cream.

Alla spicciolata. When it is hard—and it is often hard—to have, at Nan's age, the raising of a young and willful and damaged child, she thinks: Tod would be surprised. Tod, who above all counseled patience, who never lived to be a grandparent. He would find Nan changed. Well—perhaps not. But improved? Bruised; battered; but improved.

Oddly, she sometimes feels Tod's spirit hovering over Walker. As far as anyone in Bogliasco knows, Nan and Walker are married. Walker would like to make good the lie; Nan hesitates. She wonders whether, after all, being the one loved, with all its warmth and safety, isn't just a little dull. This makes her ashamed: Walker, with all his acts of light, toward her, toward Jane! But Walker seems undismayed. He's a man with a plan, a man whose reach exceeds his grasp—a happy man. The second thing Deenie left Nan in her will, he claims, was him.

Real dusk now. The shining path is fading, reverting to mere water. Three young priests in black cassocks walk past arm in arm.

"*Ciao! Nonna!*"

Jane is hanging over the iron balustrade above Nan's head, looking down. A breeze lifts her thick brown horsetail hair, grown long now, across her cheeks. Her face is shining. Claudia appears beside her; then Francesco. Three ordinary, happy children. They make a neat row along the balustrade; behind them an enormous palm tree spreads its sheltering fans, delicate but firm. The children wave in unison, hands cupped, then flying open.

Nan feels drops of wetness on her upturned face. The children shake their wrists and more drops fall. She lets them stay, little sparks of cold across her cheeks, her forehead.

"*Ciao, teppistini!*" she calls. Hi, little hooligans.

In the last brilliant rays from the sinking sun, they squint down at her, feigning aplomb. Then they dissolve in laughter.

Give me a child until he is seven, Saint Ignatius Loyola said, and I will give you the man. Imagining Deenie adding an "s" before "he" and a "wo" before "man," Nan rises. She grinds the butt of her cigarette under one sneakered foot. Her heart beats lightly, steadily. She turns away from the darkly gleaming water and begins to climb the steep stone steps toward the children.

Acknowledgments

I would like to thank the following people: Arnold Arem, M.D., Don Berger, Silvia Esposito, Laura Furman (fairy godmother), John Harbison, the late Ella Haring, Brendan Hobson, David Hobson, Sarah Hobson, Timothy Hobson, Ann Hood, Joanne Humphrey, Hester Kaplan, Sue Kelly, Linda Knight, Jarrett Krosoczka, Kathryn Lang, Frances Lefkowitz, Sally Mack, Ed Marques, Susan Mates, M.D., Dick McDonough, David McOsker, Nancy Reisman, Roberta Richman, Angel Rocha, Bruce Rosenberg, Eric Rosenberg, Lois Rosenthal, Captain John Ryan, Caterina Sama, Janet Silver, Dabney Stuart, Randall White, Janet Hagan Yanos, and—with great affection—the members of the deephearted Providence Area Writers (PAW) group.

Most of all I thank my agent, Gail Hochman, her assistant, Joanne Brownstein, and the Girl Group: Gail Donovan, Frances Lefkowitz, and Elizabeth Searle.

I am grateful to the Rhode Island State Council on the Arts, the Bogliasco Foundation, the American Academy in Berlin, the American Academy in Rome, the MacDowell Colony, Civitella Ranieri, and the Rona Jaffe Foundation for their generous support.

Parts of this novel have appeared, in a somewhat different form, in *Shenandoah*, *Story*, *Hotel Amerika*, and the *Madison Review*.